I0788428

Glimpses

A Collection of Stories

By

J.E. Taylor

J.E. TAYLOR
SUPERNATURAL SUSPENSE
& DARK FANTASY AUTHOR

Table of Contents

THE DEVIL'S OFFER

When I make a deal with the devil to save my boyfriend, I never imagined that he would break up with me two days later. Or that Lucifer himself would show up at my door, demanding payment.

What is he asking for as payment, exactly?

I must track down the last demon hunter for the devil, so Lucifer can kill him once and for all. If I do this, Lucifer will tear up my contract.

If I refuse, he will drag my soul to Hell to start my eternal punishment.

My choices suck. An eternity in agony, or lead someone else to their death in exchange for my very soul.

What would you choose?

The Devil's Offer
Chapter 1

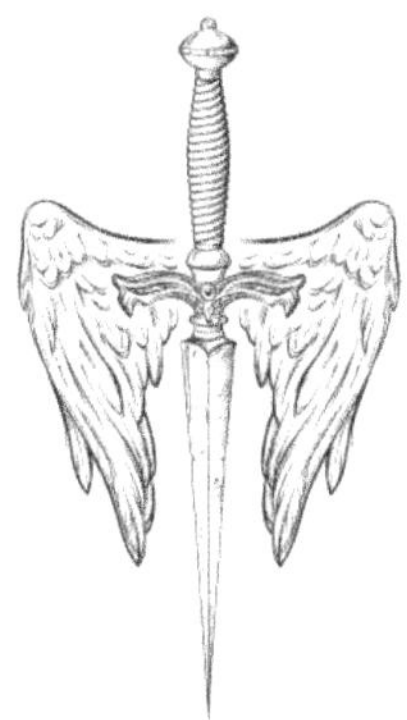

MY HANDS SHAKE AS I stare in the mirror at my disheveled state. My arm rests in a new sling, and my once spotless prom dress is now something that will end up in the trash as soon as I get home. I wipe at the red dots marring the silvery silk skirt, doing nothing more than smudging the blood stains.

My mind keeps falling back into the moment the car was hit. In that moment, Jay had been smiling at me, and not looking at the road. Lights blinded me as Jay drove into the path of a speeding car.

My brain registered the oncoming disaster, and my face must have, too, because Jay's head swiveled toward the driver's window. He slammed on the brakes, but it was too late.

Crunching metal filled my world.

I jerk again, back in the hospital bathroom attached to the room they kept me in. Still pale. Still bruised. And still alone while they worked on Jay in the operating room.

My parents hadn't arrived yet, either, but I was assured they would be here soon. *Maybe they'll be able to get information about Jay.*

"Whoever is out there listening, I'll give anything to make sure Jay makes it through this okay. Even my soul," I whisper at my reflection, searching my own haunted gray eyes. Jay had my heart and if he dies, it will crush me.

Guilt bites down hard as I close my eyes, dulling the ache in my arm. If I had said no to his begging offer of a hotel room, we wouldn't be in the hospital. My chin drops to my chest as I force the tears back.

I finish wiping my face and try to hand comb the knots out of my dirty-blonde hair, but it's useless without a brush. Instead, I turn back to the emergency exam room that I've been relegated to, with only a few bumps and bruises. I squint as I enter the room. The light creates halos in my vision. They say this is normal for a concussion, but it still unnerves me, especially when the halo encompasses an orderly.

The orderly leans against the bed with one ankle crossed over the other, looking at a clipboard as he chews on the end of the pen. His eyes lift to take me in, and a chill skitters up my spine, like someone just stepped on my grave.

"Your soul, huh?" He taps on the clipboard. "Care to seal that with a drop of blood?"

I blink at him, but the aura remains, as does his irritating drumming on the clipboard. "Excuse me?"

He shoves the clipboard toward me as he stands up straight. He towers over me like a sentinel, and I gulp before I take the offering. When my gaze falls to the words scrawled in fancy script in a language that might as well be Greek, I cock my head, trying to understand the meaning.

This was not like any medical form I had ever seen.

"I, um, I think you may be mistaken." I look up at the orderly.

"You are Layla Anderson, correct?" He purses his lips until I nod. "And you just made a wish that you feel is worthy of your soul, correct?"

I step back, wondering just how hard I hit my head. My gaze bounces between the form on the clipboard and the stranger. The meaning of his words more than the unreadable contract I hold seeps into my concussed brain, and I nod slowly.

"You might want to sign that sooner rather than later because the boss just hates bringing people back from the dead." He taps the clipboard again.

My heart lurches in my chest and I'm unsure whether it's his words or my skepticism that makes it pound in my ears like a freight train. I can't imagine this is real, and if it is, this guy must be from the psych ward. *What will he do to me if I don't sign his freaky form?*

I swallow and follow along as if I believe him. "Where do I sign?"

He points to a line at the bottom. "This is binding." He takes my finger and stabs it with the pen, drawing blood.

It takes a moment for the pain to reach my brain through the fog of the rest of my bruises. "Ouch!" I pull my hand away. I stare at the blood welling up on the tip of my throbbing finger. My gaze goes beyond my finger to the spot I am expected to sign.

A small part of me warns against it, but I ignore it and press my finger to the paper. The minute I touch the sheet, a tingle flows into my hand, up my arm, and through my entire form until I think I'm going to fracture into a thousand pieces.

The orderly smiles and takes the clipboard from my hands, and then he fades into dust, swirling away. Light blinds me and I squint, holding my hand up against the brightness. When it fades, I'm once again alone in the emergency exam room, as if the past few moments never occurred. But the blood smudged on my finger tells me it was real.

Another bead wells up from the fresh puncture, and I shiver as the truth blankets a chill over me.

I think I just sold my soul to the devil himself.

The Devil's Offer
Chapter 2

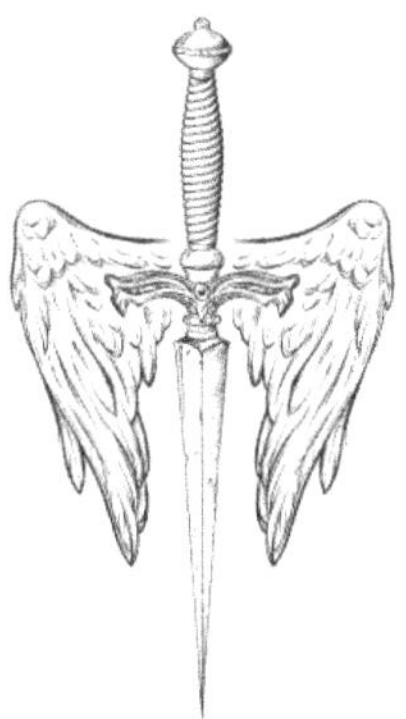

WHEN JAY STROLLS INTO the room a few moments after the mysterious orderly disappeared, I blink at him. My mind can't wrap around his unblemished clothing as I scan him from his blond crown down his athletic frame to the tuxedo pants hanging on his hips like a second skin. It's a far cry from the broken and bloodied form that had been on the ambulance stretcher next to me.

It's as if the accident never happened. Or at least his involvement in it was wiped clean. But that just set off so many alarms in my head. This is what I had asked for, but I cannot fathom the cost.

My heart jumps in my chest as if I've been hit with a defibrillator. My hands shake, and my mouth dries out to the point I don't think I can swallow without a sip of water. My soul cries out in anguish, but I ignore the pummeling strife making my insides feel bruised and battered.

"Hey," he says, and his sad eyes shoot through my chest.

I honestly never thought I would see him breathing again, and a rush of adrenaline mixed with relief throws me right into his arms. He slowly hugs me back. My hands slide along his back and his arms as I squeeze him, making sure he is solid and not another hallucination.

He sure feels real, but the image of him mangled and the medics compressing his chest to keep his heart pumping in the ambulance still clung to my memories.

"You should have let me take you home," he whispers in my ear.

I pull away. "I did." I study the darkness in his eyes.

He slowly shakes his head. "Your parents picked you up."

I look down at the splotches of blood on my dress but all I can see in my mind is the car barreling into Jay's door and the shared ambulance drive to the hospital while the medics worked to keep him alive.

"You don't remember?"

I shake my head, afraid to hear his version of the evening.

"We had a fight," he says softly. "And you ran out of the prom. I guess you called your folks, and they came to pick you up and on your way home..." He looks around the emergency room and then meets my gaze without finishing the sentence.

"There was an accident?"

"Yes." He nods. "I came to take you home."

"Shouldn't I wait for my parents?"

"No." He tries to lead me out of the room, but I resist.

The alarms in my head clang. "Why not?"

"Layla." He presses his lips together for a moment. "I saw the crash site. I saw the body bags. They were pronounced dead on the scene. I came straight to the hospital, and it's taken me a couple hours to break through the bullshit at the desk to get in here to see you." He runs his hands through his hair.

I don't fully believe him. *The deal with that orderly can't be real, can it?*

Had I signed my parents' death warrant instead of letting Jay die?

My hands went cold, and I blinked at him as my brain slowly wraps around his words. If my parents were indeed dead, they would have told me. They would have sat me down like they do on television.

"Why wouldn't the doctor come tell me this himself?"

Jay closes his eyes. "They tried. But all you kept asking was if I was okay. They said the concussion messed with your short-term memory and you insisted that I was in the operating room, and they had to find out how I was. That is the only reason they let me in here. They needed you to come to grips with the truth." He sits on the edge of the bed and rubs his face. "They said it was a miracle you survived at all, never mind with only a concussion and a cut on your arm."

My legs suddenly lose all strength and I grab the closest chair, falling into it as if I have been delivered a knock-out punch. "My parents?" I try to pull the events he outlined into my head, but I can't. The image of him near death is too imprinted on my brain.

He crosses and crouches next to me. "They asked if you had any relatives."

I meet his gaze and shake my head. Neither of my parents had any siblings and I had never known my grandparents. "No."

A moment later, a nurse steps inside the room with a bag of personal items. Personal items that aren't all mine. I recognize the rings and the purse and the wallet. My fancy purse is included, but everything else belongs to my parents. Her solemn look makes me want to scream and flee from the hospital.

"I... I need to see my parents," I say to the nurse. I can't accept this until I see them with my own eyes.

"Layla," Jay starts.

"No. I need to see them." I clutch their belongings with a lump in my throat big enough to make swallowing difficult.

The nurse exchanges a glance with Jay and then nods, leading me out of the emergency room and down the hall to an elevator. My feet are still bare and the coolness of the floor against my heels reminds me that I'm alive and this can't possibly be a dream.

When we stop in front of a curtained window, Jay steps beside me.

"Wait here," the nurse says.

"You don't have to do this," Jay says softly.

"Yes, I do." I don't expand on the fact that I need to see my parents to validate that this horror is real. I'm still stuck on this is all an elaborate dream because maybe it's me in the operating room, or worse, in a body bag. Goosebumps appear on my arms, and I rub them to rid myself of the chill that now encompasses my entire form.

The curtain swings aside, revealing two metal gurneys with black bags on them. The first is rolled close to the window and it does not look like a human body in the bag. It looks like a lump of parts. When the gurney is turned, I recognize the partial face.

It's enough to draw a whine from my throat and make my body quiver. My father's gray eye stares at the ceiling.

That is all they show of him before they zip up the bag. The next bag seems more formed to a body, and they move it close and unzip more than just a face. My mother's pale face gazes out with an expression of horror; her eyes bulge in their sockets and there's blood splattered on her left cheek. Her neck is covered with the same gore that covers her face. But it's the right side of her head that my eyes keep moving to. It looks as if it were crushed by a baseball bat.

There is no mistaking my mother. My entire form shakes, and Jay wraps his arm around my shoulder.

I swallow and nod. The nurse zips the body bag back up.

My throat tightens and my eyes sting before they blur from the onslaught of tears. Jay attempts to hug me, but I push him away. I don't deserve to be consoled. He forces a hug, and a sob escapes me.

I will never remember the events that led up to my parents' death. I will always see the headlights blinding me, Jay's battered body on the gurney next to me, and then the drop of blood on the contract for my soul.

Jay leads me away from the morgue as the terrible truth rakes its ugly claws across my form.

I caused this.

I caused my parents' death by wishing for Jay to be whole.

My world will never be the same.

The Devil's Offer
Chapter 3

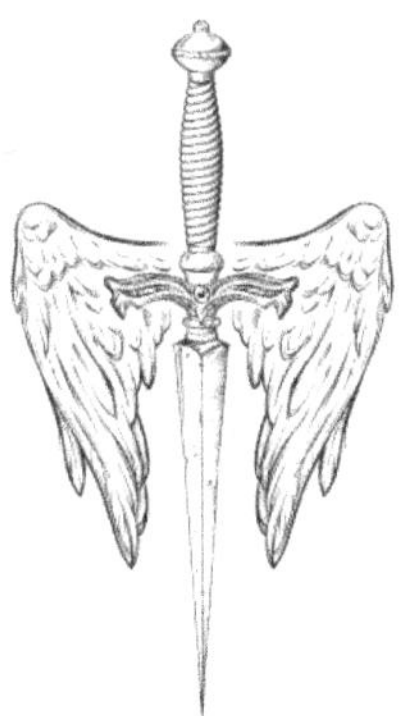

THE HOUSE IS EMPTY without my parents. Because I turned eighteen a week ago to the day, I have been told I am now the beneficiary of my parents' estate. I have no clue what needs to be done next, beyond burying my folks, but that costs money and I don't have a penny to my name.

And apparently my parents didn't either, or so the bank told me when I inquired. As a matter of fact, they still owe a hefty sum on the house I am sitting in and unless I can come up with the monthly payments, I will have to find somewhere else to live.

The doorbell rings, pulling me out of the stupor I'm in. I blink and rise, crossing to the front door. Without looking through the peephole, I open the door and stare into Jay's concerned eyes.

"We need to talk." He pushes his way inside.

I haven't seen him since the night he drove me home from the hospital. He hadn't come by until tonight, but he had tried to call. I ignored the endless ringing of both the house phone and my cell phone, feeling empty and guilty for wanting to talk to him, and at the same time, cursing my devil's deal.

"Jay, I really don't want to talk," I say, with the door still open.

He pries the door from my grip and closes it. "Why haven't you answered the phone?" He turns toward me, meeting my gaze.

"I am trying to figure out how to come up with the money to bury my parents," I snap and cross my arms over the soft flannel top of my pajamas. I haven't changed into street clothes yet. Hell, I haven't raked a brush through my hair in two days.

His eyes soften and he sighs. "Layla," he whispers and reaches to tuck the hair that has fallen in front of my face behind my ear like he always does. But he stops inches from my skin and pulls his hand away.

He's not his normal affectionate self, either. Usually, he would have already hugged me and given me a kiss even before the door closed behind him. Instead, he sidesteps me and heads into the living room, sliding into one of the straight-backed chairs. He leans his elbows on his knees.

"Seriously, Jay, they had no money and I have no idea how I am going to pay for their funeral, never mind live day-to-day here." I wave at the house surrounding me. I had been through all the bill ledgers my mother kept in the corner desk and my head still pounded from their blatant debt. I had no idea.

"I didn't come here to talk about your... situation. I came to talk about us."

Between his tone and the way he avoids looking at me, my blood turns cold, and I take a seat on the couch closest to where he sits. My voice is suddenly absent as my heartbeat thunders in my ears.

He glances out the window beyond where I sit. "On prom night, I hooked up with Tory." He looks at his hands as he speaks and only after the words tumble between us does he have the nerve to finally meet my gaze.

The night I traded my soul for his life, he hooked up with the class slut?

My brain doesn't know what to do with the information he's just fed me. "Hooked up?" I hate the pitiful tone of my voice as much as the cringe on his face.

He slowly nods.

My skin goes from chilled to hot in a flash and my hands close into fists. "Hooked up, like you slept with her?" I force myself to remain seated. Because if I stand, I am going to punch him.

His face turns red, and he stares at his shoes. "Yes, and I am still seeing her."

"My parents died because of you," I snap before I can control the fury riding my blood.

"Look, I didn't..." he starts, and I put my hand up.

I do not want his excuses, and he heeds the warning in my glare. I slowly lean back into the couch, letting the soft fabric hug me because now I don't even have my mother to hold me through the tears that I push back. I don't have my parents, or my soul, and now I don't even have the boy who I traded it all for.

"I should have let you die on that operating table," I whisper through clenched teeth.

He glances at me as if I grew a second head. "I didn't want to ghost you, especially after the accident." He stands. "I also didn't want to break up with you through text."

"Gee. Thanks." I send my death stare at him, wishing he would just explode out of existence. But I don't move from my seat. Not with the rage filling every cell. "Get out," I add as he just looks at me as if he expects me to fall apart. He doesn't move at my growled order. So, I clarify my intent by picking up the heavy globe paperweight on the table next to me. "Get out before I kill you myself."

His eyes move from the paperweight to my face, and he must have seen the storm brewing inside me reflected there because he bolts from the house before I can pitch the globe at him. If I had the ability to shoot rays from my eyes, I would have incinerated him on the spot.

The door slams behind him and I stay in place until long after the rumble of his car fades, gripping the paperweight so tight that my fingers tingle.

With each second that passes, the reality that I am alone stabs like a thousand knives. I can't move as both despair and wrath gather in my blood, fighting for control. My breath locks in my chest. My vision blurs from the onslaught of tears sliding in hot trails down my cheeks. My hands are clenched so tight that my nails embed in the flesh of my palm painfully. Tilting my head back, I scream to the heavens at the complete and utter lunacy of my situation.

How could I have been so stupid?

The doorbell shuts off my cry of anguish. I march to the door, ready to give Jay a piece of my mind. I yank open the heavy wood, and whatever harsh words were poised to shoot out of my lips die at the sight of the man in the finely tailored black suit on my doorstep.

He is tall and suave and absolutely terrifies me.

Cold air wafts from him like a freezer on a hot summer day. His eyes are a piercing blue, with flecks in the irises. I swallow hard. Those flecks are red and orange and yellow, reminding me of hellfire. Then the man smiles, and his eyes narrow slyly. He looks like a wolf who has cornered his latest prey.

"Layla," he says, in a knowing fashion that makes me feel like a thousand spiders are crawling over me and no patch of skin is spared. "I've come to collect."

My eyes are blinking so rapidly that I think they may actually create enough of a draft to make me rise off the floor. I've also forgotten how to breathe until my chest constricts painfully.

"Who are you?" I gasp through my tight windpipe before I draw in a shallow breath.

The air sparkles, and a paper appears in his hand. He holds it up so I can see my bloody signature. My gaze jumps to his. This could only be one being. I stumble back into the hallway wall, trying to figure out whether I should run, or fight, or just drop to my knees and pray for my soul.

He doesn't wait for my invitation. He steps inside and the door gently swishes closed without him touching it. "This is your signature, is it not?" He taps the paper where I've sealed my fate in blood. Even his voice, as beautiful as it is, sends ice through my veins.

I nod, still not able to utter any more words.

The devil is standing in my house.

I am so eternally screwed.

The Devil's Offer
Chapter 4

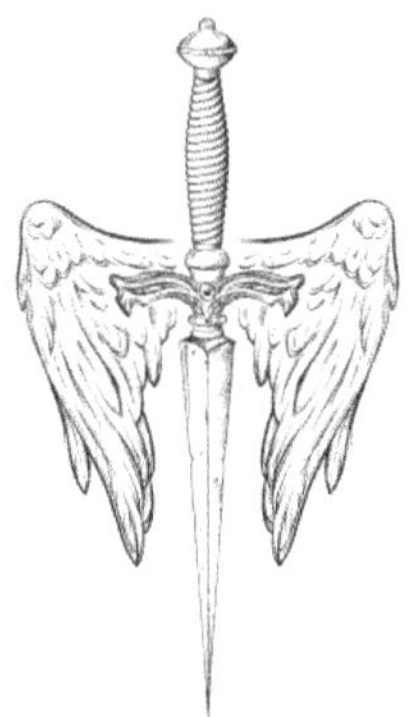

"**D**ON'T SHY AWAY FROM me, girl." He points toward the living room. "Sit a spell."

He saunters past me, and the moment his gaze moves from mine, the absolute terror gripping every cell releases. My knees buckle but the wall holds me up like a faithful friend.

"Time is ticking, Layla," he calls from the center of the house.

I force my legs to move and cross to the entryway leading into the living room. The devil sits in the captain chair that my father was fond of, with one ankle crossed over his knee. His fingers drum impatiently on the arm of the chair.

"I'm not ready." I stutter the words out. Although my problems seem unsurmountable, I do not want to stop breathing and be pulled down to Hell where my soul will be flogged for eternity.

His gaze narrows. "Did I say I was here to collect your soul?"

"I. Um. Uh." I blink rapidly again and try to recall his words.

"I said I was here to collect. If I was collecting your soul, you would already be dead, and I would not be slumming in middle class suburbia." He waves around the room.

"Um. I don't understand," I say, because he has surprised my voice back into my throat.

"Sit." He points to the chair opposite him.

I obey because I can feel the change in his demeanor from sly devil to businessman and somehow, I know if I don't adopt the same mannerisms, he might just decide to kill me immediately and forget about any other type of collection plans he had.

He leans forward, and I instinctively lean back in my chair until it feels like the seat may just swallow me.

"How far would you go to get your soul back?"

My mouth pops open and my eyebrows stretch upward. "Would that mean I'd get my parents back, too?"

"No, child. Everything has a price and that was yours for making the deal. I cannot reverse that." He slowly leans back. "My question remains."

Again, that pressure releases me, and I nearly slump in the chair. I glance down at my hands as the sorrow hits once more. My throat tightens and I swipe at the tears as they freely fall down my cheeks. "Are they..." I can't finish the sentence.

"As crappy as they are with their finances, they seemed to be strong on faith, so yes, they went to the sunny side."

I meet the devil's hypnotizing eyes. Knowing my parents are in Heaven makes a difference. I want to see them again and if I don't try to earn my soul back, that will be a wild pipe dream. "As far as I need to," I say in a small and meek voice.

"What skills do you possess?"

"Skills?"

"Survival skills, fighting skills, life skills." He throws out the words callously as if I am simple-minded.

"I am a blackbelt in jujitsu." I stop at that fact. The rest of my skills have nothing to do with survival. Unless he considers dance or cheerleading in that category.

"Any weapons experience?"

"I know how to shoot a gun, if that's what you're asking," I say in a manner that conveys my offense at his question. Especially with the hunting rifles displayed in the cabinet near the fireplace behind where he is sitting.

He smirks and glances out the window. "I like your spunk. So here is my proposal. I need you to find the last demon hunter."

I narrow my eyes at him, pretending not to be thrown by the fact both demons and demon hunters exist. "And do what?"

"You just call me and once I have torn his head from his body and stomped on his entrails until they are a juicy pulp, I will tear up your contract and you will be free." He smiles as if he didn't just paint the most awful picture in my mind.

"And where is this demon hunter?"

He leans forward, and I recoil. "If I knew, I wouldn't need your innocent ass to find him, now would I?"

The growl of his voice sends unwanted shivers through me. "Why me?"

"Because he seems to be able to sense evil. He will never see you coming, wrapped up in all that innocence, until it is too late." He tosses a close-up photo across the coffee table, and it lands facing me. The eyes on the picture scream out at me like a siren calling for a sailor. They are bright ocean-blue, but instead of flecks of hellfire in his irises like the entity sitting across from me, it looks like silver iridescent flecks. A lock of dark hair curls on his forehead. I reach for the print, but it disintegrates before I can touch the paper.

Before I look up at the devil, the demon hunter's face flashes in my memory and I have no doubt that if I run across those eyes, I will remember them. I meet the devil's gaze. "How do I call you?" I point at my cell on the table. "Cell phone?"

He chuckles, which is infinitely worse than his growl. "You just say my name."

"D-devil?" I sound idiotic, but I can't help it. I don't know this being's name. I just know I made a deal with the devil.

"No. That is my title, not my name." He adopts that same scolding tone as if I lack any bit of intelligence, and I grit my teeth. "My name is Lucifer. All you need to do is speak my name out loud, and I will be there in a snap." He snaps his fingers to emphasize his point. "And you will be free of your contract."

The world was a big place, especially for a high school senior like me. "Where do I start?" I ask, because I don't want the images of a beheaded body gutted on the ground to keep repeating in my mind and continue to sour my stomach.

"The last time this particular demon hunter killed one of my demons, he was in Prague."

"Europe?" I gawk at him. At least I know where Prague is. Some of my friends would have no clue it's the capital of the Czech Republic. But then again, I always got As in geography. "I don't even know if my parents renewed my passport."

"Well, lucky for you, I've gotten word that he is stateside. But in the event you cannot track him down here, you will need to get that passport updated." He points and scowls at me.

The United States was vast enough for me to swallow hard. "Where?"

"It's the reason I agreed to make a deal for your soul. He is here in the Northeast. I'm sure my appearance has made waves in the supernatural world, so you might get lucky."

I give him a nod and look down at my hands. Although I'd like to go galivanting all over the New England states, I have no money for gas beyond the twenty dollars in my pocket.

"I sense a problem." His tone softens.

I laugh. "One out of thousands," I mutter and meet his gaze. "My parents were in mega debt and didn't have life insurance. I have zero funds to pay off what they owe, and I have to bury them before I can attempt to get a job to pay for the gas I'll need to drive to find this demon hunter, so..."

"So, you'd like to start your penance in Hell now." He leans back in the chair and crosses his arms.

Heat spikes inside me and anger flares at his lack of empathy for the situation I am in. I bite my tongue on the derogatory comment that wants to escape my lips. That will only piss off my guest. And Lucifer is not someone to aggravate. "No. I just don't know how I can search out this demon hunter without funds to do so. Cars need gas to work. Gas costs money, and I only have enough to get me from here to maybe Boston."

"You have two feet. And didn't I see a bicycle leaning against the wall in your garage?"

This savage wants me to ride a bike around New England?

"Walking will take months," I mutter under my breath and Lucifer sighs, as if being here is such a pain in his ass. "What about my parents?"

He snaps his fingers and two urns with their names etched beautifully into the gold appear on the coffee table. "Will that do?"

I stare at them, and my mouth slowly drops. Their wills specified they wanted to be buried near my mother's parents and not cremated and kept in an urn. I guess their wishes mean nothing to the devil.

"You can put them on the mantel or have them drive shotgun with you in your car. I don't care. Now, are we done with all this human business?" He waves his hand with a frown, like their internment made him uncomfortable.

I can't rightly say no. If I do, I'll get hammered right into Hell by the devil himself. "Fine," I mutter through clenched teeth.

"You will find your bank account has a small balance. I trust that will tide you over until you find the demon hunter?"

"What?" I pick up my phone and open my bank app. I have a little less than a thousand dollars, which was far greater than the negative balance I had this morning. "Yes. This will do," I say as I put down the phone. "But what will all this cost me?" Nothing with the devil is ever free.

"Not a thing if you do your job." He stands. "I suggest you start looking for my fearless friend." He heads toward the door.

"And what happens if I can't find him?" I follow him and as soon as the words leave my mouth, the world turns dark and frigid and the things that surround me are worse than what nightmares are made of. The first nail drags across my back, peeling a scream from my lips at the unimaginable burning agony that grips me.

Within a blink, my home comes back into view and Lucifer's grin fills my vision.

"That is a little taste of what your eternity will be filled with." And with that, he leaves my house.

The Devil's Offer
Chapter 5

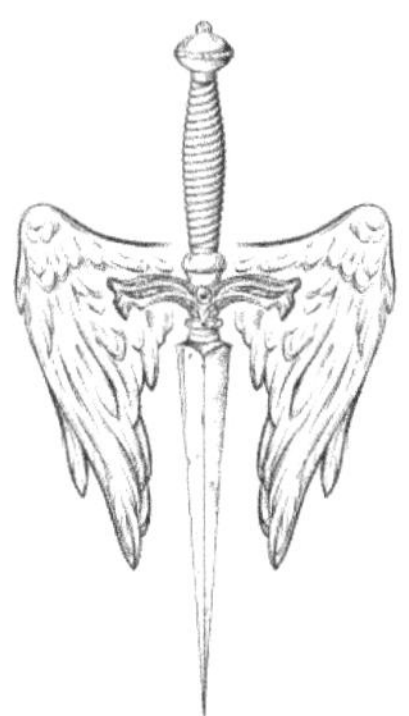

I SLOWLY SINK TO the couch as my brain rolls over the last few minutes and my back stings with the memory of Hell. But those eyes in the picture Lucifer showed me keep encroaching on my thoughts. Eyes like those are one in a million. I'm sure if I do come face-to-face with those eyes, I will know I've got the right guy.

I will do just about anything to not end up in the version of Hell Lucifer revealed to me. Although that vision motivates me, I am not sure I can knowingly sic Lucifer on someone, especially with the kind of demise he is planning for this poor soul.

If I don't, my eternity will be horrific.

I shiver and glance down at my phone at the balance in my checking account. I'm not sure it will be enough to find those blue eyes, but I better make it last. Otherwise, I *will* be walking.

Just the thought of walking hundreds of miles makes my legs ache, and I stand and stretch, trying to push the thought away.

My gaze lands on the urns. "I'm sorry, Mom and Dad," I say, but I know it isn't enough. I forfeited their future for a guy who was probably cheating on me long before prom.

The house presses down on me, tightening my chest. The thought of staying here in this town, with my overwhelming problems, leaves me just as cold as failing Lucifer.

I need to move, to get out of this house to clear my head. But I can't go anywhere in my pajamas. I head to the shower and let the warm water wash away the pain piercing my heart. I don't bother with makeup, but I do take the time to brush my hair out, so I at least look presentable to the world.

With no plan in mind beyond getting away from this crappy town, I grab the keys off the side table and head out the door, locking up the house behind me out of sheer habit.

The green compact car my parents handed down to me sits in the driveway, and I sigh as the weight of their loss presses on my shoulders. My car is the only item that seems to be paid off. Hopefully the bank doesn't repossess it for my parents' debts.

With that depressing thought, I pull out of the driveway and head toward the highway. I'm not sure where I'm going. All I know is I can't be here any longer. Not with the past few days of one bad scenario followed by another, culminating in the devil delivering my parents' ashes to my coffee table.

I need to get lost.

Lost.

The directional sign for going east comes into view, but my focus moves to the sign pointing west.

What better place to get lost than a city of millions?

Silver Flecks may be somewhere in New England, but I am heading to New York to figure out a way to give the devil the slip. When I turn onto the westbound highway, my insides tighten.

It's just an uncomfortable churning in my midsection, as if I had eaten something rotten, but the closer I get to the Massachusetts—New York border, the more my stomach squeezes. Each mile knots my belly even more until it reaches a level where I can hardly concentrate on the road.

The sign for the rest area appears and I pray I can make it. My insides feel as though something is trying to eat their way out. I take the exit ramp and fly into a parking spot, throw the car in park in the empty parking lot, and swing the door open just as acid burns its way up my throat and splatters on the pavement.

Coughing the last of the vile burning liquid out of my stomach, I spit on the ground and lean back in the seat, wiping the sweat off my face. I close the door and sit with my car idling, wondering what the hell just happened because Crunch Berries never made me sick like this before.

My stomach still feels like I was punched a hundred times over.

A huge dog jumps on the hood of my car, pulling a yelp from my lips. The thing is black as night, with a coat so short it almost looks hairless. His huge teeth bare at me in a ferocious growl, and he paws at my hood, nearly tearing the metal. His eyes shimmer red and the hairs on my neck stand on end.

I push back in my seat at the unearthly quality of the beast.

"You didn't think I'd leave you unattended, did you?"

The voice from the back of the car startles another cry from me. My gaze jumps from the hound on my hood to the rearview mirror. Lucifer's challenging eyes stare me down.

I swallow hard, trying to think up a viable excuse. But I can't.

He leans forward and runs his index finger down my cheek. "Try to run again and I'll let him tear you to pieces. He hasn't had a good meal of human flesh in months."

I can envision what those teeth and nails would do to my flesh if given the chance. I nod because my voice isn't anywhere to be found in my body. As a matter of fact, I think I'm holding my breath.

"I normally don't give anyone a second chance. Usually, I would have let my hellhounds into this car and just wait until you were juicy bits before taking you to Hell. But, given the misfortune you are dealing with, I will make an exception."

I can't tear my gaze away from his reflection in the rearview mirror. Lucifer is as terrifying as the beast on my hood.

"Turn back now and understand my hellhounds can find you anywhere you try to hide. Therefore, so can I."

I move my head in that same insane up and down motion that's making me feel even sicker. I shy away from his hand, putting enough distance between his skin and mine so that I don't feel like my cheek is suffering from frostbite.

"Do you understand?" He raises an eyebrow.

"Yes." I force the word out of my chest. I don't understand how one word can encompass the terror I feel so completely, but the devil seems to be satisfied. He and the beast pop out of existence.

Tears well up in my eyes, stinging as they leak down the back of my tight throat and heat paths down my face at the same time. There is no way out of this mess. And now I have to head back on the westbound highway before I can turn east. I don't know whether my body can take whatever pain Lucifer decides to rain on me for not going the right way.

I am not incorrect.

As I head west, that pressing anguish not only encompasses my stomach but now my entire body until I see my escape from this agony up ahead. A turn-around where police officers often sit.

Thankfully, this one is cruiser-free. But even if it wasn't I would still take the turn.

Traffic is blessedly light, and I get into the high-speed lane, checking my rearview before slowing down enough to take the turn without rolling the car. The minute I pull out onto the eastbound lane, the pain disappears.

I can almost hear Lucifer whisper "good girl" in my ear.

I shiver hard enough that I need to pull over into the breakdown lane to catch my breath. I take a moment and wipe my face of the tears that streak my skin. I have to find this demon hunter, because I cannot fathom an eternity with this type of hellish torment.

The Devil's Offer
Chapter 6

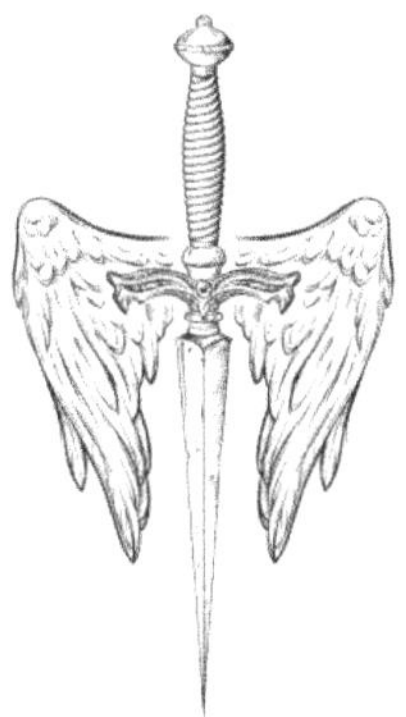

WITH THE RADIO BLASTING so loud that my thoughts can't formulate beyond the words of the old-time rock ballads tumbling from my lips, I drive nearly three hours across the state. By the time I reach Boston, my voice is a raspy whisper from belting out all the oldies that my parents loved to listen to. Secretly, I loved the old rock and roll, too, but I never admitted that to my parents. Instead, I rolled my eyes any time they cranked up the radio and sang—off tune—in the front seats.

I wish they were here and not dust on the coffee table back at the house. Overwhelming sadness grips me, and I inhale the stale air in the car, suddenly in need of a walk to distance myself from everything dear about them, including their music and the car they gave me.

I go to the only place I am familiar with: the Children's Museum near the seaport. By chance, I find a cheap parking lot to stow my car in while I walk along the seaport to get my head in gear for this unfathomable task. I have to find this mysterious stranger who will be my savior from Hell.

The ocean calms me. I love the spray that comes up whenever a wave hits the seawall, but today the harbor is relatively quiet. The lapping of the water on the wall hypnotizes me. I take a seat on a lone bench at the edge of the park, watching as the boats come and go.

My mind flows through every escape option that I can pull forth, even though I know they are all futile. My only viable option is to find the demon hunter with the eyes that will haunt my dreams forever and hand him over to the devil.

My stomach lets out a loud gurgle of neglect, and I shift in the seat, letting out a breath as my stiff muscles protest. Only then do I realize that the day has already transitioned to twilight. I blink at the darkening sky and the pink hue low on the horizon, as if I hadn't been fully aware of time's passage.

A growl fills the air, and at first, I think it's my stomach, but it doesn't come with that gnawing feeling like my abdomen is shrinking. I glance from side to side to see if whatever had made that noise came from that direction. Nothing. Which left only one other direction left to check. I glance over my shoulder. My heart jolts and my muscles freeze in place. My eyes widen at the horrid sight just beyond me, slinking in the shadows.

A beast more frightening than Lucifer's hellhound stands on its hind legs. It reminds me of Chewbacca, because of the hair all over its body. But that's where the similarity ends. Its eyes are red like a stoplight, and it has claws that would make a lion envious. I blink as my mind grabs onto the word *bear*, but that isn't right either. This thing is feral and otherworldly.

Saliva drips from its exposed teeth.

I slowly stand and face the beast, ready to defend myself as best I can against such a terrifying adversary. I fist my hands and lift them up.

"I'm not going easily." I hope the warning comes through my voice, and not the terror shrinking my muscles.

The air around me shifts, and the beast hisses and then turns and runs.

"Yeah, you turn tail and run, you coward!" I turn and run smack in to a bare chest.

"Oh, I'm…" I step back and my voice fails at the leather-clad man holding a sword like nothing I've ever seen before. But that's not what has my tongue tied. It's the magnificent wings spread from behind him, black and lush as the night threatening to fall around us.

Then my gaze goes to his beautiful face. I have never seen such a stunning man before. Hell, I've never seen a winged man before, but his beauty is beyond natural. Then I notice his eyes. Even in this low light, I cannot mistake those eyes. Ocean blue with specks of silver, just like the picture.

I lick my lips but cannot invoke Lucifer's name. Not when I am so totally lost in this being's gaze. It's as if I am hypnotized by him, and he stares at me in the same curious way.

"Did you truly think you could destroy that demon with a punch?"

Even his damn voice is like a velvet blanket wrapping around me. I let out a laugh and blink. "I don't have a handy-dandy weapon like you do." I point to the trident-like sword he's holding.

He holds up his weapon, turning it this way and that. It's really more like a double spear with some ornate metal between the two sharp blades than a sword now that I see it close up. "It was forged to kill demons and has done the job well." He looks in the direction the monster ran with a sigh. "I've been hunting *that* particular demon for a week." His gaze drops to mine.

"What are you?" I can't help the question, especially with the wings and the peculiar accent he has. It certainly isn't a Boston accent or anything near Massachusetts. It's smooth and silky, as if his voice is a deep, dark chocolate shake that heats me to the core.

He smiles, flashing teeth so white that I nearly squint. "You are not afraid of me?"

I laugh. "Not in the least." He does not instill fear in me the way Lucifer does. It's quite the opposite and honestly, I have no idea what to categorize this warmth as. It damn near has me turning to a puddle at his feet. Thankfully, my bones remain solid and keep me upright. "But you clearly were the one who scared that thing away. Thank you, for that."

"And what if I am here to reap you?" His head cocks and his eyes narrow, but that humorous glint in his eyes gives him away.

"You're a demon hunter, not a human hunter. So, what exactly are you?" I return to my original question.

His eyes cloud over with suspicion. "What makes you think I'm a demon hunter?"

My mind whirls for an answer, and my gaze falls on his weapon. "Well, if that thing was forged to kill demons and you've been hunting that demon for a week, I assume that makes you a demon hunter."

His wings fold out of sight, and he shudders for a second and then focuses back on me with slightly pursed lips. "So, you truly believed you could take a nocnik demon?"

"A what?"

"Nocnik demon. He feeds on innocence." He looks around, verifying there isn't anyone else within view. "This place doesn't usually attract the innocent after dark." When his gaze finds me again, it is piercing, like a laser boring into my soul. "Why are you here alone?"

The interest I had been feeling melts away as reality crashes down. I shuffle my feet and glance out at the bay. "I lost track of time. My parents died recently, and I just needed the quiet of the boats and the water.” I wave at the marina and shrug.

His face softens, as if I have impacted him some way, and he twists his wrist holding the weapon. It fades into the dark.

Now I really need to know what he is, besides Lucifer’s wanted demon hunter. “You never answered my question.”

“I’m just a guy who found you after you were mugged.” This time, a Boston accent inches its way into his voice.

As I stare at him, a baseball cap appears on his head and a Red Sox T-shirt materializes over his bare chest, much to my chagrin.

I shake my head to clear it, as if I am having some sort of issue from the concussion. The guy in a baseball cap is somehow superimposed over the bare-chested demon hunter. I narrow my eyes at him, focusing below the façade he put on. “You are something beyond. What are you?” I demand, tempted to say Lucifer’s name. But something I cannot put my finger on makes me hesitate.

“Jeez, I was just trying to help.” He steps around me.

I grab his hand.

Multiple things happen to overwhelm me at once.

Warmth radiates through me, as if I have just touched the purest of lights and it has bonded with me. His gaze snaps back to mine and his wings sprout. His weapon appears and he points it at me as though I’m his greatest enemy.

“What are you?” he asks in a hushed warning.

I hold tight to his hand, clasping it with both of mine as I do not want to give up this celestial touch. “I’m just a human who made a grave mistake and now my parents are dead because of my lack of judgment.” I spill pieces of the truth to keep him from impaling me with his spear.

His wings flutter, and I can't tell whether it's because he is indecisive or angry.

A crease appears between his eyes. "You can see through my glamour and are not afraid in the presence of an angel, so either you are otherworldly as well, or..." He steps away from me but does not release my hand.

"Or what?"

He blinks rapidly. "Or you are damned."

I let out a laugh but the tears surface. I blink them back as his words sink in. "An angel?" My gaze goes to our clasped hands. "Or a demon hunter?" I look back up into his eyes.

"Both. Humans aren't equipped to deal with demons." He glances at our intertwined hands. That crease appears again between his eyes. "This." He lifts our hands between us. "Is not... normal." He looks beyond our hands into my eyes, as if he's trying to read my soul.

I slowly pull my hand out of his, severing the connection between us and that warmth flees from my bones, leaving me chilled. I wrap my arms around my chest, rubbing my arms as the bite of the spring night penetrates my bones.

"Let me walk you to somewhere safe," he says while he stares at his palm, as if it carries the answers to all his unasked questions.

I let him lead me out of the park, but I steer him toward the nearest hotel.

Something deep inside me warns me not to take him to my car. A hellhound gouged the surface, marking it, and this angel will see that I am one of the devil's pawns.

I glance at the lance in his hand, wondering whether it will hurt when he spears me with it.

The Devil's Offer
Chapter 7

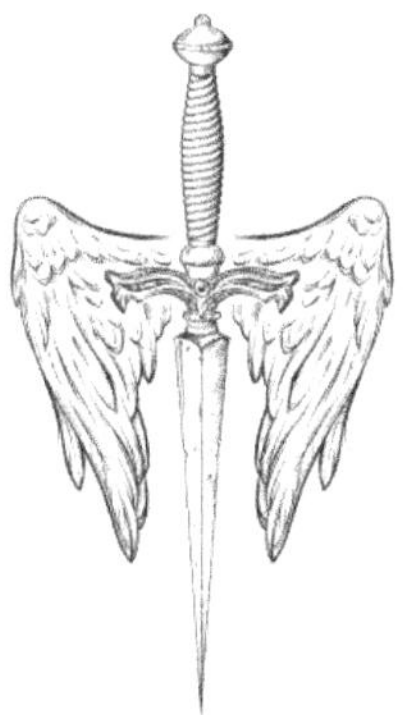

OUTSIDE THE HOTEL, I turn to him. "Thank you for escorting me this far, but I can go the rest of the way myself." I wave to the entrance as if it is where I am staying.

He nods but lingers. "What's your name?"

"Layla. Layla Anderson." I extend my hand in greeting. "And you are?"

His lip tilts to the side in a partial smile that is quite endearing. "Gabe."

He takes my hand in his in a soft handshake that is firm and warm, and I just about melt into a puddle on the sidewalk at the sensation our touching skin creates.

"Gabe what?" I ask after he pulls his hand back and the connection breaks.

He glances around us, and then leans in and whispers, "Gabriel."

"What's your last name?" I put my hands on my hips and narrow my eyes as he cocks his head. His name rings in my ears and my hands fall to my side as I stare into those blue eyes. The silver flecks seem to rotate, catching the light in such a way as to wipe any meager doubt away.

The archangel Gabriel.

My head clouds in confusion. "But your wings are black, not white." I thought all angel's wings were white except for Lucifer.

"Yes. They've never been white here on Earth. Not sure if it's the air or what, but they're only white upstairs." He points toward the sky.

"Shouldn't you be manning the gates of Heaven?" I ask as my mind fills with all my youth Bible study classes relating to the different archangels.

He laughs. It is full and musical, capturing my entire attention, just like his beautiful features. Perfection stood in front of me in every sense of the word. "I haven't manned the gates of Heaven since the birth of Christ."

I blink rapidly and then let out a high-pitched giggle. My brain finally unhinges as the reality of who I'm talking to slams home. I need to get away from this handsome archangel before I totally fall apart. "I need something to eat," I say to change the subject before my mind melts.

"They have a good pub." He nods toward the hotel. When he steps to my side and places his hand on my back to lead me inside, I stop.

"That wasn't an invitation." I don't want to spend any more time with him because he makes me feel warm and comfortable and like a total fake. I'm supposed to sell him out to the devil, but I still can't find the will to force his name from my lips. The longer I am with this being, the less interested I am in my own salvation.

Hell, I haven't been able to let Lucifer's name slip out even with the opening he just gave me. It should be easy to slip that name into conversation, but I find I'm compelled otherwise. Like a protective streak has awakened in me.

"I'm sorry. I assumed you might need someone to talk to." He shifts his feet, but he does not leave. A crease appears between his eyes, like he is just as confused about his actions as I am with mine. "I'm not… comfortable leaving you alone." His gaze meets mine. "And I'm not entirely sure why."

"Because I'm not otherworldly." I have no clue why that slips out, but it does. Which only means one other thing, and that crease between his eyes deepens.

"How are you damned?"

I stare at him for a moment too long, and then turn to head into the pub. I don't want to relive my greatest mistake. Not with it so fresh and raw.

He reaches for me, and I twist to avoid his touch. If our skin meets again, I'll spill everything and that will only make me one of his targets. But that doesn't dissuade him from following me into the building. It's amazing. As he walks through the door, he's back in the threads and hat he tried to get me to believe in the park. It's as if we passed through a portal from the fantasy to reality and I don't know which way the door swings.

"Seriously, Gabe, I don't need a babysitter." I send a sideways glance at him as he matches me pace for pace into the pub. When I take a seat at a far table, he slides in across from me.

"I've never babysat anyone in my lifetime. So, just chill and tell me what happened." He puts his hand up, waving it gently in a circle. The entire room freezes in place.

I glance around at the frozen patrons and then back at the archangel who made the room stop. I wonder whether the rest of the world is in the same condition, and a nervous flutter starts in my stomach at the continued mind-bending lunacy.

"Car accident on prom night." It's the only explanation I can give. "I came in here to eat, remember?" Internally, my heart throbs in my chest and my mouth dries enough so that I am amazed any words could escape from the Sahara that is my throat. I put my palms on the table so I won't fidget, but it's useless under his piercing stare.

His hand waves again, and motion resumed. A bubble-popping waitress approaches the table.

"My name's Shirley. I'll be your waitress tonight. What can I start you off with?" She sets down menus and silverware at the table for us.

"May I start with a water?" I pick up the menu, looking over the options. My gaze jumps from the item to the prices and then I look up at Gabe, suddenly afraid that he's going to order the most expensive item on the menu.

"I'll have a water as well. And I'll have the pub special, if you don't mind," he says smoothly, pointing at the flyer already on the table. The paper announced a bacon cheeseburger with cheesy fries at a reasonable price. "Medium rare, please," he adds as the waitress scribbles his order.

"Make that two." I hand her my menu, relieved that he didn't opt for the lobster and steak combo. Although, that actually sounds good to me. But a juicy cheeseburger sounds even better for my pocketbook.

"Lettuce, tomato, and onion?" she asks.

"No thank you," we both say in concert.

A weird sensation flows over me, and I glance toward the door, expecting Lucifer to waltz in with deadly intent. But all that enters is another couple lost in each other's gaze, and not the king of Hell.

As soon as Shirley leaves us with tall glasses of water, I take a gulp and glance back at Gabe, unnerved by his intense stare.

"You were saying something about your prom?"

I look down into my glass. "I killed my parents that night," I finally say, because saying I sold my soul for my boyfriend sounds as trite as it feels.

"Parenticide?" He jerks back in the seat with a scowl.

"It was not intentional." I meet his gaze, clarifying. "But it was still my fault."

"That could not have damned you." His eyes narrow. "Accidents don't do that."

"Well, that's the only thing I can think of that would put me in the category of damned," I snap. "I'm certainly not otherworldly." I roll my eyes to dissuade him from pursuing this anymore.

He studies me, pondering as he sips his water. "You are strange."

He pauses as our bubble-popping waitress carries out our plates. She smiles at us as she sets down our meals, and then skips off to another table with her pad at the ready.

Gabriel waves his fingers in a circle and still silence descends over the pub. Patrons freeze in place, some with food partially to their mouths or drinks frozen between the glass and waiting maws. It's odd, to say the least. Gabriel picks up his burger and glances at me.

"I like to eat in peace." He digs into his meal as if he hasn't eaten earthly food in eons.

I pick at the fries, opting for the cheesy mess first before digging into the burger. But Gabriel's mouth sidetracks me. The way he licks the juices from his lips enthralls me. It's as decadent as a chocolate fudge cake. I force my gaze back to my food while my heart flutters and my cheeks heat.

He's looking at my plate as well. "Is there something wrong with your meal?"

I smile and shake my head. The way I ate used to bother Jay, too. But I couldn't change my habit of eating from my favorite to my least favorite thing on the plate. More heat flushes my cheeks. "I kind of eat my favorite things first." I shrug, avoiding his sparkling eyes.

His low laugh fills the space between us, and he leans toward me. "So do I," he says. "One thing at a time, because mixing seems... wrong."

My eyebrows rise as I meet his gaze. "It used to drive my parents crazy."

"Well, there is something fundamentally wrong with it." He grins and those silver flecks in his eyes sparkle like the heavens above. "Instead of saving the best for last, you indulge first." He winks at me. "I bet you ate dessert first as a child."

I shake my head. "If not for my parents, I would have, though." I glance at his plate and the cheesy fries. "I'll trade you my burger for your fries."

He cocks an eyebrow and looks at my burger as if it's as good as dessert. Then he licks his lips and meets my gaze. "Seriously?"

The hopeful lilt in his voice leaves me breathless for some reason. I nod because it seems my voice has failed me. Before I know it, he has my burger in his hand and is pushing his plateful of cheesy fries in front of me.

"Do you want a bite before I devour it?"

A little voice in my head says *Oh, yes*, but I ignore the inappropriate thought that has nothing to do with the cheeseburger.

"No. This is perfect." I dig into the cheesy fries with all the zest of someone who hasn't eaten anything but dry cereal for several days. If I wasn't sharing the booth with an archangel who I was supposed to sell out, I would actually consider this the perfect date.

"You are truly an enigma." He licks his fingers clean before wiping them with a napkin. "An innocent who can see me as I am without being damned. If I didn't know better, I might suspect my brother finally found a martyr who could fool me." He leans back, studying me with his hand close to mine.

"What brother?" I say through a mouthful of fries and cover my mouth, mindful of my rudeness. My stomach tightens, and I do my best to focus on my food. When he doesn't speak, I look up.

The absence of a smile on his beautiful face shakes me, and I swallow the bite hard. His hand moves over mine, capturing it in his tight grip. He turns my hand and inspects my index finger. When his eyes return to mine, the silver specks are rotating in a strange pattern.

"Why haven't you called him yet?"

"Who?" I ask, stalling.

"Layla." He sighs and traces the mark on the tip of my finger. "How can this be?" he asks, still staring at my finger. When his gaze returns to mine, it's pained in a way that tightens my throat.

"There was a car accident after the prom..." I say softly.

He searches my eyes. And then he slowly releases my hand. "You traded your soul for someone else."

My chin quivers and my vision blurs. I look down at my lap because I cannot meet his sad gaze. I nod.

"And that bastard took your parents instead." Now his voice sounds sharp and angry.

I nod again.

"And I would bet my life that he also arranged for whoever you saved to desert you, and he offered you a way to regain your soul by serving up the last demon hunter." He crosses his arms.

"Yes."

"So why haven't you called him?"

I meet his gaze. "Why haven't you struck me down?" I ask, because I don't have a logical answer as to why I haven't called Lucifer. My sense of self-preservation is surely off-kilter.

He sighs and the air ripples with it. He touches my hand, caressing it with his finger as he shakes his head. "I don't know."

"I seem to lack a sense of self-preservation."

His lips twitch and then laughter spills from his mouth. It's full and beautiful, just like the smile that

reaches his eyes. "And I seem to have a death wish."
He threads his fingers through mine and that
physical warmth flows from him into me like a
golden sunset.

Gabriel releases the patrons as I continue to pick
at my food. I'm no longer hungry, not after admitting
I was Lucifer's pawn. But Gabriel didn't kill me. He
seems to be as perplexed with our connection as I
am.

Shirley drops the bill off at the table and I hand
her enough cash to cover it, along with a decent tip.

"You shouldn't drive tonight." He stands next to
me and clasps my hand as we enter the hotel lobby.
"You should get a room here, instead."

"Are you propositioning me?" I tease, because his
concern unnerves me.

He shifts and looks away with a shake of his
head. He can't seem to meet my gaze. "No." But his
cheeks turn crimson.

I stop in the center of the lobby, staring at the
archangel Gabriel and his bright-red cheeks. "Oh my
God. You are."

He finally meets my gaze but instead of answering
me, he says, "Just don't drive home." He starts
backing away but doesn't let go of my hand.

"Don't go." I can't believe those words escape from
my mouth. I lick my lips and shift from foot to foot as
well. "I really am not in the habit of..."

He smirks. "Neither am I." He looks at the front
desk and then back at me. "But for some reason, I
cannot seem to... leave."

"It sounds like *your* sense of self-preservation is
lacking."

He steps close enough for me to see underneath
the ruse. "And you have a death wish," he says.
"Because if my brother finds out you were with me
and did not call him, he will skin you alive." He
searches my eyes. "For all eternity."

He raises his hand and cups my cheek and without a word, he delivers a soft kiss that lights my entire world on fire.

"This is so extraordinary," he whispers against my lips and then deepens the kiss.

The Devil's Offer
Chapter 8

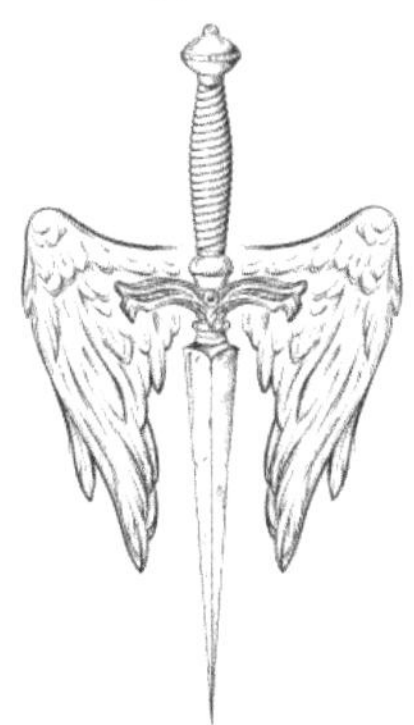

HIS KISS MAKES MY mind so fuzzy that I saunter over to the desk and ask for a room for the night. When I set out for Boston, I hadn't intended on staying at a five-star hotel. But when the concierge starts explaining pricing, I understand why.

It's the slap of reality I need.

"I'm sorry, my mistake," I say and head toward the door without a glance back at Gabriel. It isn't until I'm out on the street breathing the cool spring evening air that my mind clears.

Halfway down the block, Gabriel grabs my arm and swings me back toward him. Even his touch fogs my brain in a way that is dangerous. He is right. Lucifer will make me pay for not handing him over.

"I can't afford a hotel room." The words tumble from my lips and my cheeks heat with embarrassment.

He holds up a key. "I can."

I blink at him as if he just grew another head. "You let me pay for that meal." I point toward the restaurant.

"You wanted food. I don't want you sleeping at your house, where my brother can find you easily. So... I picked up the tab for the room."

"He said he can find me anywhere," I blurt, but my eyes are locked on the hotel room key. I do need a good night's sleep. But with Gabriel there, I doubt that will happen.

Gabriel glances down at the hand I signed the contract with. "I suppose he can, but that still doesn't negate the fact it is harder when you are not calling on him. And you do not have a convincing poker face."

His point hits like a punch. If Lucifer finds me and drills me for information, I have no hope of lying convincingly. "A hotel isn't going to protect me."

"No. But I will."

I recoil and stare at his stunning eyes. "Why? I was contracted to sell you out."

"But you didn't. You could have the moment we met in the park, and again any moment since." His soft voice lulls me like a warm hug.

"I'm going to Hell," I say equally as soft. Whatever we might find together will end, and end violently.

He stares at me. "Were you aware of what was happening when you signed your name?"

Gabriel is fishing. I can see it in his eyes as they search mine, but I have nothing to hide from him now that he knows I'm compromised. "I had a concussion from the accident and honestly, I thought I was hallucinating."

His eyes brighten, as if I gave him an opening of some sort. Hope flared and his silver flecks danced in his irises. "Did you read the contract?"

I shake my head. "It was written in a language I didn't understand. But the guy explained that in exchange for my soul, Jay would live, and he said time was ticking and his boss didn't like to revive the dead."

He bites his bottom lip and takes my hand, leading me back to the hotel. As we cross the lobby, heads turn, following us as we step on the elevator together. The concierge stares at us. His scowl says more than I want to see on an adult right now. His judgment of what he deems as two teenagers getting into trouble is clear.

Except I am eighteen, not sixteen, and Gabriel... My gaze jumps to Gabe. I have no idea how old he is, but he looks maybe twenty at best. The looks from the desk don't seem to bother him, either.

As the elevator doors start to close, frigid air fills the lobby and slips into the space with us, sending chills through me. We trade a glance and our gazes dart to the front door. I catch a glimpse of who steps into the hotel before the elevators shuts us in.

My breath locks in my throat.

Lucifer has arrived despite my inability to say his name.

I turn to Gabriel with panic seizing every muscle, and my grip tightens on his hand. His gaze is locked on the door as well, but when it turns to me, I gulp at the accusation held in his irises.

"Did you call him?" he hisses, but does not unclasp his hand from mine. It's as if neither one of us can let go.

"No." The tremble encompassing my body makes it through to my voice.

He releases my hand and runs his fingers over the elevator buttons, reminding me of a Christmas movie where one of Santa's elves does the same to make the buttons look like a Christmas tree. But Gabriel isn't doing it to make it look like a Christmas tree. His pattern is more random, and his purpose is to give us time.

Time and a way to escape before Lucifer corners us. Terror brushes a cold hand over my skin, and I can't stop shaking. If he finds us, neither one of us will fare well.

When the door opens at the next stop, he grasps my hand again and pulls me out of the elevator. We wind through the maze of hallways until we find a stairwell at the back of the building.

Relief sweeps through me as we sprint down the stairs. That reprieve ends when we get to the ground floor and the exit door has an alarm warning printed on it. Gabriel ignores it and barrels out the door into a back alley.

Alarms blare, announcing our location to anyone privy to building security, but then the door swings closed behind us, and the alarms shut off. The outer door has no handle, so if this alley is a dead end, we are screwed.

My eyes adjust to the dark, and all the hairs on the back of my neck stand on end.

"Bastard," Gabriel whispers at the pair of hounds blocking the alleyway. He pushes me behind him and puts his hand out. His weapon appears and as he steps away, the façade of the young man fades away into his true form.

The hellhounds lunge. One grabs the staff of his weapon, making it impossible for Gabriel to swing the blade at the beast. The other crouches to launch.

I react, and charge, pushing Gabriel out of the way, only to be knocked down by the hound. I roll on my back as the demon-beast growls down at me. His maw opens to strike a mortal blow, but silver swings through the air, decapitating the beast and dousing my face with hellhound blood.

I choke on it, spitting and rolling the dead body off me as I try to wipe the blood from my eyes. I am sure I'm a sight, but Gabriel grabs my hand and hauls me to my feet, guiding me around the second decapitated hellhound.

We start down the alley when the back door bangs open. Blaring alarms send my heart into overdrive.

Lucifer stands, backlit by the stairwell light, but I can see the flames swirling in his irises even from this distance.

"Brother!" Lucifer bellows.

Gabriel slows even as I pull at him to keep following me away from danger. He peels my hand out of his and gives me a nod. But before he turns away, he slips a dagger in my hand and meets my gaze. "Just in case," he whispers and then steps away, toward Lucifer.

"What?" Gabriel answers his brother. "Are you here to attempt to kill me, yet again?"

Lucifer steps out into the dark alley and the door swings closed. "I see you've met my newest acquisition." He waves toward me. "A pathetic epitome of innocence and misguided loyalty to someone who'd rather hump a whore than wait for her."

"Fuck you," I snarl, pissed by his description of me.

"Ooo. But she does possess spunk." He laughs as he steps closer reminding me more of the god of mischief than the devil. He looks past Gabriel, directly at me. "You sold your soul for someone who was screwing the school's biggest whore in the bathroom before he convinced you to go to a hotel with him so he could do the same to you."

His words scrape my soul, leaving scars as wide as this dark alley. "What?" My brain will not accept that my parents are dead because of a cheating asshole, but deep down, I know the devil speaks the truth.

It would have been more humane had he gutted me. His smile is as spiteful as he is.

Apparently, Lucifer is done speaking to me, and his attention turns to Gabriel. "And she is just the right kind of bait to flush you out. Although she will pay dearly for not calling me the *moment* she realized you were the demon hunter I sent her after."

Gabriel's wings snap open and flutter, as if Lucifer has pushed a sensitive button. His expression turns feral, and his jaw tightens before he takes a deep breath. His face smooths out, and his wings retract.

In that moment, I can imagine just how scary Gabriel can be if he isn't on your side. I thank the heavens he did see something in me that made him give me a reprieve. Otherwise, I would currently be paying my penance in Hell.

Lucifer belts out a laugh. "The little human has gotten to you in just a few measly hours? That is just priceless. Well, how about I fillet her while you watch?" He points toward me, and it's as if I am hooked onto a fishing line. No matter how hard I dig my heels in, I'm helplessly pulled toward my demise.

"Is your contract binding if the person who signs is compromised in any way?" Gabriel grabs my arm as I slide by him.

My forward progression stops. I'm not sure whether it's his words or his hand on me that kills Lucifer's hold, but I am thankful.

Lucifer blinks and points at me again, but nothing happens. And then his gaze snaps to Gabriel with a growl. "I own her soul."

"I beg to differ. A human with a concussion isn't of sound mind." Gabriel still holds my arm but his grip is light as if he could step away at any moment.

"You are trying to dictate soul contracts with me?" Lucifer's gaze narrows as his voice barrels in the alley.

"A blood signature is only binding if the person signing understands the small print. That was the deal, or at least how I understood it," Gabriel says.

I think he actually bats his eyelashes, feigning innocence.

"Do I need to call Michael down here to settle this?"

"You wouldn't dare." Lucifer glances toward the sky with something akin to fear on his face.

I rejoice in the fact the devil is quaking in his proverbial boots.

"He may beat me blind for calling on him, but you—you he's destined to kill the next time your paths cross. So, Lucifer, is today that day?" The way Gabriel cocks his head and levels an innocent smile belies the glare in his eyes.

Lucifer scrunches his face as his irises glow with hellfire. He turns that glare on me, and I just about lose my bladder. "Did you read the contract before signing it?" he snaps through clenched teeth, as if he already knows the answer.

"No. It wasn't written in English."

"Bloody fucking hell," he grumbles and then glares at Gabriel. My contract appears, goes up in flames, and his hands clench. "Her soul may be free, but I can still snuff out her life just to piss you off."

Gabriel pushes me behind him. "I'd like to see you try."

Lucifer smiles. "You didn't think I came with just two hellhounds, did you?"

I spin and gasp, backing into Gabriel as three dogs advance toward us. I regrip the knife so the blade is down and settle into a karate stance, with the knife in my forward hand. All my fear and doubts fall away and only the need to survive ignites in my blood. With grim resolve, I square up, readying myself for battle.

"If you harm her in any way, *I* will assume Michael's destiny."

"Come and try, little brother. And when I'm holding your severed head and letting my beasts dine on your entrails, no one will give a damn."

Both Gabriel's and Lucifer's exchange seems distant as I concentrate on the danger in front of me. Fear blooms in my belly at Lucifer's dare, especially with the hellhounds growling with such ferocity that

I doubt I'll see the sunrise. But just like the beast in the park, I am damned if I'll go down without a fight.

The pressure on my back releases as Gabriel steps away from me, but I don't dare turn away from the hellhounds. My survival depends on my focus, and I can't let the sounds of battle behind me deter me. Not if I have a prayer of surviving.

"Come on, then," I yell at the beasts, putting as much of a growl in my voice as I can. My outburst seems to perplex them, as if no one else in the history of mankind ever roared back in the moment before they attacked. I guess hellhounds are used to people fleeing in fear instead of squaring up for a fight. The bastards recover quickly, crouching to launch with a snarl of their own.

If all three hit me at once, I'm doomed.

There isn't much maneuverability in this alley only wide enough to fit a single delivery truck at a time, but I have enough room when they spring at me to react. I spin with the knife at the ready and a roundhouse kick trailing. I twist away from two of the hounds; one I catch with the edge of the knife and the other with a kick to the head. But their whines of pain are muffled by the third hound as his shoulder hits my side with brute force, cracking at least one of my ribs.

I stumble off-balance into the brick wall, flailing my arm with the blade in the hopes that I'll hit the beast. The hellhound jumps out of my reach at the last second.

The three hounds spread out in front of me, advancing with every intent of tearing flesh from bone.

I swallow hard and wave the knife in a slow figure eight in front of me, as I shuffle into a ready stance, balancing my weight on the balls of my feet so I can adjust my reaction to whatever comes. When they launch, I will have to move fast.

Gabriel's sword rockets through the air, slicing through one of the hellhounds and impaling the other, killing them both and leaving me with only one dog to deal with. His sacrifice shreds my very soul. By saving me, it leaves Gabriel vulnerable to Lucifer's wrath.

"No!" I cry and launch toward his weapon as Lucifer knocks Gabriel down. The remaining hellhound attacks, grabbing my arm like it's a chew toy.

I scream and try to shake him off as I reach Gabriel's sword. Searing heat grips my arm where the beast's teeth embed in my skin, and I drag my knife across the dog's snout. He retreats with a howl of pain. As much as I'd like to finish him off, I need to get that sword back to Gabriel.

One glance and my heart knocks painfully in my chest. Gabriel is on his knees, with Lucifer's arm wrenching his neck. Using my injured arm, I pry his sword from the dead hellhound and shove it across the ground toward Gabriel, praying it slides far enough for him to reach.

If not, we were both done.

The full force of the hellhound hits my chest as I straighten. I fall on my back, and before my vision is filled with fury and teeth, I see Gabriel slam the business end of his sword through his wing and into Lucifer's torso. It's enough for Lucifer's hold to fail.

I grip the knife tight despite the hound's teeth and nails shredding my forearms. His focus moves from my arms blocking him, to my throat beyond, and the hound roars as it lunges in for the kill.

I scream just as loud and slam the blade to the hilt into the hound's eye and then yank it free, ready to deliver another blow if that doesn't do the job. More blood obscures my vision and then the hound's full weight drops onto me. It twitches a couple of times and then is still.

I can't breathe with this thing on me, and if I don't get a full breath, I'm going to pass out. I use a karate move to plant my leg and roll the weight off. It takes a couple of tries and then the beast shifts onto the pavement next to me.

The world spins as I move onto my back again. I stare at the stars above as only my breath registers at first. And then a scraping sound pulls my attention toward where the battle of angels had been.

Gabriel's crawling toward me, possibly in worse shape than I am, but at least he has his weapon and that is what scrapes on the ground as he painfully moves toward me in what seems to be slow motion.

His gaze locks on mine and beyond his pain is a worry so thick I can feel it like a chilled blanket.

As he crawls closer, a dark shape rises from the ground and lifts a blade high in the air. My heart shoots a heavy dose of adrenaline through my form, enough for me to launch the knife I still hold through the air in a last-ditch effort to save Gabriel.

Time crawls. My knife slices through the air, faster than Lucifer's death strike. Before he can land the final blow into Gabriel's back, my blade pierces his throat, sending him back a few steps.

His eyes widen and the sword drops from his hand. He reaches for the knife lodged in his neck, like he can't quite believe I had it in me.

"Not today," I hiss with as much attitude as I can muster.

Gabriel swivels to his back, swinging his blade, but before he hits the devil, Lucifer turns to smoke and disappears.

My head falls back on the pavement, and I stare at the constellations above. It seems like the darkness is descending until Gabriel's face appears over me.

"No. Not today, Layla," he whispers and puts his shaking, bloody hands over me.

White light fills the alley, blinding me. I try to see through the whiteness, but Gabriel is lost in the light. It's too pure and it's invading every cell of my body, wiping out all my aches. I close my eyes, letting go.

Maybe I'll be able to see my parents again.

The Devil's Offer
Chapter 9

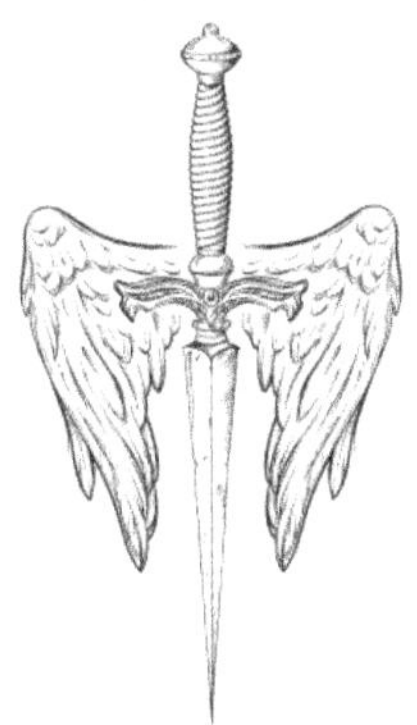

MY EYES OPEN AND I squint away from the light. The doctor snaps the flashlight off and smiles down at me. I blink and glance around a familiar room, confused. I look back at the doctor.

"Do you know where you are?"

I make an educated guess. "One of the hospitals in Boston?"

"No. You're at Mercy Hospital in West Springfield. Do you know what happened?"

I can't very well say I was attacked by a hellhound. I glance at my arms. But the sling isn't what catapults me into a sitting position. I cough at the pain in my chest and stare at the prom dress I am once again wearing. It's still marred with drops of blood, just like on prom night.

I steady myself with my hand and glance around the room again, blinking hard as if I can't quite focus my eyes on my surroundings.

Had I hallucinated it all?

"Layla, can you tell us what happened?" he asks again.

I lick my lips and look at him. "A... a car accident?" I finally say. A lump in my throat forms as fear creeps in like a stealth ninja, pummeling my insides. I don't know which accident this represents: the one in my memories or the one the devil manufactured. There is only one way to find out.

"Is Jay okay?" I need to know which timeline Gabriel dropped me back into.

"He's in the operating room right now." His demeanor seems to change, as if he shared more than he should have. "Your parents should be here shortly."

My parents. My heart fills with love and a thankfulness I don't know how to express. Tears blur my vision. If Gabriel were here, I would squeeze him in such a tight hug he wouldn't be able to breathe. But then the doctor's words penetrated through the silent joy like my knife into Lucifer's throat.

"How bad is he?" I ask, repeating the echoes of the first time I woke in this situation. But this time, my heart didn't ache for him, and my mind didn't cloud in despair.

The doctor sighed. "He is in critical condition. It's a miracle that you weren't more injured than just a concussion, a cracked rib, and a banged-up arm." He stood and jotted a few notes on my chart. "Just rest until your parents get here and then I'll be back to discuss your concussion protocol and what you can do for your rib once you're home."

I nodded. *I hadn't had a broken rib before. Had I?*

Fuzziness from the concussion blurs my vision with the nod, but after the doctor leaves the room, I slip off the bed, mimicking everything I had done before, although the ache in my side is new. As if Gabriel left me a reminder of our time. A reminder not to follow the same path as before.

I stare at my disorderly hair and try to hand comb it into place like before. Even though I replay the physical motions, the accident is not what I see in my mind. All I see is Gabriel's worried eyes as he puts his injured hands over me and that calming light fills my soul.

I don't beg for Jay's life like I had before. I just stare at my haunted reflection and try to smooth the dress as Gabriel's eyes dance in my memory.

An orderly passes by the entrance to the bathroom, and I stiffen. When I turn, it isn't the same one shrouded with a halo who stole my soul away from me. No, this orderly has a dark crop of hair and a profile I will never forget, not even if I was meant to.

"Oh, I'm sorry, I thought they said this room needed cleaning." He looks up at me, and those silver flecks dance in his ocean-blue eyes.

"Gabriel," I whisper.

He jerks and faces me with wide eyes. Everything is written in the surprise in his features, from his arched eyebrows to his open lips. His eyes shield something deeper. Something like relief.

"You really think I could forget you so easily?" I step closer, afraid he might just wisp away on the wind or something.

He shifts and looks at the open bathroom door and then at me again. "I had to be sure you wouldn't repeat the same mistake." He searches my eyes. "You only get one do over."

I shake my head. "I remember everything. I wouldn't make that mistake again." A question itches the base of my skull. "Lucifer doesn't lie, does he?" I need to know whether Lucifer had thrown bull my way to get a rise out of me in that alley.

"Sadly, he does not. He is every other despicable thing, but he is not a liar." He bites his lip and looks at the mop handle he clings to. "So, if your boyfriend pulls through?"

"Will he?" I ask, and Gabriel's eyes flare as though the question physically hurts him in some way.

"That's in fate's hands. If it's truly his time..." He shrugs. "If it isn't, then..." He looks away and his grip tightens on the broom handle.

I nod and glance around the room. "Why here?" I wave at the room.

He brings his gaze to mine. "This was the moment... the moment that you still held every last ounce of innocence before my brother meddled in your life."

I take a deep breath and step closer. "How? How did you do this?"

A frown forms and he looks at the ground. "It's a forbidden power angels possess." He doesn't meet my gaze.

I close the distance and cover his hand with mine. The same warm rush fills me and makes my mind fuzzy, but I can't see through his façade like I had in the park. I can't see his magnificent wings or his bare, chiseled chest. "I can't see through your disguise."

He lets out a nervous laugh, staring at my hand over his. "That's because this isn't a disguise. It's actually my punishment." He glances quickly at me and then back at the floor, as if his words would impact how I feel about him.

It takes a moment for his meaning to sink in. "You're mortal?" I gasp and step away.

He rolls his eyes and a smile forms on his soft lips. "I'm not otherworldly any longer, if that's what you're asking." He points at me. "And you, you should not remember all this. Are you sure you're not otherworldly?" His eyes narrow at me.

I shrug. "Not that I'm aware of. Maybe it has something to do with the concussion?" I wave at my head. "Or the broken rib you neglected to mend."

He lets out a soft laugh. "Maybe. Stranger things *have* happened."

"And your demon hunting gig?"

His eyes turn serious. "I haven't quite figured that out. I can't exactly run around Earth with that weapon. Not unless I want to end up behind bars."

It is my turn to laugh. He has a keen sense of humor. "You don't have a death wish?"

Dimples burst in his cheeks. "No. I have a healthy sense of self-preservation."

We shared a quiet chuckle. He glances at the door and lifts his hand to my cheek, caressing my lower lip with his thumb. "I don't regret my choice in the least." He meets my gaze with an intensity that takes my breath away.

"You didn't sell your angelic soul for me, did you?"

He cocks his head, and a charming half smile appears. "No. But I had to give up my wings to turn back time for you."

The weight of his sacrifice hits me. I cover his hand on my cheek and lean into his palm. "Why? Why would you do that?"

"One. It's forbidden." A small, wicked smile appears on his lips as if breaking the rules is something he's always wanted to do. "So, I walk the earth in this mortal form until *your* time ends." He points at me and his eyes dance with mirth.

My heart swells.

"And two..." He licks his lips and glances at the door as he leans in and captures a soft kiss. "Because I'd really like more of that," he whispers, and goose bumps spread across my arms. "But that is entirely in your hands."

At this moment, I wish we were at that hotel room instead of a hospital room. "I think I would like that."

He pulls away. "Then how about a real date?" He searches my eyes and then looks down at my dress. "Something a little less formal, though," he adds. "Despite you looking like an angel in that dress."

My cheeks heat, and I can't help but smile. I nod. "But give me a little time to sort out this mess."

His smile fades. "What mess?"

"Well, my parents and their finances for one, and second... Jay. If he lives, he needs a swift kick, and if he doesn't, then I have to figure out how to mourn someone who stabbed me in the back when I was already down."

"Makes perfect sense. I think." But doesn't sound convinced.

I lean forward and capture a kiss. "I'm not blowing you off. What we have isn't normal by any means, but it's where I belong," I whisper in his ear and then step back, giving him the room to process my words.

He searches my eyes and then a slow grin forms. He nods and shuffles backward toward the door. "I'll see you soon, then."

"Don't you want my number?"

He pauses and glances at the medical chart hanging from the bed with my information on it. "I already have it memorized from your chart." He slips out the door.

That's both creepy, and very, very sweet.

Before I have a chance to fully recover from Gabriel's visit, my parents walk in the room and everything Gabriel did for me strikes home. He reset my life, erasing my biggest mistake, giving me a second chance with my parents, and the opportunity for something truly amazing.

I fly into my parents' arms as tears of joy squeeze from my eyes.

Gabriel fell from Heaven for me, and for the rest of our mortal lives, I will do everything in my power to make sure he never regrets that choice.

The End

WINTER'S HEART

Myths. Magic. And a prophecy realized.

Lisa Winters is supposed to save the small town of Opal from destruction with magic she does not possess. The white tiger has awoken, and he wants revenge on the people who betrayed him, as well as the sorceress who bound him in frost.

Lisa was not that witch. And yet, everyone believes she is the fated one. The one who will finally end the white tiger's reign of terror.

Even her mentor, Herk, thinks so.

Lisa doesn't want to let anyone down, but she can barely start a fire with a match and lighter fluid, let alone do anything magical.

That is, until the moment she meets the white tiger.

His majestic beauty stirs deep within her soul. Her magic, dormant for so long, sparks to life like a shooting star streaking across the universe.

But as the burst fades, so does her strength, leaving her vulnerable to the tiger's wrath.

Winter's Heart
Chapter 1

"TRY AGAIN!" HERK CANICULA stood over Lisa like a handsome and frightening tyrant. His dark hair blew in the cold breeze, and his grey eyes looked like the ice on Opal Lake. But his demand was futile. He might as well have asked for the last drop of her blood.

"I am!" she cried, concentrating until sweat dripped into her eye, stinging.

She closed her hands and slumped on the sitting log around the great circle of fire. Except there was no fire. It was as cold as she was. She couldn't even light a damn candle with her mind, never mind light it like the prophets foretold.

She had no magic.

Not even a flicker, despite Herk's insistence that she did. She hadn't possessed it since she was a small child, and she was convinced that had not been actual magic.

The one time that she had, it was because she had gotten so mad at her parents, angry enough for sparks to snap from her fingertips. They were in a public place with enough people to start hearing murmurs about her being *that* girl. It wasn't long after that incident that a fire took all that she knew and loved and Herk's family took her in.

"This is a waste of time, and you know it. I haven't created magic since I was four, if that's even what it was." They went through this daily. This exact argument every single day since she'd turned eighteen. He hadn't left her any time for friends or fun, and she was tired. Tired of this same stale routine.

"Which is why we have been trying to help you tap into it ever since." He leaned his hands on the table next to her. "You've been able to move things with your mind before," he added. It was his way of coaxing her into continuing.

Telekinesis was very different than magic, but she wasn't going to argue with him. She could almost repeat this lecture word for word at this point. Two years of failed practices and Herk's bullying her into exhaustion. He seemed to think she was the fabled one who would beat the white tiger if it ever awoke from its long winter slumber.

The mountains buffered Opal from the rest of the world, and they were content in their little snow-filled region, so she didn't understand why parents continued to scare their children with the stories about the white tiger's return and the inevitable slaughter.

It was just a story.

She closed her eyes, and instead of willing the candle lit, she wished Herk would just give her a day of solitude and rest. This was not the way to get her mind to open. A lazy day in bed with a good book was all she needed. But that would never come to pass.

Not with Herk and his obsession.

"You can do this," he said softly, trying to coax the magic out of her.

She opened a single eyelid and stared up at him, determined to change this mundane routine of his. "I need rest. You do know the entire idea of insanity is repeating things every day and expecting a different outcome."

His lips thinned and his glare sharpened. "You think I'm insane?"

She sighed. So much for the ability to change his crazy pattern. She did not want to have words with him. Not with exhaustion licking every muscle to the point she thought she would just slide off the seat into a writhing puddle of goo.

"I am going to do something more useful than staring at a candle wick for the next six hours and expecting it to spontaneously combust." She stood.

"Sit down," he bellowed in her face and drew back as if he were going to strike her.

"No!" For the first time in years, she stood her ground and didn't flinch as the muscles in his arms tightened. "And if you so much as lay a finger on me, I will break it." She was in no mood to be bullied beyond exhaustion today. She'd had enough of his sick game.

Instead of backhanding her, he wiped his face and closed his eyes. She could almost see his mental pep-talk to rein in his anger. When he opened his eyes, they still held the dark grey of frustration, but there was something else underneath. Something more feral, like she had just ruined a much-anticipated date.

He inhaled and then nodded. "Fine. Let's head inside, and I'll make you a nice hot cup of our special tea."

"You know what? I am not in the mood for tea right now. What I need is a walk." She started towards the path, and when Herk fell into step by her side, she glared at him. "Alone."

Hurt flared in his eyes, but she was past the point of worrying about his fragile ego. All he wanted was her to save the day. To produce magic as easily as snapping her fingers. Magic that had only surfaced once, and if there was anything the years following that strange release of magic had taught her, that sorcery had been a fluke.

Winter's Heart
Chapter 2

THE BLANKET OF WHITE covering the forest floor calmed her as much as the cool breeze. Lisa knew Herk wasn't her enemy, but since she'd turned eighteen, his obsession had changed him into someone she didn't know. She wouldn't have guessed her oldest, dearest friend could become such a vicious slave driver.

She had once told him she didn't feel worthy of all the attention. She wasn't a mystical goddess who could stop Opal from destruction. She couldn't even stop water from boiling over in a pot.

He had been so determined to prove her wrong. That was what drove him to these daily practice sessions. She wondered if she had kept her thoughts to herself, would he have become this demanding tyrant?

She shook her head and drifted farther into the woods where the pines thickened, blanketing the snow with needles and sap. It smelled glorious, and she took a deep inhalation through her nose letting the evergreens fill her senses.

Something shifted in her peripheral vision, but when she looked, nothing was there. Perhaps snow had just slipped off a branch. She scanned the area, but nothing marred the perfect landscape.

Her skin tingled, and she glanced around, turning in a circle as the overwhelming sensation of being watched interrupted her peaceful walk. A plume of steam escaped from her lips with a deep sigh.

She turned, heading back to the village before the sun dipped below the mountain ridge and the icy winds picked up. She did not want to get caught in the deep woods in the dark. There were bears and wolves and other sordid creatures that came out after the sun set to hunt.

And she had been thoughtless enough to leave without any decent weapon.

Lisa hurried along, still feeling the heat of eyes on her, but when she glanced back, only white painted the ground. She slowed to a stop and stood still for a full minute, trying to shake the weird sensation.

She turned back towards the village. Snow shifted and fell in a great chunk, plopping onto the snow-covered ground, making her jump. The winds were picking up, and she quickened her pace, hell-bent on outrunning the coming gales.

A blast of warmth welcomed her along with hushed conversation as she stepped inside the Caniculas' house. Herk peeked around the kitchen doorway, his worried brow smoothing at the sight of her.

"I have some hot tea for you," he said.

She hated the tea they plied her with at least once a day. It tasted like charcoal with a hidden bitterness and always made her hands feel heavy. This tea had become a staple in her life ever since she'd moved in with them. And she didn't have the heart to tell Mrs. Canicula just how awful her home-brewed tea really was.

"I'm still not in the mood for tea." She headed towards the stairs.

"The tea will revitalize you," Mrs. Canicula said from just beyond Herk. "Come. Sit. While it's still hot." She poked her head out from behind Herk with that warm smile Lisa couldn't turn down.

She resigned herself to their imposed routine. "Fine. But just a half cup tonight." She didn't want to be up at midnight with her mind racing. The hideous-tasting tea seemed to strip her of the ability to sleep, which made concentrating for Herk's training sessions especially draining.

She sat down and steeled herself as Mrs. Canicula placed a steaming full cup in front of her. Lisa sighed and picked it up. She had tried to burn her taste buds many times to drown out the taste, but that hadn't worked. Neither had loading the cup with sugar.

There was no escaping this, so she blew on the steam then closed her eyes and quickly drank the cup, ignoring the burn that traveled all the way down her esophagus. She shivered as it plunged into her stomach like a lead ball. Her eyelids shot up as the heat hit, but she didn't make a noise. She crossed to the sink and turned on the cold water, leaned over, and gulped enough to staunch the fire in her mouth.

When she straightened and turned, the family was staring at her. Granted, she hadn't done that in years.

She shrugged. "I guess I was thirstier than I thought." She let out a nervous laugh and forced a yawn. "I'm going to head upstairs for a bit."

She went through her normal bedtime routine, brushing her hair until it shone, polishing her teeth, and rinsing the dirt and grime off her face. By the time she slipped into bed, her limbs had that heavy feeling the tea always seemed to bring.

Just as her eyelids started their slow descent, a soft knock pulled her from the edge of sleep. She groaned and glanced at the door.

Herk poked his head inside. "Can I come in?" he asked with eyes so full of concern that Lisa nodded.

He crossed and took a seat on the edge of the bed. "Are you okay?"

She sighed. "I'm just tired. Tired of our grueling days of no progress. Tired of the way the townspeople stare at me as if I'm some new revelation that was delivered from God. I'm just tired." Lisa threw her arm over her eyes before he caught the sudden mist of emotion that threatened.

"I get it, but if you're going to stop the white tiger when he wakes—"

"*If* he wakes. If he even exists." She sat up and glared at him. "This is all fables and folklore. It's not based in reality."

"Then marry me," he said.

Lisa opened her mouth to argue, and then his words settled in. She blinked at him like he'd just asked her to slit her own wrists. "What?"

His lips tilted in a half grin. "Marry me."

There were so many women in Opal who fawned over Herk, but he didn't seem interested in any of them. Even Lisa's friends at school would have gladly lain with him if he had shown interest. But Lisa had never seen him as anything but an older brother, which was the only reason she let him treat her so harshly day after day. Not once, even in her wildest dreams, did she ever envision a romantic entanglement with him.

As a matter of fact, just the thought soured her stomach, threatening to purge the tea still sitting like a rock in her belly.

"No." She pushed herself back against the headboard, putting as much distance between them as possible. Nothing about being with Herk romantically settled right.

Herk's brow creased, and his arms flexed as tight as his jawline. He stood and marched out of the room without another word.

Winter's Heart
Chapter 3

THE NEXT MORNING, LISA dragged herself out of bed, disoriented and achy from sleeping so deeply that the entire village of Opal could have been slaughtered and she wouldn't have woken to the screams.

She rubbed her face and headed into the bathroom.

She met her blue-grey gaze in the mirror as she studied her mussed-up hair. The shine from last night had faded into a rat's nest from sleep. She threw water on her face to lift the fog from her brain.

Herk had asked her to marry him? She blinked at her image, trying to decipher if it had been a dream or not. She couldn't be sure based on the stupor she had gone to bed in.

Lisa brushed her teeth as she mulled it over in her mind. The more she polished, the more she questioned whether it had happened. No way. Herk had never so much as made a pass at her.

Even as kids, he had a gruff way about him, like he was trying to not resent her for being in their home. He never handled her like she was a breakable piece of china. Until she turned eighteen, he would slide into her room to talk late at night after everyone in the house had gone to bed. He'd told her his dreams. His plans for Opal and beyond. And in none of those nightly conversations had he ever expressed wanting a future with her. And he certainly never made a move, and god knows he'd had plenty of opportunity.

They had been friends, confidants, more like siblings. She must be confusing a dream with reality.

By the time she stepped into the kitchen, she had herself convinced. It wasn't until Herk didn't even acknowledge her that her doubts evaporated. The glare he gave her before he stormed away all but screamed it at her.

"Why?" she blurted before he exited the kitchen.

He stiffened in the doorway but didn't turn.

"Because maybe I can help you attain your destiny," he muttered and marched off.

She didn't know what she expected him to say, but making it sound more like a business arrangement rather than a romantic tryst made it all the more unappealing. The man she married would be the one to sweep her off her feet. He would make her see fireworks when he kissed her, and he would be much kinder and gentler than Herk had ever been.

She slammed her cereal bowl down on the kitchen table and focused on eating, but it did nothing to calm the storm brewing inside. When she stepped outside to the start of another grueling day of training, Herk was nowhere to be found. Neither were her neighbors.

She crossed to the road and looked towards the center of town. People were gathered around the great hall. Even from this distance, a woman's cry reached her from within the crowd.

Lisa started towards the group slowly at first, but the continued wail quickened her footsteps. She pushed her way to the front and stopped short at the gruesome scene.

The town constable crouched next to one of the older women in town who was holding the dead body of her husband. Great swaths of torn flesh crisscrossed his abdomen and face. She would have guessed he was mauled by a bear until she saw the bloody footprints in the snow.

Four-toed paw prints. Two bloodied, and two pristinely cast in the snow. Bear prints have five toes and longer claws.

She looked up at Herk on the other side of the circle. His hard glare was on Lisa. Soon, everyone else's attention was on her as well.

"The white tiger has risen," he said.

A chill caught Lisa, and she wrapped her arms around her to stop her from actually shivering. It was bad enough Herk was staring at her, but now the widow and the rest of the town had started to notice that Lisa was present as a witness to this massacre.

"It appears that way." Constable Jones stood, looking at Lisa as if she had suddenly become this town's savior.

Now she wished she had stayed in bed and not bothered with starting her day. This was worse than finding out Herk had really proposed to her. Worse yet, the town expected her to magically make this tiger disappear. They expected her to fulfill the prophecy.

Herk crossed and grabbed her arm, leading her out of the crowd and back towards his training grounds before any other of the townspeople started to join in with 'what are you going to do about this' looks.

She was grateful for the exit until Herk opened his mouth again.

"It's time to tap that magic."

Was he serious? The last thing she wanted to do was stare at a cold fire for another eight hours.

"I beg to differ. It's time for me to wield a sword or pick up my bow." She yanked her arm from his grip. "If we are going to war with the white tiger, don't you think I should be able to defend myself? Or are you hoping that I'll be the next victim?"

He skidded to a halt and glared at her, pointing his finger accusingly. "You are destined to kill that thing. And magic is the only thing that can kill that beast."

"Bullshit. It's just a tiger. I can't even make sparks appear on my fingertips, never mind blast that thing back to where it came. I need to start practicing with either my bow or a sword."

"Only magic can defeat him." He crossed his arms. "Or are you missing that point."

Lisa threw her hands into the air. There was no reasoning with Herk. The lore was just as full of crap as his insistence she was *that* girl. "Then we are all screwed, because I don't possess magic," she argued much louder than she intended.

A throat cleared behind them, and they spun to see the village secretary. He adjusted his glasses and looked off at the thick woods at the edge of town.

"The council would like to speak with you," he said to Lisa.

"Tell my father I will be there in a minute," Herk said.

"I wasn't talking to you," the man said. "Your father has requested Miss Winters presence before the council."

"Oh," Herk mumbled, and his cheeks reddened. He waved Lisa to follow the village secretary.

She raked her hand through her hair and nodded, following him down the street with Herk a few steps behind like some morbid protection detail, or an escort walking her to her death.

Winter's Heart
Chapter 4

LISA WAKED INTO THE Opal hall of council, and everyone around the table stood as if she were royalty. She shifted under their worried gazes. Silence weighed on her like a heavy blanket as suffocating as their stares.

"What do you plan to do?" Randolph Canicula, the head of the council, asked. His brazen gaze left Lisa uncomfortable. And not just because he was the head of the council. It was because Randolph was Herk's father, and he had to have known Lisa turned his son's proposal down. Why else would he pin this responsibility on her?

"Excuse me?" Lisa balked and shuffled her feet. She had no answers. She had no magic to protect Opal. She only had her sword and bow, which she hadn't picked up since she'd turned eighteen and Herk started his insane training sessions. She was not prepared for the weight of the duty being thrust upon her.

"You are the chosen one. It is your destiny to rid Opal of this white tiger business." He leaned forward, pointing at her as if accusing her of killing that man herself.

"I am not the chosen one," she snapped. "I don't have any magic, and I have been trying to tell you that for years!"

A hush fell over the council, and they traded worried glances. That is, everyone except Randolph. His glare was as unnerving as the silence. When his glare moved behind her, she glanced over her shoulder at Herk still standing in the doorway.

He shrugged in a non-committal way that suddenly made Lisa's blood boil. Like he didn't care that she hadn't shown signs of magic since she was four years old. It was as if her magic had been a premonition of sorts. Days after her fingers sparked flame, her home burned to the ground with her parents inside. Lisa had not been home that day. Otherwise, she would have perished, too.

She had been at the Caniculas' house for Herk's thirteenth birthday party along with the lion share of the town's children.

"You are the chosen one," Randolph snarled. "And you will remove the danger of the white tiger from Opal, even if you have to spill your own blood to do so."

He definitely knew. Otherwise, he wouldn't have sentenced her to a sure death.

"Father." Herk's voice held a dark warning that even she couldn't ignore.

"I can fight my own battles," she said, putting her hand up to silence whatever argument Herk might launch into in front of the high council of Opal. Whatever it was, she was sure he was about to embarrass her in some way, like tell the council she would get mortally wounded if she was the one to hunt the white tiger, or something equally as mortifying.

His huff of derision jarred her enough for her teeth to ache while she gnashed them together.

"I will do my best," she said to the council. "But understand, I am not your magical chosen one. Regardless, it seems you are adamant that I be the one to hunt the monster, so I will go out there with my bow and my quiver and shoot the tiger in the eye."

"Lisa," Herk said softly from behind her. His voice was laced with something she had never heard from him. It sounded a bit like fear.

She turned and stormed past him, leaving the town hall in a march that had her footfalls echoing. The cold slapped at her cheeks as she stepped outside. She didn't even know where Herk had put her weapons. At least before she was eighteen, he had trained her with a bow and a sword, but it had been a couple years since she'd wielded a weapon.

Either way, she was on her own to take care of the beast.

That thought sobered her, and even though her feet wanted to falter, she forced her steps to continue, even with the crunch of hurried footsteps behind her.

A hand gripped her arm and spun her around.

"You aren't ready," Herk said. His eyes were a little more frantic now that the gauntlet had been dropped on her.

Lisa yanked her arm from his grip. "You heard them." She pointed at the building they had just vacated. "They expect me to take care of this with or without magic."

"I'm going with you," he said.

That's all she needed. While Herk was an experienced fighter, he hadn't trained with a sword or a bow either. Instead, he'd put all his bets on her magic and drilled her relentlessly daily.

"No." She didn't need his death on her hands, too. Besides, she had been the better archer out of the two of them. Although, he could beat her black and blue with a training sword.

His jaw tightened and his nostrils flared. He glanced at the woods in the distance. "Then at least let me train with you a little. It's been a while since you held a weapon."

She looked down at her feet, debating. The last time she'd sparred with Herk, he'd left her almost as exhausted as the daily practice of unsuccessful magic. She didn't know if she could go after a tiger with that kind of grueling test.

"Are you trying to ensure I will not return?" she finally asked. Her voice was filled with every ounce of aggravation burning through her bones.

He stepped back, and she looked up at his face. Horror stretched his eyes wide, and she immediately regretted her question.

"No. How can you say that after I asked you to marry me last night? Your death... will devastate me," he said.

Will? Like he expects me to die? What the ever-loving hell?

Lisa's head nearly exploded with anger, and the red hue covering her vision didn't help. She spun and marched away, muttering foul words under her breath. Even Herk had crossed her off. Now she was even more determined to drag back the carcass of the dead tiger, just to show this town that she was not to be trifled with in the future.

Winter's Heart
Chapter 5

"**Y**OU NEED TO GO to the funeral and pay your respects," Herk said from the doorway.

His voice held a cool warning that Lisa had no intention of obeying. She didn't need to go to a funeral to be motivated to do her duty. What she needed to do was hone her skills with her bow and arrow, but she didn't want Herk's help with that.

When Mrs. Canicula poked her head in behind Herk, her warm expression hardened. "You're not ready yet?"

"No, ma'am. I'm not feeling well." Lisa didn't like how easily the lie rolled off her tongue, but she needed to be alone. She had every intention of packing up and heading into the mountains to find the tiger as soon as everyone left for the funeral. While her skills with a bow might be rusty, she had been the best shot in Opal when she was younger.

She just hoped her steady hand wouldn't fail her. Otherwise, hers would be the next funeral this town would see.

Besides, she knew deep down that Herk would follow her if she left while he was around. And she didn't want that. He would drive her as relentlessly as he had in his training sessions, and she did not need that type of pressure.

"You need to suck it up and come with us," Mrs. Canicula said. "I'll make you some tea while you get dressed." She turned and left the room, leaving Lisa no choice but to obey the unrelenting command in her tone.

Lisa closed her eyes and tilted her head back. Escaping wasn't going to happen today, and she would just have to plan to sneak out at another time. Begrudgingly, she waved Herk out of the room and put on proper clothing for a funeral. Her wool leggings matched her dark wool skirt and her black lace-up boots that put her almost at Herk's height. Her sweater pulled the grey in her eyes to the forefront, muting the blue. She smoothed her skirt and made her way downstairs where the rest of the family waited.

Mrs. Canicula held out a cup of the black tea.

Lisa shook her head and held a hand up. "I'll be fine."

"You should have a little before we go," she said.

Lisa sighed and took the cup into the kitchen, pretended to take a sip, and then dumped the rest down the drain. This wasn't the way she wanted to start the day, but she did not want to deal with a sour stomach on top of the nerves already skittering under her skin.

She turned back to the family waiting in the doorway, pasted a smile on her face, and followed them to the church in the center of town.

The somber mood even bled out into the sky, pulling the clouds overhead and blocking the sun from shining down on the valley. It made for an even more heart-wrenching display. The closed coffin looked like an ominous premonition, and Lisa slumped in the seat, trying to disappear from the eyes of the congregation as they sought her out for reassurances she could not give.

Even the widow's gaze found hers when she stood next to the casket. Her eyes pleaded in a way that moved Lisa's soul.

She would not let this happen to another citizen of Opal.

As soon as the funeral was over, Lisa bowed out before she could get cornered at the reception. She made her way back to the house and closed herself in her bedroom to pack a sack for later that evening. Going out into the deep woods at night was not the smartest thing she thought to do, but it was necessary so she wouldn't have to worry about Herk or anyone else who decided to take up arms with her against the killing beast.

The soft knock on her door jerked her around, and she slid the backpack under her bed before she crossed and opened the door. Herk gripped both sides of the doorjamb and stared at the floor. The muscles in his arms bulged under the tight dress shirt covering them.

When he finally raised his gaze to her, she shivered at the resolve in his eyes.

He didn't speak. Instead, he moved into the room and kicked the door closed as he grabbed her arms and pinned her against the wall. Before her brain caught up to his actions, his lips were on hers.

Her eyes widened and she tried to shove him away but only succeeded in trapping her arms between them when he pressed his weight against her. She jerked her knee up, right into his family jewels. His grip on her dropped as he groaned and fell to his knees, gripping his balls.

"Don't you ever do that again," Lisa seethed and scooted away, putting distance between them before she decided to dropkick him.

He put his head on his arm and stayed that way for so long that Lisa took a tentative step forward. He put his hand out to stop her.

"I'm fine, just..." he said with a voice tight with pain. "I thought..." He wiped his face and looked up at her.

"You thought if you kissed me, it would change my mind?"

His old half smile that made him more than endearing appeared, and he shrugged.

She took a seat on the edge of her bed. "Herk, I've never seen you as anything other than an overprotective big brother." She finally voiced the silent narrative ranting in her head. "You're my oldest friend. You and Molly down the way were the only ones in this town who seemed to accept me when I arrived." She looked down at her hands. She hadn't seen Molly since Herk started his insane magic training sessions. "I think the last couple of years has clouded that enough to sour me even on a friendship with you. What we have is not healthy the way it once may have been. It's more of a rivalry to you. Your proposing just seemed... wrong."

"And you could never see beyond friendship?" Hurt flared in his eyes and bled into his voice.

She shook her head. She did not want to give him false hope. Better to squash it now than to lead him on and have to do it later. "No." She refrained from expanding on the age differences or pointing out his unflattering obsessions.

His gaze hardened, and he gave her a nod like he was somehow coming to terms with her words. "You're going to be twenty-one next week," he said as if that was the end of the world.

In Opal it might have been. By twenty-one, most maidens were married. But Lisa wasn't most maidens. In the years when she should have been dating, Herk had her trying to start a fire where there wasn't any. It had been like asking her to get blood from a stone, and if that was his idea of courting a woman, god help the girl he finally settled down with.

"And?" she asked, even though she knew it was a loaded question that he would happily shoot at.

"You have no other prospects." He stood tall, crossing his arms. His face still held some of the redness from when she had kneed him, but the blotchy spots were probably more from anger than physical pain.

"So what? I'm supposed to get all aflutter at your magnanimous pity proposal? Just get out." She pointed at the door.

He took a step towards her, and she stood, shifting into a fighting stance. He smiled at her, and an utterly inappropriate, mischievous light flared in his eyes. They narrowed as if she had become his prey.

"What the hell is wrong with you?"

"I like it when you get all feisty," he purred in a way that shot fear through her. "Besides, if you're going to go after the tiger on your own, don't you want to know what it feels like to be with a man before you die?"

She clenched her fists tighter as he took another step closer. "Get out."

"That is something I can successfully teach you." He reached for his belt buckle.

"I swear if you come any closer, the next shot I get in will break something down there permanently." She looked at his crotch and then back at his face pointedly. "And if that doesn't work, I'll claw your eyes out," she added when he continued to pull his belt from the loops.

The sound of the front door closing downstairs paused Herk's progress. It also seemed to clear the darkness from his features. He glanced over his shoulder and then back at Lisa. He pointed at her and then turned, storming out of the room before his mother or father came upstairs.

Lisa sagged back onto her bed on shaking legs. If they hadn't come home when they did, she wasn't sure what Herk would have done. Something had snapped in his mind, because her oldest friend would have never gone on attack mode like that. He would have protected her to the death.

She had to leave as soon as the opportunity presented itself. Otherwise, she was leaving herself vulnerable.

Winter's Heart
Chapter 6

"LISA?" MRS. CANICULA'S WORRIED voice came through the wooden door. "You didn't come for dinner when I called," she added, and then the door swung open. Mrs. Canicula smiled as she carried a tray into the room with a steaming bowl of stew and sliced bread.

"I wasn't hungry." Lisa straightened, but her stomach betrayed her, rumbling at the delicious scent coming from the dinner.

"Sounds like you are now." She smiled and set the tray at the foot of the bed. "Are you and Herk fighting?"

Lisa didn't quite know what to say to Herk's mother. If she said yes, the woman was sure to pry into why they were fighting, and she didn't want to tell her that her son was becoming a monster.

"He's been harder on me the last few weeks," she said, leaving it at that.

"Well, he's just trying to protect you." She turned to leave and pointed at the tray. "I'll be back in a little while to grab that when you are done."

She dug into the food and finished it faster than she had eaten in a while. She wished she had been downstairs for dinner and could've had seconds, but she could not face Herk after his earlier near assault.

She picked up the teacup and walked to the bathroom, dumped the tea down the drain, and then replaced it on the tray. That was the only benefit of eating in her room. There was no oversight, and she did not have to choke down the tea. Maybe she would do this more often when she got back from her mission. It sure beat hurting Mrs. Canicula's feelings.

Lisa brought the tray downstairs and put it in the sink while Mrs. Canicula was preoccupied with the laundry in the backyard. On the return trip to her room, she grabbed her winter coat and boots and stowed them under her bed along with her backpack and duffel with a warm waterproof sleeping bag.

As soon as both Mr. and Mrs. Canicula went to bed, she was leaving this house. She would brave the bitter winter wind over waking up with Herk climbing on top of her in her sleep. If he was out drinking, that was apt to be the end result when he got home. She had more of a chance surviving the white tiger.

She remained awake until the whispered good nights came through her door. When the hall lights extinguished, Lisa went into action. She pulled on her warmest pants and laced up her boots. She tucked in her thermal nightshirt and pulled on a thick sweater before slipping on her jacket and gloves. The heavy scarf easily wrapped around her head and neck before she pulled up her hood.

Lisa bound the duffel bag to her backpack and then put it on, clipping it and securing it tight. She moved as silently as possible to the door and gripped the knob.

Her heart jumped into her throat at the sound of the front door below, and the stumbling that followed had her shuffling to the window. She had climbed out it once on a dare from Herk and nearly broke her leg. But she hadn't been as tall as she was now. She'd have to toss the backpack out of range before she jumped out. Otherwise, she *would* break her leg.

Rushing, she pushed the window open, unclipped the backpack, and heaved it out the window. It sailed far enough away to not impede her drop from the sill once she got outside.

Herk's footsteps reached the stairs, and she could hear him murmuring but didn't wait to find out what he was saying.

Her heart drummed in her chest, and she threw her leg out of the window and turned, sliding her other leg out as she gripped the sill with her gloved hands. The moment she slid out the window, her door opened. She didn't wait. She lowered herself to her full length and let go.

Herk's hand slammed down on hers, pinning her in place. He glared down at her from her window. "Where do you think you're going?" he asked with breath that stank like a brewery.

Lisa tried to wiggle her hand free as he reached out with his other hand. She swatted it away and curled her fingers so his grip would slide off her glove. Just like that, the fabric slipped off her hand, and she was freefalling to the ground.

Herk's face disappeared from the window, and then she hit the ground, stumbling back onto her ass. She stood on shaking legs and grabbed her backpack in an all-out run towards the woods. If Herk caught her, she knew what he would do. She saw enough in his drunken eyes.

His lumbering footsteps crunched the snow behind her.

"If I catch you, you will regret saying no to me!" His growling voice echoed off the snow.

A yank on her backpack jerked her, and she glanced back at Herk. He had a strap in his hand

and an insane smile like he had just caught the brass ring at the fair.

She let go of the pack and put everything she had into running as fast as she could. She was sure it wasn't just her virtue on the line. If he caught her, that was not the only thing he would do to her.

She didn't stop once she breached the forest. She dodged the tree branches and hurdled over the low bushes. Her heart thundered in her chest and her breath wheezed.

Still, he came after her, sounding like a wrecking ball taking on the forest. She darted to her right and slid beneath a prickly thistle bush. Covering her mouth, she forced herself to breathe as shallowly as she could.

Herk barreled by her, but his pace slowed down to a stop a few hundred feet away, illuminated by a patch of moonlight. He circled around looking at the pristine snow surrounding him.

A bitter wind rustled through the trees, blowing the snow around and covering her slide under the bush. It was almost as if the gods didn't want Herk to find her either.

"I will hunt you down, Lisa," he shouted. "And when I do, I am not taking no for an answer. Do you understand me?"

She shivered but remained silent as he stomped his way back to the edge of the woods.

"And if the white tiger gets you, I will not mourn your loss," he added.

The crunching snow became more distant with every step away from the woods. It wasn't until she heard the door slam that she let out a breath and crawled out from under the bush.

She had nothing. No sleeping sack. No clothes beyond what was on her back, and no weapons. And she couldn't go back to the house to try to retrieve her bow from the shed like she had planned to do before she snuck away.

She was on her own, weaponless, and her pocket wasn't going to keep her ungloved hand warm enough in the whipping wind. She stood on shaking legs and headed away from the house. It was the only direction where she had a slim chance of surviving the night unscathed.

Winter's Heart
Chapter 7

THE NIGHT BLANKETED LISA in heavy doubt. She had used Herk's footprints to the clearing, but she knew his tracking skills. No matter how much the wind blew, she knew he would eventually find her. She just hoped she wouldn't run into a bear or a pack of wolves in the meantime.

She dragged a tree branch she found behind her to try to obscure her footprints, which was fine in the woods, but now that she was in an open meadow, there was no hiding the path she took.

That itch between her shoulders started in again, and she spun, scanning the woods for the owner. She prayed it wasn't Herk because she didn't have the strength or speed, even with the head start, to reach the other side of the tundra to make it to the safety of the woods.

Nothing but the wind.

She took a deep breath and slowly let it out as she did one last sweep of the woods behind her. When nothing out of the ordinary happened, she turned back to her destination.

Trudging through the heavy snow slowed her down, and when she finally made it to the woods, she glanced back towards town. The path she'd crossed was no longer visible. She glanced at the branch. It had served her well covering her tracks, and it might provide her some sticks if she could find a rock to shave the ends. Her survival depended on her having something to defend herself with.

It might not be against the wildlife either.

She needed to reach the catacombs of shallow caves and find one to protect her from the unrelenting wind. Her entire body ached, and she needed to hunker down and get some rest before sunrise came.

She let the woods swallow her. The snow thinned here because the canopy was so thick, and not even the moon penetrated. She slowed and closed her eyes to try to let them adjust. If it weren't for the snow blown in from the tundra reflecting some ambient light, she wouldn't even be able to see the trees.

She picked up her pace, trying to recall the route through the trees. The only sound was the crunch of her boots and the brush dragging behind her. She prayed it was enough to keep the predators away.

Just as she reached the clearing with the caves in sight, rustling behind her stopped her in her tracks. She slowly turned, changing the grip on the tree branch to bring it up like a stickball bat at her shoulder. As silently as possible, she backed away from the woods under the bright light of the full moon. Each crunch of snow was as loud as a branch snapping, and she cringed.

Above her frantic heartbeat drumming in her ears, she heard low growls. Whatever was on the hunt was not a single beast. If she ran, she would be brought down like a wild antelope. She continued her retreat, and after a dozen steps, eyes peered out from the dark forest. She gripped the branch tighter and gulped down her fear.

"Well, don't just hide in the woods. If you're going to attack, attack," she snarled and checked her footing to make sure she would get a full sweep with her makeshift weapon.

The lead wolf stepped out from the shadows with his lips drawn back from his deadly canines. Then a half dozen more fanned out on either side of the alpha, all snarling just as harshly.

If they attacked as one, she was doomed. Her chest tightened, and she dared to take a step back, and then another, and another. With each step, she reset her grip on the branch. They advanced at an equal pace, fanning out even more.

She knew the drill. She had seen wolves take down a moose before. These bastards were trying to get behind her, and then they would attack.

Out of the corner of her eye, she saw something move. She swung towards it, but nothing was there. She swung the branch wide as she turned back to face the wolves, and they jumped back.

A ball of heat formed in the pit of her stomach, and her breath quickened. The wolf to her left launched, and she swung the branch again, giving it everything she had. The crack of wood against bone filled the air, followed by a sharp yelp. The branch snapped in half, leaving her with a piece that was shorter than her arm, making her even more vulnerable to their attack.

It was as if the pack sensed her mounting fear. Another wolf rushed forward. When she swung, it grabbed the end of the broken branch between its teeth and yanked it right out of her grip. Now she was defenseless against the pack.

She backed away and splayed her hands in front of her. "Easy now," she said, trying to keep the tremble out of her voice. Her heartbeat ran wild.

That shadow in the corner of her eye crept close enough that she couldn't ignore it. She pulled her gaze away from the wolves and froze in place at the sight before her. A beautiful and terrifying white tiger approached on silent paws, but his gaze was not on her. It was focused on the wolves.

She looked back in time to see the alpha launch at her.

Light, hot and deadly, flared from both her palms, blinding her. The magic she did not believe she possessed shot forth like a flame thrower, turning the wolf to dust before he reached her. It blasted from her as if she were a human bomb, depleting every drop of energy she had.

When the light faded, a wave of dizziness took hold. She took an unsteady step, trying to blink away the white spots dotting her vision.

"Damn," she whispered, and then darkness fell over her with the force of a falling anvil.

Winter's Heart
Chapter 8

LISA WOKE WITH A start, disoriented by the gray walls and the small fire burning near her. But it was the skinned squirrel slowly roasting over the flames that made her sit up straight. Another wave of dizziness hit, and she nearly collapsed again.

A soft chuff came from her right. She jolted, spinning around to an entry of a cave. Lying in the snow like a sentinel guarding her was the famed white tiger. His blue eyes remained locked on hers for a moment before he looked back out at the dawn-streaked sky.

She did not understand how she got here, or even how she'd started a fire and obtained a meal with no weapons, never mind skinned and impaled it on a stick.

She huffed. The tiger obviously wasn't capable of doing these things. Lisa looked around for any indication someone else had been here. Footprints. Clothing. Anything. But there were no signs of her benevolent savior.

She glanced between the fire and the sentry, unnerved. This was the beast attacking her town. Targeting the weak. She shook her head, bothered by the dichotomy of that versus the silent sentry posted at the entrance. Such a heinous beast surely would have killed her when she was unconscious. But instead, he was... protecting her?

He glanced back at her, his blue eyes shining bright in the low light. It was almost as if his eyes were human. They held kindness. Those were not the eyes of a killer.

Troubled, she focused on the food. Delicately, she removed the cooked squirrel and waited until it cooled enough to peel a piece off. The meat inside was tender and juicy, and after her first tentative bite, she devoured the entire thing until there were only bones and sinew left. She tossed it all in the fire and leaned back against the wall.

She stared at her hands. Had she produced magic? Or had it been a trick of her imagination?

The tiger chuffed as if she had spoken aloud, but he did not look her way. His ears twitched at something outside, and he stood facing the morning light letting it bathe his beautifully fierce face. His fur reflected oranges and pinks as the sun rose into the day. When he stretched, his lithe form stirred something deep inside Lisa.

It was as if the wild beast was speaking to her soul. The language was unfamiliar though. Still, the warmth inside her had nothing to do with the embers of the fire. It was as foreign to her as this predicament.

She climbed to her feet. Her legs shook, and she wasn't sure if it was weakness or nerves. Normally, she would run in the opposite direction of danger, but she couldn't help the draw pulling her toward the tiger.

He stood from his stretch and turned his head towards her, following her as she approached but he showed no signs of aggression. When she stepped beside him, she looked out over the valley. Her gaze drew to the woods, and she gasped at the blackened landscape. A half-moon of devastation had imprinted on the land. Even the snow hadn't blown over it. It was as if the blast had killed the wind.

"Did I do that?" she asked.

The tiger nodded his head as he chuffed at her.

"Holy…" Her legs gave out, and she fell to her knees, woozy. She held her hands out and stared at them. "I've never…" She couldn't think clearly enough to form a coherent sentence.

As much as she hated to admit it, Herk had been right, although it took a near-death experience to unlock the magic. She wiped her face, still staring at the blackened land.

"And you saved me from the wolves?"

The tiger shook his head. Very slowly. When his gaze fell on her she shivered at the hardness reflected in the blue of his eyes. He looked back at the scar on the land and poked his chin out before his gaze returned to hers. He stretched out on the ground next to her, his regal head held high as if he knew she was in awe of him.

She reached out and touched his silky fur. Just the connection filled her with warmth and stole her breath. His eyes closed, and he chuffed softly, almost like a purr. Her duty to kill this beautiful creature did not sit well.

"Did you kill a villager down there?" She pointed towards Opal in the distance.

He shook his head and glanced at her. There was a horror lit in his eyes that didn't belong on a tiger's face. Deep down where that warmth lit her soul, she knew the tiger was telling the truth.

Which meant there was some other evil plaguing the town. Something so heinous that they blamed the filthy lore. Lies passed on from generation to generation fueled someone's homicidal tendencies.

Who would do such a thing?

She didn't have an answer, but she needed one, even if it meant having to deal with Herk again. But she would wait until the sun was high enough in the sky that the town was awake and active. Otherwise, she might end up locked somewhere as Herk's plaything.

"I need to go back," she said, even though that chilled the warmth right out of her bones.

He leaned his big tiger head into her and rubbed her with his jaw, nearly knocking her over.

She climbed to her feet, and he stood as well.

"You can't go. They'll kill you." She knew the townsfolk too well. If she walked into town with the white tiger by her side, they would shoot him on sight, and she didn't know what they would do to her.

At least this way, she could fight for him without putting either of them in danger.

"I will return. I promise." She gently patted the tiger.

She wanted to figure out what this draw was all about and why when the tiger had shown up, her magic flared as if the door holding it in place had been ripped off by a twister.

Winter's Heart
Chapter 9

THE TREK BACK TO Opal was uneventful in comparison to the night before. The tiger had followed her into the woods, but at the entry to the tundra, she pointed back towards the caves.

"Stay. Please. I do not want to be responsible for you getting hurt." She waited until he had slunk out of sight before she headed across the snow without worrying about covering her tracks like she had the night before. If Herk was waiting for her, there was nothing she could do except fight.

She stepped out of the woods a little south of where Herk's house was. The quiet hit her. Usually by the time the sun was this high, the town was busy with the noises of living. She bypassed the Caniculas' house and walked down the middle of the street.

It wasn't until she got to her friend Molly's house that the hushed whispers from the back reached her ears. The pattern of too many footprints pulled her along, and when she rounded the corner, a small crowd had gathered around another body. Her brain stalled at the bloody snow and the red-stained animal prints.

She gasped. "Molly," she whispered as she stared at the body of her friend.

Constable Jones turned towards her with his hat tipped farther back than normal. His jaw was tight and his eyes suspicious.

"When?" she asked, still unable to draw a complete breath. Her only friend left in this godforsaken town was dead. Slaughtered like an innocent lamb. She drew a painful inhale of frigid air and tried to plow through the confusion clouding her mind.

Could the tiger that protected her really have done this? Horror, loss, and building anguish crested inside her. It didn't help that Herk was eyeing her from across the yard, and she couldn't quite bring herself to make eye contact, either. She knew the moment she did, the stinging tears she was holding back would escape.

"She had gotten up to feed her animals before work and never came back in," Constable Jones said.

Molly worked the early shift. She always got there just as the sky was painted with the sunrise. If that were the case, Lisa's tiger couldn't have done it because he was keeping watch over her in the cave. She swallowed the bile lining her throat and looked closer at the kill site.

"You need to stop this tiger before he kills again," Herk said from the other side of the crowd.

"How do you know it was the tiger?" she asked, still looking at the snow all around them.

Herk, along with Constable Jones, pointed at the tracks surrounding Molly. They were clearly tiger tracks, but she hadn't seen a sign of paw prints leaving the town, never mind a path of blood that was sure to stain the snow for at least a few feet. But outside of the prints around the body, there was no visible sign of exit, not even in the trampled path she had come on.

"Where are the footprints coming in or going out?" She waved at the snow in the backyard. The only pawprints were around her dead friend. "Did the tiger drop from the sky and then fly away?" She dared to send a sideways glare at Herk.

Red bloomed in his cheeks. "Lisa wasn't at the house at all this morning, and her bed didn't look like she even slept in it."

Anger surfaced. How dare he try to pin this on her.

She crossed her arms. "First it was the tiger who did this? Now you're trying to pin this on me?"

"Where were you?" Constable Jones asked, which given his job, made sense since he was investigating the death, but the fact Herk had put that seed of doubt there irked her.

"I was out there in the woods trying to stay alive, no thanks to Herk." She waved at him, but she still had a thread of loyalty for their former friendship left. "You'll find my footprints across the tundra to the far woods and beyond if needed," she added when Constable Jones narrowed his eyes.

"Your backpack was in the yard," Herk said, and a crease appeared in his brow.

"Yeah, well you scared me, and I dropped it," she said, but didn't explain any further. She didn't want to tell Constable Jones she was actually running away from Herk. That wouldn't look good considering they all were standing around a dead body.

Herk cocked his head like he was trying to remember the prior night.

"I went to try to find the tiger," she said softly.

"Alone?" His eyes widened in horror.

She didn't know whether Herk was acting or not. If he was, he was doing one hell of a job.

She raised her eyebrows. "Yes. The town council made it clear I needed to fix this problem or die trying, or were you not listening to them yesterday?"

She did not want to tell them that she had released some kind of magic last night. She didn't want to give Herk the satisfaction of being right after what he had pulled.

Could she forgive him for his drunken ramblings?

She had shot down his proposal, so he could have just been acting out. She let out a huff and glanced at her dead friend, and the loss hit, misting her eyes with unshed tears. Her chin started to tremble, and she turned and trudged out of the backyard, hell-bent on figuring out who, or what, was killing members of her town.

A hand landed on her shoulder, and Lisa instinctively yanked away, spinning to look Herk in the eye.

"Don't touch me," she hissed and swiped at the wet heat streaking her cheeks.

He pulled his hand back quickly. "Sorry," he mumbled and looked at the ground. "I know she was your friend."

More tears covered her eyes, blurring her vision. She nodded. She only had a few friends in Opal, and it seemed she had lost both of her close ones in the last twenty-four hours.

"You don't remember last night, do you?" She sniffled and wiped her nose.

He bit his lower lip and shook his head. "I had a real bender." He kicked at the snow again. "I found your backpack this morning. And then I heard Molly's mother screaming..." He looked at the ground.

Lisa swore there were tears in his eyes, but he blinked them away just as fast as they came.

"I thought the worst." He met her gaze.

"Then why did you make that comment about me being gone last night to the constable?" She didn't buy his innocent act, at least not all of it. He did look a little green this morning, and she hoped his hangover was as hellish as he had made her night.

"Because I'm still mad that you said no to my proposal," he said. "But not mad enough for my heart not to hammer in my chest at the thought of you getting hurt." He shuffled in place and crossed his arms as if he were protecting his very soul from any more harm.

"You are a very mean drunk, Herk. I ran because of you." She stabbed a finger into his chest, unable to contain the anger any longer.

His eyes widened, his arms fell, and then sadness and shame washed over his face. "I didn't..."

"No, you didn't. I got away before you could do anything you could never take back, but I saw a side of you that I had never seen before. I've seen you drunk, but not like that. And I detest that person who threatened to take whatever the hell he wanted. You may be the son of the head of the town council, but you are not above the law." She forced her voice to stay hushed so the lawmen in the vicinity wouldn't hear her.

"So why didn't you tell the constable?" he grumbled and glanced towards Molly's backyard.

"Because you were once my dearest friend, and I still have some insane loyalty to you and your family." She glanced at the people still milling around Molly's and decided the conversation about the prior night was over. "The white tiger did not do that." She looked back at Herk. "I don't know what did, but I'm going to find out."

She marched towards the Caniculas' house to get her backpack. As she rounded the corner, she saw it sitting next to the door along with Mr. Canicula.

Mr. Canicula stood and glared down at her like he believed she was some sort of criminal.

She slowed to a stop at the foot of the stairs. "It isn't the tiger," she said, looking up at him trying to gauge his reaction. His lips were thinned like he was pissed at her even approaching the house.

His eyes narrowed. "I have half a mind to lock you up for Molly's death."

Her mouth dropped in stunned silence. How could he think she had killed her friend?

She glanced down the street and back at him in confusion. "I didn't kill Molly," she said. "I don't know who did."

"It was the tiger, and you damn well know it."

Something deep inside her warned her not to say more. Not to tell this man that she knew it wasn't the tiger because he had been protecting her in the caverns. She didn't understand the voice inside her, but she obeyed and snapped her jaw closed. She took another step and reached for her backpack.

He shook his head and pointed towards the mountains. "Do your duty, or reap the repercussions," he growled.

"I'm planning on it, but I'd like to figure out who is killing people here before I go." She stared up at him, blocking the door and her pack.

"If you stay, you are going to jail for the murders." He crossed his arms and clenched his jaw.

She didn't understand why he was doing this. People in town were being killed, and it wasn't from a fabled beast like he seemed to think. "But..."

A wicked smile appeared, one that she had never seen before and one that spawned a thousand alarms in her head. When he leaned forward, she stepped back, putting distance between them as her flight response started blaring.

"I can put you in jail for life." He tapped his lips and looked at the sky. "Actually, I could put you in front of a firing squad, and then my son would move on and settle down with someone more his style."

So, it was about her refusal to marry his son. "You bastard," she said.

"I've been called that a time or two, but just so you don't think too badly of our family, my wife insisted you take this with you." He tossed her a thermos. "Now go. Kill the tiger like you were meant to, and then maybe I'll rethink my position."

She stared at the silver canister in her hand and debated. Stay and get put in jail for something she didn't do, or go back to find the white tiger and figure out what really happened, both in town as well as with her magic? The choice was easy.

"Can I at least have my backpack and bow?"

His smile turned even meaner if that was even possible. "No. And I'll give you to the count of three to get moving before I change my mind."

Lisa turned towards the woods with only the canister of black tea that she knew would make her sick. But it might serve in a pinch if she couldn't find food.

What she really needed was that warm fire and answers that she would not find within a jail cell in Opal.

Winter's Heart
Chapter 10

WITH HER FOOTPRINTS STILL trackable in the snow, she found her way back to the area outside of the woods. She thought this was where the wolves had attacked, but the blackened earth was gone. The snow drifts were large enough to make her doubt her location. The mountainside of caverns didn't help, either. There was no telling which of the shadows facing Opal had been the one she was in earlier.

Her arms dropped by her side as she stared.

"Can I help you?"

She jumped and spun towards the deep voice. Sparks danced across her fingertips, and she clenched her fists, shocked at the sudden appearance of magic. She stared at her hands, dumbfounded, and then jerked her attention to the man standing near her.

People in Opal thought Herk was all the rage, but this man made Herk look like the ugly stepsister. His jet-black hair reached his shoulders and had a natural curl that most women would die for. His strong jaw was dabbled with stubble that she was sure would be scratchy against her skin. She was ashamed to admit she wanted to find out for sure. Both his hair and unshaven face made his eyes stand out even more. She had never seen eyes that bright blue. They glimmered like a glacial stream or the sky at noon in the fall. Deep. Penetrating. Intoxicating.

She blinked and stepped back. She *had* seen eyes that specific shade of blue before. She had seen them this morning, but they weren't a man's eyes. They were the eyes of the white tiger. Her heart pounded and her stomach rumbled like she hadn't eaten in days. She licked her lips but couldn't stop staring.

"Can I help you?" he asked again, and a smile toyed with his lips, making him all the more devastatingly attractive.

She giggled and heat rose in her cheeks. His question finally knocked her out of her stupor, and she turned her gaze back to the wall of caves, silently cursing her lack of being able to get her brain and mouth to work together to articulate.

"I... uh... I was looking for the cave that I woke in this morning."

"I can help you if you'd like." He held his hand out to her. "My name's Elijah."

She stared at his outstretched hand for longer than customary, and when he started to pull it back, she grabbed it and shook like she had zero manners. She stared at the connection in shock as her entire body filled with magic, as if whatever had been keeping it dormant had finally burst free. *What the hell?*

It engulfed her, and she breathed deeply. The scents surrounding the two of them were wild, like a raging river, or the air right before a thunderstorm. With it came the undertones of his unique musky scent that put her hormones into overdrive. Along with thrilling her, his touch was also calming, like the cadence of the sea.

His smile faded and his eyes widened. "You are the fated one." He seemed to squeeze a fraction tighter as if he never wanted to let go.

Her moment of awe ended like a crack of thunder on a clear day. She yanked her hand away. "I am not killing the tiger," she snapped.

His smirk deepened. "I would hope not," he said with a chuckle. "Come on, let's find a fire and get you warmed up." He started walking towards the caves.

She hesitated. He was a stranger, after all.

He stopped a few steps away and glanced over his shoulder. He reached down and pulled a knife out of a sheath on his leg that she hadn't noticed, and her heart lurched.

This could be the killer!

He flipped the knife around and held the hilt out to her. "I promise I won't bite, but if you need something to feel more secure about following someone you don't know, here."

She stared at it and slowly took it from him, unsure of whether she felt safer or not with a weapon in her hand. In all of Herk's physical training, he had proven how easily someone could be relieved of their weapon. She narrowed her gaze.

There were no warning alarms going off inside her like there had been at the Caniculas', and she had to trust her instincts. They usually didn't lead her astray. She nodded. "Normally I don't follow strangers, but a warm fire does sound nice."

He smiled and she nearly melted in the snow with the effect it had on her. Warm and gushy like holding a baby for the first time, and she wanted to smack herself. This wasn't like her. She was more the cynical one and not the one to get mushy or drool over a man. Plus, the warm and wild connection she felt when they were shaking hands was something she couldn't ignore.

The path wound up the mountain passing by some of the lower indentations. When he stepped into the first real cavern, she hesitated at the sight of the smoldering fire. She thought she could make out bones in the ashes, but he threw a couple more logs on the embers, burying whatever she thought she saw.

He leaned over and blew on the fire to fan the flames to life, and her brain stalled when his gaze found hers. Just watching him stirred things inside Lisa that she had never experienced before. It was almost on the edge of euphoria, but that made no sense. She shook the thoughts out of her head and stepped inside near the fire as he settled back on his knees.

Lisa set the blade on the rock next to her, glancing around. "Is this... yours?" She waved at the place.

He nodded.

"So... you're the one who brought me here last night and cooked a squirrel for me?"

Color filled his cheeks, and he glanced at the fire with a small nod.

"Thank you," she said with a mouth that was suddenly so dry she considered Mrs. Canicula's tea. She wanted to ask about the tiger, but her tongue stuck to the roof of her mouth. She needed a drink and opened the thermos.

Elijah's head snapped up the moment she unscrewed the cap. He nearly jumped over the fire and grabbed the container from her. "You brought their poison here?" he bellowed.

Lisa's eyes went wide, and she scrambled for the knife, jumped to her feet, and pressed herself into the wall. Her knife hand shook just as much as the rest of her trembling body.

He dumped the contents in the fire, and instead of dousing the flame like the tea should have, it acted as an accelerant, turning the small fire into a blaze.

"Where did you get this?" He held the container out like it was as deadly as the flames licking the ceiling of the cave.

"Mr. Canicula," she said, steadying the knife in case he dared to get any closer. She had had enough of being the victim with Herk. She wasn't going to let a stranger get the best of her. "I know it's awful tasting, but poison? Really?"

He gave her a deadly glare. "And you were going to try to give it to me?" he growled, and even in his anger, he was beautiful to behold, like an angry angel might be.

She nearly hissed at her inappropriate thoughts, growing just as irate as Elijah. "No. I was thirsty!" she yelled at him. "I was going to have a drink and look what you did!" She pointed the knife at the blaze.

"You drink *this*?" He shook the container at her, acting more like Herk than the gentleman she met at the edge of the woods.

"Not by choice," she snapped. "But it is all I was given when I was driven out of Opal. So, sue me if I wanted a drink."

He recoiled with wide eyes and seemed to calm again. "You really drink this?" he asked, and a confused crease marred his perfect forehead.

She shrugged. "I was never fond of it, but the Caniculas have made me drink a cup every day since my parents died."

He slowly paled. "When was that?" he asked with a voice so full of trepidation that she almost laughed and would have if her heart wasn't pounding in her throat from the adrenaline rush.

"Since I was four."

"Jesus." He turned and pitched the thermos out the cave with a growl.

He paced the entry, mumbling under his breath. It looked like he was having an argument with himself. Every time he stole a glance in her direction, she gripped the knife tighter. She didn't know what to think of him, and if she had a different place to hunker down, she would have been gone in a heartbeat.

He finally stopped and stared towards Opal. His shoulders dropped as if the wind had whispered a calming truth. When he turned, he was wearing the mask of the kind man she'd met at the edge of the woods.

"You said something when I called you the fated one." He approached the fire again. "Why would the fated one kill the white tiger?" he asked with genuine curiosity.

"Haven't you heard the fable about the white tiger?"

He nodded. "That's why I'm asking. I don't understand."

She cocked her head. "That's the lore," she said as if he were shy a few marbles. "The white tiger wakes and slaughters the innocent. He wants to destroy Opal, and only the fated one's magic can kill the tiger and stop the reign of terror."

With each word, his eyes saddened until a tear slipped from the corner of his eye, and all she felt was his despair.

He slowly sank to his knees facing her. "No, child. That is not the true prophecy." He wiped his face and stared up at her. "You've been fed poison in more than one way."

"What do you mean poison?" She lowered the knife but wasn't ready to sit back down and leave herself vulnerable.

The fire still blazed sending white and red embers like rain.

"Tea steeped with tar." He waved at the fire to make his point. "Did anyone else in the house drink it?"

Lisa went to nod, but tilted her head trying to remember Herk drinking his mother's tea. Herk's parents drank wine or water and rarely had a teacup in front of their seats at dinner. Now that Elijah mentioned it, she was sure she had been the only one that drank Mrs. Canicula's tea.

Finally, she shook her head. "But why would they poison me?" She continued to stare at the fire.

"Tea steeped with tar is a magical eliminator. It kills magic and then kills the host." His lips pressed tightly together. "By all standards, you should have died before your fifth birthday."

"Bullshit." She reset her grip on the knife. She shifted away from him. She didn't know this man, and the suggestions he was making made her skin itch with unease.

"The true prophecy, the one that was written in the history books by scholars of long ago, stated that when the white tiger woke from a long winter's sleep, he would unite with the fated one to rid Opal of all forms of evil and bring true peace to the region." He bit his lower lip and looked at the ceiling. "But it seems the monsters who initially bound the tiger in frost have been very, very busy." His voice turned feral, and he pressed his lips together shaking his head. Elijah climbed to his feet and glared at her. "Tell me everything."

"Why should I tell you anything?"

He stared into her eyes with an intensity that made her take a step away from him. "Because I am the white tiger, and the people who imprisoned me were named Canicula."

"How is that even possible?" she spit out.

He stared at her but didn't say a word.

Lisa leaned back and laughed. He was talking gibberish. That would mean he was hundreds of years old, and he really was some type of strange monster that looked like a twenty-five-year-old man. That was just not possible.

"Right. And I'm the Queen of Sheba."

"Proof it is." He closed his eyes, and the wind picked up, sending a funnel into the small cavern, spraying smoke everywhere. A fresh breeze cleared the smoke, and the white tiger stood right where Elijah had been. The tiger cocked his head and raised a single brow, challenging her.

She stumbled back and fell on her ass. The knife clattered on the rock next to her. Her wide eyes matched the shock pounding her heart in staccato beats.

Her mind stalled at the implications. "But... how?"

The wind blasted through the opening again, and she squinted trying to blink through the blinding smoke. This time when it cleared, Elijah stood tall and crossed his arms. His eyebrow remained cocked the way it had as a tiger.

"I am a tiger shifter." He shrugged. "The Caniculas were my people's natural enemy. I am the last one of my kind thanks to those vampires. They thrive on chaos and fear, and when desperate, they will drink the blood of the innocent. They are the true evil haunting Opal."

She laughed again and picked up the knife to give her some edge against Elijah if she needed it.

She could not see the Caniculas in the same light that Elijah was painting them. Herk's father was an asshole, so maybe he could be some long lost relative of those he was describing, but vampire? Come on. They didn't even have pointy teeth.

"If you had told me they were power hungry bastards, I would have believed you, but monsters, like out of a fiction book?" She shook her head.

He licked his lips. "Randolph Canicula?" he asked, and her smirk faded. "And his lovely wife

Serinya whose hair looks as smooth as ancient Egyptian hair plates? Not a usual name these days, I'm sure, but it was fairly popular when she was created."

She narrowed her gaze. "You could have heard their names in Opal or seen her on the street." She was beginning to doubt this man had any honorable intentions like she'd originally thought. "They practically raised me after my parents died, so why should I take the word of something that is supposed to be evil? That's supposed to have killed people in my town. My home. Give me one good reason why I should stay here. Why should I not do my duty and kill you?" She pointed the blade at him.

"Because I have not breached the barrier since I woke three years ago." He pointed towards Opal. "And I have every reason to. Randolph Canicula burned my fated mate at the stake at what they call the great fire circle just before he dragged me to the mountains and bound me in ice for three hundred years. But I didn't because revenge is not justice." He sent a glare at her and wiped his mouth. "And because deep down you know that tea was poison." He pointed at her.

As much as she didn't want to admit it, in the very essence of her soul she knew he was telling her the truth. And with Mr. Canicula's reaction to her today, she conceded that Elijah was more trustworthy than either of the men who had lived under the same roof with her since she was four.

"Have you ever killed before?" she snapped, still gripping the knife like it was her last hope.

"I've killed to eat."

She recoiled.

He rolled his eyes. "Squirrels, pigs, deer, all manner of beasts."

Her eyes narrowed, and mistrust laced her mouth with bitterness. "Define all manner of beasts."

"Bears, wolves, other large cats. But your real question is, have I killed people?"

She nodded.

"I have never killed a human being, and I do not intend to start now." He took a seat on the opposite side of the fire and waved for her to sit.

Deep down in her soul, she recognized the truth.

"Then who is killing the townspeople of Opal?" she asked and lowered the knife. She took a seat on the ground and put the blade down to show she was willing to trust him, but it was close enough to leave the alliance uneasy.

He shrugged and reached behind the nearest rock. She tensed until she saw a canteen in his hand along with some dried jerky.

"You said you were thirsty." He offered her the canteen and half the food.

She took it and tested a small sip from his canteen. Cool, crisp water washed over her tongue, and she took a longer pull of the refreshing drink. It flowed down her tight throat, easing the dryness of the fire-heated cave. She put the jerky aside, not ready to eat just yet. Her stomach was in too many knots.

"So, what's your story?" He took a bite of the jerky, and just the action of his lips pressing against the dried meat sidetracked her for a moment.

She shook the thoughts away and focused on his blue eyes, but that was no better. "What do you want to know?" she asked, trying to focus on anything else but the shifter across the fire.

"Let's start with your name." He smiled, and it completely disarmed her.

"My name is Lisa. Lisa Winters."

"Lisa, please start at the very beginning," he said in a soft voice that almost lulled her into trusting him.

She took another sip from the canteen and handed it back, avoiding the food he had offered. Her stomach was nervous enough, so food would just turn it into a roiling mess, especially if she was going to start at the beginning of her own short tragedy.

Winter's Heart
Chapter 11

WITH A DEEP BREATH and an internal pep talk, she glanced at the cave's opening. A snow squall had just started, wiping out the vision of Opal in the distance. The snow didn't reach where they were. Neither did the howling wind, but it provided the perfect backdrop for her to start her sad story.

"I wasn't born in Opal. I was born in the lowlands where it never snowed. I still remember the vast green fields and the even greener trees lining the winding river that our house was on. It was just as stunning a view as Opal's white opulence." She traced her finger on the rock floor, taking in the natural chill radiating from the surface. "I was four when the floods came. Our house was destroyed when the river rose, and we were left with nothing but the clothes on our backs." She wrapped her arms around herself and shivered.

Elijah threw a few more logs onto the fire. The blaze devoured the wood, warming the rock and her surroundings.

"My father decided it was time for us to see his home." She smiled. "I was amazed by the mountains and all the white blanketing the land." She closed her eyes. "Did you know snow has a scent?"

"Yes."

His soft answer opened her eyes, and the wistful look on his face made her want to cross over and wrap her arms around him until he smiled again. Instead, she dropped her gaze to the flames and continued.

"Newly fallen snow has the same smell as a freshly cleaned baby, and I can remember stepping out of the carriage and inhaling. That was the first taste of Opal I truly had. And it was glorious until the scrumptious smells of the bakeries mingled with the scent of the snow. It was a lot for my four-year-old self to take in all at once. I had wanted to cherish each one separately, but they layered together, cheapening the experience."

She let out a small chuckle at the memory of that first day. Lisa had been awed by Opal. She could still feel the tingle that traveled her spine as she took in the town center.

"By the time we got to the town center, I was so in awe of the place that I stopped walking and just stared up at the grandeur of the town hall. I had never seen something so tall." She sighed. "My parents were in a hurry to get to the house we were staying at, but I didn't want to leave that spot. It was as if the place called to me. When they tried to move me along, I don't know what came over me. Maybe I was tired from the trip or had sensory overload, but I jumped right into tantrum mode and my fingers started shooting sparks, like mini strips of gun powder being lit. The sensation overwhelmed me." She glanced at Elijah. "That was the last time I had the ability to tap into magic until last night."

"I'm surprised you were able to produce any at all." He took another bite of food. He nodded to her pile, but she shook her head and offered them to him. "You should eat a little." He pushed her hand back.

She broke off a small piece and chewed on the end. "I don't know how I did it. I've been drilled in so many failed training sessions since I turned eighteen and not a flicker."

"The tea should have made it impossible."

Lisa bit into the jerky, taking a bigger piece of the salty hide to make the memory of the black sludge on her tongue go away. "I should have known." She looked at him. "That stuff, it was gross. And Mrs. Canicula kept telling me it would help me find my magic." She shuddered.

"What happened at the town hall?" he asked, pulling her back to the conversation.

Lisa appreciated the redirection. "Nothing really. Just a few murmured whispers before my parents whisked me away to our new home. It was much sparser than the house on the river. But then again, we didn't have much left, and Opal was the only place we had relatives."

"So, you had family here?" He leaned forward.

"Had being the operative word. By the time we arrived, my grandmother was on her death bed. My parents wouldn't let me go into the sick room for fear I might catch whatever it was that was wasting my grandmother away. I only saw a glimpse of her through the cracked door, and she looked like a skeleton with a human skin stretched over it. It gave me nightmares for years, and I've seen that same affliction a couple of times since my grandmother died. It was as if their life was being slowly drained from their bones, and there was nothing they could do to stop it."

Elijah nodded as she talked, like there wasn't anything said that he didn't expect or see in his lifetime either.

"Grandma passed away within days of our arrival. I met Herk at the funeral, and he was such a fun boy. He wanted to know if I wanted to come to his birthday party in a few days. There was a nine-year difference between us, but he talked with me for a very long time. Looking back, it seems a bit strange." She bit her lip and wondered why he hadn't gone to play with the kids his age instead of sitting and talking to the lonely new girl. She shook the thoughts away. "Well, my mother thought that was a wonderful idea, but my father was skeptical. When Herk said the party was just for kids, my father gave me permission to go."

She smiled. "I remember my mother sewing a beautiful party dress for me, and she did my hair nicely before both my parents walked me to the party. I thought the town hall was the big thing. Well, Herk Canicula's birthday parties were spectacular, especially for a four-year-old who'd never had more than a cupcake and my parents singing 'Happy Birthday.' I didn't know where to look. Bright, shiny balloons hung from posts leading guests to the actual party spot."

Lisa's smile faded as the memory came barreling back in full color in her mind. The bittersweet memory shed tears from her eyes. "I didn't even say goodbye to my parents. I just ran towards the colorful chaos."

She met Elijah's gaze, and he handed her the canteen. She was grateful and sucked down a mouthful of water, letting the coolness coat her mouth before she returned it to him. She wiped her face, erasing the tears that had formed.

"I wish I had hugged them goodbye. If I had known I would never see them again…" She looked out at the swirling snow and pressed her knuckle to her lips.

Elijah moved closer and took her hand. The calmness of his touch gave her control again, and she squeezed his hand before releasing it.

"Thank you," she said, cleared her throat, and stripped her jacket, laying it over the rock next to her. "My parents were late in picking me up, and Mrs. Canicula brought me into the kitchen and handed me a cup of her black tea. She waited until I choked it down before telling me that my parents had died."

She picked at a hangnail on her thumb while Elijah waited for her to continue. Her mind shot off like a rocket exploding in a million different directions as she started scrutinizing her memories.

A slow burn started in the pit of her stomach, making her feel sick. All the hidden things she should have seen were starting to swirl in her head, and she climbed to her feet. Pacing helped and then horrible truths started revealing themselves until the tingling of sparks on her fingertips drew her out of her own reverie.

"They poisoned me every day since I was four." The verbal confirmation sent her heart into overdrive as her fingers ignited and flames warmed her skin.

Elijah sat unaffected by her display. It was as if he had known these things but needed her to figure them out on her own.

He raised an eyebrow and nodded. "For someone who has been fed poison for sixteen years, you most certainly have a huge untapped reservoir of power." He hopped to his feet.

She stared through him as a new horrifying thought surfaced. "They killed my parents?" she asked and then focused on his blue eyes. "And fed me lie after lie about you?" Her voice rose higher.

He put his hand on her arm in an attempt to calm her. The connection doused the fire sparking from her hands, but it did nothing to stave off the building fury inside her.

"Why would they lie? Why would they..." She paused, and her eyes widened. "Would they kill the people of their own town?" She searched his kind eyes.

"Caniculas are evil creatures escaped from the bowels of hell. Those skeletons with skin stretched over them are the victims of Canicula greed. The fact they bore an offspring while I slept is even more concerning." He glanced out towards the town. "If they are the same soulless bastards they were back when I walked this earth the first time, then I wouldn't put it past them to kill members of the community in an effort to frame me." He met her gaze. "Especially since they had to have known I was awake, or at the very least waking soon."

"How did they know that?" She scoffed, still uneasy with the idea of them being actual monsters.

He pointed at her. "You. You're turning twenty-one next week if I'm not mistaken."

She took a step away from him and nodded, expecting the type of pep-talk that Herk delivered the other night.

"If they truly believed you were the fated one, they know the fable and would do anything to stop the prophecy from coming true. They knew the white tiger would claim you on your twenty-first birthday."

"Wait. What?" She took another step back. Her mind spun with doubt. Doubt for which fable was truth. Doubt for everything she had been taught, for every conversation. For every single lie she was fed. All because a handsome stranger was feeding her a line.

"What the hell do you mean by claim me?" She glanced across the space at the knife where she had been sitting kicking herself for not grabbing it before she had her mini rant. "I am not claimable," she snapped and set herself in a fight stance.

He let out a soft laugh and moved back to his seat by the fire. "I guess men don't claim women anymore?" Elijah shrugged and leaned against the wall. "But that's not an option. They've made that impossible now."

Her stomach dropped to the ground at the disappointment raking her skin. Just a moment ago, the thought of being claimed rubbed her into a frenzy and now that he'd proclaimed it was impossible, she was disturbed? *Make up your mind, girl.*

Confusion shadowed her thoughts, and she stepped farther away from him. "Why is it impossible?" she asked, and she despised the pout in her voice.

"They poisoned you. Hence any union would poison me in a way you do not want to witness." He kicked at the dirt. "Theoretically speaking."

"What the hell does that mean?"

"It means that maybe you're not toxic, but I'm not willing to find out, especially since you seem so dead set against the idea."

When she didn't dignify him with a comment, he continued, "Theoretically, you should not have been able to produce an ounce of magic. Yet you did." He waved at her like presenting a gift.

She stared down at her hands and cocked her head. If she had been poisoned with a serum that was supposed to kill off her magic, why didn't it work? Was the white tiger the one who was lying to her?

She crossed to the opening of the cave and swept her gaze over the forest below. Elijah had been nothing but a gentleman to her. If he wanted to claim her as callously as Herk had wanted to, she wouldn't have been clothed and cared for this morning. He had ample time and opportunity to take advantage of her. But he hadn't.

Besides, he wasn't lying about killing her friend. The timing of Molly's death just so happened to coincide with his display of kindness.

However, the thought of the Caniculas being evil didn't mesh with the fact they'd taken her in and given her a home. They provided food and clothing and a roof over her head. They provided her with a lifelong friend in their son.

And yet, Mr. Canicula had sent her to what he thought was certain death. Why?

"What happens if you are killed?" she asked with her back to him.

Elijah remained quiet and she turned around.

"Their evil will spread outside of Opal. Deaths will increase tenfold from what you saw in Opal. They've been cautious because of the small community, but that will end if the boundary is destroyed. I'm the only thing keeping them bound to this location."

"And if I die?"

His lips formed a grimace. "Then if the lore is true, I would die, too. I'm as bound to the fated one as they are bound to this town."

Lisa reached for the wall. "And what if I was to marry a Canicula?" she asked in a hushed whisper, meeting his gaze.

His rosy cheeks paled, and his eyes widened in true horror. He shook his head. "The Caniculas would inherit your magic, and all would truly be lost."

Lisa's knees weakened and she dropped to the ground. She knew Herk's ambitions. She knew his obsession with her magic. And she glimpsed the monstrous side of him the other night. Could he truly be that manipulative?

"I am such a fool."

Hands landed on her shoulders. "Tell me you aren't married to one of them," he said with a strained voice that matched his tight grip.

"No. But their son *did* ask me to marry him. He said he wanted an alliance. A partnership to defeat the white tiger." She let out a high-pitched laugh.

"And you said?"

"I said no. He's too much like an older brother to me. Everything about it was all wrong."

Elijah's face relaxed.

"But it all makes sense now. The tea, the relentless failed magic training day after day. And then the recent deaths made to look like tiger attacks, and the final straw was Mr. Canicula's sending me out here to basically die."

"Either way, it suits their purpose," he said. "If you are the fated one, your death would kill both of us. If you aren't, then it is the perfect way to get rid of you."

Her stomach rolled, but she swallowed the bitter bile. Good God. Every scenario, every facet of her life to this moment had all been a grand manipulation in the pursuit of Canicula power.

Winter's Heart
Chapter 12

"I HAVE TO GO back to Opal," Lisa said as she grabbed her coat and slipped it on. She headed towards the opening.

Elijah scrambled off the floor and stepped in front of her. "You should try to harness your magic a little before you step into a hostile situation." He put his hands out, splaying his fingers in an effort to stop her. "Please."

"What if they kill again? Do you want that on your head?" She finished buttoning her coat and glared up at him.

Elijah closed his eyes. "Think about what you're doing."

"I am." She went to step out of the cave.

"I can't let you go," he said, and stepped in front of her. He had yet to physically manhandle her, but the warning in his eyes conveyed that might change if she kept pushing.

Each time she moved, he mirrored her, blocking her ability to get around him. "Get out of my way."

He pressed his lips together and shook his head. At least he had the decency to look conflicted. "They will kill you."

She blinked at his calm statement. If he had used force to stop her, she wouldn't have thought twice about leaving, but the calm way he delivered that sentence made her stop and stare at him. If the lore he believed was true, then if she died, he died.

"And then they will poison the rest of the world. That is their end game."

The gentleness of his voice was as convincing as his words, and she glanced over his shoulder at the woods. Still, she couldn't let more people die because of the Caniculas' greediness. She had already lost too much to them.

"Then come with me."

He wiped his face. "Without control over your magic, we are bound to lose."

She lifted her hand, and she willed sparks to dance across her fingers. They obeyed her silent request.

He laughed. "I know you possess it, and obviously can control it while things are calm, but I'm not sure you really want to vaporize the town if you go into panic mode like you did last night with those wolves."

She folded her hand in on itself, dousing the flames. Despite the hit to her ego, Elijah was right. She'd exploded the night before and wiped out the wolves along with some of the trees. The blackened mark on the land that was now covered with snow was a reminder of her lack of practice. She didn't want to take that chance in town. She did not want to be a killer of the innocent.

"Then teach me how to control it." She studied his expression and how the tightness around his mouth relaxed. "But we can't wait too long, because if they are the ones doing the killing, they will get the townspeople riled up enough to come hunting for you. And Herk is an excellent tracker."

"If this Herk is a Canicula, he will not be able to breach those woods." Elijah pointed towards the barrier separating the tundra from the mountain caverns they now sat in. "The farthest he can go is the barren fields. That was the curse that I made just before the ice took my last breath. I bound *them* to the town of Opal, just as they bound me in ice."

Her eyebrows rose, and she glanced at the ground trying to recall their hunting adventures as children. Every time they got close to the outer woods, he would say he wasn't feeling well and wanted to head back. Even when she had gone into these woods with her bow, he stayed in the field instead of following her. He always seemed so envious when she came back, but she thought it was the kill she carried or dragged with her.

"Come. Sit." He waved towards the spot near the fire. "It's time to master the magic you can tap, which seems to be fire related, which may be the one thing that has saved you from falling ill to their tea."

"How so?" Lisa took a seat, and he followed, sitting close enough for her to feel the heat from his leg. She had an urge to reach out and touch him again but refrained. Petting a tiger was different than rubbing a man's leg.

"Well, tar melts under flame, and soot and ash are fire-born material, so perhaps under stress, it burned through the poison that built up over the years."

She made a derisive noise. "It wasn't the magic. It was having you near that allowed it to reach the surface. Herk had me training day after day for a very long time, and the only significant thing I did was roll a pencil a few inches across a table, but even that could have been attributed to the wind."

Elijah sucked in his bottom lip as he seemed to contemplate what she'd said. "If that's true, that means I have to be near you at all times in Opal. At least until we can identify and eradicate all the evil."

He stood and collected some wood, then set it up in a small dip in the rock floor before returning next to her. He pointed his chin at the logs. "In the meantime, we have work to do. Start the fire, please."

She went to stand, but he put a hand on her knee, keeping her in place. When she lifted her hand to blast the logs, he shook his head. His strong fingers clasped hers, forcing her to lower her arms. This time when she conceded, he didn't remove his grip on hers, and she didn't want him to.

"With your mind." He lightly tapped her temple. "That is where your power is. Your hands are just the messenger. Your mind is where you will be able to see true evil and destroy it, so we need to strengthen that muscle." He lifted her hand. "And we may need to work on using this, too, but that will be later. Now light the fire."

"How?"

"Use your imagination. Visualize. Envision the spark and then the flame under the wood as if you just stuffed the spaces with paper and lit it with a match."

This felt way too much like Herk's training sessions, except Elijah's tone was calm and soft versus Herk's loud commands.

"Close your eyes and see it," he said, nodding at the wood. "And once you actually see it in your mind's eye, command your magic to make it so."

She studied the small wooden teepee he had built and then closed her eyes, doing exactly as he'd described. In her mind, she stuffed paper in between the logs and leaned over, striking a match. She held it to the paper until it was burning before dropping the stub left between her fingers.

A low whistle came from Elijah and Lisa opened her eyes. She hadn't just started a fire. She'd started a blaze.

Elijah smiled. "That was more controlled than last night, but you nearly made that wood explode. The fact you didn't is a step in the right direction, though. Now, control the flame." He pointed.

"Control it how?"

"Make it into something. Anything will do. A bird, a heart, anything. Just manipulate it." This time his voice carried some exasperation.

Lisa pressed her lips against a smile and closed her eyes. She envisioned a tiger made of flame.

"Jesus," he whispered in an alarming tone.

Her eyes popped open and widened at the mammoth flaming tiger in front of them. She slid back at the heat radiating from it. When it turned its head and snarled at the two of them, he grabbed her wrist.

The flames snuffed out completely.

Lisa looked at his hand on her wrist and then at him. Her heart thundered in her chest. She had created that thing, and somehow, just for a moment, it seemed to get away from her control.

"How did you do that?" She waved at the smoke still hanging on the air.

"I wished it so, but I had to be touching you to diffuse your magic." He smiled at her. "I cannot imagine what you would be like today if this had been allowed to be cultivated. You are most certainly the strongest elemental I have ever encountered." Interest sparkled in his blue eyes.

Lisa shifted away from him and stuffed her hands in her pockets. Again, she wondered if this man was the one she should be afraid of and not the Caniculas. Her mind drifted back to Molly and the lack of footprints leading away from her murder scene. He had some magic if he could bind the Canicula's to Opal and stop her flames from going out of control.

"Can you go from one spot to another in the snow without leaving footsteps?"

"No. I cannot wish myself from one spot to another. I am not capable of teleporting elsewhere. The only things I can do is transform into a tiger and neutralize out-of-control magic by touch. I didn't even know I was capable of creating a binding spell until I woke a couple of years ago. Unfortunately, I was not within reach of those miserable Canicula beasts when they slaughtered my soulmate and cast me in ice." He pressed his lips together and inhaled before he glanced at Lisa. "And it only took you three hundred years to bind your soul to magic and return." He let out a soft laugh.

Lisa blinked rapidly. Her mind stuck on his words, and his crooked smile did nothing to stop the chill that crawled down her spine.

"Fire and ice," he said. "I guess it is appropriate and perhaps why their poison was ineffective in squashing your gifts."

"I'm sorry. I'm having trouble understanding this. You think I'm your soulmate come back from the dead?" Had she traded one crazy for another?

He chuckled and looked down at the floor of the cavern. "This was prophesized long before either one of us were born. I did not believe it. Not until I woke up and felt the barrier protecting the rest of the world from the Caniculas. *That* was when I believed the prophecy, and I knew someday I would be standing here with you."

Lisa stared at him, unsure of what to say.

He shrugged. "I just didn't know what kind of force you would become."

While her mind rebelled against his every word, the cells in her body hummed like being this close to him was where she was meant to be. It was all too crazy, but then again, she had powers she didn't quite understand, and she needed to if she was going back into the belly of the beast.

Winter's Heart
Chapter 13

THE NEXT FEW DAYS consisted of hunting, resting, sparring, and practicing her magic. Being with Elijah had a calming effect on her. He made her feel whole again, filling that missing piece that had been gone since she had been told of her parents' death. Although his absence of vengeance against the Caniculas made her look at her own emotions.

The more she worked with Elijah, the more she trusted his version of the truth. And the more she used her magic, the more she resented the Caniculas. Elijah coached her on control, not just of magic, but of her moods and her mind as well. Only in letting go of her anger would she be able to see the true measure of their hearts.

The way to win this coming battle was not to give in to bitterness.

"Let's try something different," he said as he skinned the rabbit they had caught during their daily hunting jaunt. He put it on a cooking spike over an empty firepit and stepped away. "Tonight, I want you to try to do two things at once with your magic."

"Excuse me?" Just when she was getting comfortable with her magic, he had to throw a wrench into the mix.

"I want you to cook the rabbit for us, not charbroil it, and I want you to create a ring of fire near the entrance big enough so my tiger form can jump through. You'll need to give me enough room so I don't just jump off the ledge, though, okay?"

How in the world was that okay? She let out a laugh, like he must be joking.

"I'm serious, Lisa. You've done well with just one task, but we need to up your game before we set out for town."

"You're coming with me?"

"Don't sound so surprised. You said you thought being near me was what unleashed your magic, so I'm not taking any chances. But I will stay hidden, because I don't want them to recognize me. At least not until I can prove my innocence. Now stop sidetracking and do as I ask." He waved to the firepit and to the entry to the cavern before shifting into the beautiful tiger. His blue eyes gleamed in the semi-darkness as he waited for her to do as he'd bid.

Lisa took a deep breath to calm the sudden hammering of her heart that seeing him in tiger form always seemed to produce. She concentrated on a point on the wall between the firepit and the entrance, trying to ignore the stress crawling on her skin like a thousand fleas. If she failed, they either wouldn't eat or at the very worst, she would cook Elijah instead and end up freeing the Caniculas.

She closed her eyes and envisioned the circle first. His chuff echoed softly in the cave, and she opened her eyes to a circle she couldn't even fit her own hand through. After another cleansing breath, she willed the circle to become bigger. The fire obeyed, and she halted when the circle was almost the circumference of the cave entrance. If anyone was down below, they would think this cave was on fire. She pulled back on the inner part of the circle, leaving a space large enough for Elijah to jump through.

He did. And then turned and jumped back inside. He didn't stop like she thought he would. He just kept jumping in and out of her flaming circle.

Lisa knew he wanted her to continue. To start the fire under the rabbit just high enough to slow roast the carcass. She tore her eyes away from Elijah and looked at the empty firepit. In the back of her mind, she kept the vision of the ring of fire intact. At the same time, she willed sparks to ignite below the rabbit. It was difficult without a source for the flame to feed on, and she pushed harder.

Elijah yelped at the same time a blaze jumped up under the rabbit, scorching the outer layer of meat. The smell of burnt rabbit and singed fur filled the cavern. She closed her eyes, dousing both flames herself without his help.

"Why did you stop?" Elijah said in a strained voice.

Lisa opened her eyes and glanced at him as he inspected the angry red burn on his arm.

"That's why." She crossed to him, staring at the damage she had done. "I was supposed to cook the rabbit, not you."

He smiled. "I'm only singed. And you did sear the rabbit, but it isn't charred." He piled some wood underneath the rabbit and gave her a raised brow. "But it still needs to cook a little more."

With a flick of her wrist, the wood ignited.

"What did you learn this time?" he asked as he retrieved some snow from outside and packed it on his arm.

"That I can't take my eye off of what I'm doing?"

"Well, sometimes you have to, but in most cases if you aren't fully concentrating and in control, things will go awry. You will need to split your attention at times, but you need to understand the ramifications if you can't control the magic." He held up his arm.

"I am so sorry." She reached out to his reddened skin.

He didn't flinch at her touch, and that fresh feeling of the air before a storm surrounded them. They both stared at the connection and then met each other's gazes. The heat that built between them caught her breath in her throat.

Elijah leaned towards her, his eyes sparkling in a way she hadn't noticed before.

A shuffle outside the cavern startled both of them. They spun to the sight of one of the children from the village. The girl's hair was matted, and her face streaked with tears as she shivered in only her night shirt and socks. It was cold enough outside to be frostbite weather.

"Dear lord," Lisa whispered, and rushed to the girl. "Cheri, is that you?" she asked, scooping the girl into her arms.

The child's shakes were so bad that Lisa had no idea if she nodded or not. She moved close to the fire and grabbed her coat off the rock to wrap Cheri in it.

She rubbed Cheri's arms, trying to get the blue to recede from her fingers. "What in the world are you doing so far from home in just your nightgown?"

"He killed my family," she whispered through chattering teeth. "Slaughtered them one by one, but my momma told me to run. She said I had to find you. You would be able to stop him." Her dark eyes stared at Lisa.

"Stop who?"

Tears fell again. "The white tiger." Her gaze moved to Elijah. "But not a real tiger like I saw in here when I was climbing the mountainside. This one stalks on two legs and carries claws." She brought her gaze back to Lisa, and her chin trembled as fresh tears fell. "I saw his face."

Lisa traded a glance with Elijah. "Who killed your family?" Lisa asked, dreading the answer. She thought she knew who was doing the killing. He had been at both scenes, and she had caught a glimpse of his dark side.

"Mr. Canicula," she whispered.

"Herk?" she asked just to make sure.

Cheri shook her head. "No. Mr. Canicula."

Lisa sat back on her haunches, and a measure of relief swept through her. She had been so sure Herk had been the killer. Even with Elijah's stories of his parents, they had never been nasty to her the way Herk had been in his drunken state. She didn't know how much Herk knew, but she prayed he hadn't known of his parents' plans. She didn't think she could handle his duplicity on top of everything else.

She didn't want to hurt Herk if she didn't have to, but Mr. and Mrs. Canicula were another story. They had to be stopped at all costs.

"Have there been any other attacks since I left?" she asked Cheri.

"Mr. Canicula told the town that the white tiger is trying to weed out the fated one." She spit on the ground. "Four families with girls died before he attacked my family. He is driving everyone into a frenzy with the purpose of hunting the tiger, except he is the one doing the killing." Her face transformed into a mask of fury.

Lisa gasped and stared up at Elijah. "We have to stop them from killing anyone else."

Elijah nodded with a tight jaw. "Will you tell the town what you told us?" he asked Cheri.

Her eyes widened and she gulped, but she nodded. "If you promise to protect me," she said in a small fear-laced voice.

"With my life," Lisa said. "But we need more than just a scared child's word. We need irrefutable proof."

Her mind raced. Mr. Canicula wouldn't keep weapons in the house, especially those used in such public murders. They would be too easy to find, and his sheds were no better. He never kept those locked, so unless he had lost a few marbles, he wasn't compromising his freedom by keeping them local. She glanced out the cavern entrance while still rubbing Cheri's arms and legs.

There was one place that was far enough away from the town to be a possibility, and it was on the Opal side of the tundra. It was well within Elijah's barrier, too. The Canicula hunting cabin. And there was even a locked trunk that neither she nor Herk could ever find the key for. They were sure that was where his father kept his hunting rifles, but now she guessed that locked trunk contained something darker.

"I think I know where you might find evidence." She looked up at Elijah. "But I'll need to provide some sort of diversion so you can check it out."

"I don't want you walking into that town alone."

"I need to. And you need to take Cheri with you and keep her safe." She glanced at the girl's clothes. This wouldn't do. She couldn't let Cheri outside without proper clothing against the harsh elements. "Do you happen to have other clothes anywhere?" She started to undress. She handed Cheri her boots and pants along with her shirt, until all she stood in was the nightshirt she had on under her clothing when she'd jumped from her window.

Cheri gratefully pulled on the clothing even though it was far too big for her pre-teen body.

Elijah stared at Lisa, slowly taking her in as the wind fluttered the thermal fabric around her. He blinked and met her gaze before nodding and disappearing down a tunnel she had never ventured into. There were a couple of tunnels that led deeper into the mountain. Maybe when this whole ordeal was over, she would explore his interior domain a little more thoroughly than she had.

When he came back, he carried a beautiful fur-lined outfit that looked as if it was new, but the moment she touched it, she knew it was as old as he was. "It was my love's favorite hunting outfit," he said. "I'm not sure if they will recognize it or not, but..."

As soon as she slipped on the pants and boots, she turned and peeled off her nightshirt, then put on the matching top and cape. Arm bands and long gloves came next and when she turned, Elijah sighed so heavily that she almost took the outfit off.

When his eyes met hers, he held out a bow and quiver that with the same patterns as those on her arm bands. "You are ready, my fated one."

Winter's Heart
Chapter 14

T HE SUN HADN'T YET crested the mountains, but a deep crimson hue stretched over the town like an ominous premonition. It was enough to give Lisa pause as she took stock of her little band of warriors. Cheri, looking just as scared as she had when she'd whispered the name of the man who slaughtered her family. Elijah, who was dazzling in his fur bomber jacket and black pants. And herself, who looked like some ancient Amazon queen stepping out to battle. They made an odd group, but it would have to do. She couldn't let anyone else die while they played magical games in the cave.

"Ready?" Lisa asked Cheri.

The brave girl nodded and looked up at her in awe. Lisa gave her a quick squeeze before leading them down the mountain path. They timed it so Lisa would be walking into the center of town at the time that Mr. Canicula would be rallying the crowds like he had done at the same time each day, according to Cheri.

Just before the barrier, Elijah stopped and pulled Lisa into his arms, hugging her tightly against him. "Be careful."

His embrace bathed her in warmth, and she squeezed him back. "You, too."

Lisa begrudgingly stepped away. Elijah and Cheri veered towards the Caniculas' hunting cabin, and she waited until they were out of sight before focusing all her concentration on what she was walking into. It was likely to be a witch hunt if Elijah was correct, and she prayed she wouldn't need to use the bow he had given her against the people she was prophesied to protect.

She crossed through the barrier, feeling the tingle of it now that she knew where it was. As she stepped onto the tundra, her exposed skin prickled from the cold, and her cape billowed around her. The quiet whisper of the wind was the only noise filling the valley, like nature knew a magical showdown was about to happen and was holding its breath.

She passed by Cheri's house and the bloody mess left on the snow-dusted porch. Not even Constable Jones remained. It was all as Cheri had described the last few mornings, and she knew where the town had gathered. It wasn't the town hall like she had expected. He gathered them at the great circle, using the sacred grounds to rally the crowd.

The legendary place where good would triumph against evil. Even in the Caniculas' version of the lore, this was where the white tiger would be defeated. The gathering spot where the fated one would finally light the pyre.

Mr. Canicula's voice carried over the crowd telling them the same bullshit Cheri had said he had been feeding them. As Lisa approached, the people closest to the back of the crowd glanced over their shoulders at her. Their chants silenced, and they parted, as did the rest of the group until a path cut straight to where Mr. and Mrs. Canicula were standing.

In the center of the great circle stood a single post surrounded by mounds of cut logs. Iron shackles swayed from the post like a ghost was dancing in the breeze. There was enough firewood to create a bonfire, or roast a tiger, which from Mr. Canicula's tirade was exactly what this display was for.

A hush fell over the crowd. When Mr. Canicula turned to see why silence had fallen over his minions, his voice faltered. His eyes widened at the sight of her, and she recognized fear before he had a chance to mask it.

She stopped at the opening and stared him down.

"Well, if it isn't the traitorous whore." He crossed his arms.

"I'm not the one slaughtering his own people," she replied.

Confusion appeared on the few faces she could see. Looks were traded, and gazes bounced from her to Mr. and Mrs. Canicula.

"She is the one responsible for the deaths in this town!" he bellowed and pointed at her. "She has never fit in and has used the prophecy for her own nefarious activities!"

The crowd turned towards her, their faces going feral. How soon they forgot she was revered as the fated one who would stop evil from overshadowing Opal.

Oh, the bastard knows how to twist a tale all right.

"Murderer!" His voice thundered over the crowd. "Grab her!"

No one moved.

A noise behind her startled her. She spun towards it, trying to get her bow off her shoulder, but she didn't have time. Herk barreled into her, knocking her to the ground. Fortunately, Elijah had practiced escape moves in various situations, and this was one of them. Herk had also made her practice this type of move once upon a time as well.

She used their falling inertia to throw him over her head.

She scrambled to her feet and glanced at her bow on the ground out of reach and the arrows sprinkled around from the impact.

The crowd moved back, clearing the way for this battle of brawn versus brains. Lisa knew she didn't have a prayer without a weapon, but at least she had a few new moves up her sleeve thanks to Elijah. She set her feet in place, ready for his next attack, and kept her ears open for any attempt to blindside her in the event someone else decided to jump into the fray.

He stepped in and swung his fist. She parried, blocking the first punch, but she missed the gut shot. It was so hard that it picked her off her feet and yanked the air from her lungs.

The crowd's cheers turned to hisses when she spun away and landed a kick on the side of Herk's face. He stumbled back and cupped his cheek where she'd hit him. A playful smile formed along with a spark in his eyes. She hadn't ever landed a strike like that in the past, and it seemed to fuel whatever twistedness made Herk tick.

This time he approached more cautiously, his fists loose, matching the easy smile on his face. "You've been practicing?"

Lisa shrugged and gasped for air as her stomach throbbed. "I'm just paying attention," she said breathlessly.

His next swing grazed her cheek, but she moved quickly enough to knock him off balance. She swept his feet from under him and squared herself again, mindful of keeping her distance from anyone else.

Herk climbed to his feet and dusted himself off within striking distance, but she didn't take advantage of the open shot he gave her. When he glanced up, he cocked an eyebrow and faked to one side. But then he surprised her by tackling her full-on. He landed on top of her, and before she could twist under him and roll like she had been taught, he pinned her arms next to her head.

The crowd went wild with cheers.

"Why did you do it? Why would you kill those people?" he asked, staring down at her with confusion in his eyes.

"I didn't kill anyone." She didn't trust Herk to believe her, but she wasn't about to reveal the real culprit until she had proof. The crowd would scoff at her declaration of innocence, especially if she pointed a finger at Mr. Canicula without evidence.

Iron cuffs clasped around her wrists, and she glanced up to see Mr. Canicula's mean smile. Herk climbed to his feet as Mr. Canicula dragged Lisa to the wooden post.

"It's time to pay for your crimes," he snarled loud enough for the crowd to hear.

They cheered like this was a game. He hauled her arms up over her head and secured them to the post.

She kicked out and hit his shin, but all he did was grimace.

He stared down at her with a sneer. "I told you what I would do if you crossed me," he said in a low rumble.

The crowd chanted "Burn her" as if they had been put under some dark spell.

Herk approached. "What are you doing?" he asked his father. "You said you would put her in jail until her trial."

Lisa laughed as she kept her eye on the crowd. They were far enough back to not be able to hear their exchange, especially over the continued call for her death. "Your father's a monster."

"This *is* her trial." Mr. Canicula spun towards the crowd. "What say you?" he bellowed, holding his arms wide.

"Burn the witch!" they yelled, caught up in the frenzy. The noise was deafening.

"No!" Herk shouted above the crowd.

His father glared over his shoulder at him. "Shut your mouth boy and step away."

Herk stepped closer to her. "Do you have proof that she did it?" Doubt painted his features, and he glanced at her before looking at the bloodthirsty crowd surrounding them.

"Son, step away," Mrs. Canicula said softly from the side of the pyre. "She is not worth this fight."

"Says the woman who poisoned me for years with tea made of tar." Lisa stared down her false accusers.

Mrs. Canicula's eyes narrowed.

Lisa glanced at Herk. "Did you know?"

The shock on his face screamed innocence just as his current stance against his parents' need to destroy her. It was as if he really, truly did care for her.

"Know what?" He eyed the restless crowd from his place next to her on their makeshift bonfire kindling.

"That her black tea was actually poison meant to kill my magic and eventually kill me," she said.

"She said it was special to help you tap magic if you had it." His wide grey gaze met hers before it shot to his mother. "And that's why I could never have any."

"Herk, step away," she said, her features hardened. "Now."

He looked back at her, his eyes pleading, but for what she had no idea.

"I've never lied to you," Lisa whispered. "Even when I knew what I had to say would hurt."

"We can't just publicly execute her!" he shouted over the crowd's chant.

"Sure, we can," Mr. Canicula snarled, "and if you don't get off this pyre, I'll just burn you right along with her."

Mrs. Canicula's face registered the same shock Lisa felt.

"Randolph, please," Mrs. Canicula begged.

He glared and pointed at her. "This is your doing."

"Don't hurt him," she whispered, pleading.

"Then get him off this wood stack before I set it on fire."

"Herk, come down here now." Mrs. Canicula held out her hand.

Herk looked at his mother and then back at Lisa. He shook his head. "This isn't right. This isn't following the law like you've always preached."

His father grabbed his wrist and shackled him as well. "You fool."

While some still chanted, others stopped at the new development. All eyes were glued to the scene before them. It was not only their perceived murderer, but now it was the Canicula's son on the pyre.

Mr. Canicula stepped off the wood pile and lit a match, but before he could toss it on the wood, Mrs. Canicula blocked him.

"Please," she pleaded, but his stare was colder than the midnight wind.

"Father?" Herk pulled at his bound wrists.

"I am not your father," he snapped and pushed Mrs. Canicula aside. "Your mother fucked a human." His gaze moved to Lisa. "Your father slept with my wife long before he met your mother. The bastard ran before I had a chance to skin him alive. Too bad the fool came back to Opal."

Lisa's blood chilled. In so many words, Mr. Canicula had admitted to killing her father. She sucked air in between her teeth, containing the sudden swell of fury that clawed at the surface. She glanced at Herk, and for the first time, noticed that his eyes were the same shade of grey as hers. The same shade as her father's.

This wasn't another lie. She could see the devastating truth in Mrs. Canicula's eyes as Mr. Canicula threw the match.

She had a brother. The thought struck her hard as the match traveled through the air and landed on the wood.

"What are you doing?" Herk cried and pulled at the chains holding him to the post.

The crowd gasped and cheered as the wood burst into flame in more of an explosion than a slow burn as if Mr. Canicula had treated it with an accelerant.

Mrs. Canicula threw herself forward, but Mr. Canicula caught her around the waist and pulled her to safety. Still, she wailed at the sight of her son in mortal peril.

Heat filled the space around them, and Lisa closed her eyes, leaning her head against the wood post. Herk yanked at the chain holding him in place, pleading for help, but there was no help coming from Opal.

She was the only one who could get them out of this predicament, and they had chosen fire to try to destroy her. Fire. Her chosen element. She smiled.

The first thing she needed to address were the chains. She couldn't hold the fire at bay forever and being bound in the middle of the danger zone wouldn't fare well for either of them if she lost control of it. Iron could melt and that is what she concentrated on. Heating the cuffs to the point their structural integrity wasn't enough to keep them bound.

The burn of hot metal made her wince, but in a matter of moments, the cuffs holding her in place were weak enough for her to tear her hands from. She grabbed Herk's arm and yanked, despite his howling.

He just stared at her and grasped his wrist.

In the distance, a tiger charged towards them surrounded by children. And even through the wall of flames obstructing most of her view, she saw the panic in Elijah's eyes.

Herk went to move, and she grabbed his arm. "Don't run."

She concentrated on pushing the flames to the edge of the wood pile. It still blazed high enough for people to step back. Mr. Canicula held Mrs. Canicula against his chest and smiled in triumph at the wall of flames. Lisa could see him, but he couldn't see through the block she'd created.

"Are you—"

"Shush," she interrupted Herk.

When she thought she had total control of the blaze, she looked beyond them at the Caniculas and willed the fire to encircle them. The fire obeyed, trapping them in a circle of flame before they understood what was happening. Gasps came from the crowd, almost making Lisa's control falter.

"We need to get off this wood," she said as sweat dripped from her forehead. She kept her hands splayed and her focus on the fire ring.

Herk gently took her arm and kept her steady as he helped navigate them from the pile. When they reached the ground, he let go of her.

"Do not harm the tiger," she yelled without breaking her concentration. "The only thing about the lore we've all been fed over the years that is true is that the fated one would rid Opal of evil. The tiger is *not* evil!"

"But..."

"She's right," Cheri said, stepping into the crowd. She threw a bloodied fake claw on the ground in front of Constable Jones.

He gasped. "We thought you were dead."

"That's exactly what Mr. Canicula wanted everyone to think about all of us." Cheri waved at the other children surrounding the tiger. "That was in Mr. Canicula's hunting cabin along with the other kids."

"The tiger has put them under a spell," Mr. Canicula yelled, but his words had an empty effect on the crowd.

"Shut up!" Herk snapped venomously and pointed a finger at him. "You were willing to burn me to a crisp because I wanted due process for Lisa. You chose to be judge and jury and sentence innocent people to death. So just shut your mouth."

Some of the flames shot back to the pyre before she could harness them again, and Lisa gave Herk a side-eye.

"I saw the man who killed my family!" Cheri pointed towards the circle of flame holding the Canicula's prisoners. "He slaughtered my family with that thing." She nodded towards the bloody man-made claw. "Mr. and Mrs. Canicula are the real monsters in this town."

Even Constable Jones seemed frozen with indecision.

The townspeople were no better. Just like Herk, they seemed to be grappling with the poison they had been fed for generations. And they all seemed to be looking to Herk for direction.

No one knew quite what to do now that the white tiger was here and not living up to the expectations painted for centuries.

Herk looked down at the bloodied man-made paw as well as the pristine one another child held. Both looked rudimentary. He pointed to the one that another little girl named Mary held. "Press the end in the snow."

Mary did as Herk asked. When she pulled it out, she said, "Mr. Canicula killed my family, too and he and Mrs. Canicula came to the cabin and killed Tommy and Joe. They drank their blood." She scrunched her face. "And then told us we were next."

Lisa clenched her fists, and the fire flared brighter. It took her a moment to get it back under control. Luckily it didn't devour Mr. and Mrs.

Canicula. She was not the judge and jury and would not be the one to take justice into her own hands, even if that was what she wanted to do.

Herk wiped his face and paled as he stared at the pristine tiger footprint. "Where in the cabin did you find this?" he asked Cheri.

"The locked trunk."

"If it was locked, how did you get it open?"

While Herk seemed unconvinced by the evidence and even his parents' actions, Lisa knew better. Herk asked lots of questions when his mind was having trouble reconciling the truth in front of him with his feelings. She was sure this was as much of a loop as it was for her.

"He picked the lock." Cheri pointed at the tiger.

The children seemed to move closer, each putting their hand on his fur in both a protective and grateful manner.

"Cheri found us in the caverns. She ran all the way there in her nightshirt," Lisa said, knowing he would understand just how frightened this child must have been to flee without winter protection.

He stared at her and then glanced at his parents.

"Don't believe that lying witch," Mr. Canicula snarled.

"The hunting cabin was the only place I could think of where your father had a place to hide things. And we never could figure out where the key to that trunk was," she added softly, bringing up memories of their childhood adventures in the woods while he processed everything.

He swiped his hand down his face, and Lisa could tell that the past few minutes were spinning in his head by the way his eyes seemed to widen as he stared at the bloody man-made paw. His gaze lifted to the white tiger in the center of the group of children, and his gaze narrowed. He took a wobbling step towards the beast.

Lisa grabbed his arm, steadying him the way he had helped her when they climbed off the wood pile meant to be their death. She had always felt a connection to Herk, always thought of him as a big brother, which was why his proposal threw her so hard, and even now as he stood debating on his loyalties, she felt that connection.

"Don't do anything stupid, brother," she said, keeping the lion's share of her focus on the ring of fire burning around his parents.

He stared into her eyes for a long time. "He tried to kill me."

She nodded.

Herk turned to his parents. "Lock them up. Their trial starts tomorrow."

Lisa snuffed out the flame and Constable Jones and his deputies descended on Mr. and Mrs. Canicula like flies on spoiled meat.

Winter's Heart
Chapter 15

LISA SAT ON THE couch in one of the empty homes near the town center with both her arms bandaged. The burns from the melting iron still itched and would be a reminder of this entire ordeal. The six orphaned children, including Cheri, sat on the floor with crayons and paper, coloring as they waited for the sentencing of Mr. and Mrs. Canicula.

The past few days had been reveal after reveal of the atrocities the Caniculas had delivered to Opal over the centuries. From the burning of Elijah's love at the same stake they had tried to sacrifice Lisa and Herk on, to the slaughtering of families over the years, including Lisa's parents and grandparents.

Mrs. Canicula had cooperated. Spilling truth after ugly truth, including poisoning Lisa with tar-tea to destroy the magic inside her. She didn't know why it didn't work. And all throughout her testimony, Mr. Canicula glared at her from the defendant's box.

The most damning evidence was the children's testimonies. They didn't divert from one another. Each one witnessed their parents' death and then

Mr. Canicula swept them away to the cottage, tying them up for his amusement. They were vampires alright, and with the children, they chose to make their deaths a display of blood and gluttony.

Lisa's stomach had churned and almost spilled their contents at the description. She looked at the children, silently admiring their bravery for facing those vampiric monsters.

Elijah stepped into the doorway leading to the kitchen. "Breakfast is ready."

Crayons were dropped, and a flurry of arms and legs filled the space as everyone ran to the kitchen table. Lisa followed and stopped next to Elijah, watching as the children climbed up on chairs and started helping themselves to bacon and eggs that Elijah had whipped up.

"Are you okay?" he asked and brushed a piece of hair out of her face.

She shook her head. "Not particularly."

The Caniculas had been found guilty on all counts. If sentenced to death, it would be her duty to annihilate them with her magic. Which meant death by fire, and that was never pretty or humane.

A knock at the door interrupted them and she crossed to open it. Herk stood on the other side, his face drawn with exhaustion. Finding out he was the son of an immortal had seemed just as hard as his father's betrayal.

He was flanked by two officers, and his arms were behind his back.

"Death." He grimaced as he said that lone word. Then he met her gaze.

Lisa swallowed hard.

He let out a little laugh. "They aren't sparing me either."

She blinked and her eyes widened.

Herk didn't do anything. Why are they sentencing him to death?

"What?" she asked to make sure she'd heard him right.

"Guilty by association. Monster blood and all." He shrugged a shoulder.

Her gaze hardened, and she shook her head. She turned toward Elijah. "This is not right—" She waved at Herk in the doorway. "—He did nothing wrong."

Elijah's open jaw was enough to announce his equal shock at the sentencing. "But he's innocent."

She looked back at Herk and the guards holding him hostage. She couldn't let this happen. "Killing an innocent man is not part of the deal."

"I'm sorry, Miss Winters, but the jury demanded the complete destruction of the Canicula bloodline."

"And what of the Winters' bloodline?" she asked and stormed out the door past the guards.

She marched towards where the crowd was forming. This town seemed to have a taste for public executions, and it had to stop. It was as if the Caniculas had truly destroyed the humanity of this little town.

She made her way through the crowd until she stood before three posts and more wood piled than before. The middle post was empty, but Mr. and Mrs. Canicula were bound to the other two and struggling in their bonds.

When the guards with Herk went to pass her, she put her hand out. Flames licked her fingers.

"Do not go any farther," she said. "He is not one of them. He is my half brother."

"But he is also a Canicula," the judge said from her station to the right of the pyre. "And therefore, must be eliminated."

Chants of "burn them" started behind her, and she realized the Caniculas' evil had spread to the human hearts of this community.

"Herk is not evil. I will not abide by this ruling." She turned towards the crowd as the chants continued.

The frenzied looks in their eyes saddened her, and when Elijah stepped into her sight in tiger form, his eyes magnified her despair.

"My job as the fated one is to rid Opal of evil." A tear escaped, sending a hot path down her cheek. "What I see and hear before me is evil." She choked on her words. "This bloodlust is evil." Tears now flowed freely as her voice echoed above the chants.

She turned towards the pyre and pointed. "They are not the only ones who harbor evil in their hearts. If you cannot recognize it in your own soul, there is no hope for Opal."

Only a few catcalls of "Burn them!" remained. The rest of the crowd looked shamed at their actions.

"Justice is not the same as bloodlust. Executing Mr. and Mrs. Canicula is just. Executing Herk makes you no better than them." She pointed behind her at the pyre. "I am willing to be the hand of justice, but I will not murder an innocent man because of your unfounded fear." She gave one last glance at the crowd before turning to the judge. "Rethink your sentence."

The judge recoiled, her face reddened and scrunched in anger. "The judgement stands."

Lisa clenched her fists. Magic swelled inside her, and she met Herk's gaze, shaking her head slowly before she closed her eyes. The tiger roared, but she ignored him. Evil must be annihilated, and the innocent must be protected.

"Justice." She concentrated.

White light filled her vision and all she saw were human hearts. Nearly a dozen of them were blackened and shriveled, including the judge's, but the multitude of them carried vessels filled with the light of hope.

Screams filled the air along with gasps. She opened her eyes, and the people with evil shriveling their hearts became human torches in the crowd. Lisa turned towards the pyre. Mr. and Mrs. Canicula smiled at the pandemonium, drinking it all in until they realized Lisa was looking at them.

Lisa only saw the root of evil blackened and sickened within these two monsters. Fire leapt from her, sweeping forward like a wave, leaving only ash floating on the air where the Caniculas had once been bound. Not even the iron shackles remained.

Herk's wide eyes stared at her. She turned back to the crowd now bathed in ash. Wind swirled and Elijah stepped from the grey mist. He started running towards her, and she couldn't understand the horror in his gaze.

When he was close, he leapt through the air, turning into the tiger before he hit her, slamming her down to the ground with the force of his weight. She smelled singed fur just before everything went black.

Hushed whispers surrounded her, penetrating the blackness, but Lisa could not make out the words, nor could she escape the darkness pulling her into oblivion.

Winter's Heart
Chapter 16

ACOOL DAMPNESS CARESSED her forehead. Lisa moaned and tried to open her eyes, but her lids seemed crusted closed. She lifted her hand to wipe them, but a cloth swiped across her eyes instead.

"Shhh," a deep voice softly cooed and then that heavenly dampness wiped her eyes again.

She blinked them open but couldn't quite see clearly. It took her a few blinks to focus on the face hovering over her. Blue eyes peered down from a face that held deep creases of concern.

"You scared us all for a spell." Elijah continued wiping her face and neck with the cloth before dipping it into a bucket next to the bed she was laid out on.

"What happened?" she whispered with a voice hoarse and raspy.

"You became the hand of justice smiting evil. It was something to behold." He smiled, but his concern still hung on the air. He kept methodically wiping her face and neck with the cool cloth that smelled of honey and peppermints. His lips held tightness even though he tried to smile for her.

"What aren't you telling me?" she asked after another swipe of coolness.

His smile faded and he sighed. "I didn't react as fast as I should have." He closed his eyes for a moment and then went back to washing her gently with the cloth.

She lifted one of her hands and stared at the bandages covering her skin. What she saw was red and angry with patches of blisters poking out from under the gauze. Her last memory of singed fur surfaced, and she looked closer at him. His arms had bandages that looked like those on her hands, and her gaze jumped to his.

"I burned you?"

He sighed. "Rest. You're pretty doped up on medicine right now, and you need the sleep." He gave her a grimace of a smile.

"But you're hurt." She started to sit up. Every muscle protested with a scream of pain, and she fell back.

"I'm fine." He swiped her shoulder and arm with the cloth. "But we nearly lost you." This time when his gaze met hers, tears glossed his eyes. He swallowed and closed his eyes for a moment before looking back at her. "The doctor should be back to check on us in a little while."

She relaxed back into the bed and glanced around at their surroundings. Her heart lurched in her chest at the metal bars surrounding them.

"Jail?"

His smile softened. "This was the only place they could really sterilize to address our wounds. The doors aren't locked, and there hasn't been anyone in the jail for a while. We can control infection better here than at the doctor's office or someone's home."

A throat cleared from behind Elijah. He turned and Herk appeared at his side.

"Hey," he said. The side of his face looked like he had fallen asleep in the sun.

Lisa's stomach dropped. "I hurt you, too?"

His hand jumped to his face. "Nothing more than a sunburn," he said with a nervous laugh. "Most of us who were near you ended up like this, but it will eventually clear up." He crossed and took a seat at the foot of her bed.

"What else is happening out there?"

Herk looked over his shoulder at the open doorway and sighed. "The townsfolk are somewhere between awed and scared." He locked gazes with her. "They keep coming to me like I have answers." He shook his head. "I don't know how to put people at ease. I just know how to beat the crap out of people. Or run them ragged until they tell me to..." He looked at her pointedly.

"Sod off?" She snorted laughter.

He smiled. "I think I've come to terms with you being my little sister. It certainly explains my insane need to push you and protect you at the same time."

"So, you agree you were being unreasonable?"

Elijah's lips formed a smirk, and he raised an eyebrow at her as he wiped her other arm with the salve.

Herk glanced at Elijah and then back at her. "Considering what you actually did, I don't think I was being unreasonable at all. I just didn't know my mother was poisoning you." He looked down at his hands. "I had some time to talk to her alone. She didn't want to talk at first, but I told her she owed it to me considering I was sentenced to death alongside her, just for being her son. She opened up. Told me about her affair with our father. She said he was kind and pure-hearted, just like you are. And he didn't shy away from her when she told him what she was. He asked a lot of questions, so you have a great deal of him in you, but when Randolph found out, she made your dad leave town. He never knew my mother was pregnant.”

That did sound like her father. He always told her to question everything because that was the only way to get to the truth. She nodded.

“When you and your family came back, it devastated my mother. Your dad had given his whole heart to your mother, and the minute you stepped into town, my father knew magic had intruded on Opal and the prophecy was imminent unless he could change it in some way. He apparently wanted to kill you right then and there, along with your parents, but my mom couldn’t abide killing the child of someone she cared a great deal for. Although, she gave my father some bullshit excuse that worked because...” He waved halfheartedly at her.

“I guess I am glad she had a heart,” Lisa said.

He nodded. “I’m glad, too. Although I wish she had clued me in before I made a royal ass out of myself with you.”

“You didn’t know. It was kind of creepy because I just couldn’t get past seeing you like a brother.”

“Thank god.” He shivered at what might have transpired had Lisa said yes to him. “Anyway, it seems every day was a battle for my mother to keep you alive. It wasn’t until I showed interest that my father backed off because he thought that was how we would be freed. She didn’t know when he figured out I wasn’t his son. He manipulated us all. He knew I would have done anything to keep Opal safe, even try to go after the tiger with you. Which, according to Elijah, would have killed me if I forcefully tried to go through the barrier. So...”

“He wanted you just as dead as he wanted us,” Lisa said.

“Apparently.” Herk chewed the side of his lip. “When that failed, he fed me doubts about you and seeded the thought that you might be the one killing people here especially when you pointed out the lack of animal footprints around Molly and then told me the tiger didn't do this." He glanced at Elijah. "I thought you had some magical ability to pop in and attack and then be gone." He laughed under his breath. "But that's beside the point. I guess what I'm trying to say is I'm sorry I ever doubted you." He met Lisa's gaze.

"I'm sorry I ever thought you were a part of this." She tried to sit up.

"Lay your ass back down," he snapped at her and then pointed at Elijah, acting more like the Herk she was used to. "Make sure she rests."

"You can count on that." Elijah continued to administer salve to her exposed burns.

"We'll have to figure out this sister-brother thing when you are better, but I've got to say, having a tiger as your protector is actually pretty cool." He stood and glanced at Elijah. "And he seems pretty fond of you," he added before he wandered out of the room.

She yawned, exhausted from the conversation, and met Elijah's gaze. "I'm pretty fond of you, too."

This time his smile was more natural, more dazzling. "We will have to explore this mutual fondness a little more when you are back on your feet."

"Oh, you can count on that!" She smiled and closed her eyes, wishing she could experience Elijah's kiss.

It was as if he had read her mind. His soft lips pressed down on hers, and the connection created a warm heat in the center of her heart. Sparks danced on the back of her eyelids, and her entire body tingled. This was something that could become all consuming.

She wrapped a bandaged arm around his neck and opened her mouth to deepen the kiss.

He pulled away with a chuckle, and she opened her eyes to his bright blue ones that held the same spark igniting inside her.

"Rest and heal first," he whispered in a voice that had turned husky with need. He ran his thumb across her bottom lip and smiled. "That was just a tiny incentive, so you get better as fast as humanly possible."

That was one hell of a stroke of motivation.

That little peck was not nearly enough for Lisa. She wanted so much more from her white tiger.

She wanted forever.

The End

MESSIAH

An Ancient Prophecy.
A forbidden love.
Now, there's nowhere to run.

André's abilities have always marked him as special, but fulfilling an ancient prophecy is enough to have him ostracized into the cosmos. Love was his motivation for preventing his parent's execution, now in Earth's refuge, love is his undoing again.

The Commander's daughter is off limits, but this kind of love is destiny, forcing Katrina and her alien paramour to elope.

Word of André's survival reaches his home planet when his image is broadcast across the universe. This time, his very existence may well trigger the destruction of a planet, his haven, Earth.

Messiah Chapter 1

*M*AY 2255
 God, this is mass suicide.

The auditorium filled with Commander Robbins's special task force; an elite team built for the sole purpose of keeping humanity from extinction.

He glanced to his side, taking a deep breath and meeting his son's somber gaze.

This is not your fault.

His son scoffed in response and looked away.

Returning his attention to the auditorium, Commander Robbins scanned the murmuring crowd, and steeled his emotions, locking them behind a barrier, hiding the roar of his heart and the nerves causing his mouth to lay as dry and wasted as the world outside the domes.

Messiah Chapter 2

*A*PRIL 2233
First Colonel Matthew Robbins picked up the phone in his office.

"We still haven't received a response from the ship, sir."

He paused and looked out the window toward the bright sky. The president's orders were clear: seek and destroy unless contact could be made. The precarious existence of the human race couldn't tolerate another unknown, and with each and every attempt at communication falling on deaf ears, the government wasn't taking a risk.

Not with the first alien contact in history.

He was expected to carry out the order alone. "Get my ship ready." He hung up the phone. The soldier in him was thrilled to take another space jaunt, but he also tasted the metal tinge of fear.

The first leg of the trip was uneventful. Bursting through the Earth's atmosphere into space always filled him with a sense of awe, but this time, it was short-lived. His ship's tracking mechanism homed in on the alien craft, calculating time and distance and the trajectory that would put his spacecraft in the path of the unknown.

Hours passed and the small dot in the window grew as he drew closer. Sweat pooled in Matthew's armpits and at the small of his back. His tongue scraped the roof of his mouth like a rough patch of sandpaper, and he swallowed trying to alleviate the dryness.

Shaking his head, he admonished himself. *I'm a colonel in the United States Armed Forces for God's sake!* Matthew shoved the fear into a small lead ball that found its way to the pit of his stomach.

He focused on the craft, studying the data the computers were spewing. There seemed to be no thrusters navigating the sphere. As he drew closer, the readouts showed no discernible windows and communication was still non-existent. He stared at the small craft and wondered again if there really was life inside it, especially since it wasn't big enough to carry more than a couple human beings at best. He checked the statistics again and they confirmed a life-form—or at least an energy source—onboard. One that had diminished since they first discovered the craft.

Circling the small sphere, he studied it, the smooth surface reflecting the shining light. Using the extension crane, he plucked the ball out of space and pulled it into the loading bay of his spacecraft, watching the controls. Once the panel indicated his cargo was secured, he sealed the outer doors and started pressurization. When the oxygen display returned to an acceptable level, he punched in coordinates and switched the ship on autopilot, heading home.

Matthew closed his eyes and took a deep breath, calming the clamor in his chest before stepping through the doors and into the loading bay. Cool steam, like an open batch of dry ice, drifted off the ship. He circled it, sliding his fingers along the smooth, unbroken surface. It was cold, cold enough to numb his digits, and he pulled his hand away, rubbing his fingers to his palm to get the feeling back.

"Hello?" he called, still circling.

No answer.

He put his hands on his hips and looked down. There, barely visible in the satin skin, was a break. Matthew crossed to the crane controls and slowly rolled the sphere. When the panel the size of a small hatchway was completely exposed, Matthew returned to the sphere, studying the hatch. He rubbed his hands together and felt the door, looking for a release, a button, a way in.

The hatch door didn't contain a release valve, so he moved his search to the outer rims and halfway down the frame of the door, he felt the skin of the ball compress and he pushed on the spot. The hatch popped open.

Noxious fumes escaped from the craft and Matthew coughed, covering his mouth and shooting back a few steps. The heart of a sewage plant would have smelled better. After a few shallow breaths, he approached the dark opening. Matthew pulled a light stick from his pocket, snapped it on and stepped inside the craft.

He glanced around, confused. The inside of the craft was cold like the inside of a refrigerator and seamlessly round as the outside. The sphere had no control panels or any form of mechanical means to contact the outside world and it was filthy. Layers of waste, blackened by time, lined the surface and mounded in the center of the room. Empty cartons of what looked like rations poked out haphazardly from the mess, along with something akin to plastic water bottles, all empty and decayed. His hands shot over his mouth again as the stagnant air full of methane assaulted his nostrils, making his eyes water and his stomach roll.

He scanned the room again and his gaze landed on the mound in the center of the sphere. The temperature skyrocketed and the widest, bluest eyes he had ever seen peered out of the filth. Eyes attached to a smear-covered body equivalent to that of a ten-year-old boy.

Shit, how'd I miss you? He almost laughed at the sudden thought. The boy uncurled and crouched in the center of the sphere; his eyes carried caution layered with fright. His gaze bounced between Matthew's face and his uniform, specifically the United States Armed Forces insignia on his right breast pocket.

"Hello," Matthew said after a moment, unsure of anything else to say.

The boy remained squatted. His eyes narrowed in an expression of distrust, and he brushed his stringy bangs out of the way.

"Can you understand me?" Matthew asked.

The boy nodded slowly. He looked at Matthew's uniform, intently singling out the flag on the right breast pocket. A crease appeared between his eyes.

Matthew smiled. A fraction of relief layered under his skin. *At least the lines of communication are open.* "I won't hurt you," he said, trying not to gag at the smell seeping into his clothing. He put his open palms in front of him to show the boy he had nothing in his hands, but the light stick clutched between his thumb and forefinger.

The boy nodded. "I know," he said in a weak, scratchy voice.

Another notch of ease swept through Matthew. The kid understood English. "What's your name?" he asked and stepped toward the boy. A jolt from an electrical force field zapped him and he recoiled, dropping the light stick in the slime at his feet. "Jesus!"

The boy's eyes widened.

Matthew rubbed the back of his hand, wincing at the reddened skin. He surveyed the room again, slower this time, looking for the controls to the force field surrounding the boy. When his visual search came up empty, he focused back on the child. "How old are you?"

A shrug. "I don't know."

Puzzled, he glanced at his singed hand and back. "How long have you been in space?"

Another half shrug and the boy's eyes turned toward one of the sphere walls. He followed his gaze and stared at the counting sticks drawn in the muck, hundreds of them. He shifted his eyes back to the boy, watching his lips silently count and then press together in frustration, trembling. "A long time, almost too long."

Silence filled the small space and Matthew nodded. The state of the capsule was evidence of an extended period of time, perhaps years. "Do you know how to turn the force field off?"

The crease between his eyes became more prominent.

"The controls, the switch, you know—a button?"

The boy shook his head, still wearing a perplexed expression, like Matthew was one shy of a deck of cards. "There isn't a button."

Shit. How do I get him out of here?

A slight laugh filtered through the sphere. "The force field isn't created by this thing." He waved a skeletal hand at his surroundings and the effort seemed to suck a fraction of life from his eyes.

Shock skittered across Matthew's skin, pooling at the base of his spine and morphing into a slight chill. The only other explanation, one that defied logic, popped out of his mouth. "Did you do that?"

The boy nodded and Matthew inched a step back toward the opening, the president's directive echoing in his mind. *Seek and destroy.* Matthew's mind reeled, taking in the now shaking form of the filthy boy; his eyes widened as if he was reading Matthew's thoughts. Matthew blinked, swallowed and took a shallow breath.

If this truly was a child, he couldn't kill him, no matter where he came from. His duty was to serve and protect those who couldn't protect themselves. "Do you remember how old you were when you were put in here?"

A shadow passed over the boy's face and he nodded. "Six."

Matthew did some rough calculations and came to the conclusion that the kid had to be at least eight, maybe older, based on the slim carvings counting the passage of time, and that cinched his decision: dangerous or not, he couldn't destroy this child.

"Do you know where you are?" Matthew asked.

The boy's expression changed to guarded confusion, and an eyebrow rose, shifting the layer of muck on his face. He glanced around the windowless craft, shaking his head.

"You are in the Sol System. What we on Earth call the Milky Way. Your..." He paused, looked around and then returned his gaze to the boy. "Your ship is in the loading bay of my star cruiser."

"Earth?"

"Yes, Earth." Matthew crouched down so he was at eye level with the boy. "Where are you from?"

The boy just stared at him.

"Do you know where you're from?"

He nodded, still wary, his eyes bouncing between Matthew and the insignia on his shirt and beyond at the opening.

"Do you want to get out of here?" Matthew asked, hooking his thumb over his shoulder to the open hatch. He wanted out of the vile sphere. He wanted to scrub the scum off both the boy and himself, to feel clean again and not have the stink permeating in his nose.

The boy's eyes shot to his face and widened. His teeth slid on his lower lip and for the first time since he entered the sphere, he saw a light in his eyes.

Hope and fear mixed in his expression, and he nodded.

"What's your name?" the boy croaked.

Matthew stood. "Colonel Matthew Robbins. What's yours?"

"André," the boy replied and the slight electrical crackle filling the sphere suddenly cut off. He pushed himself off the ground, but his legs wobbled beneath him, and he sat down hard on the floor.

Matthew's heart went out to the kid. He certainly showed signs of bravery and resourcefulness, surviving in a windowless pod for so long. But he wondered if André would trust him enough to help. "Will you let me help?"

The conflict was clear in the boy's eyes: the want, the hope, the fear all screaming from the blue depths as he finally met Matthew's gaze and nodded. Matthew leaned down and scooped up the boy and a measure of alarm shot through him. The kid weighed less than fifty pounds. Much less. *God, how did he ever survive out here?*

Matthew offered a smile, sweeping the concern from his face, and focused on getting out of the pod. He carried André into the decontamination room and set him down, closing the doors before hitting the button. Warm soapy water sprayed from all sides, blasting years of filth from the boy's skin and soaking Matthew's clothes. He helped André to his feet, steadying him, watching his eyes close and his head tilt into the warm stream.

After several wash and rinse cycles, including using the exfoliating system, André stood clean, his skin the color of a deep Texan tan, his hair reminding Matthew of raw sienna. With a physique identical to that of a ten-year-old boy, Matthew guessed he could easily pass as a human child and for the first time since he stepped into the pod, he had an idea of how to protect this kid, but he needed agreement from his superiors and that would be sticky.

André flashed a line of straight shiny white teeth in his direction and without the layers of dirt, his eyes shone bright azure, bordering on metallic. They held gratitude. Gratitude so deep that Matthew cleared the lump from his throat and flipped the drying jets on, closing his eyes against the powerful blast of air.

Rummaging through the cabinet, Matthew grabbed a shirt and handed it to André. The material covered his emaciated body almost to his bony knees. Refreshed and clean, Matthew led him into the cockpit, pointing to the co-pilot seat and nodding as André slid onto the soft cushion.

Staring out the window with his hands on the controls, Matthew's mind raced. All the B-rated horror movies about aliens filtered through his head and he shot a glance at the boy.

André stared at him, his eyes wide and a grin playing on his lips. "You have moving pictures too?"

Matthew's gaze snapped to his passenger. *You can read minds?*

"Yeah, can't everyone?" André glanced back at him like he had two heads and a forked tongue.

Matthew shook his head. *First the force fields, now mind reading. What else can this kid do?*

"A lot of things. That's why I was exiled," André answered.

"Exiled?" *What the hell have I gotten myself into?* He turned toward the loading bay, wondering about the lack of any instruments in the alien ship.

"It's not a ship. It's a death capsule."

Matthew's eyes shot to André's. Revulsion snaked across his skin, and he blinked, his mouth dropping open to speak but no words formed. He looked back at the loading bay doors and collected his flying thoughts. "Were you alone?"

"Yes." He looked at his hands fidgeting in his lap.

Alone. Years in a death capsule—alone. Matthew couldn't fathom why anyone would do that to a child. "Why in God's name would anyone exile a six-year-old?"

"My father told me once that I was gifted." His voice cracked with emotion and he stopped talking, his eyes welling up with tears.

Matthew recoiled, his eyes widening as thick drops of blood flowed from the corner of André's eyes. "Jesus! Are you okay?" Matthew reached for him, but André put his hand up, stopping Matthew.

He swiped his hand over his eyes. "I'm just crying," he said.

"Your eyes bleed when you cry?" Matthew grabbed some tissue and handed the wad to André, still skeptical even though he nodded. Maybe the kid just needed hydration. Matthew turned, pressing a few buttons on the side panel. A moment later, a tall bottle of cool water popped into the order tray. He unscrewed the top and handed the drink to André. "Maybe this will help."

"It's normal," André answered and took the bottle of water. The first sip turned into a guzzle, and he downed the entire bottle of water within seconds. "Thank you." André looked at the empty plastic container. "Can I have another one?"

"When was the last time you had something to eat or drink?"

He shrugged in answer and handed over the empty bottle.

"If you're anything like we are, you might want to wait a few minutes..."

André scrunched his face and doubled over. Matthew reacted quickly, grabbing a container from the corner and putting it under André's face just in time to catch the spew of water that came from the boy's stomach.

Once he finished retching, Matthew stood and disposed of the contents. When he returned, he punched in the command for another bottle and this time he gave a warning. "As I was saying, if you're anything like we are, and it looks like you are, your stomach won't take too kindly to a rush of food or water after not having any for an extended period of time. Drink slowly this time."

Taking a small sip, André leaned back in the seat and squeezed his eyes closed. His lower lip quivered and his jaw line clenched. A slow stream of bloody tears rolled down his cheek.

"You're going to be okay," Matthew said, even though he wasn't sure how close to death the kid was. He shook his head, kicking himself for not insisting on a medic for the trip. He placed his hand on André's shoulder and gave it a quick squeeze before focusing back on the loading bay doors, wondering again what this kid could have done to be sentenced to death.

Without prompting, André continued, "The emperor believed in an old Zyclonian legend, one that foretold the end of our civilization. I guess I fit the description and he figured I was a threat. He had both my parents and me arrested." Again his voice hitched and he took a sip of water. "He charged my parents with treason and killed them and then he sealed me in the capsule. At least they gave me a little food and liquid, but it wasn't enough to last long. He expected me to die...alone."

The rush of anger that filled Matthew surprised him as much as the tightened grip on the controls. "You were just a child. Hell, you still *are* just a child."

André shrugged. "Yeah, well, the emperor didn't care." A measure of sarcasm laced his voice and Matthew returned his focus on the boy.

"If I ever see him again..." His eyes glimmered with red tears and radiated a hatred so strong Matthew felt it fill the small craft. "I will kill him."

A smile spread across his lips, one that never should have graced the face of a child, and Matthew shivered. He cleared his throat and looked at the bay doors again. Matthew reached across the instrument panel and pressed a button. The sucking sound of de-pressurization leaked into the cockpit as the loading dock outer doors opened, emptying the contents of the room into space. Their attention diverted to the monitor and the sphere meant to be André's coffin drifted away from their ship.

The transmitter squawked. "Colonel Robbins, come in."

He flipped the channel open. "Colonel Robbins here."

"Can you confirm the success of the mission?"

Matthew inhaled. He turned his attention toward the sphere and pressed another button on the control panel, lining up the trajectory between the spacecraft and the death pod with the mouse controls. He glanced at André and squeezed the trigger on the control; a second later, the pod vaporized.

"Mission success confirmed," he said, keeping eye contact with the boy, wondering just how far up shit's creek he was going to be when he got back home with his visitor in tow.

"Confirmation received." A pause. "Colonel, we're showing another life-form aboard your craft."

"Affirmative."

"Please advise."

Now for the shit storm. "I found a boy onboard the alien craft."

"Sir, your orders—"

"—I'm aware of my orders," he interrupted the officer on the other end of the transmission. "I'll deal with Commander Lawrence when I land. In the meantime, the spin to the media is this was a rescue mission for one of our own." *I'm going to get my ass handed to me on a platter.*

"Excuse me, sir?"

"Tell the media a kid got stuck in a waste pod and we successfully retrieved him."

"Word already leaked out, sir."

Damn it. "Then I suggest you correct the mistake."

Silence greeted his statement.

"That's an order."

More silence.

Matthew closed his eyes and sighed. "It's just a kid."

"But, sir, your orders."

He raked his hand through his hair and glanced at André, knowing full well the kid was reading the flurry of thoughts and memories spinning through his head. He was disobeying a presidential directive. Deep shit didn't begin to describe it. This was more like a deep grave.

"I'm aware of the orders and if I had been met with hostility, I would have carried them out without issue. But I'm not in the business of terminating children, no matter what their origin. Tell Commander Lawrence he can start court-martial proceedings if he disagrees." More silence. "I need a medical transport when we land. The kid is in bad shape." He scanned the boy. "Physiologically, he's similar to our race and I need someone who will have the utmost discretion."

"Yes, sir."

Matthew closed the communication channel and directed the spacecraft toward Earth, giving André the first look at his new home. His eyes went wide with wonder at the mixture of swirls of white overlaying a deep blue background and sporadic masses of brown, green, and white. "Earth," he whispered.

ANDRÉ STARED AT THE planet in the window, the colonel's conversation and his thoughts all forgotten in the wake of the beauty before him. He blinked, wondering when this hallucination would give way to reality. He'd had so many over the last couple of years, but this one beat them all. Even the drink, what the man next to him had called water, felt so real. Cool and refreshing going down but hot and acidic coming back up. His eyes dropped to the bottle in his hand and he squeezed it, listening to the crumple of plastic under his fingers.

How can I trust this?

Sighing, he took another sip. Cool liquid slid down his sore throat, coating, calming the burn and causing his stomach to rumble, drawing Colonel Robbins's attention away from the controls.

"What types of food do you eat?" Colonel Robbins asked.

André stared at the colonel. *This has got to be a dream. Why else would I be able to understand what he's saying?* The irony caught him off guard. The odds of this being real were insane and he knew it, but the dream was so damn tangible, the thought of food caused his saliva glands to kick into gear and he decided to go along with wherever this vision would take him. "Mainly protein," he answered. "My mother tried to get me to eat vegetation, but I don't really like it."

Colonel Robbins let out a small laugh. "What about fruit?" he asked and produced a round red sphere out of the food compartment, handing it to André.

The sphere weighed a few ounces and he studied it, running his fingers over the smooth surface and rolling the stub of a stem through his fingers, twirling it until it broke from the center. A delectable scent drifted from the fruit and he brought it to his nose, inhaling the sweet perfume.

Again, he was struck by the vivid sensations of this dream and his gaze drifted to the approaching planet. André looked at the fruit in his hand. An apple, according to the colonel's thoughts, and he sank his teeth into the red flesh, relishing the tangy sweetness as juices bled into his mouth with the chunk he bit off, setting his hunger reflex into overdrive.

Here's the part where I wake up.

But he didn't. Instead, he devoured the apple, down to the small hard nub on the bottom and licked the juice off his fingers. "Can I have another?"

Colonel Robbins nodded and smiled, handing André a second apple before returning his attention back to navigating the ship.

André stared out the window, splitting his attention between the apple and the approaching planet, still waiting for the dream to end when a new thought dawned on him. *Maybe I'm already dead.*

He didn't have time to explore that further. The engines revved and the ship plummeted through the clouds, darting toward the deep blue mass of water. To their left lay a beige landmass that reminded André of the sand dunes on Zyclon.

"We're flying over the Atlantic Ocean," Colonel Robbins explained waving a hand toward the vast blue expanse of water. "In a little while you'll be able to see the eastern shoreline of North America, where we live."

The radio squawked again. "Colonel Robbins, please adjust your course and proceed to the southeastern landing strips."

"Will do," he replied and closed the transmitter. "You're in luck André; you get to see the ruins of our nation's capital today."

André smiled, sifting through the colonel's thoughts. History had been one of his favorite subjects and the demise of the great capital of the

United States was one the colonel studied until he could recite it word for word.

The decay of mankind started some two hundred years before, precipitated by religious zealots who got a hold of nuclear weapons, launching them at the colossal giant. The United States returned in kind and then other nuclear nations jumped in and an all-out holocaust ensued. But what drove mankind to near extinction wasn't the nuclear winter, but a meteor strike that flooded the entire eastern hemisphere, submerging Asia, Europe, Africa, and Australia, annihilating life in that part of the world. The northern ice cap shifted, covering Alaska and Canada in a glacial sheet that continued to creep toward the United States. The rain forests of South America withered, leaving a burning desert in its wake, and tipping the balance of oxygen in the atmosphere to almost nil, threatening all remaining life forms on Earth.

The creation and construction of domes rose out of these disasters and had been the American way of life ever since.

"There's the Virginia shore." Colonel Robbins pointed to the white sands, turning the space ship in the same direction.

The pristine beaches gave way to the wreckage that was once Washington DC, the capital of the United States. Broken structures rose out of the overgrowth, but none as majestic as the solitary unbroken golden dome of the Capitol building lying on the wasted shoreline.

The colonel sighed, his gaze locked on the gold dome until they passed over it.

"You live in domes?"

Colonel Robbins turned toward André, one eyebrow cocked higher than the other. "Are you reading my thoughts again?"

André's cheeks grew hot at the piercing stare and he swallowed, nodding.

"My thoughts are not for you to filter through, young man."

"Yes, sir," André responded and sunk further into the chair.

The colonel nodded curtly and returned his gaze to the windshield, navigating the aircraft home. "Yes. We live in a network of domes because there isn't enough oxygen outside to support us for very long. Domes cover quite a few American cities: Denver, Chicago, Phoenix, Nashville, St. Louis, Las Vegas, and Dallas-Fort Worth, which is where I live."

The forest below gave way to stark plains with tall, pale grass bowing with the breeze, and in the distance sat Dallas-Fort Worth. The clear opaque dome reflected the sun's rays, spitting off tiny rainbows of light.

André closed his eyes tightly and inhaled, not trusting the feel of the craft landing, or the sound of the engines throttling down. Hope was something he couldn't afford. Like all his hallucinations, waking was the hardest part. Shattered hope smothered his will to live, to take another breath, and if this turned out to be another one, he didn't want to wake.

Slowing to a stop on the tarmac, Colonel Robbins shifted the craft into neutral and turned toward him. "André, I've got a medic on standby and he's going to need to run some tests to determine what you need to get better. That might mean staying in the hospital for a few days."

A shrill echo of his former life came back and along with it came the mistrust, and he shot his eyes between the dome and Colonel Robbins, unsure of what to feel. "Can't I stay with you?"

"Not right away. We need to get you healthy before we cross that bridge."

"When I'm better, can I stay with you?"

Colonel Robbins inhaled, turning his gaze toward the dome. When he met André's questioning stare, André saw hesitation and underneath, the need to protect him. He heard the flurry of thoughts accompanying the uncertainty and understood what he was asking was next to impossible.

Even so, the colonel nodded and said, "Yes, you can stay with me."

That declaration eased André's fears. The man next to him just made a promise, one that could likely land him in a world of trouble, but he made it just the same.

"Just so we have things straight. I'm a colonel in the US Armed Forces and if you live with me, I expect you to obey my rules, and don't think for one minute I won't punish you if you step out of line."

The stern temper of his voice shrank André's confidence and he shifted in the chair, nodding assent. "Yes, sir."

"I want to prepare you for what's waiting for us inside the hangar," Colonel Robbins said. "Based on the information I received earlier, I'm pretty sure we're walking into a media circus."

André cocked his head to the side. "Media circus?" He wasn't sure what that phrase meant.

"Reporters. Do you know what a reporter is?"

"I think so."

Colonel Robbins waited with his eyebrows arched. "Without pulling the info from my head?"

Caught again. This time André let a small smirk form and he shifted his gaze to the dome. "Without reading your thoughts, no, I don't know."

"A reporter reports the news and they think you're news worthy. An alien from outer space is news worthy, but we're going to give them a rescue of a boy who slipped into the wrong container."

The dome entrance opened, and they taxied in. "Think you can handle that?" he asked and cruised into the docking bay.

André nodded.

True to his word, the media was out in force and the sheer number of people overwhelmed André.

Colonel Robbins carried him through the sea of reporters, ignoring the microphones shoved in their faces and questions shouted at them. "No comment," he repeated as he cut his way through the crowd and into the base.

"Media circus?" André asked, looking back at the doors with the dozens of faces pressed to the glass, combined with the tiny camera lenses.

The colonel let out a small laugh. "Yes. They're piranhas."

"What's a piranha?" André asked.

"A flesh-eating fish."

André giggled. He could see where they would be likened to flesh eating fish. Before he could react beyond a giggle, a medic with a wheelchair swung next to the colonel.

"I can take him from here."

"Thanks, Cal," the colonel said.

André wanted to scream no, but the colonel sat him in the chair and nodded. "I'll be by in a little while to check on him." And with that, he turned, leaving André alone with the stranger.

Messiah Chapter 3

MATTHEW GLANCED OVER HIS shoulder just as the medic wheeled André into a room. Worry still lined his stomach, making it a well of acidic slosh. He didn't know how he was going to make good on the promise he made to that boy.

"Stupid idiot," he muttered under his breath. Turning, he marched to the commander's office and slid inside, standing at attention until the commander finished his phone call.

"What the hell were you thinking disobeying a direct order?" Commander Lawrence bellowed and slammed the phone down.

"He's a boy," Matthew snapped, glaring at his commanding officer. "And I didn't sign on with the Armed Forces to kill children."

"He could be a spy for all we know."

"Bullshit, sir."

Commander Lawrence surveyed his colonel and closest friend. "He is an alien."

"Who has been drifting in space for years with no food or water. If he hadn't come into our solar system, he would have died out there. Alone. In the dark." Matthew took a deep breath, squashing the fury building inside; the injustice of what was done to André was too much to abide. If he ever got his hands on those responsible, he'd gladly carry out his orders to exterminate them. "He is only a boy," he repeated.

"He is a ward of the United States now."

Matthew nodded. "As an officer of the United States Armed Forces, I would like to take responsibility for the boy."

The commander gawked at Matthew. "He's going to the lab in Denver so we can study him and his species."

Matthew clenched his jaw and his hands followed suit. "He isn't some animal to poke and prod under the microscope. He's a kid who is scared shitless on a planet he doesn't know."

"He's an alien," Commander Lawrence repeated.

"Yes, but—"

"—No buts Colonel."

"He's been through enough, sir. You can't just imprison him for the rest of his life. It's not right. It's not the American way," Matthew said, knowing full well it would push the commander's buttons.

Commander Lawrence leaned back in his chair, crossing his arms, and studied Matthew. "What exactly is the American way, Matthew?"

"Our history has always welcomed those from other nations with open arms, sir. The words are still inscribed on the remains of the Statue of Liberty. *Give me your tired, your poor, your huddled masses yearning to breathe free, the wretched refuse of your teeming shore. Send these, the homeless, tempest-tossed to me, I lift my lamp beside the golden door!* He deserves a chance at a life and not in some lab, under inspection like a rat."

Leaning forward, Commander Lawrence narrowed his eyes. "What if he's dangerous?"

"I'm willing to take that risk, sir."

"What the hell am I supposed to tell the president?"

"Tell him it was a mistake. The boy got locked in one of our waste containers. That would explain the lack of communication," Matthew said. He had enough time on the return trip to come up with a logical situation. "As for labeling it an alien craft— well, the fact a life-form was onboard drove that assessment. I'll take the heat for that." He shifted his weight and added, "Sam, he's just a kid."

Commander Lawrence exhaled. "Why? Why would you risk your entire career for an alien?"

"Because a child was sealed in a tin can and sent into space to die but somehow, by the grace of God, he survived. I'd like this kid to have a chance at a life and I'd like to be the one to offer him a home."

Commander Lawrence sighed. "Matthew, we have known each other for a long time," he started.

"Yes, sir, we have."

"Are you sure this doesn't have anything to do with the fact Linda can't have children?"

Matthew hesitated before he spoke. "That has nothing to do with it."

"Now who's bullshitting who, Colonel?"

ANDRÉ STARED AT THE meal on the tray before him. The entire presentation of the steak, mashed potatoes, green beans, a side salad along with silverware and a napkin perplexed him. The smell of the cooked food assaulted his senses and made his mouth water, but he was unsure of what to do with the metal utensils. Relief swept through him at the sight of the colonel and he picked up the utensils, shooting a questioning gaze in his direction.

A mental image materialized in his head, courtesy of the colonel, and he adjusted the fork in his hand to the vision drawn for him. Sticking the tines into the mashed potatoes, he pulled a small amount to his lips. He sniffed it and then took a taste. The creamy consistency flowed over his tongue and like the apple, his hunger dictated his actions, and he licked the rest from the fork enthusiastically, digging in for another bite.

Colonel Robbins approached the side of the bed and glanced at Officer Cal Grey fiddling with readouts. "How's he doing?"

Cal turned, trading a glance with André and then back at the colonel. "He's definitely dehydrated and malnourished. I was able to find a vein and we're hydrating him now." He waved toward the intravenous line and the bag of saline hanging from the t-bar on the bed. "I want to monitor him for the night and make sure he doesn't have any adverse reaction to either the food or the saline."

"Thanks, Cal. I appreciate the discretion here."

Cal nodded. "You were correct. His physiological makeup is very similar to ours, but there are subtle differences, like his blood type. It isn't compatible with ours, so he's at risk if he ever needs a transfusion." He jotted a note on the computer screen.

"Can I go home with you?" André asked around a mouthful of food.

"Not yet, kiddo."

André paused, meeting the colonel's gaze. He hadn't won the argument with the commander. They were still at an impasse, which meant his future was still in a "to be determined" status, which didn't surprise him. Usually the direction his dreams went was from utopia to nightmare and this was sliding fast.

His vision warbled, transitioning to a red film, and he blinked the tears away.

"I'm working on it." Colonel Robbins placed his hand on André's shoulder. "Besides, Officer Grey here will take good care of you tonight, isn't that right?"

"Absolutely," Cal replied, offering a warm smile.

"I will be back in the morning and then we can talk about what's next."

And with that, Colonel Robbins disappeared through the door.

André swallowed the lump in his throat and focused back on the meal in front of him. His appetite raged, and he downed the meal within minutes, even going so far as to lick the plate.

"Hi." A soft female voice said from the doorway.

André froze in place when he saw her, the glass of white liquid they referred to as milk half way to his mouth forgotten in the wake of her beauty. He had never seen yellow hair and the contrast with her soft, tan skin left him speechless; her eyes, a striking green with small veins of brown straggling through the irises, flicked in his direction.

Katrina Lawrence stepped into the room.

Cal cleared his throat from the far corner.

"Oh, hi Officer Grey," she said, moving her gaze to the officer, her cheeks blooming red.

"How'd you get in here?"

She let out a little laugh and shrugged, looking at her feet for a moment before raising her eyes again. "I snuck in."

Her laugh sounded like the sweetest music to André and his lips curved into a smile. He brought the glass to his mouth, remembering he was in the process of finishing what was on the tray when she interrupted. His heart fluttered, both in his chest and on the readout next to Cal.

"Your father will have your head, young lady." Cal stood, crossing the room toward the girl.

She bit her lower lip, a move that shot tendrils of heat into André's stomach, fishing outwards like a tornado overtaking his body.

"Please let her stay," André said.

Cal paused, glancing between the two children. His eyes flicked to the monitors, and he shook his head. "Not tonight. Maybe in the morning after you get some rest." He turned toward Katrina. "And you—you need to beeline it home, young lady."

She rolled her eyes and sent a half smile in André's direction as Cal led her out of the room.

Soon after she left, Cal dimmed the lights, ordering André to get some sleep, but all André could do was stare at the ceiling and see her teeth shimmering between her pretty pink lips.

Messiah Chapter 4

OFFICER CAL GREY SAT in the dim light, poring over the test results. The X-rays showed open growth plates and bones that had lost density but could be revived with the right mix of vitamins and minerals. Cal just had to figure out what that right mix was. The hydration routine along with intravenous vitamins therapy seemed to sit well with the boy, and he certainly looked stronger than he did when Colonel Robbins handed him over.

His organ placement mimicked that of a human and his honey-bronzed skin looked like the tone of a healthy tan. In other words, the kid snoring in the bed could have been any normal eleven-year-old boy, save a few distinct traits. His blood type wasn't a match to any known on Earth, the kid's tear ducts produced blood along with saline when he cried, and his eyes shimmered almost neon blue when he had seen Katrina Lawrence.

Colonel Robbins had stuck out his neck for this kid and he could understand why. There was something special about André, beyond the fact he survived in space for so long. Cal mulled that over, turning it every which way in his head. To survive in a pod with little food and air required a state akin to hibernation, something humans can't accomplish, but somehow this boy did, conserving energy and oxygen for an extended period. In short, his survival was a miracle and he felt compelled to protect the kid.

André hadn't talked much and the way he looked around, curious but not as much as he should be, alarmed Cal. It was almost as if André didn't believe he had been saved, that some level of his subconscious dubbed this experience a dream. He jotted a note on the case tablet to run André through a psych review before releasing him.

Voices in the hallway caught his attention and he glanced at the clock. Eight in the morning and the argument grew louder. With a quick glance at André, he slid out of the room into the hallway, heading toward the ruckus between Commander Lawrence and Colonel Robbins.

"You can't put him under lock and key in some institution, Sam," Colonel Robbins snapped.

"I've got the paperwork to do just that right here." Commander Lawrence waved the forms in his hands.

"Excuse me, gentlemen," Cal said as he approached.

"What?" they both snapped in Cal's direction.

"The paperwork submitted on the boy states his name is André Robbins and Colonel Robbins is listed as his next of kin. As such, I can only release him to Colonel Robbins."

Both of them gawked, speechless and then Commander Lawrence sent a glare in the colonel's direction.

"You didn't."

Colonel Robbins shifted. "I had to put something on the forms."

"And you know the laws better than any of my subordinates."

Cal watched the colonel's shoulders raise and lower. He knew the laws just as well as Cal did. That's why the paperwork was submitted through the system, so Matthew Robbins could claim legal guardianship over his long-lost nephew.

"I should throw the book at you," Commander Lawrence snarled.

Colonel Robbins spread his arms. "Go ahead, Sam, but what will that look like to the public? Hmmm? He's a kid. What will incarcerating him do to your political aspirations?"

Cal saw the gears turning in the commander's head, along with the burning red spreading from his nose to his ears. Colonel Robbins hit a sore spot and he hoped like hell the gamble he played would be enough; otherwise, he'd be court-martialed for his part in this ruse.

Messiah Chapter 5

A SOFT HAND SLIDING into his jerked André from sleep and he sat up, his eyes darting around the dim room and falling on Katrina.

She offered him a smile and squeezed his hand. "You snore."

André blinked and rubbed the sleep out of his eyes before scanning the room for Cal. When his scan came up empty, he turned his attention back to Katrina.

Katrina looked down at her feet. "I'm sorry for waking you," she said. "I just wanted to…"

"Talk to an alien?" André said, his voice raspy from sleep.

"Yeah," she admitted and met his gaze.

He smiled at her. "You're not afraid of me?"

Katrina rolled her eyes. "No."

"What's your name?"

"Katrina. What's yours?"

"André."

"André," she repeated.

Between her speaking his name and the soft warmth of her hand, the monitor went from a steady beep to a quick staccato beat, mimicking that of his heart. She was a new introduction in this hallucination, one that left his soul wanting, begging for this to be real. He pulled her hand to his lips and kissed her palm, drinking in her fresh scent.

"Am I what you expected?"

She shook her head. "No."

"Sorry to disappoint you."

"You didn't."

The door banged open and both André and Katrina jumped. The lights flicked on, and Commander Lawrence glanced from his daughter to André and back.

"What the hell are you doing here?" His voice carved the air, filling up the small hospital room with hostility.

"Daddy, I, um..." She looked at André, pulling her hand out of his grip and turning toward her father in one smooth move.

"I dropped you off at school this morning." His teeth clenched at the obvious disobedience.

"I know. I just wanted to see him, Daddy," she said, waving toward André.

Commander Lawrence shot a glance at André. "You've seen. Now get back to school and we'll talk about how long you're grounded tonight," he said.

"Please let her stay," André said, alternating his gaze from Katrina to the commander.

"Maybe some other time," Colonel Robbins said as he and Cal stepped into the room.

"Please, Daddy," Katrina begged.

"No, Katrina, you have school." Commander Lawrence crossed the room and took her by the arm, leading her out of the infirmary, closing the door on her imploring eyes.

André turned his attention to Colonel Robbins and Cal. "She woke me up." As if that could explain the girl in his hospital room. A girl who was as much a delusion as anything else that was happening.

"She snuck in here last night, too," Cal said, crossing to the monitors and scanning the readouts. "You're doing much better this morning."

Before André could respond, Commander Lawrence walked back into the room and stood at the foot of the bed, inspecting André.

"André, I'd like you to meet Commander Lawrence. Commander, this is André," Colonel Robbins introduced.

Doubt and suspicion radiated from the commander.

"Nice to meet you," André replied.

Commander Lawrence gave a curt nod. "My daughter is of no interest to you," he said to André. "Understand?"

André nodded his head slightly, his eyes drifting between the commander and Colonel Robbins. *She certainly is of interest to me.*

"When I ask a question, I expect an answer."

"Y-yes, I understand."

"Good, because you are not allowed to go near my daughter."

The order, while par for the course in his hallucinations, still shook André. He wanted to see her again, to get to know her, to grow old with her and if this was indeed real, nothing on this planet could stop him.

Commander Lawrence studied André further and seeming satisfied, moved on to his next question. "Young man, what brings you to our solar system?"

"Luck," André said, wondering if this was the precursor to being exiled again. It was either that or being torn apart by vicious animals or being slowly suffocated. That's how the dreams usually ended, bringing him back to the dark pod.

"Why do you say that?"

André's gaze darted between Colonel Robbins and the commander. "Because I don't know how much longer I can last out here," he replied. His voice choked, and a red sheen filled his vision. He blinked and hot tears rolled down his cheeks.

Commander Lawrence gasped.

"It's normal, sir." Cal pulled a sheet of tissue from the box next to the bed, handing it to André.

André closed his eyes, wiping his face with the soft cloth.

"How long have you been in space, son?" Commander Lawrence asked, his tone softening.

André shrugged. "Officer Grey thinks I'm eleven and if that's the case, I've been drifting for five years," he said.

The commander rubbed his chin in thought and turned toward Colonel Robbins with a slight nod. "Colonel Robbins will be responsible for you from here on in." He left without another word.

Cal and Colonel Robbins exchanged a glance, and both exhaled.

"Do I really have to stay away from Katrina?"

Colonel Robbins returned his attention to André. "Yes, you are to stay away from Katrina Lawrence." He turned to Cal. "Is he ready to be released?"

André noted the hesitation and something about a psych evaluation crossed the officer's mind, but instead of voicing his concern, he nodded.

"I think that might be best."

"Thanks, Cal. I couldn't have done it without you." The colonel reached across and offered his hand to Cal.

"No problem. He's a special kid." He leaned toward the colonel and whispered in his ear, so André couldn't hear but his thoughts rang through loud and clear.

"Be careful, Matt. I'm not sure he knows what's real and what isn't yet."

André glanced between the two men. He couldn't help but feel the tendrils of hope wrapping around his heart.

"Will do," Colonel Robbins answered and grabbed the wheelchair in the corner.

"I can walk," André said, swinging his scrawny legs over the side of the bed, still wearing the hospital Johnny they put him in when he arrived.

Colonel Robbins shook his head with a smile. "I don't think you want the world's first real view of you to be a bare ass as you walk past."

Cal burst out laughing at the colonel's comment. "I think I can drum up something for him to wear." He disappeared into the adjoining room. He came back a few minutes later with a pair of underwear, denim jeans, and a t-shirt that was an exact match with André's eyes.

"Thank you," André said, taking the clothes from Cal and looking at the wardrobe. Colonel Robbins sent him a mental note on how to dress.

"I remember how to put clothing on," André said. "Do you mind?" He looked at the two men standing in the room.

Both men turned their backs on André, amused by his modesty.

André slipped into the clothing, relishing the clean fabric. He ran his hands over the t-shirt; the soft cotton brushed his fingertips and he swallowed, not allowing himself to believe, not yet. "Okay," André said, shaking the hope away and waiting for the dream to morph.

Colonel Robbins turned and nodded. "Now you're presentable." He led André out of the infirmary.

Katrina trotted up next to André as he followed Colonel Robbins out of the building. "Hi," she announced and fell in step next to them.

"You should be at school, Katrina." The colonel shot her a glance. "Your father wouldn't approve."

"Screw my dad," she said, shocking both of them. "He isn't the boss of me." She flipped her hair back over her shoulder.

"That's pretty disrespectful." André kept walking.

She grabbed André's arm and pulled him to a stop. "I'm sorry."

Her big, green, sincere eyes melted his heart, and he looked over at Colonel Robbins.

"Katrina, your father would not approve of you being here with us," he said again.

"I don't want to upset your father," André said. "He doesn't trust me, and this will hurt any chances I have of ever gaining that trust."

Katrina looked down at her feet. "I'm sorry," she said again. "I just wanted to..." She trailed off.

"Talk to the alien?" André smiled.

"Yeah," she admitted with a smile, and skipped in the opposite direction, her hair bouncing in a way that stirred a need deep within him.

With a smile plastered on his lips, he turned back to Colonel Robbins.

"Don't even think about it." He put his hand on the back of his neck, leading him away.

"Too late," André said.

Messiah Chapter 6

MATTHEW WALKED INTO THE house with André in tow and pointed to the living room couch. "Have a seat." He went to find his wife.

Linda stood over the kitchen stove, whipping up dinner, preferring to do it herself, rather than dictate the menu to a computer. Wonderful smells drifted through the house.

"Hi honey," he said from the kitchen doorway. "Remember what I talked to you about last night?"

"Yes." Linda turned her fair, freckled face toward her husband. Her pale blue eyes stared at him through a couple fallen strands of strawberry blonde hair.

"Do you have enough for three?"

"Really?" She took the pot off the stove, placing it on the cool counter surface.

Matthew glanced over his shoulder. "Yes, really. I think I've pretty much screwed any further advances in my career, but..." He turned back toward her, locking eyes. "He needs a home. Come on." He led her into the living room.

André studied the pictures that graced the mantel and he turned and smiled at Matthew's wife. "Hi."

Linda's eyes went wide, and she turned to Matthew. "He looks so... so human."

Matthew smiled, nodded and shrugged.

Her eyes flashed with both hope and fear.

"My name's André," he introduced himself, extending his hand like he saw Matthew do in the hospital.

Linda's tight, nervous features relaxed. "I'm sorry, it's just that...it's just that I didn't think Matthew was serious," she said, embarrassed, offering a small smile. "Welcome home, André." She walked over, ignoring his outstretched hand. Instead, she wrapped her arms around him in a warm hug.

WARMTH AND QUIET RESIGNED acceptance radiated from her, and André glanced at Matthew through a red sheen of tears. "Thank you," he said.

Linda pulled away and put her hand on André's face. "Why are you crying?"

He wasn't sure he could formulate the words, but he tried anyway. "I've never had a home," he said, wiping his face. His parents had been on the run for so long before the emperor found them. He had no memory of anything else. They were never in one place for any length of time before word got out about the blue-eyed boy.

"Well, you do now." Linda glanced at Matthew and back. "Are you hungry?"

André nodded. Gratitude encompassed him and he offered a forced smile, sniffling and swiping his face again. "Thank you."

"You might not feel that way once we talk about rules," Matthew said.

André laughed a little and he followed Linda into the kitchen.

"I'm not kidding," Matthew said.

"Leave the boy alone, Matt." Linda leveled a stare over her shoulder at her husband.

André sat where she indicated and waited for his food, watching the pleasant dynamics between the colonel and his wife.

Matthew sat at the table in front of his meal and looked over at André. "The rules," he began.

"Matt," Linda started.

Matthew held up his hand. "The rules," he said again. "First, we need to get you enrolled in school."

André's jaw dropped with his fork halfway to his mouth and his eyes glued on Matthew's.

"Second, you will come home from school and do your homework. Then you will help with whatever Linda needs you to do." He took a bite of the food. "This is great, honey," he deviated from the rules for a moment. "Bedtime is by nine pm," he added. "When you make friends, and I'm sure you will, you can play only after your homework is done. Understand?"

Dumbfounded, he nodded, although he had never been to school, and he was never any place long enough to make friends.

"We can tell the school that you are Matthew's nephew—you lost your parents and are living with us now. I'll make sure transcripts are produced so your real identity is kept under wraps," Matthew added. "They won't know unless you tell them."

André looked down at his food. The prospect of being a normal kid overwhelmed him; this deviated so much from any vision he had to date, and doubt began to creep in. Maybe this *was* real. "I don't know," he said, unsure of himself.

"You don't know what?" Matthew asked.

"I've never been to school," he said, putting his fork on the side of the plate and picking up his glass.

"Don't they have schools on your planet?" Linda asked.

André nodded.

"Why didn't you go?"

André shrugged and took a sip of his milk. "We were never in one place long enough." He placed the glass back on the table and stared at the plate. He couldn't bring himself to look at her, afraid of the questions in her eyes.

"Why did you move around so much?" Matthew asked.

"Because..." André looked back at Linda. Her eyes were blue too. "Because my eyes are blue," he admitted sheepishly and returned his gaze to his food, the embarrassment heating his cheeks.

"You have the most beautiful eyes I have ever seen," Linda interrupted.

André shrugged a little. "I was different," he said. "My parents died because I was different."

When Linda took his hand, he glanced in her direction, surprised as much by the gesture as what he saw.

Her eyes reflected a deep sadness punctuated by clear tears that rolled down her cheeks. "Oh, honey," she whispered.

André slowly withdrew his hand and finished what was on his plate.

"Can you read?" Matthew asked after he had finished his meal.

André shook his head. He couldn't read his own language, never mind this civilization's.

Matthew sat back in the chair and blew out a stream of air.

"I can teach you to read," Linda offered before Matthew could comment. "It's not hard once you learn the alphabet."

"Alphabet?"

"The letters that make up the words," she explained as she stood and cleared the dishes. "I'll show you in a few minutes." She smiled over her shoulder, popping the dishes in the sanitizer. She walked out of the room and returned with some lined paper and the alphabet books she used in her classroom.

Matthew retreated to his upstairs office while Linda worked with André.

André wandered into the office an hour later, now able to recite the letters of the alphabet in order and recognize a few of them by sight. "Why are you doing this?" he asked, interrupting Matthew.

Matthew looked up at him and took off his reading glasses. "Doing what?"

André tilted his head and raised his eyebrow. "You know what I'm asking."

Matthew leaned back in the chair. "Please close the door," he said.

The door closed behind André without physical intervention.

Matthew let out a bark of a laugh. "That freaks me out a little," he admitted.

"Why are you doing this?" André asked, sensing an underlying agenda.

Matthew sighed. "Because my wife can't have children," he admitted. "And adoption wasn't in the cards either. I'm not in a line of work that allows that." He leaned back in the chair. "You need a home; she needs to be a mother." He shrugged. "It just made sense."

André sat down in the chair opposite the desk and looked around the room. The walls were lined with books, and he recognized some of the letters that Linda had gone through with him, which made him smile. "What do I call you and your wife?"

"What do you want to call us?" Matthew asked.

André shrugged.

"You can call us Matthew and Linda, if that's what makes you comfortable," he replied.

André nodded and stood up. "Thank you." He licked his lips. "Matthew," he said, not quite feeling right about using the man's proper name.

Matthew stood and escorted André to the guest room. "This will be your room," he said, flipping the light on. He pointed toward a doorway in the corner. "You have a bathroom over there." He turned toward André. "Another rule. No locking your bedroom door.

A locked door means something is going on inside that I wouldn't approve of," he said sternly. "Are we clear?"

"Yes, sir," André replied looking around the room. It was more than he ever had in his young life. "Thank you."

"Goodnight, André." Matthew messed up his hair.

"Goodnight, sir," André said.

Matthew cleared his throat and raised his eyebrows at André.

"Goodnight, Matthew," André corrected. He waited until the door closed behind Matthew before he let the sob escape. Gratitude and fear snaked over his skin, combining to a crippling combination, and he fell to his knees on the plush carpet with his face in his hands.

He never expected to live long enough to see a planet, never mind meet people willing to take him in, to offer food and a place to sleep, to offer kindness and make him feel safe. He didn't trust what he saw, what he felt, and wondered if this was just another last-ditch hallucination or if it truly was real.

It was too much for him and he let the tears come, staining his shirt and pants as they fell through his fingers. Fear kept his palms to his face—afraid if he moved them away, he'd still be in that god forsaken death ship.

Messiah Chapter 7

AUGUST 2239

"What do you mean I can't go out for the football team?" André slammed his glass down on the dinner table.

"After what happened on the soccer team last year, I don't think that's such a good idea," Matthew said. "You nearly killed that goalie. You were so caught up in winning; you forgot just how dangerous you can be."

André glared at his father but said nothing.

"You didn't just kick that ball, did you?" Matthew yelled when André said nothing.

"Fine! I gave it a little push—so what? We won the championship."

Matthew threw his napkin on the table. "You shouldn't have won. You used the power you have and that wasn't a level playing field. It was cheating." He stormed out of the room and slammed the door to his study, leaving André sitting at the table with Linda.

"Your father is right, you know," she said softly, picking at her food. "You should have never taken advantage of the situation like you did. Winning isn't everything."

André glanced over at her. "But Mom," he whined, "I really want to play football."

"I know, honey, but you don't always get what you want. Life doesn't work that way."

"Why the hell not?"

"Because that's just the way it is." She stood and paused in the doorway. "Your father cares a great deal about you, André. He's only doing what he thinks is best."

"Bullshit. He just wants to control me," André snapped.

Linda turned on him; the anger flared in her eyes. "Just because you're seventeen, doesn't mean you can talk that way in our house."

André looked down at the floor, his face heating with shame for pushing her to the point of anger. "I'm sorry."

"Do you understand why your father is saying no?"

"Yeah, but—"

"—I didn't ask for excuses. Do you understand why?"

"Yeah," he said, still staring at the floor, unable to meet her angry gaze. "I wanted to win, and I didn't care how I did it."

"Precisely." She turned on her heels and left the kitchen.

MATTHEW PACED AND CURSED under his breath. Only André could push him over the edge like this. Up until the boy turned sixteen, the house had been calm and quiet and fun to live in, but at sixteen it was like a switch had been flipped, and he and André were constantly at each other's throats. He just didn't understand it.

Linda interrupted his thoughts, closing the door to his study behind her.

"What am I doing wrong?" he snapped.

"You're not doing anything wrong," she replied, validating his approach. "He is just a teenager, Matthew. They all act like that."

"He can make me so angry." Matthew looked out the window.

"Yeah, well, it goes both ways."

Matthew spun toward the voice and his gaze landed on André standing in the doorway. "Your mother and I are talking."

"I know," André began. "I screwed up, all right?" He stepped into the room and flopped down on the leather couch.

Matthew bit the response that was begging to let loose and the fact that he didn't say what popped in his mind didn't matter. He knew André heard it anyway.

"I know it isn't all right, Dad," he answered the unspoken dig. "I fuh...," he started and checked himself before he continued. "I screwed up royally. But don't you think I can learn from my mistakes?"

"André, you take competition to a level that's hard to overlook. It's like you constantly feel you have something to prove. I don't doubt that a part of you regrets hurting that kid, but as you just so eloquently articulated, so what, your team won the championship. What the hell would you do if you were in my shoes?"

André looked at his mother and then back to his father. "Okay, I get it." He stood and walked out of the study, leaving Matthew and Linda alone. André's door slammed and music followed, loud enough for Matthew to feel the vibrations in the floor. He clamped his teeth together, trading a glance with Linda before he marched down the hall.

The bass beat shook the portraits on the wall in the hallway and Matthew reached for the doorknob. It didn't budge. The fact the boy locked the door, disobeying one of his first rules, sent a fire of irritation through his muscles and he tensed against the adrenaline rush of anger.

He pounded on the wood grain. "Open this door right now, young man!"

ANDRÉ IGNORED THE POUNDING and tried to shut out the angry, ranting thoughts. He clamped his eyes tight and willed the stereo louder, drowning out even his own thoughts.

The door splintered as it sailed wide from Matthew's booted kick and André tensed at the fury radiating from his father. He hadn't been subjected to that kind of wrath since they sealed him in that tin can of a pod, and fear layered on top of his anger, freezing his muscles in place.

Matthew stormed across the room and ripped the power cord out of the wall, turning on André. "Look at me!"

André couldn't move. Tonight was the first time he disobeyed outright and he lay in terror of retribution. A hand grabbed his arm, flipping him on his back, and he stared into his father's furious eyes. Fueled by his fear, a small burst of power escaped, and Matthew sailed into the far wall.

Horror freed his paralysis, and his hand flew to his mouth. "I'm, I'm, I'm sorry," he stuttered.

Matthew stood and glared at André. He walked out of the room without a word, his silence more deafening than the bellowing anger coming out of his mouth when he was pounding on his door.

André couldn't take the silence. Silence reminded him of being locked in space. It spread a suffocating layer over him and he had to get out, to run. André bolted out of his room, past Linda and down the stairs.

"Where do you think you're going?" she asked before he reached the front door.

"Out." He looked at her through a red haze. Hot tears streaked his cheeks, and he closed the front door behind him. André ran, with no idea where he was going and when he passed the lakeside beach a few miles from his house, he stopped.

The lake looked inviting and a glance up and down the street confirmed no one was around. André scaled the fence, ignoring the sign stating trespassers would be prosecuted. He crossed the soft sand and crouched down at the water's edge, splashing the cool liquid on his face, washing away the hot tear streaks. He sat back on the sand, wiping his palms on his pants, still in a state of panic and self-loathing.

"I never figured you for a troublemaker."

He jumped and turned his head toward the familiar voice, offering a small smile. "What are you doing here?" he said, shifting his weight against the shock of seeing Katrina Lawrence on the same beach.

"I sneak in here all the time, especially when my dad is in one of his moods."

André took a deep breath. "I'm sorry about your mom," he said. "I was gonna call, but..." He trailed off and shrugged.

"But your dad wouldn't let you."

He nodded.

"Still, it meant a lot to me that you came to her funeral."

André sighed and looked out at the water, feeling the sorrow in Katrina's heart, and wished he could wipe it away. The last three years had been hard on her, and he didn't know which was worse, watching your mother waste away with cancer or having her executed before your eyes.

Every time he saw Katrina, he wanted to take her in his arms and tell her she was the only one who made his heart skip, the only one who could render him speechless, but he had respected his father's wishes and kept his distance.

Silence settled between them along with an undeniable electrical current.

She sat down next to him on the sand. "So, what's up with you?" she asked, flipping her thick blonde hair back over her shoulder in the same arrogant gesture he adored.

He shook his head, glancing sideways at her. "I had a fight with my father," he drawled in the deep Southern accent prevalent in the Texas dome.

"About what?"

"I want to try out for the football team and he said no."

"Well, that's just stupid," Katrina said.

"I agree," André said. "Speaking of our fathers, your dad wouldn't be very happy with you, talking to me and all."

Katrina grinned. "Yeah, well, once a troublemaker, always a troublemaker."

"My dad would be pissed," he replied and stretched out on the sand, looking up at the stars visible through the clear dome.

"I thought you always listened to your father?"

Before this evening, he would have said yes without hesitation but tonight he just smiled in return. He went to sit up and Katrina pushed him back onto the sand, positioning herself half over him, looking straight into his eyes. She leaned close.

"You don't want to do that," André said just before her lips touched his. He put his hands on her shoulders, stopping her despite his racing heart.

"Why not? You afraid Anna would find out?"

Her breath caressed his face smelling like sweet licorice. "No. I couldn't care less about Anna," he answered, still conflicted and holding her above him. He wanted her from the moment she stepped into the infirmary six years before and this was just way too tempting.

"Then why not?" She glanced at his lips and then back to his iridescent blue eyes sparkling in the dark.

"Because I won't stop." His lips curved in a slow easy smile. "And don't you already have a boyfriend?"

"Not anymore. Besides, maybe I don't want you to stop."

His body reacted to her; heat pooled in his belly and lust lined his skin. It took everything he had to hold her at bay. "You shouldn't tease me like this."

"I'm curious." Katrina stared down at him. "Are you anatomically the same as men on Earth?"

The glib question along with the mischievous sparkle in her eyes goaded him. "You already know the answer to that, don't you?" he said, his voice husky with the need that filled his entire body.

She grinned. "I've heard some rumors."

"And what? You thought you'd find out firsthand?"

She shrugged. "I've always been curious about you but could never seem to pin you down." She licked her lips and smiled down at him.

That was all he could handle, and he gave in, pulling her to him, kissing her hard and rolling her over onto the sand under him. The sweetness of her lips drew air from his chest and for a moment, he lost himself in the exploration of her mouth and the kiss was everything he always imagined it would be. His hands slid down her sides to her waist before he regained control and pulled away, smiling as he stood up.

Katrina stared up at him with wide eyes full of surprise. "Where are you going?" she asked, hopping to her feet and following him.

He stopped and looked over his shoulder at her. "If I stay, your curiosity will be satisfied and I'll be up shit's creek without a paddle," he drawled and turned away again, reaching for the fence.

"Come on, André. We've been playing this game for years and we're finally somewhere alone without our parents. Please, don't go."

He hesitated, still with his hand in the chain link. "I have to go." He leaned on the fence, glancing at her feet as she walked up to him. His entire body fought for control over his senses, and he closed his eyes, taking a deep breath before scaling the fence as quickly as he could. He walked away, leaving her silent and thoughtful on the other side. He didn't glance back right away; her thoughts still clung to him, and he snuck a peek just before he rounded the corner that would block the view of the beach.

Katrina was less than ten feet behind him.

André stumbled, fell and willed himself to stop just short of the pavement, stopping what would have been a nasty impact. He righted himself and turned to find her giggling at him. "What the hell are you doing?" he gaped.

"Following you," she answered.

"Why?"

"Because I don't want to play games anymore."

André continued in the direction he had been heading, and she resumed her stalking behind him. He slowed a little, allowing her to keep pace. He glanced over at her staring, probing eyes. "I'm not a fucking bug," he snapped.

Katrina blinked but didn't look away. "What was it like?"

"What was what like?"

"Space." She glanced at the sky.

"I don't know," he said. "I only saw a little of it and that was from my father's ship when he rescued me."

"Really?" she said, astonished. "But you were out there for so long."

He nodded. "Yeah." He glanced over at her. "It wasn't fun," he said, not wanting to elaborate on the terror he felt each day, wondering if it would be his last one alive.

Silence settled between them as they walked.

"Five years?"

André nodded. "Sealed in a tin can."

"How'd you not go crazy?"

"Who said I didn't?" he countered, giving her a hint of a smile.

"Seriously," she said. "How does someone get through that?"

"Don't you have somewhere to be right now?" he asked, slightly annoyed by her line of questioning and even more so by her train of thought. Her close proximity messed with his mind, setting his skin on fire and he knew if she continued to follow, there was no turning back for him. No staying away anymore, despite what either of their fathers said.

"No."

André stopped walking and leaned on a nearby tree, crossing his arms. He sighed as his eyes grazed her. "I guess my will to live overpowered everything else and I was smart enough to not eat what was provided all at once."

"I don't know any six-year-old with that kind of willpower." She stepped closer.

"Please don't," he said softly as she reached out to touch him.

Katrina smiled and ignored his plea.

"Kat, I don't have that kind of willpower where you're concerned."

"Are you like this with all your girlfriends?" she asked as she moved closer, leaning her body against his.

He shook his head. "No, only you can do this to me." He swept her in his arms and kissed her, rolling his tongue gently in her mouth as his hands traced her back, stopping at her waist. One of his hands found its way back up into her hair and the other slid down her hip to the edge of the very short skirt she had on, grazing the skin of her thighs with his fingertips. He pulled her closer, kissing her deeper, searing his soul to hers.

"What the hell do you think you're doing?" Matthew yelled, stepping from the hovercraft a few feet away.

André and Katrina jumped away from each other, both panting with the power that still coursed through their veins. *Oh shit!*

Before he could say anything, Matthew's hand grasped the scruff of his neck and hauled him to the hovercraft.

André glanced sideways at Katrina and offered her a small shrug as they pulled away, watching her in the side mirror. She continued to watch the hovercraft until they pulled around the corner out of sight.

"I have told you a thousand times to stay away from that girl," Matthew growled.

André didn't say anything. He just slouched in the passenger seat with his hands in his pockets and looked out the window. He heard all the thoughts flying through his father's head loud and clear. When the silent accusations flew, he spoke. "I went to the beach, and she happened to be there."

"How did she know where to find you?"

André willed the hovercraft to stop.

"Stop that," Matthew snapped.

"I have followed the rules you laid down for the past six years, Dad. I know she's off-limits, but..." He took a deep breath. "But she just happened to be at the place I ran to. I had no idea she would be at the beach and if I did, I wouldn't have gone there." He released his hold on the vehicle and it lurched forward again. "One thing led to another..." He trailed off. "I'm not staying away from her anymore," he announced as they pulled into the driveway.

"You are to stay away from that girl," Matthew ordered as he stepped out of the hovercraft and slammed the door closed.

"No, I am not staying away from Katrina." André stood his ground. "I've been in love with her since the day I set foot on this planet."

Matthew stood at the front door with his hand on the doorknob, his back to André, struggling with the anger raging through him. He silently counted to ten. "She's bad news, André," he said. He had heard the commander bitching about the things she had done on a daily basis and Matthew didn't want André exposed to such a rebellious child.

"I know she has a reputation for being a little wild," André said, "but I really don't give a damn."

Matthew turned. "I do."

"You won't let me play football; you won't let me date Katrina. What next? What are you afraid of?"

"That you'll get in trouble and the government will take you away from us," Matthew snapped.

André took a half step back and blinked, hearing the truth in Matthew's voice and in his mind. "They could take me away?"

"If they find out what you can do, yes," Matthew said.

"Kat already knows what I am, and she hasn't said a thing for the last six years."

Matthew took a deep breath and exhaled.

"Besides, I'm going to marry her," André added.

Matthew laughed. "You are only seventeen."

André shrugged. "I know what I want and she's it."

"You want her because I said you couldn't have her."

"No, Dad. I want her because she's the one and I've dated plenty of girls since I came here but not one of them does what Katrina does to me, not even Anna."

"What I saw back there was moments away from getting into a world of trouble, André. If that's what she does to you, it's just another reason for me to put my foot down. You are too young for that." Matthew pointed in the direction where they had come from.

André tried to suppress a grin but didn't do a very good job.

"Wipe that grin off your face. Seventeen is too young."

"Too young for what?" André asked innocently, just to see his father's reaction as he leaned on the porch banister, crossing his arms, the amused smile still on his face.

Matthew glared at him. "Sex. You are too young for sex," he clarified. "Now go to your room. I don't want to see or hear you until the morning. Got it?"

André nodded and walked through the door Matthew held open for him. His grin spread as he bounded up the stairs and closed his broken door. *What he doesn't know won't hurt him and if he ever finds out just how much I've screwed around, Jesus, he'd blow a gasket.*

He pulled his cell out of his pocket and stared at the half dozen texts he ignored for the past couple of hours and sighed. It was time to cut Anna loose, especially after what happened with Katrina. He shot over a message, knowing Anna wouldn't take too kindly to him breaking up with her by text, so after he pressed Send, he shut his phone off, tossing it on the nightstand before flopping back on his bed.

André stared at the ceiling in the dark room, his thoughts drifting to Katrina and all the things he'd like to do with her.

A soft knock on his window interrupted his thoughts and his eyes flew open. He crossed to the window and slid it open, staring into her hypnotizing eyes.

What are you doing here? He sent the thought into her mind. Surprise registered and she teetered on the tree branch, but André reached out and caught her before she fell, hauling her in the window and putting his finger on his lips. *Don't speak; just think it and I'll hear you.*

Katrina looked around the room and then back at him. *You can hear my thoughts?*

I can hear everyone's thoughts. André smiled at the bloom in her cheeks. *What are you doing here?*

I'm not sure. She glanced at the broken door. *Let's blow out of here.* She looked toward the window and back at him.

André tilted his head and let his eyes graze her from head to toe. He looked over at his bed and raised an eyebrow. *Why? The bed's right there.*

Katrina let out a small quiet laugh.

Isn't that why you came? To satisfy your curiosity? André pulled his shirt over his head and tossed it on the floor.

Katrina scanned his bare torso and licked her lips. A slight sweat broke out on her forehead, and she drew in a deep breath. *Is it hot in here?*

He chuckled and tilted his head. *I took my shirt off. Now it's your turn.* He leaned against the bed waiting.

I don't know. Katrina looked at the door and bit her lower lip.

Don't worry. I'll hear them if they come this way. Let's see what you've got.

Katrina hesitated.

André sighed and moved across the room, taking her in his arms. "Isn't this what you want?"

"I, uh…"

"Because it's what I've wanted since I first laid eyes on you." He didn't wait for an answer; his mouth covered hers, tasting, tongues intertwined in a dance that left him trembling and wanting more. Her skin, like silk under his fingertips, lit a fire in his abdomen and he broke the kiss, smiling down at her upturned face.

He tasted the curve of her neck, grinning when her skin broke out in a batch of goose pimples followed by a shudder, and he peeled her shirt off. With a flip of his fingers, her bra unclasped and followed the path of her shirt to the floor. He found her skirt zipper and slowly unzipped it, kissing his way down the front of her body before he slid the garment to her ankles.

Standing, he maneuvered her to the bed, covering her neck with kisses and stretched her out underneath him. With a glance in the direction of the hallway, his nightstand slid, blocking the door and reducing the chance of a surprise entrance by his folks.

You've done this before.

André chuckled against her throat and moved his lips to hers, kissing her, losing himself in the feel of her mouth, her skin, her body. He throbbed against the fabric of his jeans, and he shifted when her hands fumbled with his belt, giving her access to undo them, the progression of the zipper sounding like a jackhammer wrapped in the frantic rush of their breath.

With a rustle of fabric, he was free of his pants, settling between her legs, his heart hammering in his chest as he gazed in her surprised eyes.

I guess you are anatomically correct.

He grinned. No one had ever complained about what he had to offer. His smile faded as he scanned her face, his gaze falling on her full lips before returning to the green eyes he dreamed of night after night. His body ached for her, but she *was* a virgin and the seed of doubt formed. *Is this what you want?*

She pulled him to her lips without speaking, her mind answering him as loud as the pounding of her heart against his chest, but he had to be sure this wasn't just the heat of the moment, not just his wishful thinking.

Not with her.

He broke the kiss. "Are you sure?" he asked, reining in the lust raging through his blood.

"Yes, I've wanted you from the first day we met, too," Katrina whispered, and that was all he needed.

Her jaw clamped with the first thrust, a crease appearing between her eyes as he christened her, but it soon smoothed out with each gentle circle of their hips. Heat consumed him and he sped up, each stroke sending tingling sensations through his core, and her eyes closed, her lips pressing together, turning her moan into a sensual purr that drove him mad.

When her eyes opened, they flew wide and her breath hitched, her gaze locked on his, but he didn't care; he was too far gone to worry about his eyes or the shock rippling through her.

"Katrina," he whispered, his lips curving into a smile; the sensations overcame him, and he clamped his eyes closed, shuddering. "My Katrina," he corrected when the aftershocks subsided. He opened his eyes and looked down at her, satiated.

You've done this before.

André smirked and shook his head. *Not quite.*

I know you're not a virgin, so what do you mean by not quite? Katrina tilted her head.

"I've never lost control before," he answered.

"What are you talking about?"

I've never let anyone see me.

Katrina raised her eyebrow and smiled, lowering her eyes to their melded bodies and returned her gaze to his a moment later.

The real me, and you know what I'm talking about, Kat. I saw it in your face, in your mind. My eyes—they turned, didn't they?

Katrina's smile faded and she nodded.

You would have heard about that by now, don't you think? He pulled off her and put his underwear and pants back on, the smile on his face faltering as his gaze shot to the door. He swiped her things off the floor and handed them to her, pushing her toward the bathroom. *Shit. Bathroom, now.* He moved the dresser back soundlessly as she disappeared behind the bathroom door. Jumping on the bed, he stretched out on his back, covering the small red stain on the comforter she left behind. He snapped his eyes closed.

Matthew poked his head in the room.

André made his chest rise and fall in the rhythm of sleep, praying Matthew would buy it. But his father's gaze traveled from him to the window, and he stepped inside the bedroom.

André opened his eyes. "I'll close it later, Dad," he said, startling his father and slowing his progress across the room.

"I got it." Matthew stopped between the bed and the window. He reached down and picked up the discarded bra, looking over at André with scrunched eyebrows and parted lips. "What the hell is this?"

André sat up, refusing to move from his place on the bed. If his father saw the stain, he'd know and at this point, he just suspected some less than innocent petting. "I, uh..." André looked between the bra and his father.

Matthew's eyes narrowed and his glance darted to the only logical place a girl could hide. He crossed to the bathroom, shooting André a warning glare. Flipping on the light, he caught Katrina frantically adjusting her skirt.

His jaw tightened and he held out the bra. "I assume this is yours," he said.

Katrina traded a glance with André and nodded, taking the bra from Matthew's outstretched hand.

He closed the door so she could reassemble herself and spun in André's direction, pointing his finger at him. "You have no idea how much trouble you are in right now," he growled. "Downstairs when she is finished. Understand?"

André nodded, avoiding Matthew's eyes. After his father left the room, he flopped back on the bed with his heart hammering in his throat. When Katrina opened the door, he stood and grabbed his shirt off the floor and slipped it on. "Shit."

Katrina bit her lip. "I'm sorry."

"Why?"

"I got you in trouble."

"You didn't get me in trouble, Kat. I did that all by myself," he answered, catching a kiss before he led her downstairs where Matthew and Linda waited.

No one spoke. Neither Matthew nor Linda knew what to say and André didn't dare utter a word with the angry thoughts going through their heads until Matthew glanced at Katrina, silently blaming her.

"It was not her fault." André glared at his father, unconsciously stepping in front of her in a protective reflex.

"But you...she..." He trailed off.

"Blame me, not her," André said, a little softer. "I'm the one with the experience."

Both Matthew and Linda stared at their son, dumbfounded by the admission.

"Yeah, I'm only seventeen, but I've been around the block. She hasn't."

"How far did you go up there?" Linda gasped.

André dropped his gaze to the floor, his cheeks flaring with heat, and he stole a sideways glance at Katrina. She stared at the floor with the same guilty expression he imagined he wore. Her hands gripped his and he sighed, bringing his gaze back to Matthew's, offering an apologetic shrug.

"Jesus Christ!"

Katrina cowered against André and tears created a glossy sheen on her eyes. "Please don't tell my dad," she whispered, her voice shaking.

"How did you get in?" Linda asked.

"I climbed the tree," she admitted. "I wanted to see if he was okay."

"And you couldn't have done that with your clothes on?" Matthew snapped.

"I'm taking her home." André started toward the door.

"The hell you are." Matthew quickly blocked the exit path. "I called her father. He's on his way."

Katrina let out a muffled sob.

"Nice going, Dad." He glared and then wrapped his arms around her, kissing the top of her head in a gesture so sweet, it brought a fresh wave of tears from Katrina.

Matthew's gaze bounced between André and Katrina, his thoughts racing over the brief conversation and then his eyes narrowed, locking with André's. "How many?"

"That's none of your business."

Matthew took a step in his direction, reining in the need to launch at his son. His jaw tightened and he spun to the window overlooking the front yard, the fury wracking his every thought transmitting to André like a beacon in a dark storm.

André retreated, leading Katrina away from his stewing parents into the family room. He pulled her down next to him on the couch. "I think I'm grounded until I go to college," he whispered, gleaning Matthew's angry thoughts.

"My dad is going to kill you," she said, wiping her face with her hands.

The doorbell rang and they traded a glance. Dread wrapped around his heart, and he took her hand in his, walking toward the entry like he was navigating death row.

Commander Lawrence waited in the front hall. "Katrina Lee Lawrence," he barked, and she buried her face in André's back, refusing to step into view of her father.

His eyes narrowed and his jaw clamped shut as he shot a deadly glare in André's direction. "I told you once a long time ago to stay away from my daughter."

"Sorry, sir," André said. "I stayed away as long as I could."

He looked at Matthew. "What happened here?"

When no one answered or met his inquisitive gaze, he knew and he turned his sights on the teenager before him, launching himself at André, his hands curled into claws, hell-bent on reaching around the boy's throat and squeezing the life from him.

André held up his hand stopping the commander, suspending him in the leap. His bangs hung in his eyes, and he stared through them, grinding his teeth against the murderous thoughts filtering through the commander's mind. A chill skittered across his skin and memories of the hostility on his home planet raged. This man was no better than the Zyclonians who exiled him. "Tsk, tsk, you shouldn't lose your temper like that. That's setting a bad example," he said, his voice toying but laced with a coldness that made everyone in the room shudder.

"André, let him go," Matthew ordered.

André turned his hard gaze to Matthew. "Katrina and I are together. End of discussion."

"Fucking alien," Commander Lawrence seethed, still frozen in mid-air. "I should have locked you up the day you arrived."

"You shouldn't talk to your future son-in-law that way."

"Over my dead body, you son of a bitch," Commander Lawrence snapped back.

"Please don't hurt my father," Katrina said, finding her voice and breaking through the deadly layer of frustration building around André.

He softened at the shake in her voice and turned, locking his gaze with her wide eyes. Fear had exploded inside her, and he felt it. "I wouldn't hurt him, Kat." He lowered his hand, setting her father on his feet in the process. *I didn't mean to scare you.* "Sorry." He shrunk inside his skin. He stepped away from her, suddenly vulnerable and ashamed of his display of power.

Her father grabbed her arm and dragged her out the door without another word.

André sat down on the stairs and put his head in his hands. That last stunt of his scared her, and he wasn't sure if he would ever see her again, never mind hold her in his arms. "You had to call her father," he yelled from behind his hands. "You had to ruin my fucking life." He flew up to his room.

Her scent permeated his bed sheets, and he gripped his pillow in his arms, inhaling the sweet essence of her shampoo. Tears blurred his vision, brimming and cutting hot paths down his cheeks as he stared at the open window.

Linda stepped into the room and sat on the edge of the bed. Her hand ran across his back, and she sighed. "What are you doing, André?"

He turned his head toward her. "I don't know," he answered and turned his head away again.

"Can I ask a personal question?"

He nodded without looking. "I did until tonight with Kat," he replied before she could verbally ask.

"You didn't use protection tonight?" she clarified her question.

"No," he answered. "We didn't."

"Matt doesn't know what to do with you right now."

"He wants to send me away." André turned to his adoptive mother. "I don't want to go anywhere." He wiped the tears off his face, smearing blood over the back of his hands.

"André, for the past year you have been a completely different person."

"Mom, I don't want to leave Dallas," he replied again. "Katrina is here."

Matthew leaned against the doorjamb. "You might not have a choice."

"What do you mean I might not have a choice?"

"Commander Lawrence may revoke our privilege to keep you here," he answered. "He was livid, André. Livid." Matthew turned and walked away without voicing the other thoughts rattling through his brain, thoughts of what Commander Lawrence might do, all of which encompassed unpleasant outcomes.

"Jesus." André closed his eyes.

"Actions have consequences, honey."

He nodded acknowledgment.

Linda stood to leave. "Despite what you may think, both your father and I care a great deal about you, no matter how angry or disappointed we are in what you have done." She walked out and closed his door.

André looked at the open window and thought of the options his father had entertained, all of which meant never seeing Katrina again. Sending him to a military base in another section of the country wasn't an option. No way he'd allow anyone to study him under a microscope for the rest of his life, and the alternatives were even worse.

Closing his eyes, he sighed, falling back on the only instinct he knew.

Survival.

He opened his eyes and stared at the window, contemplating his odds.

Messiah Chapter 8

ANDRÉ WENT INTO ACTION, packing some things in his duffel bag before he changed his mind. He clasped his watch, slid his wallet into his back pocket, and then tied his sneakers. As an afterthought, he grabbed a baseball cap and slung it into the bag before he zipped it up. He tossed the bag from his second-floor window, and it hit with a solid thump. André looked back at his door with a pang of guilt and slid his legs out the window. He gripped the sill and lowered himself out, hanging his full length. Letting go, he fell the extra fifteen feet, landing solid. He grabbed his bag and hauled it over his shoulder, jogging quietly away from the house. Glancing over his shoulder, he inhaled.

"Bye," he whispered, focusing his mind on Katrina, and headed in her direction.

André left his bag in the woods behind her house and snuck close to the foundation, unsure which room was hers.

"Katrina?" he whispered, sending the thought out to her and waited.

A light on the second floor flipped on and André moved under the window with a quick glance at the first-floor sliders a few feet to the left. He hated to think what the commander would do if he caught him in his back yard. Thoughts of shotguns and blood filled his mind, and he focused back on the upstairs window and Katrina's surprised face in the glass.

She glanced over her shoulder before pushing the window open. "What are you doing here?"

"I'm not going to let them lock me in a lab for the rest of my life, but I'm not running without you."

Katrina bit her lip and glanced behind her again, considering his implied invitation, her thoughts rolling to their earlier transgression. She sent him a sly smile and disappeared from view.

A few minutes later, an overstuffed duffel bag dropped, and he caught it, smiling up at her backlit form. Another item dropped and he snagged it from the air, her pocketbook. He set it next to the duffel bag, casting a worried glance at the kitchen sliders again.

She swung her leg out the window and reached for the rose trellis on the side of the house like she had done a million times, but this time she miscalculated the distance and lost her balance.

André's heart lurched and he stretched his arms out. "I got you," he whispered, willing her into his arms. She landed right into his grasp with a small oomph, her eyes wide and frantic with panic pumping in her veins. He just smiled at her and set her gently on her feet.

He glanced at the doorway again and handed her the pocketbook before slinging her bag over his shoulder. Grasping her hand, he led her into the woods where he grabbed his bag as well. "Where do you want to go?"

"I want to see New York City," she whispered.

"That's outside the domes, Kat."

She smiled and nodded.

"You're out of your mind. There's no oxygen out there."

"You don't know that for sure," Katrina said. "That's just what we've been told. If we go up to Chicago, we can get out of the dome through Lake

Michigan." She glanced at him as they navigated the thick woods.

"Then what?" André asked.

Katrina smiled. "Then we begin our adventure."

André laughed. "That's if we live long enough to see the East Coast," he drawled. He shook his head a little. "I can't believe I'm agreeing to this," he said aloud and glanced sideways at her.

They stepped out of the woods. "It would be really cool if we could steal a hovercraft."

"No." André shook his head.

"What are you, a fucking Boy Scout?"

"It's not right," he said, getting his bearings. He looked around and then over at her.

She pulled her hand out of his. "How do you suggest we get there?"

"Hitch."

She gawked at him. "I'm not getting into a hovercraft with a stranger."

"But you'd rather steal one and end up in jail?" He raised his eyebrows.

"And you'd rather be kidnapped and killed?"

André smiled. "No one's going to harm us, Kat."

"How can you be so sure?"

"Did you not see what I did to your dad at my house?"

She went to say something and then thought better of it.

"I can stop anything," he said.

"You can stop a laser gun?"

"I can stop anything on Earth." He grinned and put his arm around her shoulder. "So could you, if you tried."

"Yeah, right," she said as they walked to the edge of the road.

He escorted her across and began walking north. André turned at the sound of a hovercraft coming in their direction. He stuck out his thumb and the craft stopped.

"Where you headed?"

"Chicago," André answered.

The driver hesitated. "That's a long way from here."

"My aunt is up there and she's sick. Andy was kind enough to agree to go with me but neither of us has a hovercraft and I'd really like to see her before she dies." Katrina's eyes filled with tears, and she offered a sad smile.

The driver nodded. "All right." He unlocked the doors and André dumped their bags in the hatch, sliding in front with the driver. Katrina took a seat in the back.

"I didn't want Katy taking the trip alone." André glanced back at Katrina, amazed at her acting ability.

"I'm Paul, pleasure to meet you." His eyes drifted to the rearview mirror at Katrina in the back seat.

André smiled a little. "Don't even think about it, dude," he said, seeing the look on Paul's face and hearing his feral thought process.

Paul glanced over at him, sizing him up and smiling like he didn't just have thoughts of carnal activities with the girl in the back seat.

"Where are you headed?" Katrina asked.

"St. Louis," Paul answered. "That's as far as I can take you tonight."

"That's perfect," Katrina said.

"So, Paul, what do you do?" André asked.

"I'm in sales," he answered, again glancing at Katrina.

André looked out the window, his mood turning dark at the stranger's thoughts. "What kind of sales?" he asked, his voice a little strained as the anger ebbed its way in.

"Sales." Paul glanced over at him. "What's it to you?" he asked as they entered the connector tunnel between the Dallas and Topeka domes. Paul hit the hyper-drive and they shot through, faster than the speed of sound, the sonic boom absorbed in the material of the shaft.

André shrugged. "Just making conversation," he replied, putting his hands up in the air. He already knew what type of sales and it figured. Katrina was right about the dangers of hitchhiking. This man was a slime bucket who sold body parts to the highest bidder, and he had plans for the two of them when they got to their destination. Killing André was first on his agenda and Katrina was another story. The things he planned on doing to her made André see red, but he took a deep breath, calming the rising fury in his belly.

He looked around at the hovercraft. "Nice craft," he observed.

Paul smiled. "Thanks. Do you two have a place to stay in St. Louis?" he asked as they entered the Topeka—St. Louis tunnel way.

André shrugged. "No. We really want to get to Chicago before morning."

"It's not that far from St. Louis," Paul said over another sonic boom. "You can catch some Zs at my place if you'd like," he offered. "That way you can have a fresh start in the morning." He glanced back at Katrina.

"Thanks, but I think we'll pass," André answered.

"You sure? Because your girlfriend is sacked out in the back," he said, glancing at André.

André looked over his shoulder and back at Paul with an easy smile and shrugged. "We'll see." He had every intention of making Paul regret he ever picked them up and scooping up this hovercraft for the rest of their trip. He just hoped that Katrina wouldn't wake up when he made that happen.

"There is no aunt, is there, Andy?" Paul asked, glancing in his direction.

"What makes you think that?"

"I've seen my fair share of runaways and you two fit the bill."

André laughed. "What kind of sales did you say you were in?"

Paul glanced in his direction, pulling out a laser gun and pointing it at André. "I didn't say." He smiled as the hovercraft began to slow down. "Now be a good boy. Just sit there and keep your mouth shut and you won't get hurt."

André morphed his expression into one of fear and his eyes flicked from the end of the barrel to Paul's demented smile.

"Didn't your parents ever tell you not to hitchhike?" Paul asked and pressed the tracking button on the dash, putting the hovercraft into autopilot. He turned his full attention to André, keeping the gun trained on him.

André tilted his head. "Didn't yours ever tell you about the dangers of picking up a hitchhiker?" he countered, the fear no longer visible, replaced by a slow, evil smile of his own.

Paul leveled the gun to André's forehead as they pulled into the stream of busy city traffic. "I'm going to have so much fun with your girlfriend." He smiled and pulled the trigger.

Nothing happened and Paul looked at the gun, his eyes blinking rapidly. When he looked back at André, he screamed.

André felt the transition and knew from the horrified expression that his eyes had turned as red as the laser beam meant to explode through his head.

"Get out," André ordered, and the driver's side door swung open. They were traveling at close to one hundred miles an hour and roughly thirty feet from the ground.

Paul looked out the door and then back at André. "I'll die if I jump."

"You'll have more of a chance of survival jumping than if you stay here," André said. "Now get out," he ordered, loud enough to stir Katrina.

Paul glanced back at the drop and then at André's red, murderous eyes. Opting for the remote chance, he jumped.

André slid over to the driver's seat, closed the door and turned off the tracking system. He swung back toward the northern tunnel, glancing in the rearview mirror as the red hue diminished from his eyes, returning to the bright blue he was used to seeing. His gaze moved to the backseat, meeting Kat's shocked green eyes.

"What have you done?" she gasped.

"Rid the world of one sick bastard," he answered after a moment's hesitation. "And gotten us a ride that no one will report missing until long after we're in Chicago."

"Stop," Katrina yelled. "Stop the craft!"

"Kat, he was going to kill us. Do you know what he did for a living?" André asked and continued before she could answer, "He sold body parts, and he had no problem killing healthy runaways to get those parts." André shuddered, his adrenaline fading. "Hitchhiking probably wasn't such a good idea."

"How do you know what he intended to do?" she asked, and the high pitch of her voice matched the tears streaming down her cheeks.

"He put a laser gun to my forehead and pulled the trigger. If I had been human, I'd be dead right now." Reality settled into his bones, hitting him with its full force. The shakes started in his hands and worked their way up his arms and into his shoulders just about the time his stomach decided to roll. He pulled the craft down to the side of the road and threw the door open, shooting vomit onto the pavement below. Spasms racked his body and the knowledge he just killed someone slammed into his conscience hard.

He spit and then closed the door again, leaning back in the seat. Tears stung his eyes, blurring his vision and the tremors continued with the tears. "Holy shit." He looked into the rearview mirror, wiping his face and shaking the bloody tears from his hand.

Kat's eyes went wide. "You're bleeding."

"I'm fine," he answered when the shakes subsided. "Do you have any gum?" he asked, still tasting the bile in his throat.

"No, but I've got a mint." She pulled one out of her pocketbook, handing it to him as she climbed into the passenger seat. He swiped the bloody tears from his cheeks, wiping his hands on his jeans, leaving a maroon stain on the blue fabric, and pulled the hovercraft back into the stream of traffic.

"You bleed when you cry?"

He nodded without looking at her. Emergency lights blinked in the rearview mirror, and he focused on the lane in front of him.

"He was going to kill us?" she finally asked after the silence had wrapped itself around them.

"Yes." André glanced at his watch. "What time do you usually get up in the morning?"

"Why?"

"Because it's almost five."

"I must have slept."

"You did for a while."

"Did you?"

"Hell no." He raised his eyebrows at her. "I wasn't giving him an opening like that."

Katrina took a deep breath and glanced out the window.

The hovercraft sprung forward into the last tunnel, and he pushed the controls beyond eight hundred miles per hour, creating another sonic boom in their wake. Thirty minutes later, they entered the Chicago dome with the sun rising over the horizon.

"Now I need some sleep." André slowed the hovercraft down. He cruised at street level and punched "Nearest Hotel" into the tracking system. A few minutes later, they pulled into the Millennium hotel chain. André pulled out his wallet and flipped through the bills he had stashed. He glanced over at Katrina. "I don't know if I have enough."

"I do," Katrina answered. "Come on."

André took the keys and grabbed the bags out of the back. He hesitated and glanced at her before activating the security controls. He hoped that all it took to deactivate was just a push of the button.

"We'd like a room," André said, approaching the counter. His eyelids drooped and he imagined he looked every bit as tired as he felt. Twenty-four hours without sleep, along with the emotional rollercoaster of the last twelve hours, was finally taking its toll.

The concierge looked up at him.

André heard his train of thought and closed his eyes, sighing. "You will rent us a room," he said softly, pushing the concierge mentally.

"And how would you like to pay for that?" The concierge smiled at him.

"Cash."

"Certainly." He nodded and punched a few keys in the panel. "That will be three hundred and fifty dollars."

André glanced at Katrina and then back at the concierge. "Don't you mean thirty-five dollars?"

The concierge's smile faltered. He looked down at the paperwork and scribbled the fee. "Thirty-five dollars."

André handed him the money and took the room key, leaving the concierge smiling and clueless that he had just been hustled.

Katrina didn't say a word until they were in the room. "What did you do to the desk guy?"

"Influence." André flopped down on the bed. The minute his head hit the fabric, blackness overtook him.

ANDRÉ WOKE HOURS LATER, disoriented until he glanced her way. The prior evening came flooding back and he wrapped his arms around her, pulling her against him and burying his face into her hair. He dozed again with the smell of her cascading into his nostrils.

Knocking on the door roused him from sleep.

He pulled himself free and opened the hotel room door.

The manager stood with the concierge. "I'm sorry, sir, but there seems to be a problem with your bill."

André smiled. "You had a special and I qualified." He pushed the influence on the manager and concierge and watched them blink, look around and then down at the bill the manager held and back up at him.

"Thank you again for staying at our hotel." The manager smiled, folding up the bill and pocketing it. "I hope you have a pleasant stay." They wandered away.

André closed the door and glanced at the clock. They had been sleeping for six hours, long enough for his parents to know he was gone. He wondered how relieved they were to finally have him out of their hair. He couldn't imagine them being upset by his disappearance; angry at the disobedience was probably more accurate.

He sighed and stepped into the bathroom to clean up, letting the warm water wash away the sleep from his body. He leaned his hands on the front of the stall, closing his eyes and thinking about New York City.

What if she was right and there was oxygen outside the domes?

What if there wasn't?

At that thought, his eyes popped open, and he straightened, running his hand through his drenched hair. "What am I doing?" No answers came.

He shut off the water, towel dried before leaving the steam-filled bathroom and pulling out a pair of jeans.

Katrina stirred and rolled, burying her head under her pillow, mumbling. After he slid his jeans on, he sat on the side of the bed and rubbed her back until she uncovered her head and opened her eyes.

"Last night was real?"

"As real as it gets," he said. "Shower's free if you want to clean up."

She nodded and he moved, watching her disappear into the bathroom before sitting down at the table to count the money they pooled together.

Two hundred dollars.

Not enough to fade into obscurity.

He rubbed his face. "I didn't think this through very well," he muttered under his breath and swept the money off the table, stashing it away in his wallet. Instead of beating himself up for his piss-poor execution, he flipped the television on and settled back in the seat, hoping the droning of the news would keep his mind occupied away from their current situation, especially with the thought of Katrina naked in the shower just a few steps away.

It was all he could do to not act on the building need pooling in his lap, and when Katrina stepped back in the room with the towel wrapped around her, still dripping, he smiled, scanning her with his eyes, captivated. He pointed the remote at the television to turn it off and paused at Katrina's picture filling the screen.

"Shit." Instead of clicking the off button, he raised the volume. The reporter warned viewers that Katrina's abductor had a violent history and should be approached with extreme caution and then his picture popped up on screen. "Goddamn it!" He tossed the remote onto the table and shot a glance in Katrina's direction.

She wrung the water out of her hair, not looking concerned in the least by the news story or their pictures splashed across the airways. "My father is an asshole." She crossed toward André.

"Kat." He scanned her, torn between the instant lust and the need to run. "We don't have time for this now," he added as she straddled his legs and leaned on the arms of the chair, her wet hair dripping on his jeans.

She grinned and sat on his thighs. "What's another half hour?"

Heat radiated off her. "Kat," he whispered, his hands drifting to her legs and his heart pounding against his ribcage.

"André." She seductively licked her lips. "Marry me. Today."

André stared at her. "Why?"

"Because it will piss off my father."

He went to push her off his lap, annoyed by the answer. The idea of having her as his wife was a lifelong dream that started the moment he saw her in that infirmary, and she just shot all his romantic notions to hell.

She pushed him back against the chair. "I'm serious." She ran her hands down his bare chest. Her thoughts were as jumbled as the nerves in his stomach.

He leaned forward, kissing the soft flesh of her neck, wanting her with every fiber of his being, but afraid she just wanted him as a tool to make her father miserable. "Do you love me?"

"Yes. I love you, André," she said. "I always have."

He pulled away and met her gaze. "Why? Why do you love me, Kat?"

She sighed and placed her palm on his cheek. "I don't know. I just do."

"You sure it's just not the curiosity speaking? Or a way to piss off your father?"

She pulled her hand away. "Yes, I'm sure. I was curious when I walked into your hospital room, but the minute our eyes met, I don't know, it was like I knew you were meant just for me."

"And then your father forbid you to see me." André ran his hands through his hair, leaning his head back on the headrest.

"Why the hell do you think I've been such a nightmare at home? I was frustrated and you... you slept with anything with a skirt and hardly looked at me anytime I passed. That pissed me off."

"I was trying to find a way to get you off my mind." A smirk found its way to his lips.

Katrina slapped his chest.

"Seriously, Kat. My father forbade me from seeing you too, so I didn't have much of a choice. And you're right. I screwed my fair share of girls, but not one of them came close to making me feel the way you do," he said, turning serious. "You stole my heart in that hospital room and I haven't been able to recover since."

"Bullshit."

"You really want to marry me?"

She studied him and her smile faltered.

His smile disappeared, gone in the flash of her thought. He stood and pushed her away from him, gathering his clothes and shoving them into the bag. He glared over his shoulder. "You're the one who crawled through my bedroom window. I didn't coerce you into having sex; you wanted that just as much as I did. If you think for a minute I'd use the influence on you, you're insane." He zipped up his bag and threw it on the floor. He picked up hers and threw it in her direction. "Get dressed; we have to get out of here."

Katrina's chin started to quiver, and the tears spilled over. She rifled through her bag, looking for clothing to pull on. "You influenced the people here so easily..." She trailed off.

"It kills a part of their brain every time I do that," he said without looking at her. "I could end up making someone a vegetable if I'm not careful."

"I'm sorry." She began to sob.

André turned. "Don't cry," he said. "Don't fucking cry," he repeated, and the emotions caught up to him. A rollercoaster was as accurate a description as anything he could put his finger on. The highs and lows of the last twenty-four hours were enough to send him spiraling out of control and he sat on the edge of the bed, watching her pull her clothing on between sobs.

"You want to go back."

She nodded and then shook her head. "I don't know." She sniffled, getting control again. "Ever since we ran into each other yesterday, it feels like I jumped on a rollercoaster and can't get off." She wiped her face with her hands and looked at him.

He blinked and stared at her. It was almost as if she read *his* mind. "Why did you use that example?"

She shrugged. "It just popped in my head."

Her answer brought a low chuckle from his chest, and he looked down at the floor. Maybe she did have a touch of ESP, just like his father and that was something he could work with.

"What is so funny?"

He glanced at her. "That's exactly what I was thinking."

She opened her mouth and closed it and then just stared at him. "What are you trying to tell me?"

"You can read minds too."

"Bullshit."

"You are closer than you think, Kat. I can teach you if you let me."

She raised her eyebrows. "You can teach me? How?"

"Let's get out of here first. I don't want to fry their brains any more than I already have, okay?" André said.

"Okay," Katrina said, pulling a shirt over her head and packing up her clothing. She glanced at the bed as they stood to leave. A sigh escaped and she looked back in his direction. "Where are we going?"

"City Hall."

"Why?"

"We're getting married."

"We are?"

André paused and looked at Kat, his hand on the doorknob. Doubt swarmed her mind, and he dropped his hand, turning toward her. "Do you love me?"

She bit her lip and looked down at the carpet.

The swirl of her thoughts kept him holding his breath, praying she felt the same and this all wasn't just a ruse to get back at him for some unknown transgression. A small part of him wanted to push her into it, to make her do his bidding, but he couldn't do that. He needed her to make the decision on her own without his influence. He needed to know she accepted him for who he was. A rush of air escaped when she nodded and met his gaze.

"I know I asked, but..." She shifted and turned her back on him, looking out the window.

"But what?"

"I need to know what else you can do."

"I'm really not sure. I can read minds, I can influence minds, and I can control physical things around me."

"Can you kill?"

André thought about Paul and sighed. "I'm capable if I'm pushed. But then I imagine everyone can kill if pushed to their limits."

She turned back toward him. "Can you kill with your mind?"

André looked out the window, unable to meet her questioning stare. "Probably." He met her gaze. "Do you still want to marry me?"

A deep breath and a nod, and his fears dissipated. She wanted to marry him. A slow smile spread on his lips. "Let's go."

In the parking lot, André took out the keys and pressed the button, unlocking the hovercraft and throwing their bags in back. The clock blinked on, flashing a little after two in the afternoon, and he punched in two destinations into the navigation system—one for a pawnshop and the second for City Hall.

Twenty minutes later, they walked into a local pawnshop just around the corner from City Hall.

"Hi, I'd like to see some wedding bands," André said, draping his arm around Katrina's shoulders, his Southern accent, thicker than usual because of the nerves jumping under his skin like Mexican jumping beans.

"Sure thing." The pawnshop owner pulled out a tray full of bands.

André scanned the mishmash assortment and singled out a gold ring with diamonds embedded in the band and picked it up. "Let's see if this fits," he said, glancing at Katrina, and she put her left hand out. The ring slid on her finger like it was made especially for her. "Do you like it?"

She smiled and nodded. "What about yours?"

"You pick."

After studying a few rings, she settled on a simple thick gold band with a solitary diamond chip and slid it on his left ring finger. The fit was perfect, and they grinned at each other.

"We'll take these," André said.

"That'll be a thousand dollars."

André inhaled and glanced at the video cameras, willing a glitch in the recording while he reached for his wallet. He pulled out a hundred dollars and put it on the counter, pushing with his mind as he slid the bills forward. "This ought to cover it."

The owner smiled and counted out the money with a nod before he slid it away in the cash box. "Thank you for doing business with us." He wandered toward the back of the shop.

André put his arm around Katrina's waist and led her out of the building without another word. They slid into the hovercraft, glancing at each other as he flipped the tracking back on and the hovercraft headed for City Hall.

"I really hate doing that." He sighed.

Katrina studied the ring on her hand and sent a smile in his direction. "Thank you."

"You really want to do this?" he asked as he parked in front of the building.

"Yes, but only if you want to."

He laughed. "Asking me if I want to marry you is like asking if I want to breathe, although sometimes when I'm around you, I find it impossible to catch my breath."

"Aww." She put her hand over her heart. "That's the sweetest thing anyone has ever said to me."

He rolled his eyes and smiled. "So, you're good?"

"Yes."

They entered the grand atrium and scanned the directory, homing in on the justice of the peace located on the third floor. André led Katrina up the stairwell. "Can I have your ring?" he asked when they stood in front of the room.

She peeled it off her finger and offered it to him in exchange for his.

He stared at the ring in his hand and glanced at her, wondering if this was a dream and for an instant, he had the surreal feeling that if he opened the door, he'd be back in that godforsaken death pod and all these wonderful years on Earth would have been nothing but an elaborate dream. Fear saturated his cells, and he clamped his eyes closed, praying this was real.

"André?"

Her voice broke through his terror, and he opened his eyes. "Ready?" he asked.

"I am," she said.

He opened the door and relief swept through his bones at the mundane office and the judge draped in black robes behind the desk. They stepped in.

Judge Simpson looked up from the papers strewn on his desk. "May I help you?"

"Yes, we'd like you to marry us," André said.

"Do you have a license?"

André pulled out his driver's license and handed it to the judge.

The judge chuckled and studied the identification. "You're a little young to be getting married," he said, handing the license back to André.

"Yes but we have our parents' consent."

"Do you have the approved application for marriage?" he asked.

André slipped his license back into his wallet. *Shit, here we go again.* "You've got it there on your desk." He waved toward the papers, willing the judge to do his bidding.

The judge pulled out a blank marriage license and filled it in according to André's silent instruction and when he finished, he turned it to André with a dull, distant look in his eyes.

André sent a sideways glance at Katrina and closed his eyes, tapping into his mother's mind and scrawling her signature in the slot for parental consent. Commander Lawrence's was harder, but he managed to get a ghost of a glimpse and signed his name as well. A small headache formed behind his right eye, and he slid the paper back to the judge.

The judge nodded, smiling as he picked up the form, focusing on the document in front of him. "Ah, yes, yes, I do indeed, and it looks like everything is in order."

"Yes, sir." André smiled, giving another push.

The judge stood and pressed an intercom. "Betty, can you and Harry come in here to witness a marriage ceremony please?" He smiled as they waited. An elderly woman and a middle-aged man came into the room and glanced between the young couple and the judge.

André smiled and stifled a yawn. Even the little pushes wiped him out, but this was worth every second of exhaustion.

Judge Simpson began the simple civil service. "Do you, André Robbins, take Katrina Lee Lawrence to be your wife?"

"I do," André replied.

"Do you, Katrina Lee Lawrence, take André Robbins to be your husband?"

"I do," Katrina said, looking up into André's eyes and he sighed with relief.

"Take the ring and slide it onto her finger and repeat after me. This is a symbol of my love and fidelity." Judge Simpson waited.

André positioned the ring at her first knuckle and looked into her green eyes. A mix of emotions sprung forth and he took a deep relaxing breath before speaking. "This is a symbol of my love and fidelity," André said with a slight tremor in his voice, and he slid the ring on her finger.

Judge Simpson looked at Katrina.

Katrina slid the ring on André's finger. "This is a symbol of my love and fidelity," she said without being prompted.

"By the power vested in me by the grand state of Illinois, I now pronounce you husband and wife," he said. "You can kiss your bride."

André leaned over and kissed Katrina. He smiled as he stood back up. "May I have a copy of the marriage license?"

The judge smiled and nodded. "They'll give you a copy in the clerk's office." He had the witnesses sign the certificate as well as Katrina and André before he signed and stamped the marriage license with the state seal. "Just ask for a copy when you drop this off at the clerk's office on the first floor."

"Thank you, Judge Simpson," André said, and they headed out of his office, stopping in the clerk's office to file the certificate and get a copy.

When they stepped outside into the bright sunshine, Katrina asked, "Was that legal?"

"Yes, as long as our parents don't charge us with forgery." He stared at the copy of the marriage certificate in his hand. The fact he broke the law yet again weighed heavy on him, but when he glanced at her, it all made it worthwhile. She was now his wife, and he folded the certificate, sliding it into his wallet. "Where to, Mrs. Robbins?"

"Lake Michigan." Kat smiled. "But first, you look like you're in need of a hotel."

She didn't know the half of it. All that mind bending had left him in a state near collapse and while she had visions of more carnal activities on her mind, all he wanted was an hour of sleep to get his bearings back, and then he'd gladly comply with her silent wishes.

THE DOOR BURST OFF the hinges and André shot up, his arms tightening around Katrina. A squadron of police barreled into the luxury honeymoon suite of the hotel bordering Lake Michigan. Fifteen guns trained on them, and Katrina yanked the sheet up, covering her naked form and uncoupled from the straddled position she fell asleep in.

Commander Lawrence stormed to the end of the bed, his gun drawn and pointed at André.

André didn't flinch; he just glared at his father-in-law, looking from the end of the barrel to his face. "I married her today, sir," he said.

The gun never wavered. "Get your hands off my daughter," Commander Lawrence growled.

"Dad, I married André." Katrina spoke, causing her father's gaze to fall on her. "I'm his wife." She held up her left hand, showing him the ring.

"The marriage certificate is in my wallet," André said. He looked around the room at the wall of cops. "Do you mind?"

"André Robbins, you are under arrest for the kidnapping of Katrina Lawrence," the closest officer began.

"He didn't kidnap me!" Katrina yelled. "I married him."

"You have the right to remain silent…"

André traded a glance with Katrina. This wasn't working. No matter what he said, he'd either be arrested or shot based on the commander's instructions. He sent a small push. "This is a family matter, not a police matter."

Collectively the officers blinked, and all the guns lowered except Commander Lawrence's. After a quick gaze between André and Commander Lawrence, the squadron filtered out of the room, closing the door behind them.

Commander Lawrence watched in dumb fascination before he snapped his gaze back to André. Fury etched into the commander's features, transforming his handsome face into an ugly mask of rage. He pulled the trigger and a flash shot out of the laser gun.

André only had a fraction of a second warning and tackled Katrina, pushing her down on the mattress, out of the way of the laser beam. The shot cut through the headboard where his head was moments before, and anger leapt to the forefront of André's mind.

He let loose, vaporizing the gun and singeing the commander's hand in the process.

The pain in his head grew to a throbbing pulse at the exertion. He reached for the bathrobe on the edge of the bed, handing it to Katrina without taking his gaze from the cursing commander standing at the end of the bed, shaking the burn from his hand.

After Katrina eased off the bed, he grabbed the other bathrobe and threaded his arms through the plush fabric, tying the robe before sliding from the bed. He crossed to the table, grabbing his wallet, and plucked the marriage certificate from the folds, holding it out to Commander Lawrence.

Commander Lawrence cradled his burnt hand to his chest, his breath coming in harsh rips matching that of André, his gaze jumping from the piece of paper to his eyes. He snatched the sheet from André and scanned the document, his jaw tightening with every word.

"In Illinois it's legal," André said. "You don't have to be eighteen if you have parental consent."

The commander stared at the form, his face taking on the same tone as a fire engine. "I don't care whether you think it's legal or not. You are a goddamn alien, a freak," he growled. "You don't have any rights here."

He turned full toward the commander, his jaw dropping at the discriminatory slant.

Katrina stepped in front of André. "Daddy, I love him."

"You are sixteen. You have no clue what love is," he spouted back at her.

"You told me you met Mom when you were sixteen."

His lips thinned and his eyes narrowed. "What I had with your mother isn't even in the same league as this. You don't even know him."

Katrina looked down at the floor. "I know enough that I want to spend the rest of my life with him and you forbid me to see him. What else were we supposed to do?"

Commander Lawrence gaped at his daughter. "Katrina, you are coming home with me."

"No, Dad, I'm not."

He took a step toward her, and André stopped him short with an invisible wall.

"No way," André replied. "I'll take her somewhere where you can't find us," he warned.

MATTHEW FLEW INTO THE hotel room, out of breath, praying he wasn't too late. The commander had left swearing he would kill André when he got his hands on him. He slid to a stop as he took in the scene.

Commander Lawrence glared at him, flinging a piece of paper in his direction.

Matthew caught the paper and looked at it. His eyes nearly popped out of his head at the title. "A marriage certificate?" He looked up at André, receiving a nod, and he returned his gaze to the signatures, Linda's signature. His gaze shot back to André. "Your mother never signed this." He held it out.

"Are you sure, Dad? She was in my room for a while last night. Who's to say she didn't sign the consent form?"

Matthew dropped his gaze to the form, confirming again that his wife's distinctive scrawl graced the page. Doubt crawled under his skin and his eyes drifted to André's left hand, where a wedding band glimmered.

He knew his wife.

He knew she'd never do this behind his back.

Clenching his jaw, he raised his eyes to meet his son's defiant glare. "You are in a world of trouble, young man," he said, handing the paper back to his son.

"If you try to break us up, we'll run away again."

"André, you can't run. Your picture is all over the television."

André looked at his father. "Who said we'd run inside the domes?"

Outside? Is he out of his goddamn mind? "She'll die on the outside," Matthew said. "There isn't enough oxygen."

André cocked his head in challenge, raising an eyebrow. "How long has it been since someone tried?"

"That's how we enact a death sentence, André. The last one was sent outside the dome in Texas three weeks ago. He lasted less than twenty minutes before he died," Matthew said.

André closed his eyes and rested his chin on the top of Katrina's head, his arms still protectively around her. "I'm not going home unless Katrina is with me," he whispered into her hair as he opened his eyes and met his father's gaze.

Matthew put his hands on his hips and studied the patterns in the plush rug.

"I swear Matthew, I'll have you court-martialed," Commander Lawrence threatened.

"I'll tell the president that you tried to kill my husband without justification," Katrina countered, glaring at her father.

"He needs to be locked up, Katrina. He's dangerous," Commander Lawrence growled at his daughter.

"Bullshit!" Katrina yelled.

André's eyes narrowed and a small red ring formed around his iris. "If you try to lock me up, I swear to God, I'll wipe out any memory you have of me," André said, trumping everything else. "And that may end up sending you to the loony bin for the rest of your life."

Silence filled the room and Matthew stared at André. This was a new power he wasn't aware of. Dangerous if left unchecked, and for the first time since he brought André home, he wondered about the wisdom of his decision.

"It's up to you, Commander," André replied, breaking the uncomfortable silence. "Your memories and possibly your sanity or letting us go?"

Commander Lawrence cursed under his breath and turned his attention to Matthew. "This is your fault. You brought him here instead of terminating him on his ship like you were ordered to."

"He was just a child."

"And now that *child* has brainwashed my daughter."

"Jesus Christ, Dad. He did *not* brainwash me. This was my choice. I asked him to marry me, to get me the hell out of our house. It's a nightmare living with you," Katrina yelled, the anger filling the room.

Commander Lawrence looked at André, his face still an angry shade of red, but not the heart attack red it had been a few minutes before. His gaze bounced between André and Katrina, and he uncurled his hands. "Katrina, he is dangerous."

"I'm only dangerous if I'm pushed into a corner, sir," André said.

Silence filled the room, all parties at an impasse and the commander turned to Matthew.

Matthew guessed he was going over everything including the altercation at the house, all of which happened so fast, his brain was just now catching up. When his hardened gaze returned to Matthew's, he knew he was in deep shit.

"You've been hiding his abilities for the past six years, haven't you, Colonel?"

He nodded to his commanding officer.

"Why?"

"I knew you would want to use the boy to make him into a military weapon. He was lost and needed a home, not some institution that would brainwash him and turn him into a killing machine."

"And yet he still turned out to be a menace to society."

Matthew sighed. "André's a good kid, sir. Despite all this." He waved his hand at the two teenagers.

"I left him in your care, Colonel, and this is how he turned out?"

Matthew stiffened and shot a glare in André's direction, silently telling him to shut up before his son could even open his mouth. "Yes, sir," he said, knowing any other response would be a futile effort.

"You realize I could have you court-martialed and tried for treason," the commander said.

"Yes, sir," Matthew said.

"You'd give up your life to protect him?"

Matthew met the commander's gaze, searching his own soul for the answer. His heartstrings were tightly wrapped around André, as much as they would have been if André was his own flesh and blood. He inhaled and nodded. "Yes, sir, I would. Just as you would for your daughter."

TREASON.

The word triggered nasty memories, memories of tortured screams, of frantic pleas, of painful promises and the air sucked from his lungs. He knew more about that word than a child had a right to, along with the accompanying consequences. Treason meant death and the commander just threatened his father with it. He couldn't pull enough air into his seized lungs, only a high-pitched wheeze that pulled attention from everyone in the room.

"What's wrong?" Katrina turned out of his grasp, and he dropped to his knees, meeting Matthew's gaze.

André put his hands on his knees and concentrated on getting his breathing back to normal, his eyes never leaving his father's. "Treason,"

André gasped again, and his eyes filled with tears. "My parents," he hissed through the gasping breaths.

"The commander isn't serious, André. He was just reminding me of the possible consequences of my actions." He glanced over at Commander Lawrence. "Right, sir?"

Commander Lawrence glared at Matthew without answering. His gaze shot to André. "Your parents were convicted of treason?"

"Yes, sir," André said, looking at the floor, regaining control over his breathing.

"Why?"

"Because of me, sir," he answered, still staring at the carpet. His lungs loosened, air drawing back and leaving him dizzy, expecting this world to shatter, leaving him alone and cold in a sludge filled space ball.

"Why?" Commander Lawrence pushed.

"Because my powers were so refined and my eyes, sir... my eyes are blue," he said.

The steam evaporated from the commander and his eyebrows rose. "Did you say your parents were tried for treason because your eyes are blue?"

André nodded. Shame laced its way through him, and his face heated with it.

Commander Lawrence looked at Matthew, still not understanding. "His eyes?"

"Unfortunately, yes," Matthew acknowledged. "His parents tried to hide him from the government because he was different. That's why they were killed, and André was exiled."

Commander Lawrence returned his gaze to André, studying him like a lab technician would study a unique and dangerous virus.

"I'm not a threat, Commander," he said, regaining his faculties and standing.

"I'll make that determination," he snapped, crossing his arms.

"My actions should be enough. If I *was* an actual threat, I would have taken both you and the entire police force out. And believe me, I hold that capability."

"What would prevent you from doing that in the future?" Commander Lawrence asked.

"Because I know right from wrong and this is my home, sir. The only real home I've ever had."

"And yet you pulled this irrational stunt." Commander Lawrence waved at the room. "That doesn't give me a lot of confidence in your abilities to discern right from wrong."

André shifted from foot to foot and traded a sideways glance with Katrina. "She asked and I really couldn't say no. Not with the way I feel about her, sir."

Commander Lawrence let out a bark of a laugh and approached André, so he was toe to toe, towering over him. "I will never accept you into my home and I sure as hell am not letting my daughter stay with you." He reached for Katrina's arm, and she stepped away.

"I'm not going home with you, Dad," Katrina said.

"You'll let her come with me and you won't do anything to my father either." The words tumbled out of André's mouth and with it, an influential push.

Commander Lawrence blinked and took a step back, his face paling before the angry hue returned. He glared at Matthew. "This is your problem now," he directed at Matthew and strode out of the hotel room, leaving the three of them alone.

MATTHEW WAITED UNTIL THE door closed and shot a glare at his son. "What the hell were you thinking?" he yelled and stepped away, letting the anger and frustration he felt ever since he walked into his son's room this morning take hold. He paced, letting it flow. "You forged your mother's signature on that document." He glared at the two of them. "Both of you. I can't believe you pulled this shit."

"Go get dressed," André said to Katrina, pushing her gently toward the bathroom and out of Matthew's angry ramblings.

Katrina grabbed her bag and headed into the bathroom, closing the door behind her.

André skirted around his father and found a pair of underwear in his bag, slipping it on under the bathrobe. He pulled a pair of jeans on next and sat on the edge of the bed. "I love her, Dad," he said. "You don't seem to understand what that means to me."

Matthew laughed. "I don't give a shit what that means to you right now." He didn't know what was going through André's mind, but he wasn't about to allow them to live as husband and wife under his roof. André's gaze snapped in his direction. "I'm serious," Matthew said. "If you're under my roof, you will not sleep together until you are both eighteen. I don't give a damn what that paper says."

"Then we'll find an apartment."

"Good luck with that," Matthew snapped. He never imagined the boy would do something this impulsive. "You can't get a job without a work permit, and I won't sign one for you, not under these circumstances. And so help me God, I'll throw your ass in jail if you forge another signature."

"But, Dad—"

"—No. Stop now. This was one of the stupidest things you've done since coming into my home and frankly, I don't give a damn what your excuse is. You disobeyed me outright and I told you I wouldn't tolerate disobedience. I really have no clue what to do with you right now." Thoughts of military school swarmed his mind.

"I'm not going to military school."

"You don't have a choice."

"You know damn well you can't make me go."

Matthew took stock of his temper and counted to ten, calming himself down before he spoke again. "You have to finish high school and if you refuse to obey the rules I outlined, military school is the only other option." He knew he was boxing his son into a corner, but he didn't care.

André glared at him.

"Don't expect the next year to be easy, either. Just because I agreed to let her live in the same house does not mean I'll slack off and let you two act like husband and wife. Understand?"

ANDRÉ DIDN'T HAVE THE energy to argue. The expenditure of power in the last half hour, along with the sudden fizzle of adrenaline, wiped him out and he took a seat on the edge of the bed, nodding and waiting for Katrina to come out of the bathroom so he could clean up.

A layer of relief settled his clenched stomach and while the prospects of the next year seemed dim, it was eons better than waking from another hallucination.

He met her gaze when she walked out of the bathroom and offered a strained smile.

At least I'll get to see her every day.

Messiah Chapter 9

*O*CTOBER 2239

Katrina's stomach cramped and she raised her hand.

"Yes, Katrina?" Mr. Mills asked.

"I don't feel so well. Can I go to the nurse's office?"

He nodded his round, bald head and returned his focus to the history lesson. Katrina stepped out of the classroom, her books in her arms and her eyes at half-mast. She clenched her teeth against the bile threatening to burst from her stomach and made it to the bathroom just in time for her breakfast to come up. Again.

Screw the nurse's office, she thought and stood, spitting the last of the rancid taste from her mouth. *I'm going home.*

The walk home took longer than normal. Every few hundred feet she had to stop, close her eyes and will her stomach not to expel the last of the acid boiling up her esophagus. No one was home when she stumbled in the front door. She made it upstairs and into the bathroom before collapsing over the toilet, dry-heaving over and over and over, tears sprouting from her eyes at the intensity of each empty hurl.

Too weak to continue, she curled up on the floor and closed her eyes, sending out a silent cry for help.

ANDRÉ STOOD IN THE lunch line at school, looking around for Katrina. After a moment he did a quick mental scan. She wasn't in the area. Turning his attention back to the array of desserts, he reached for a slice of pie and jumped a mile at the volume of her cry, nearly knocking the entire display over. His heart pumped in his chest. The scare was worse than any of those pop-up Draculas you find at cheesy haunted houses. He inhaled and offered the kid behind him an awkward smile and turned, leaving his full tray on the conveyor. "Where are you?" he whispered as he headed out of the cafeteria.

A girl in front of him looked back at him. "Are you talking to me?"

"No, sorry, just thinking out loud." He skirted around her and into the hallway.

Home.

Her thought was wrapped in agony and André picked up the pace, hitting an all-out run by the time he reached the pavement in front of the school. Ten minutes later, he bound into the house. "Katrina?"

"Bathroom," she whispered.

André ran up the stairs and pushed the door open. Her head rested on the lip of the toilet, her face ashen, giving her misery-filled eyes a living-dead quality.

"I'm sick."

"I can see that." He walked over and picked her up in his arms, carrying her to her bedroom. He set her on the bed and ducked out for a moment. When he came back, he had a wet washcloth and an empty garbage can. He put the can on the floor and sat on the edge of the bed, wiping her face gently with the washcloth. "Can I get you anything?"

"Is there any ginger ale?"

"I'll go check." André put the cool cloth on her forehead, kissing her cheek gently. He left the room, returning a little while later with a glass for her. He sat on the edge of the bed and helped her take a sip.

"I feel like shit." Katrina sunk back on the bed. Dark circles surrounded her eyes.

"You pretty much look like shit too."

"You're not supposed to say stuff like that," she said, her eyes filling with tears.

"Sorry." He smiled down at her. "I love you anyway."

Katrina began to cry.

"What is wrong with you?"

She shook her head. "I don't know. I'm tired all the time and now I'm nauseous all the time."

"How long have you felt this way?"

"Just a couple weeks, but it's getting worse," she said, wiping her eyes.

"Maybe we should get you checked out," André said.

"It's just the flu." Katrina reached for the glass again.

André put his hand on her forehead. "You don't have a fever." He had seen his mother with a stomach virus enough times in the past six years to know what to do.

"Have you ever been sick?" Katrina asked.

André shook his head. "No."

"Must be nice to be you," she said sarcastically, closing her eyes and rolling on her side.

"I need to get back to school, Kat."

She rolled and looked at him. "Can't you stay?"

"I've got a test in twenty minutes, but I'll be back after, okay?"

Her eyes welled up with tears but she nodded.

"You have the ginger ale, and the garbage can. I'll be back just as soon as I can." He kissed her cheek. "If you need me, just call."

KATRINA WATCHED AS HE left her room, biting her lip and swallowing the tears burning her throat. The brief encounter in his arms felt like coming home, even if it was just to carry her from the bathroom floor to the bed. Five weeks of living under the same roof but not being able to be in each other's arms took its toll on their marriage and her constant exhaustion and volatile moods didn't help.

Neither did the fact André was adamant about following his father's rules while they lived there. Gone was the impulsive guy she married, the one who defied his parents, threatened her father, and cleared an entire room of hostile police officers as easily as waving a dismissive hand.

No, that guy had been replaced by an obedient, ultra-responsible, uber popular football player. Practice, homework, a little television, and a good night's sleep in separate rooms. She hated it, missing the feel of his arms, the brush of his kiss, and that playful laser that encompassed his irises when he was horny.

She took a sip of ginger ale and curled up on the bed, drifting into an exhausted slumber.

ANDRÉ WALKED BACK INTO the house an hour later and pushed her door open. *God, I miss her.* They lived in the same house, but since they returned, the air between them grew tense with sexual frustration and dissent. Every encounter ended with her huffing and stomping upstairs. She just didn't understand how close he came to being sent to military boarding school in Denver and he didn't want to tempt his father by disobeying him again.

He stared at her sleeping form and sighed. Torn, he looked at the stairwell and back at Katrina, deciding a few hours with her in his arms was worth getting yelled at. He stepped inside and closed the door behind him.

Crawling onto the bed behind her, he slid his arm under her neck, wrapping it around her and pulling her to his chest. He ran his fingers through her hair, sighing at the feel of her against him. "I love you, Kat," he whispered.

She mumbled the words back to him and snuggled closer.

"God, I miss holding you," he whispered, inhaling the fruity essence of her hair.

"I miss being in your arms." She reached up for the glass, taking a sip of the ginger ale and then returning to the comfort of his grasp. "I still feel like crap, though."

André kissed her shoulder. "I'm sorry, babe." He went back to combing her hair.

"That feels good."

He continued, feeling the texture of her fine locks against his fingertips, the soothing strokes helping her slip back to sleep.

He wasn't sure how long he lay holding her but when Linda opened the bedroom door, André shook his head and put his finger to his lips. Sliding his arm from under her, he slowly rolled away, climbing out of the bed with as little disruption as possible. Outside the room, he closed the door.

"If your father had caught you in there…" Linda began.

"Kat's been throwing up all afternoon." André glanced at his watch. "I was waiting till you got home before I left for practice," he said, skirting down the stairs. "Keep an eye on her for me, okay, Mom?"

KATRINA WOKE TO THE smell of chicken noodle soup. She sighed, catching a glance of herself in the mirror. Her eyes still held the dark shades of exhaustion, and her left cheek was marred by small red blemishes where her face scrunched into the pillow. She did look like shit. She picked up the glass and wandered down to the kitchen. "Hi, Mrs. Robbins." She set the cup into the sanitizer.

"How are you feeling?" Linda asked, glancing at her.

"Eh," she replied and sat at the table. "I'm so tired."

Linda crossed the room and pressed her wrist to Katrina's forehead. "You don't have a fever."

"That's what André said earlier," she said. "He took care of me today."

"I know. I caught him in your room."

"I'm sorry."

Linda went back to stirring the soup on the stove. "It's okay. I'm not going to tell Matt."

"You're not?"

"No. André was just trying to make you comfortable." She looked back at Katrina. "Right?"

Katrina nodded and put the back of her hand to her mouth, bolting to the downstairs bathroom, sliding onto the floor in front of the toilet as the ginger ale came flowing up. She put her forehead on the cool porcelain. "I can't seem to keep anything down today," she said as Linda appeared in the doorway.

Linda's brow creased. "How long have you been feeling this way?"

"I've felt sick for a couple of days, but I've been exhausted for the last couple weeks." She proceeded to dry heave.

Linda picked up the phone, calling her doctor. "Can I bring her down now?" she asked after explaining the situation. "I'd really like her checked out," she replied. "Yes, I can have her there in ten minutes." She hung up the phone, collecting Katrina from the bathroom floor, and helping her to the hovercraft, before zooming to the doctor's office.

After providing both a urine sample and a blood sample, Katrina headed back into the exam room where Linda waited for her. "Thanks." She stretched out on the table.

Linda nodded from the chair in the corner.

The doctor came in a few minutes later, consulting Katrina's chart. "Well, it seems you are dehydrated, little lady, and we need to get some fluids into you."

"Dehydrated?" Linda asked, standing and crossing to Katrina's side.

"Yes, dehydrated." The doctor turned back to Katrina. "You need to drink at least sixty-four ounces of liquid a day in order to keep hydrated in your condition," he added. "Especially in the early stages."

Katrina blinked. "What condition?"

The doctor looked at the chart and back to Katrina. "You're pregnant."

Katrina's mouth fell open in shock. *Pregnant? I can't be pregnant. I'm only a junior in high school.*

She met Linda's gaze as the doctor fed the intravenous line into her arm. The first emotion she recognized was disappointment but underneath, she swore she saw a flash of envy. She sent a reassuring smile her way and Katrina offered a bleary one in return. She was not ready to be a mother, at least not yet. Too many questions, too many fears fluttered through her mind, and she bit her lip, her vision tripling behind the sheen of tears.

"Do you want me to go get André?"

Katrina nodded, not trusting her voice.

"I'll be back with the father in fifteen minutes." Linda turned on her heels and walked out of the doctor's office.

Fifteen minutes later, André walked in, his eyes landing on the IV attached to her arm. "Are you all right?" he asked, bringing his gaze back to hers.

"I'm pregnant."

André broke out in a smile. "Really?"

"It's not a good thing." She wiped her face.

André walked over to her. "We're married, remember?" He sat on the edge of the bed. "Is everything all right with the baby?" He pointed at the IV line.

"Yeah. I'm just dehydrated. I need one more bag and then I can go home."

André nodded and the grin returned.

"Stop smiling like that."

"I'm sorry, Kat, but this doesn't upset me at all," he said. "Quite the contrary."

"I'm scared."

"I'm here." André took her hand. "There is no need to be scared."

"I'm not ready for a child."

He listened to her train of thought and sighed. "My DNA is very similar to human DNA." He kissed her hand. "I think the gestation is close to the same too," he said, "and it's our child."

Katrina looked at him. "We're still in high school."

André shrugged. "So."

Katrina closed her eyes. "How are we going to afford a child?"

"Don't worry about that. I'll think of something," he said, his expression growing serious. "All the things you're worrying about aren't the issue, are they?"

Katrina looked into his blue eyes. She loved him but she was scared to death because of who he was and what that could mean in a child. "What if the baby isn't right? What if the combination of our DNA produces a monster?"

André tilted his head, his eyes showing the depth of his love for her. "What if it produces an angel?" he drawled softly, countering her fears. "What if we produce a new beginning for the human race? One that can exist outside the walls of the domes?"

Katrina closed her eyes and took a deep breath. When she opened them, she smiled a little. "I guess we're having a baby."

The smile reached his eyes, making them sparkle. "Does my mom know?"

Katrina nodded.

André looked toward the door, wondering why he hadn't picked that up from her on the way over. She was usually so easy to read. He crossed to the door and pushed it open. Linda was leaning against the wall. "Hi, Mom. You can come back in if you'd like." He smiled as he held the door open for her.

She looked at him as she passed. "I haven't called your father."

André nodded. "I want to be the one to tell him."

"He's not going to be happy."

André shrugged. "You know what, Mom? I don't care. I'm happy and Kat's happy and that's all that really matters."

Linda sat down. "It's not all happiness and sunshine, André," she said. "Having a child is a lot of work."

He nodded. "I know. It's the second biggest commitment, next to marriage."

"No, it is a bigger commitment than marriage," she corrected. "The welfare of your child comes before anything else." She paused and looked at them both. "It comes before football and homework, prom and graduation. A child is first. Their wants and needs trump all."

André took Katrina's hand and squeezed it. "I know," he said, looking at his mother.

Katrina put her free hand on her stomach and looked up at Linda. She didn't have the same conviction as André, but she nodded.

The nurse came in and changed her IV bag. "You should be good to go in about a half hour."

Linda stood and handed André the keys to the hovercraft. "I need to get supper ready for your father."

"We'll be home once they let her go." André turned back to Katrina. The color was back in her cheeks and the circles under her eyes had faded a bit. "How are you feeling?"

"A little better."

The doctor came in. "I assume you are the father?"

"Yes."

The doctor took note of the wedding band on André's hand. "You two are married?"

"Yes, sir, we are," André answered. "For a little over a month now."

The doctor scanned the chart. "It looks like your wedding day prompted more than just nuptials."

"When is she due?"

"May, June time frame. When was your last period?" he asked Katrina.

"I'm not sure. Beginning of August?" she said. "But I can tell you the date that we probably conceived. It was either August fifteenth or sixteenth," she said, reciting the day André made love to her for the first time as well as the day they were in Chicago.

"Then we are looking at roughly around May fifteenth," he answered, plugging the dates into the chart.

Katrina raised her eyebrows. She might not make it to finals and that irritated her, along with the prospects of going through senior year with a child. But André was so damn happy about this that she sighed and focused on what the doctor was saying.

"...prenatal vitamins and you will need to drink lots of fluid so you don't get dehydrated again." The doctor scribbled on the screen and the prescription came out a few moments later. "Do you have any questions?"

André opened his mouth and then closed it, biting his lip like he did when he was trying to formulate a delicate question. "What kind of complications could we be facing?" he asked, taking a seat on the edge of the bed.

"Your wife is a healthy woman in great physical shape, so she is at a lower risk for complications," the doctor began. "However, with that said, there is always the risk of miscarriage in any pregnancy but that risk gets lower after she completes the first trimester. Warning signs to look for throughout the pregnancy include serious cramping, spotting, and dehydration. If any of those occur, you should bring her here immediately." He handed them the bottle of prenatal vitamins. "Try to maintain a healthy diet, and I want to see you every month if all goes smoothly. If we hit some bumps, I'll want to see you more frequently." He looked at the IV bag. "I'll send the nurse in to take that out and before you leave, please make your next appointment." He headed toward the door. "If you have any questions, don't hesitate to call the office."

"Thank you," André said, and then turned his attention back to Katrina. "You look so much better."

"I feel so much better than I did earlier," Katrina said as the nurse came in.

The nurse removed the IV and handed them an instruction sheet before showing them out of the office.

"My father is going to blow a gasket," Katrina said as they got into the hovercraft and headed toward the house.

André shrugged. "My dad isn't going to be happy either, but we'll deal."

Katrina pulled the visor down and glanced in the mirror. "I look like shit."

"No, you don't." He grasped her hand and kissed it.

MATTHEW PULLED UP AS they were getting out of the hovercraft, and he sent a glare in André's direction. "Where were you?"

"Tell Mom I'll be in in a few minutes." André waited for Katrina to trot up the steps and enter the house before turning his attention back to his father. He took a deep breath, ignoring the intimidation inspired by the full military attire Matthew wore. He leaned against the hovercraft. "We need to talk, Dad."

Matthew nodded for him to follow and placed his briefcase on the porch, sitting on the steps and indicating for André to do the same. "What's on your mind?"

André took a deep breath. "A few things. First, I'm not real happy with the arrangements," he said, picking at a hangnail on his thumb.

"Tough."

"I think since I'm gonna be a father, I should be able to share a room with my wife." He leaned back to watch Matthew's reaction.

Matthew went to speak but stopped as the words sank in. "What the hell are you talking about?"

"Kat's pregnant." André crossed his arms. "It's time to change the living arrangements."

Matthew shook his head. "No, the arrangements are not changing."

André uncrossed his arms, the bite of anger creeping in. "She's already pregnant, Dad. You don't have to worry about that variable anymore."

Matthew glared at his son, and then stormed into the house.

André immediately followed. "Dad, you're being ridiculous."

Matthew stopped in his tracks. He turned slowly toward André. "My roof, my rules," he replied. "You don't like it, you can leave," he added and headed toward the master bedroom to change.

André mumbled something unintelligible under his breath and stormed into the kitchen. He sat down, the moody air rippling around him conveying to his mother and Katrina that all did not go well with his conversation. "Can you talk to him?" He looked up at his mother, exasperated.

"About what?" Linda asked, stirring the soup and looking over her shoulder at him.

"The living arrangements."

Linda raised her eyebrows. "This doesn't change anything, André."

Katrina and André exchanged a look and she silently asked him to let it go. "We are married, damn it!"

"You are also just seventeen," Linda said as she turned her attention back to the pot on the stove.

"We are going to be parents!"

Linda glanced back at him and shrugged. "While you are under our roof, you play by our rules." She recited the mantra she and Matthew had agreed upon that first night. They planned to stick to their guns no matter what was thrown their way.

"Do you and Dad fucking practice that?" André snapped.

Linda turned on him. "That language is not to be used in this house!"

André stood up. "Fuck you!" he screamed and turned to storm out of the kitchen.

Matthew stood in the doorway, his face red with anger, and his open palm connected with André's cheek, the loud slap silencing everyone in the room. "You do not talk to your mother that way."

André's hand flew to his cheek, his eyes wide as both the sting of the slap and the surprise at finding Matthew blocking the doorway sunk in.

Katrina burst into tears and skirted by them, pausing long enough to give André a look conveying her disdain before bolting up the stairs.

André started after her but Matthew grabbed his arm. "Sit your ass down," Matthew growled and pointed at the kitchen chair.

André looked toward the stairs and back at his father. "No, Dad. I need to go talk to my wife." He yanked his arm, but Matthew's hand clamped around his biceps like a vise.

Matthew swung him around and into the kitchen chair, planting his face within inches of his. "Right now I don't give a damn what you want," he began. "You have royally screwed up that girl's life." He pointed toward the stairs. "You don't even have a clue, do you?"

André shrank away from him, confusion overtaking the anger. "What are you talking about?" he asked, his voice barely a whisper.

Matthew took a step back from André. "Whatever career aspirations she might have had, you have screwed. Do you know how hard it's going to be for her to finish high school with a child? Do you?"

André slowly shook his head.

"And college is going to be damn near impossible for both of you."

"So," André replied.

"How are you going to support your family?" Matthew asked.

André nodded toward Matthew. "The same way you do."

Matthew blinked. "You think Commander Lawrence is going to allow you in the military after what you've done to his daughter's life?"

André looked at his hands and shrugged. "Yeah," he mumbled, sheepishly looking up through his bangs.

Matthew laughed. "André, I have a doctorate in aeronautical engineering. I was in college for eight years before I enlisted. I wasn't a high school dropout. Do you know what happens to dropouts?"

André shook his head.

"They become losers living off society or criminals who end up either in prison or worse. So, what makes you think you can live the way I live? What makes you think the commander would give you any sort of chance?"

André looked at the floor. "Because I can teach people to do the things I can."

Matthew took a step backwards when André raised his eyes.

Fire red blazed over his eyes; his battle to hold in his anger began to waver. "I am smarter than any of the kids in my class and not one of them can do this." He tilted his head; the entire kitchen set lifted into the air. He smiled and set it back down. "Imagine being able to stop any threat aimed at you or someone you love without scrambling for a gun." His voice rumbled in his chest. "How much do you think that's worth?"

"How the hell are you going to do that?" He pointed at the kitchen set. "No one on Earth has that power."

"I can teach anyone to tap into their inner strengths, even you," André snapped.

"Bullshit," Matthew said.

André shrugged and got up to leave the kitchen. "Whatever," he said over his shoulder and wandered away, leaving Matthew and Linda in the kitchen staring after him.

MATTHEW SPUN TOWARD HIS wife. "Do you think he can?" His eyes grew wide with the possibilities. "Do you think it's even possible?"

Linda looked at the empty doorway and back to her husband. She took a deep breath. "Yes. I think he can do anything he puts his mind to, Matt," she said with a sigh. "André may not be all that swift on the common sense side of things, but academically, he is far superior to kids his age. And he has more insight into the human spirit than either of us. So yes, I think if he sees it, the possibility is there."

Matthew digested her answer and looked toward the door thoughtfully.

Linda stared at her hands, struggling with the next thing she wanted to say. "He may be seventeen in years the way we see them, Matt, but I think he's much older than that underneath."

He looked back at Linda.

"Sure, he still does some of the stupid things a normal teenager does..." She trailed off. "But..." She shook her head. She turned toward the forgotten dinner, turning the burners off and formulating her thoughts. "I've stood by the rule you laid down when they came back, but with this new development, I think they should be together," she said. "They're going to need each other, Matt."

Matthew sat down at the table.

She faced him. "We don't know how this pregnancy will work," she said bluntly. "And I'd rather André be with her. He'll know if something is wrong."

Matthew closed his eyes. "But he's just a child."

"That's where you are wrong, Matt. He isn't a child anymore," Linda replied.

"So we just give in to his every whim?" Matthew countered.

"No. But we have to trust that he's learned something from us. He's always had a clear idea of right and wrong." She walked over to Matthew. "What he did with Katrina wasn't wrong—stupid, yes, but not wrong." She smiled a little. "It was actually a bit romantic if you think about it."

Matthew rolled his eyes.

"Don't roll your eyes at me, Matthew Robbins," she scolded, putting her hands on her hips.

Matthew smirked, humor returning to his eyes after what seemed like weeks. "I'll roll my eyes any time I please," he replied, standing up and pulling her toward him. He kissed her gently. "So we give them what they want?"

She nodded. "In this case, I think it would be for the best."

Matthew sighed. "You want to tell them?"

"No, it needs to come from you."

"Crap," he muttered under his breath.

Linda heard the mutterings. "You dished out the punishment; you also get to be the one to give back the privileges. That's how it works, honey."

"Yeah, yeah," Matthew said as he headed out of the room and up the stairs. He hated the very idea of giving in.

ANDRÉ SAT ON THE bed with his arm around Katrina, looking expectantly at the doorway to Katrina's room when Matthew stuck his head in.

"You knew I was coming," Matthew stated.

André nodded.

"Do you know why?"

André half smiled and nodded, trying not to gloat.

Matthew sighed and nodded. "No sex."

André raised his eyebrows and looked at his father through his bangs. *Yeah, right.*

Katrina hit his stomach with the back of her hand, giving him a cross look.

"I'm serious, André," Matthew said.

"I know you are," André replied but he had no intention of agreeing to the stipulation.

Matthew went to leave but paused and looked back. "You can really teach people to control things and read minds?"

André nodded and glanced toward Katrina. "Show him."

Katrina bit her lip, glancing at Matthew. She turned her attention to the desk, staring at the pen that lay on her math book. A thin layer of perspiration broke out on her forehead as she willed the pen to move. She let out a hiss of air from her lips and the pen spun around in a circle. She smiled, but the effort obviously wiped her out.

André kissed her cheek. "Good job, babe." He looked over at Matthew.

Matthew's gaze bounced between the pen and André and back. "How long did that take?"

"A week," André answered.

Matthew's jaw dropped and he blinked rapidly, trying to grasp the concept. "How?" he asked when he recovered his composure.

André debated on telling him the process. "You didn't believe it was possible," he stalled and got up. "I need to get her a drink." He walked past his father and down to the kitchen, coming back in time to hear his father drilling Katrina.

"How, Katrina?"

Katrina shook her head and wiped her face with her hand. "I'm not sure. But now if I concentrate, I can do stuff. I can read minds, too, if I try." She looked at her hands. "I think this may be the reason I got sick, though. It takes a lot out of me."

André stepped in with a glass of orange juice and handed it to Katrina. Taking a seat next to her, he turned his attention to his father. "I can teach almost anyone," he said. "The only caveat is that the person has to trust me."

"Why is that?"

"I have to get into their head," André replied.

Matthew's brow furrowed. "Say again?"

"I have to get into their mind."

Matthew sat back. "Mind control?"

"Not exactly," André answered. "Mind control screws people up. It scrambles their brains a little." He shrugged. "This is different. It's more like opening a door that's been locked since birth." He studied the hangnail again and then glanced at Katrina. "I guess it hurts a little, too." He looked back at his father when Katrina nodded.

Matthew glanced between the two of them. "Okay, go for it." He leaned back with his arms out.

"Huh?" André grunted.

"Teach me," Matthew said, putting his hands on his thighs.

André blinked and glanced sideways at Katrina.

"It hurts," Katrina warned.

"You got through it." Matthew shrugged. "How bad can it be?"

André turned away from Katrina as a small laugh escaped his lips. His father just set her off with that statement.

"What, you think girls are wimpy?" Katrina shot back at her father-in-law, the anger in her eyes making Matthew smirk and shrug. She stalked out of the room in a huff, leaving André and Matthew staring after her.

"You just pissed her off," André replied with a grin.

"Seriously, how bad can it be?"

André shrugged in response. "Do you trust me, Dad?"

Matthew considered the question. "For the most part, yes."

"But not completely?"

Matthew shook his head. "No, not completely. There are some things that I don't trust you with. Katrina, for instance." Matthew pointed over his shoulder.

André blushed, shrugged and nodded. His father had good reason not to trust him with Katrina.

"But as far as putting my life in your hands, I trust that you wouldn't intentionally put me in harm's way."

André nodded. "I wouldn't." He sighed. "But if you have any doubts at all, I could end up really hurting you."

"Tell me how this works."

André shifted uncomfortably. "First I have to access the point where the brainstem attaches to the spinal cord."

"Define access," Matthew demanded.

André looked at the floor and back up. "I stuck a needle in Kat's neck."

The color drained from Matthew's face. "Then what?"

"Then I remove the needle and plug the cut with my finger. And from there, I'm able to access the person's mind." He shrugged. "Once I'm in, I break down the barrier that prevents humans from getting to the natural powers each of you already has." André wouldn't meet his father's gaze.

Matthew took a deep breath. "What aren't you telling me?"

André scanned his hand. The cut on his finger had healed from his venture with Katrina. "In order to get to your mind, I have to infuse my blood with yours."

Matthew digested what André told him; his eyes narrowed, and his brow furrowed. "And how'd you know this would work?"

André hesitated. He didn't have a reasonable answer to the question. "I just knew."

"You put Kat's life on the line on a whim?" Matthew balked.

"No. I can't tell you how I knew what to do or that it would work. I just did. Maybe I saw something similar when I was a kid but I can't be sure." He took a deep breath. "Do you want to do this or not?"

Matthew stood up and walked to the doorway. He paused with his hand on the door, shaking his head slightly at the internal debate. What Katrina had done was amazing. Finally, he closed the door, sweeping the doubts away and turning back to André. "Where do you want me?"

André pointed at the chair. "Face the back of the chair," he instructed. "And you can't move at all when I do this," André said. "Not even a fraction."

Matthew nodded and sat down just as André instructed. "I must be crazy."

André smiled a little and opened his top drawer, pulling out what looked like a long, thin sewing needle that measured roughly six inches in length. "Hang your head a little lower," André said, gently pushing his father's head down, clearly exposing the spinal cord on the back of his neck. "That's good," he said. André closed his eyes and took a deep breath as he ran his fingers along his father's spine, searching for the point on the base of the skull that he needed. His eyes opened when he found his mark. Glancing at the needle, he willed the tip to heat up. When the tip glowed, he swiftly plunged it into the point where his finger had been.

Matthew didn't move despite the sting of the needle and the sudden debilitating pain exploding in his head.

André yanked the needle out and slashed his finger with it, dropping it on the table as he covered the pinhole in his father's neck with the bloody tip of his finger. Closing his eyes, he let his mind follow the path of his blood into his father's brain.

Matthew sucked in air between his teeth audibly, the blood burning its way into his mind along with André. Bright patches of light replaced his crystal-clear vision as André's blood reached his brainstem. The pain he initially felt began to subside.

André followed the blood to the dark recesses of the brain, finding the film-like fiber separating the unconscious from the conscious psyche. With his mind's eye, he willed the barrier to shatter, watching it fall into microscopic bits on the floor of his father's mind. He felt Matthew's pain; the lights dancing on his eyelids increased in speed and frequency and he felt the physical flood of power filling his father.

"Jesus," Matthew said, letting a small protest of pain escape while he gripped the chair.

André worked quickly before the pain immobilized him. He swept the pieces into a pile and willed them to dissolve, leaving no trace of the original barrier. André physically and mentally pulled away from his father, breaking the contact between them. He sat down on the bed, getting his bearings back. His finger was still bleeding, and he put it in his mouth so the crimson liquid would not drip onto the carpet.

Matthew blinked his eyes open when the contact with André broke. The pounding in his cranium overrode all other sounds as blood and oxygen hydrated the long dormant recess of his brain. He felt like someone had taken a baseball bat to his head. "Sweet Jesus," he muttered and glanced over at André. "How long does this last?"

André pulled his finger out of his mouth. "Kat's headache only lasted an hour," he replied and reached for the tissues on the edge of the desk, wrapping one around his injured finger. "You probably should go lay down."

Matthew went to nod, and the pain exploded through his head, causing him to moan.

"You need help getting there?" André asked.

"Yes," Matthew replied, still partially blind from the pain.

André helped his father to his bedroom.

Matthew stretched out on the bed. "Tell Kat I'm sorry for giving her a hard time," he whispered, closing his eyes. "This hurts like a bitch."

Messiah Chapter 10

*D*ECEMBER 2239

André and Katrina walked into the complex hand in hand, heading toward Commander Lawrence's office. Matthew looked up from his desk, surprised when they walked by. Scrambling, he bolted into the hallway.

"What are you doing?" he asked, catching up to them.

"I thought I'd tell my father before I started to show," Katrina said.

Don't. Matthew sent the thought into both of their minds.

André and Katrina stopped and looked at Matthew.

"Today is not a good day." They had just enforced another death sentence and the commander was in a particularly foul mood.

"It's almost Christmas," André said. "Kat hasn't seen her father since we came back from Chicago, Dad."

Matthew nodded. "I'm aware of that." The commander asked about Katrina every day but refused to come to the house to see her or pick up the phone and call. He was still angry about the whole situation, and this would not help. "But you shouldn't ambush him at the office."

Katrina glanced toward her father's office. "He's always moody after an execution."

"So, we do this another time?" André asked.

Katrina nodded and turned to leave.

Commander Lawrence stopped when he saw Katrina, André, and Matthew in his path.

"Too late," André whispered as he and Commander Lawrence locked eyes.

"What the hell are you doing here?" The commander glared at André.

"Hi, Daddy," Katrina said trying to run interference.

The commander had every intention of throttling André, and Matthew stepped in front of the kids, blocking Commander Lawrence.

"Colonel, get out of my way," the commander said, switching his gaze to Matthew, the anger that had been simmering inside for the past four months bubbling to the surface.

Matthew shook his head. "You don't want to do what you're thinking," he stated, hearing the commander's thoughts. Since André performed his barrier-breaking ritual, Matthew could read others' thoughts without trying.

Commander Lawrence glared at Matthew. "How the hell do you know what I'm thinking?"

"Because it's written all over your face," Matthew replied. "Sir." Matthew snapped to attention as an afterthought.

Commander Lawrence returned the salute with a glare. He focused his attention back to André and Katrina.

"Dad, your office may be a better place to talk than the hallway," Katrina said.

Commander Lawrence nodded and headed to his office with Katrina and André in tow.

Matthew stayed behind against his better judgment. He watched as Commander Lawrence closed his office door, but not before the two men exchanged eye contact. "Shit." Matthew turned toward his office. He paused and shook his head to clear the waves of thoughts assaulting his mind, concentrating on only the few he wanted to hear. His eyes widened and he turned back, heading toward the commander's office slowly at first, and then breaking into a run as his internal alarms sounded.

"Dad, no!" Katrina screamed.

Matthew flew into the room in time to see the knife the commander held run into André's stomach. His anger flashed, unleashing a power burst that sent the commander sailing across the room, away from his son. Matthew bolted to André's side, assessing the damage. "What the hell do you think you're doing?" he yelled at his commander, glaring in his direction. He looked at Katrina. "Call 911," he ordered as he pressed his hand on the cut and looked at André's ashen face.

"I guess he really doesn't want to be a grandfather." André laughed and then grimaced in pain.

Commander Lawrence stood up. "The freak threw me across the room." He still held the bloody knife.

"No, I did." Matthew glanced back at him.

The commander's eyes narrowed. "You?"

Matthew nodded and returned his focus to his son. "How are you doing?"

Katrina hung up with emergency services and returned to André's side. She cast a glare at her father. "I can't believe you tried to kill him, Daddy."

Medics and military police barged into the commander's office, interrupting the family squabble.

"Arrest him," the commander bellowed, pointing at André.

Matthew stood up, blocking the path of the military police. He shook his head. "No. Commander Lawrence attacked this young man without provocation." He looked at his long-time friend. "Sam, you crossed the line."

"He got my daughter pregnant—that's plenty of provocation," Commander Lawrence snapped.

"He's my husband," Katrina said, standing up as the medics took over.

André looked at the nametag of one of the medics and smiled as he raised his eyes to the familiar face. "Hi, Officer Grey."

The medic studied the boy's face and offered André a smile. "It's Captain now, son," he said.

"Think you can fix me?" André asked, his complexion pale as shock threatened to take over.

Cal inspected the wound. "Not a problem." He looked back up at the scene unfolding in the commander's office.

"He stabbed my husband," Katrina snapped, pointing at her father. "He's the one who needs to be arrested."

The confused MPs looked between Matthew, Katrina and the commander. The commander still had the weapon in his hand and that clinched the decision.

"Drop the knife, sir," Captain Shaw, the head military police officer ordered. He put his hand on the laser gun at his side.

"Excuse me?" Commander Lawrence balked.

"The knife, sir. Please drop it," Captain Shaw said for the second time, unclipping the laser and setting it to stun in one motion. He pointed it at the commander.

Commander Lawrence glanced at the bloody knife that he still gripped and then around the room at the faces. His eyes fell on André. "Son of a bitch," he growled and took a step toward them, the knife still clamped in his fist.

"Stand down, sir!" Captain Shaw shouted and when Commander Lawrence ignored him, he shot the laser gun, slamming a debilitating shock into the commander's chest, knocking him backwards onto the ground.

André's expression changed, his eyes widening as he watched the commander convulsing on the floor. "He's not okay." He his eyes to his father. "Dad, he isn't okay."

Matthew turned toward the commander. "Cal, the commander needs help!" he said loud enough to call the attention of everyone within earshot.

Cal turned. "Shit." He bolted across the room, leaving André in the hands of the second medic. He grabbed the flailing arm holding the knife and pinned it to the floor under his knee. The commander's face turned blue, and his eyes rolled back in his head as he flopped like a fish out of water. Cal forced open the commander's jaws, reaching in, grasping the tip of his tongue and yanked as the commander's teeth clamped shut on his fingers. "God damn!" he screamed, trying to free his crushed fingers. He forced open the commander's jaws enough to yank his hand out, pulling his bloody fingers to his chest. "Sandy, I need your help with this one, otherwise we're going to lose him," Cal shouted.

The commander stopped convulsing and his chest remained still, his eyes wide and glossy, staring at the ceiling and Matthew shivered, almost feeling the commander's passing.

The medics worked frantically to revive the commander, but with each failed attempt, his son's overwhelming sadness permeated his mind, and he glanced over as Katrina knelt beside him.

"I'm sorry, Kat." He glanced in her direction, his face hot with red-tinged tears. "I'm so sorry."

Katrina's expression slowly registered what was happening and she glanced back at the medics working on her father. She sat down hard on the floor by André.

All this seemed to flow in slow motion and Matthew looked at the small crowd peering into the room from the hallway. He stepped to the door and closed it on the curious onlookers, turning back to the room and focusing on Captain Shaw.

"I had the laser on stun," he said, showing Matthew the setting.

Matthew nodded. "I wasn't accusing you of anything, Captain."

"It was on stun," the captain repeated.

"I know," Matthew replied. He glanced back at André and Katrina. André was pale, with streaks of bloody tears running down his cheeks. He turned his attention back to the military police. "Captain Shaw, what's the protocol here?" he asked, trying to get his focus away from the medic's vain attempts to revive the commander.

"You are second-in-command, sir." Captain Shaw said. "Ordinarily when the commander retires or passes on, the second-in-command takes the post."

"This isn't an ordinary situation, Captain."

Captain Shaw nodded, staring at his dead commander on the floor. He returned his gaze to Matthew and then beyond the colonel at the two teenagers. Taking a deep breath, he returned Matthew's questioning stare. "It looks like the commander had a heart attack while visiting with his daughter," he stated.

Matthew's eyebrows creased. "What about my son?"

"An accident that resulted from the heart attack," Captain Shaw replied.

Cal looked up at Matthew and Captain Shaw. "Accident, my ass. He stabbed that kid."

Matthew shot a warning glance at Cal. "As far as everyone in this room is concerned, it was an accident. Got it?" he said with authority.

"It was an accident," André echoed from behind Matthew.

Captain Shaw holstered the gun. "Are you all right?" he asked the boy.

André shrugged.

Cal looked at his partner. "Call it," he said.

"Time of death fifteen forty-five," she said as she glanced at her watch.

"Captain Shaw, you are dismissed." Matthew picked up the phone on the desk, placing a call to the president to inform him that the commander had passed away.

Cal crossed to André checking his wound and meeting his gaze. A flurry of questions flew through his head, including why the commander had stabbed him.

"Just patch me up and forget about it," André said under his breath and received a slight nod in response.

Cal glanced at Katrina and back to André. "You're married?"

André nodded. "Four months ago."

"Aren't you a little young?"

André shifted under the weight of Katrina. "Ouch," he responded as the pain exploded in his side. The room started to spin, and André blinked. "Shit." He passed out cold, slumping onto Katrina.

Cal pushed Katrina out of the way and laid André on the ground, cutting the shirt away.

Matthew looked in their direction, still holding for the president. He felt the blood drain from his face at the sight and considered hanging up as the president himself picked up the line. "Sir, I'm calling to inform you that Commander Lawrence had a fatal heart attack in his office," he said, his voice absent of the concern racing through him.

Cal grabbed the medical bag and found a bottle of iodine, dumping it in the cut and praying that André wasn't allergic to the sterile liquid. "Sandy, hold the wound open." He reached for the cauterization laser. He handed her the lighting instrument after she opened the wound with a retractor. Shining the light inside illuminated the path of the knife and Cal blew out a stream of air. Carefully, he pointed the laser and cauterized the cut on the large intestine. He looked up at Sandy. "Can you turn it to make sure we got the entire cut?"

The color drained from Katrina's face as she watched the medic reach in to inspect André's guts.

"Looks like you got it, Captain," Sandy said.

"Okay, remove the retractors, please," he instructed. When the skin flapped back together, Cal used the laser to cauterize the entry wound, leaving a dark black line of melded skin where the gaping knife wound had been.

André's breathing remained shallow through the impromptu surgery and Cal picked up André's wrist, searching for his pulse. The result was sporadic at best, and he took a deep breath, closing his eyes. "Come on, kid, I can't lose you too."

Matthew's eyes went wide with those words, especially in concert with Cal's thoughts, thoughts centering on blood transfusion and the conversation they had years ago about risks. He hung up on the president and crossed the room, falling to his knees next to André and leaning close to his ear. "Don't you die, you hear me?" he demanded of his unconscious child. "You hear me?" His command filled the room.

André's eyes fluttered open. "I'm not deaf, Dad." He looked up at his father, weariness reflecting in his eyes.

Katrina let out a startled laugh and threw herself onto André, covering his face with kisses and tears. "You scared the hell out of me." She sat back up.

Cal still had the fingers of his good hand on André's arm, feeling the pulse in his patient return to normal. "Glad to have you back."

"It still hurts like hell," he said. "But you did a pretty good patch job." He looked at the scar on his side. "And I wasn't even close to dying," he replied. "I did pass out, but I thought it was better for me to stay checked out while you did your thing."

"You were aware of what we were doing?"

André nodded. "Yes. I did the same thing on the ship. I slowed down my body functions to conserve energy." He shrugged. "It saved oxygen."

Cal sighed. "You still amaze me, kiddo."

Matthew focused on Sandy. "None of this is to leave this room, understand?"

Sandy looked at Matthew, and then back at Cal. "Who is this kid?"

Cal glanced at her. "You don't have clearance," he answered, keeping the secret in check.

Sandy sat back on her heels, surprised by the response of her superior officer. "And you do?"

"Yup," Cal replied and winked at André. "And if you breathe a word of this, I'll have you court-martialed." He glanced at Sandy.

"Yes, sir," she answered with an unhappy pout. She looked over at André and he shrugged a little in her direction.

The phone on the desk rang, making all of them jump. Matthew answered it before the second ring. "I'm sorry, sir, I had an issue to attend to."

"I'm an issue now," André whispered, allowing a crooked smile to grace his features. He glanced at Katrina and his smile disappeared. "I'm sorry about your father."

Katrina's chin began to shake, and she nodded as fresh tears spilled from her eyes.

André reached for her, putting his hand on her cheek. "Ah, baby," he whispered, forgetting that there were others in the room. He leaned forward and kissed her gently on the cheek.

"He'll never know his grandchild."

"Kat, I'm not sure he would have anyway," André replied.

Cal and his partner were packing up the medical supplies and he looked in the direction of Katrina and André. "You're expecting?"

She nodded in response.

He glanced at André, and then at the covered deceased commander and back. He raised his eyebrows. *Is that why?*

André heard Cal's thought and shrugged. *Please let it go.* André half nodded and glanced in the direction of Sandy.

"Corporal, you're dismissed," Cal stated and watched as his partner shuffled the supplies out of the office, closing the door behind her. He glanced in the direction of the colonel and then at André. "You can read minds?"

André sent a glance in his father's direction and then back to the captain. He figured if his father and Cal schemed to get the commander to agree to letting him stay with Matthew, he could level with him without worry. "Yes."

"He can teach people to do the things he can," Katrina said, wiping her face.

Cal rubbed his chin with his uninjured hand, considering the possibilities. His left hand still dripped from the bite wounds the commander inflicted, blood staining the carpet where he stood, his mind whirling.

Matthew slowly hung up the phone and glanced at André and Katrina. He moved his eyes to Cal. "I know what you're thinking," he stated. "I thought the same thing but it's a big responsibility."

Cal shifted his gaze back at André. "What else can you do?" he asked, looking down at his hand.

"I can't fix your hand," André replied to the question in Cal's mind. "The power to heal is a myth; the power to control your body functions so a wound doesn't kill you isn't." He stood up with the help of Katrina, glancing at his father. "You're the Commander now?" he asked.

Matthew nodded glancing at the covered body of his friend on the floor. The president had promoted him over the phone. "Yes." He finally verbalized the reply.

"So, are you going to let me enlist?" André asked.

Matthew gaped at his son. "You have to finish high school," he replied. There was no leeway in his answer.

André took a deep breath. "I can help you create a special force of soldiers, Dad."

"To do what?" Matthew snapped.

"To protect and preserve the laws of the United States."

"André, this is not a discussion I am having with you. You have to finish high school first before I will even entertain such a thought." He glanced at Katrina. "Besides, you'll have a child in six months. Your priorities may change when you're a father."

Cal still stood in the center of the room. "Once you teach someone, can they teach someone else?"

"No," André answered. "I mean, once the barrier in a person's mind is broken, yes, they can help teach someone to use their own powers, but I'm the only one who can break the barrier."

Intrigued, Cal asked, "Why?"

André allowed a crooked smile. "Because I'm not from around here."

Cal looked at Matthew. "I'd like to volunteer."

Matthew shook his head. "Not now, Captain." *Maybe in a few years.*

Cal nodded and saluted his commanding officer. "Yes, sir." He glanced at André once again as he picked up his radio. "I need someone to come collect the body of Commander Lawrence," he transmitted.

"Already on the way," a voice squawked from the other end. A knock on the door sounded in unison.

"You two need to get home," Matthew said to André and Katrina.

"Yes, sir." André led Katrina out of the room as members of the coroner's office converged.

Messiah Chapter 11

*M*AY 2240
Matthew was in his office when the call came in.

"Dad?" André's voice came over the intercom.

"Yes?" Matthew said. He was reading a brief and wasn't giving the call his full attention.

"Kat's in labor," André said, his voice strained, and near panic.

Matthew's attention snapped to the phone as both the words and the emotion from his son reached the recesses of Matthew's mind. "What?"

"Kat's in labor. What do I do?"

"Where are you?"

"We were at school when her water broke. I brought her home."

"Where's your mother?"

"I don't know," André said. "She's in labor," he repeated.

"Get her to the hospital, you idiot," Matthew said, shooting out of his chair. "I'll meet you there."

THE SIMPLICITY OF WHAT his father just said made him laugh aloud. He panicked to the point of stupidity. "Okay. I'll see you there," André replied and hung up the phone.

André collected Katrina and brought her to the hospital.

"It's going to be okay," André said, pulling up to the emergency room. He put his arm around her waist and led her into the hospital, escorting her to the reception desk. "My wife's in labor," he announced.

The nurse looked up and her brow furrowed.

"My wife is in labor," he replied. "Her water broke at school," he added, looking in Katrina's direction.

Katrina groaned as the next contraction ripped through her.

The nurse responded immediately, coming around and leading Katrina to a room nearby and getting her settled on the bed with a soft pillow and a blanket, explaining the process. "Once the doctor takes a look, we'll transport you up to the maternity ward." She left the two of them alone.

Katrina squeezed André's hand so hard, he thought it would break, but he didn't say a word, just smiled at her and wiped the hair out of her face, keeping his frantic thoughts to himself.

"Something's wrong," she gasped.

André put his hand on her stomach and his smile faded. She was right; something was very wrong. The emotions he picked up from their child were not the simple contentment he had felt over the last four months; no, this was alarm wrapped around agonizing pain. Pulling his hand away, he lifted the blanket. The bedding under Katrina was soaked with blood and the flow just kept coming.

"Jesus," he gasped, and his gaze shot up, meeting her wide, scared eyes. "You need to slow your body functions down, Kat," he ordered. "I'll be right back. Just concentrate on what I taught you. Okay?"

"Don't leave me!"

"I have to get the doctor. Slow your heart down, Kat. Right now," he commanded and bolted out of the room.

André's eyes darted both ways down the hall, zeroing in on a doctor leaning on the nurse's station, flirting with the nurse who had brought them to the room. "My wife is bleeding," he announced as he flew to the doctor and grabbed his arm. "You have to do something."

"Hold up, son," the doctor said, trying to pull out of André's grasp.

André shot a warning look at him. "She is hemorrhaging. There's blood all over the bed. You need to get the baby out and fix her. Now." He shoved the doctor through the door into the room.

The doctor's irritation ended abruptly at the sight that met him. "Nurse!" he yelled and went into action.

The nurse stepped into the room and stopped in her tracks, the amount of blood daunting even to a professional, but she recovered, turning to André. "Sir, you need to leave while they work on your wife," she said.

André shook his head and moved closer to Katrina, putting his hand on the top of her head. "She's my wife. I'm not leaving her," he insisted, threading his fingers into her hair. *Come on, baby; you can do it. Just hang on.*

"She needs surgery, and you can't go in with us," the doctor snapped.

"Yes I can. All you have to do is get me scrubs."

The doctor shot a glance at André as they began to roll Katrina out of the room.

"I'm not leaving her," André insisted. "I promised her I wouldn't."

"She won't know any different," the nurse said as they rolled by.

André glared at her and pushed. "Get me a pair of scrubs, now," he growled low.

She blinked, nodded and wandered away, coming back a few minutes later with what he asked for.

André changed into the thin, sterile fabric, putting the mask over his face and the cap over his hair. He walked into the operating room and sat down near Katrina's head. "I'm here." He closed his eyes, putting his forehead against hers for a moment. "Just don't die, okay?" He kissed her temple and pulled away, allowing the anesthesiologist to put the oxygen mask over her mouth and nose. The IV was already in her arm, pumping medicine, anesthesia, and precious blood into her system.

Surgeons converged, paying little attention to André, who stayed close to Katrina's head with his gloved hand lying gently on her shoulder. Within minutes, they pulled his child from Katrina's abdomen and handed him off to the nursing staff before returning their attention to finding the hemorrhage site and stopping the bleeding.

André turned his attention away from the flurry of thoughts in the surgeon's head to the nurses and the child they were cleaning and swaddling. A boy. His son. He bit his lip and squeezed his eyes closed, dousing the tears from starting. Joy and trepidation lined his stomach, and he shot the thought to Katrina. *A son. We have a son, babe.*

The baby let out a healthy cry from the other side of the room and André smiled. "The baby's just fine," he whispered in Katrina's ear.

"Damn it, her blood pressure's dropping," the surgeon swore. With seconds to decide, he did the only thing he could to save her life; he took out her uterus.

André understood what happened even without the doctor's frantic thoughts. Any chance of another child died with the doctor's actions and for a few precarious moments, Katrina almost followed, but the doctor was able to find the source of the hemorrhage and cauterize it, closing down the uncontrollable fountain of blood.

Hanging his head, he let the tears slip out, but contained the sob that threatened. Relief, joy, and sorrow all culminated into a perfect storm of emotion; he swallowed the cyclone, diffusing it for the sake of his son. He glanced in the direction of the wailing child and wiped his face with the hem of his scrubs, standing and heading in the direction of the noise.

The nursing staff frantically rinsed and re-rinsed the baby's eyes, trying to stop what they thought was bleeding.

"He isn't hurt," André said. "He just takes after me." His son's wails ceased at the sound of his voice and the tiny blue-eyed gaze landed on André.

"Hi." André smiled, pulling his mask down so his son could see his face.

The crowd of nurses stared at André. "You shouldn't be in here," one of them said.

André glanced up, his eyes shining with a film of bloody tears, and shrugged. "I wasn't leaving my wife." He reached down, picking up his son for the first time. "Hey, little man. Your mama is going to be just fine." André glanced over his shoulder at Katrina.

The doctor finished cauterizing the wounds with the lasers and stepped away, peeling off his gloves. "You've been here the whole time?"

When André nodded, the doctor exchanged a glance with the ER nurse who was supposed to escort him to the waiting room. He turned back to André. "Do you understand what happened?"

André nodded. "You saved her life," André said with his son safely propped against his shoulder. He gently rocked, trying not to let sadness overtake the joy. His son could feel it as well and let out a sorrowful squeal. His gaze shifted from his wife to the baby in his arms. "We have this little guy," he added with a small smile, but a tear betrayed him, cutting a hot path down his cheek despite the cold operating room. He kissed the top of the baby's head.

"What's his name?" one of the nurses asked, pulling a chart off the wall and a pen from a hidden inside pocket.

"Samuel Matthew Robbins," André replied. He and Katrina tossed around names for the past six months and decided on naming the child after their parents, whether it was a girl or boy. The only thing that had still been undecided was the order of the names but André alone made that decision with his son in his arms. "When will Kat wake up?" He pointed his chin at his wife.

"In about an hour," she replied. "We'll bring her into the maternity ward once she wakes. They have a room all set. Follow me."

André stepped into the maternity room, still in full scrubs with Sam in his arms.

MATTHEW TURNED. "YOUR MOTHER'S on her way," he said.

"We have a son." André cradled Sam in his arms so his father could see. "Samuel Matthew," he added.

Matthew looked up at André, touched by the gesture. "How's Katrina?" His gaze returned to the baby.

André took a deep breath. "She can't have any more."

Matthew's head shot up, his eyes meeting André's.

"She almost died." André handed his son to his father. The levity of the situation hit him like a meteor storm.

"Is she ok?"

André nodded and sat down in the chair, burying his face in his hands. "I almost killed her." Tears dripped from his palms while sobs ripped from his chest.

"Son, you can't blame yourself for this," Matthew said.

"She almost died giving birth to my son," André said, looking up at his father. "If I hadn't gotten her pregnant…"

The baby let out an unhappy wail.

Matthew put the baby against his shoulder and patted his back, cooing in his ear. He turned his attention back to André. "Even with all the advancements we have in medicine, women still die in childbirth, André. It happens. Be thankful she's alive." He rocked his grandson.

André sniffled and wiped his hands on the front of the scrubs, smearing the bloody tears across the fabric. His father was right; he should be thankful instead of homing in on the scariest part of the day. He had a son. They had a son.

Wandering into the bathroom, he peeled off his shirt, tossing it in a bin on the floor before splashing his face with cold water and washing the tracks away. He gave a strained smile to his reflection and stepped back into the room, shirtless. "I don't know where my clothes ended up." He put his hands out for his son.

Matthew relinquished his grandson into André's capable hands. "I'll go see if I can find them for you."

"Hey, little man." André smiled down at his son. "Are you getting hungry?"

Sam cooed and kicked his legs, flailing his tiny arms and prompting a grin from André.

"All right, let's see if we can get someone to give us a hand." He headed out of the room to the nurse's station.

The young nurse looked up when André cleared his throat. Her eyes went a fraction wider like a switch flipped, putting André in a spotlight. He shifted. Her lingering gaze and her dirty thoughts made him squirm.

"Um, how can I help you?" A predatory smile surfaced.

"My son is hungry," he explained, blushing at the forwardness of her inspection, and the kinkiness of her thoughts.

She nodded and disappeared for a second. When she returned, she handed him a bottle. "Here. Do you know how to feed a baby?" She gave him the once-over again.

André shrugged. "I'll figure it out." He hurried away, knowing the nurse was watching him, his ass in particular, and he sighed a breath of relief when he cleared the door into the room. Taking the corner seat, he propped the bottle in the baby's mouth.

Sam suckled immediately.

André looked down at his son and back at the door, still privy to the nurse's fantasy and he could feel the heat in his cheeks. When he looked down at Sam again, he had finished the bottle and was now sucking air. He pulled the bottle out, setting it on the table and put Sam on his shoulder. Rubbing the baby's back, he smiled when Sam let out a gargantuan burp.

Matthew walked in just as André finished swaddling Sam in the crib.

"I found your clothes." He handed the garments to André.

"Thank you." André grabbed them from his father's grasp. He disappeared into the bathroom and came out fully dressed a couple of minutes later.

Matthew gently rocked his sleeping grandson and looked up at André. "What's wrong?"

André started to laugh a little. "I really have no idea." He glanced out in to the hallway and caught sight of the nurse at the desk. He looked back at his father. "I think the nurse came on to me," he said, and the disbelief was rampant in his tone.

Matthew tilted his head, glancing into the hallway and back at André. "You're kidding?"

André shook his head. "I went to get a bottle for Sam and it was like I turned on a light switch. She was looking at me like I was her next meal."

MATTHEW KEPT HIS MOUTH shut. He saw the iridescent glow in his son's eyes when he came in the room, the one Katrina referred to as his booty call gaze. Instead of voicing his skepticism, or giving André a warning about stepping over the line, he chose to focus on his sleeping grandchild, but that was short-lived.

Linda walked in the room and smiled, taking notice of André, perking up in his presence like she'd never done before. "Hi there," she said, ignoring Matthew and approaching André. *Yummy.* Her eyes drifted over her adoptive son as if she were seeing him for the first time.

"Jesus, Mom," André said, pushing the chair back into the corner with his feet. He looked at his father for help.

"Linda?" Matthew said, interrupting her disturbing train of thought.

André pointed toward the baby in Matthew's arms. "My son," he said, not knowing what else to say.

Linda turned toward the sleeping baby in her husband's arms.

I told you. André sent his wide-eyed glance in Matthew's direction.

Flabbergasted by the iridescent glaze of André's eyes and the horny look on Linda's face, Matthew stared between the two, picking up Linda's silent fantasies and André's horrified reaction.

"What's his name?" Linda asked.

"Samuel Matthew," André answered and exhaled when her thoughts turned away from explicit sex tricks to her grandson, but he felt dirty just the same.

RELIEF WASHED OVER ANDRÉ when they wheeled Katrina into the room. Her eyes stood at half-mast, groggy and unfocused until they landed on him. Then it was as if a tidal wave washed away the haze, leaving only her and André in the room.

André and his booty call smile.

He shot to his feet and approached the bed. "Hi, babe," he said, taking her hand and wiping the offending smile off his face.

She pulled him to her lips, planting a deep, hungry kiss, one she shouldn't have been capable of in her post-operative state. Breathless, she gasped a quick hello when he pulled away from her lip lock.

"We have a little boy. Samuel Matthew. Do you want to hold our son?"

Katrina nodded, still staring at André, her eyes glued to him and her mind rampant with desires to the point he stopped halfway to the crib, sending her a *stop that* look, his pointed gaze traveling from her to his father and back. *He can hear you.*

Blinking, Katrina shook her head, trying to rid the dirty thoughts before her father-in-law caught them, but from the look on his face, she was too late. Instead, she focused on the baby André gathered in his arms.

Their son.

Their perfect tiny bundle.

Once in her waiting arms, she gazed down at the small heart-shaped face, her breath taken away by just how beautiful he was, just like his father. Her gaze wandered back to André. "He is perfect."

André offered a smile and kissed her cheek before exchanging a quick glance with Matthew. "Kat, did the doctor talk to you yet?"

Katrina tore her eyes away from her son. "No, why?"

He inhaled and bit his lip. Both actions lit her up, spreading a familiar heat through her and her thoughts digressed, drifting back to their wedding day.

"Stop thinking about that," André said. His thoughts jumped there right with hers and his lips tilted in a slight grin before he banished the memory and continued, "You were in serious trouble, Kat," he said, his eyes growing sad. "The doctor had to do more than just a C-section."

His sincerity and sorrow bit into her, knocking all thoughts of their prior escapades out of her mind. "What does that mean?"

André tilted his head. "We can't have any more kids."

The words cut through her as effectively as a knife. "What?" she said, knowing full well what he just told her but unable to fully digest the information.

"We won't be having any more kids," he repeated. "On the upside, you won't ever have to worry about your period."

His attempt at levity was lost on her, and her gaze dropped to the baby in her arms. "He's the only one?"

"Yes," André replied. "He is a very special little boy."

Katrina glanced back at André, tears blurring her vision. "He certainly is." She absently wiped one as it slid down her cheek. "I tried to slow down my heart like you said."

"You did. The doctor said it was a miracle you lived. You should have bled out before they got you to the operating room." He touched her face. "I almost killed you," he whispered, his eyes taking on the red sheen of tears.

"Bullshit. Even if it *was* the nature of the pregnancy and not a fluke, I would do it again in a second if I could." She touched their son's face and his little eyes fluttered opened, revealing the iridescent blue that matched his fathers at the moment. "Hi, angel boy." She kissed her son on the forehead.

THE DOCTOR DISRUPTED THE moment as he bound into the room. "Well, well, well, you're awake. You gave us all quite a scare, young lady." He stepped to her side, picked up her wrist and checked her pulse the old-fashioned way. Satisfied, he continued, "I'm not sure how much you recall from last night, but in order to stop the hemorrhaging, we had to perform an emergency hysterectomy." He looked between André and Katrina. "Do you understand what that means?"

Katrina nodded. "André said we can't have any more kids."

"That's correct." He opened the chart and scanned the list of her vitals before returning his focus to them.

"It looks like you're doing well; however, we still want you to stay for another night to make sure there are no complications relating to the transfusion. We can talk about what restrictions you'll be under, tomorrow."

"How long will she be under restriction?" André asked, more curious about what she was limited to.

"Six weeks. She won't be able to lift anything heavier than your son for six weeks or participate in any strenuous activities. Which means sexual intercourse is also on hiatus during that period." He closed the chart. "Any questions?"

"No sex?" André asked, ignoring the look from his parents.

The doctor nodded. "Usually with a C-section, it's eight weeks."

It was André's turn to raise his eyebrows. "Eight weeks?"

"Six in your situation," the doctor clarified.

"A year," Matthew said, gaining the attention of everyone in the room. "Not until you're both eighteen."

André laughed aloud and looked back at the doctor. "Six weeks," he agreed with shimmering eyes.

The doctor smiled. He checked the cauterization on her stomach and pressed lightly on her abdomen. "Does this hurt?"

"No," Katrina answered, her eyes glued on André and his smile. Her heart fluttered under his stare and everyone else in the room disappeared. The cry of her son broke through the haze, and she dragged her eyes away from her husband to her little boy.

"He's hungry," André said. It was the same tone of discontent the baby had earlier.

Katrina raised her gaze to the doctor.

"I'll send the nurse in with some formula. I'd rather you not breastfeed until after you are medicine free." He disappeared and the nurse who flirted with André earlier came in.

"Hello. I'm Nancy." Her gaze meandered toward André. She let her eyes drift over his body and then directed her attention back to Katrina.

Katrina took note of the way the nurse looked at André and shot a questioning glance in his direction. He shrugged in response and stepped away so the nurse could hand Katrina the bottle of formula she carried. The nurse left with a lingering glance in André's direction.

"What did you do to her?" Katrina asked.

On that accusatory note, Matthew and Linda left the room.

André shrugged. "I don't know. Ever since Sam was born, the women around here have been acting funny," he drawled and sat on the edge of the bed. "Including you," he said, reaching out and touching her face.

Katrina closed her eyes at his touch and her body ignited. "Holy crap, André, you have got to stop doing that." Her cheeks took on a rose hue and she opened her eyes.

"Doing what? I'm not doing anything."

"Turning on the sex vibe," she said. "It's rolling off you." Katrina shifted Sam, propping him a little lower and making sure he wasn't sucking air along with formula.

"The sex vibe?" The ridiculousness of her statement sent him over the edge, and he doubled over, laughing so hard that his eyes misted red.

Her reaction was less than humorous; her pouty lips thinned, and her mind filtered to the word *jackass.*

André wound down, still chuckling and staring at her. "Sex vibe?"

"Yes. Sex vibe." She pulled the empty bottle out of Sam's mouth and propped him on her shoulder, gently patting his back like she had done while babysitting the bratty neighbors when she was in junior high.

"I'm sorry to disappoint you, babe, but I ain't doing anything different."

She raised her eyebrow. "When you can turn me and every other female on in a ten-block radius with only a smile, you're doing something different."

"Baby, I don't know what to do with that," he said, still chuckling.

"Stop with the vibe."

"I'm not doing anything!"

"Yeah, right." The skeptical eyebrow remained arched.

André scoffed and reached, taking Sam from her and putting him on his shoulder, patting gently, and was rewarded with a burp. The prospect of a sex vibe emanating from him was as ludicrous as him taking flight. Still, beneath the unhappy expression lay a smoldering fire and he sent a smirk and a wink in her direction before cradling his sleepy baby in his arms. "We have a little boy, Kat." His smile softened as he took in his son, running his finger gently over his little features. He looked back at his wife. "Our son." The reality ebbed in.

Katrina put her hands over her heart, realizing she was the luckiest woman on the planet to have his love and devotion. She sighed and closed her eyes, giving in to the sudden exhaustion.

When André looked up, Katrina was sleeping peacefully with a slight smile on her face. "Your momma is one tired lady," he whispered to Sam and got a coo in return, followed immediately by a yawn. Sam settled into his father's arms and drifted off. André soon followed both his wife and son into sleep.

ANDRÉ WOKE HOURS LATER in the dark with empty arms and Nurse Nancy kneeling between his legs. Her hands found his zipper and tugged, and it took André a few seconds for his confused sleep-infested brain to understand this wasn't a dream.

With a blink and a shove, he pushed her away, zipping up his pants. "No," he hissed.

"Shh, no one has to know."

"I'll know." He tried to push the chair farther into the corner to put some distance between him and the minx in front of him, but he was trapped, and she was determined.

"Get out," he gasped, pointing at the door.

"You don't want this?" She pouted and slid her finger between her lips, pulling it out slowly, suggesting what she had in mind.

He knew a locker room full of guys who would give their right arm to wake up to an older woman with her head between their legs, but he wasn't one of them, especially with Katrina less than an arm's length away. "No," he said. "I don't." *You don't want me.* He pushed the thought harder than he meant to and she winced at the power of it.

The nurse blinked in confusion and got to her feet, straightening out her uniform before wandering out of the room without comment.

André went into the bathroom and closed the door, exhaustion overtaking his confused mind. "What the hell?" he asked his reflection and then splashed cold water on his face to erase the images from behind his eyelids. "Sex vibe?" he muttered and finally understood what Katrina alluded to. "Shit. How long is this going to last?" He took a deep breath, almost laughing aloud.

He wiped his face and stepped back in the dark room, crossing to check on Sam. The baby slept peacefully in the crib next to the bed and André looked down at him with a small smile, gently laying his hand on the baby's head before he slid into bed next to Katrina. Pulling her against him, he kissed the back of her neck as she slept. She let out a soft moan at his touch and burrowed closer but didn't wake. André closed his eyes.

The cry of their son filled the space and André sat up, disoriented by the bright, sunny room.

Katrina rolled over next to him, blinking and wiping the sleep from her eyes. "What time is it?" She yawned.

"I have no clue," André replied, his voice raspy from sleeping. He got out of the bed and wandered over to the portable crib. "Hey there," he croaked, smiling at his crying child. He changed the diaper and brought Sam to Katrina along with a bottle, crawling back into the narrow hospital bed.

André smiled up at Katrina. "Morning," he said as an afterthought and kissed her gently.

"Morning." Her smile faded with his silent confession.

"You let her?" She gasped.

"No. I was asleep and when I woke, she was there. I stopped her before anything happened. I wasn't thinking straight, and I used the influence on her, much harder than I meant to, so I don't think she'll remember a thing." He sat up and swung his legs over the side of the bed, wiping his face with his hands.

"I hope you scrambled her fucking brains," Katrina snapped.

"Kat, watch your language."

"Bite me."

He reached out to touch her face and she knocked his hand away. "Not now." The edge of a smile curved her lips as his vibe began to affect her. She shook her head angrily. "Stop that," she said, blushing.

"Stop what? I'm not doing anything!" He stood and began to pace around the room, stopping at the window to watch the last of the sunrise.

"You are," Katrina said, her aggravation diffusing with his predatory gait. *You really don't know what you're doing, do you?*

André sighed and shook his head, glancing back at her. "I've got no clue."

"Well, just don't let it happen again."

André snorted, like he could control whatever was going on, but he nodded anyway. "I have to go into school today," he said, glancing back at her. "I've got finals."

"I'll have to reschedule mine." The baby burped in her ear and she shifted him in to her arms.

"I'll only be gone for a couple hours."

"Don't you have practice?"

André offered a small smile. "Yeah but being here is more important."

"You're so full of shit." Katrina laughed. "You're just trying to win brownie points."

André glanced at her sideways, his crooked smile charming her. "Is it working?"

"A little."

He went to her side and gently took his son from her arms. Taking him to the crib, he checked the diaper and grimaced at the brown sludge inside. André undid the diaper and got a chest full of urine as the stream arced from the baby. Sam cooed and kicked his legs.

"Ah, come on," he said to his son, looking down at his soaked shirt.

Katrina burst out laughing until tears squeezed out of the corner of her eyes. She held her stomach in obvious discomfort, but the hilarity of the situation struck a chord, and she couldn't stop laughing.

Chuckling, he finished changing Sam and then stripped his wet shirt, dropping it on the floor and using a couple of baby wipes to clean his hands, chest and stomach.

Her laughter stopped the moment his shirt peeled over his head, and he shot a glance in her direction and picked up Sam.

She was on her feet, approaching him with that hungry look.

The one she used to give him at the house.

The one that set his blood boiling in his veins, throbbing through his skin.

The one that drove him over the edge and this time was no different.

"Oh no, you don't. The doctor said six weeks."

She didn't stop, closing the distance within seconds, faster than she should have been able to move under the circumstances. She reached him, running her fingers over the front of his pants.

"Kat." He chuckled and stepped away, his eyes burning, and he knew they went full-fledged iridescent, maybe even laser red.

Katrina stepped closer. "I want you," she whispered.

André sidestepped away from her. "You can't have me right now. Besides, not in front of the baby."

"Ah, but you want me."

"Damn straight. But I can't have you for the next month or so." He licked his lips and tilted his head a bit. "When I do...baby, when I do, I want to hear you in the next county," he drawled, his voice low and sultry as the urge to throw caution to the wind almost engulfed him. He looked down at his son and raised only his eyes back to meet his wife's before handing her their son and disappearing into the bathroom. He flipped the lock. There would be no telling his libido to shut down if she cornered him in the shower, no matter what the water temperature.

He dialed the shower to the coldest setting and stripped; stepping inside, the sting of the freezing water nearly ripped a yelp from his chest. He forced himself to stand under the icy spray until shivering and no longer teetering on tearing her clothes off. He turned off the water and looked up at the ceiling. *Lord, please give me the strength to obey the doctor's orders.*

Katrina waited outside the bathroom with Sam in her arms and when the door opened, she handed the baby to André and slipped inside without a word, grabbing the bag with her clothing before she shut the door behind her.

"Hey, little man." He put his finger in the baby's hand and Sam immediately grasped it.

Matthew knocked on the door, peering inside. "Good morning." He stepped into the room. "Where's Kat?"

"Shower." André pointed with his chin. "Where's Mom?"

"She'll be in later. I figured I'd swing in on the way to work to say hello to my grandson." He marched across the room and put his arms out for Sam.

André handed over his son. "What time is it?" he asked as his father pulled Sam to his chest.

"Almost eight," Matthew replied.

"Shit, I have to go," André said, looking at the bathroom door. "I've got an exam in less than an hour and I still need to swing home and change."

"Go on, I'll wait till Kat gets out." Matthew smiled and settled into the chair his son just vacated.

André glanced at the bathroom door on the way out of the room. *I'm heading out. Dad's here with the baby,* he silently conveyed to Katrina in the shower.

I'll see you in a bit. He heard her voice in his head and smiled.

ANDRÉ DIDN'T BOTHER CALLING out; he just bound up the stairs and into the bedroom, swinging the door closed behind him. He stripped and tossed his clothes into the corner, before pulling on a fresh set of boxers and jeans. Turning to sit on the edge of the bed, he caught Linda staring at him from the wide-open door and he froze in place. His mind had been too preoccupied with what he needed to do for his exam to hear her thoughts, but now they shined through the haze like a lighthouse in a storm. "How long have you been there?"

Linda grinned. "Long enough." She went to step inside the room.

André put up his hand in a stop signal and with it, an invisible wall. He recognized the wanting in her eyes and her thoughts. "Cut the shit, Mom," he snapped, and resumed putting his socks on while keeping the barrier intact.

Linda walked smack into the barricade, her jaw going slack with surprise.

André ignored her and slid his sneakers back on. He grabbed a shirt and the keys to the hovercraft and turned toward her. "Mom, you have to move." When she didn't, he physically moved her aside with his mind. He shot her a get-a-grip look and disappeared down the hall and out of the house.

"Jesus, what the hell am I transmitting?" he muttered under his breath and put the hovercraft in gear, heading toward the school.

André pulled into the parking lot with fifteen minutes to spare and leaned back in the seat, rubbing his face with his hands and trying to focus on the advanced calculus exam. He got his mind set and stepped out of the craft. All motion around him stopped and every female in the parking lot and in front of the school turned to look at him. "Shit."

Two of his ex-girlfriends were already making a beeline toward him. He sidestepped them, walking directly into the school. A line of women followed and converged on him before he was able to get to the classroom.

They steered him into an empty room, groping and pulling at his clothing.

"Stop!" he yelled, but no one listened. The aggravation brewing shot out of him and the group pushed away as if a giant broom swept a five-foot arch around him. He stood in the center of the open space, glancing around. "What the hell is wrong with y'all?"

He singled one of the girls out with his eyes. "Hannah, you're Kat's best friend."

"When the cat's away, the mice will play," Hannah purred.

André glared at them. "You do not want me," he muttered and pushed the thought on the group.

Most of the girls blinked, looked at one another and at André in confusion. They dispersed, leaving only a handful who had been out in the hallway. They approached André, stalking him as they circled, blocking his path to the door.

"Girls, I have an exam right now," he sighed, exhausted.

"A physical exam," Anna said, slipping up to him and running her hands up his chest.

Her brown eyes sparkled, much more than he remembered, and his mind went back to their fling a year ago. She was one of his more memorable conquests: lithe and athletic, her cheerleading skills translated well into the bedroom. Shaking the thought from his head, he took a step back, right into the big desk in the front of the classroom and said, "Anna, I'm not in the mood."

"Seems to me I recall you're always in the mood." She rubbed her hands over the front of his pants and the other girls stepped closer.

André let out a nervous laugh and his body responded to her touch despite his better judgment.

"Mmmm," Anna purred. "Five-on-one. I bet you never dreamed you'd ever get this chance."

André raised his eyebrow and blinked, pulling his gaze away from Anna and the other cheerleaders caressing his clothing. He squirmed away from the desk, trying to break free of their insistent hands. "I can't do this," André whispered without the conviction needed to break the spell. He shook his head to clear it and peeled the girls off him, heading in the direction of the door.

Anna grabbed his arm and spun him toward her, planting a hot, wet kiss on him.

André's resistance was at the limit and he closed his eyes, allowing her to explore his mouth with her tongue. Hands reached and rubbed and it was only when his shirt hiked up his chest that he broke the spell, pushing Anna away and yelling, "No!"

He stalked into the hallway, heading straight for his calculus exam. The bell rang just as he slid in to his seat and he tensed against the budding frustration itching just under his skin. His frustration increased a notch as all eyes bore into him. "Come on," he mumbled and rolled his eyes.

Mr. Samuels, his calculus teacher, stared at him with a slack jaw.

"What?" André growled at the intense stare.

"Your eyes."

The teacher's terror filled his head and André bit down on the angry retort to all the rampant thoughts flying around the room, from the hot, seductive thoughts of the girls to the stunned fear in the male population. "I know. Just hand out the fucking test," André snapped. He closed his eyes and hung his head for a moment, concentrating on calming his emotions. When he looked back up, he scanned the classroom and finally met the professor's gaze. "Apparently, having a baby makes my eyes freak out," he added, trying to throw a brief bone of levity into the room.

"Kat had the baby?" Adam, one of his teammates, asked.

"Yeah, yesterday." He glanced back at Adam.

"And it did that to your eyes?" Adam gasped.

André smiled. "Yes and no," he said. He looked back at the professor. "Are we taking an exam today?" He leaned back in his seat, crossing his arms.

The professor fumbled with the papers on his desk.

"Or do we all get A's?" André pushed the thought into the professor's head. He watched as the professor blinked, looked down at the blank tests and his grade book and then up at the class.

"You all have an A average. I don't think an exam is necessary." He wandered out of the classroom.

The students stared at the empty doorway with wide eyes and slack jaws, their collective gaze slowly focused back on André.

André's smile faded. *Oh crap!*

"How the hell did you do that?" Adam asked.

"Yeah?" The resounding response from thirty students sounded at once.

André shrugged and took a deep breath. "I dunno," he mumbled and looked at his hands.

"I don't care how you did it." The girl who was sitting behind him slid out of her seat and knelt on the floor beside him. She ran her hands up his legs.

André grabbed her wrists and glanced over at Adam. His jaw clenched as he took note that a few of the other girls were heading in his direction. He closed his eyes. *You do not want me,* he thought and sent targeted pushes to the women heading in his direction. When he opened his eyes, the girl kneeling on the floor stared at him with the same dazed confusion the professor had on his face before he left the room.

"What are you?" Adam whispered.

André let out a laugh. "I'm a seventeen-year-old father." He stood to leave.

"Bullshit," Adam said.

André turned back toward Adam and the rest of his class; any hint of amusement vanished with the accusatory stares. "Look, I've had a long couple of days. I'm tired and this isn't a discussion I'm inclined to participate in," he said with a voice thick with the Texan accent. Thoughts accosted him with words like monster, freak, and alien, the last sending chills up his spine. A warning prickled his neck, and he spun back toward his class, raising his hand and caught the apple sailing toward his head.

Adam leaned back in his seat. "You ain't one of us."

André tossed the apple in the air and caught it. "Maybe not, but we wouldn't have made it to the championship this year without me." He shined the apple on his shirt and then took a bite before heading out into the hall. *Kat, I royally screwed up,* he thought and took another bite, stepping outside. *Royally.*

How so? Her voice resounded in his head, and he faltered, flustered by the clarity in her thought broadcast to the point he wondered if she actually could read his mind at this distance and hoped like hell that wasn't the case.

They saw my eyes.

You screwed around on me? Her voice carried through his head.

"No. I was ambushed," he said aloud from the confines of the hovercraft. *And then my class saw my eyes and they saw me use the influence on the teacher.* "So I think my secret may be out sooner than anyone anticipated," he said to himself.

André walked into the hospital room fifteen minutes later.

Katrina's eyebrows furrowed. "Since when do you wear lipstick?"

André headed into the bathroom and took a quick glimpse in the mirror, letting out a laugh at the traces of pink lipstick on the corner of his mouth, cheek, and neck. He grabbed a paper towel and erased the damning evidence. "I don't know what's happening to me. All I know is this thing is out of hand." He tossed the towel into the garbage and stepped back in the room. "It's like all the females I come in contact with are affected by a weird aphrodisiac and I'm the benefactor." He met her sour gaze. "I didn't ask for this, Kat. I didn't ask for the entire female population of our school to corner me in a classroom either."

"You let them close enough to leave lipstick?" She pushed her chin out in irritation, her lips pursing with disbelief.

André looked at the floor, heat filling his cheeks. "I guess."

If she had been standing, her foot would have started tapping the floor with impatience. Instead, she pressed her lips together, leveling a hostile gaze that spoke volumes to the tumult inside her.

"I sent a wave of influence through the room and everyone inside stopped, but I didn't think to send that web farther, like through the entire school, so when the masses left, the cheerleading squad cornered me. That's where I got the lipstick marks."

"Anna," Kat said, her tone laced with disappointment and a dash of jealousy.

"Yep." André flopped into the chair, leaning his temple on his fist, closing his eyes as the exhaustion weighed on his muscles, dragging him down toward sleep.

Katrina let out a small laugh. "I don't know about your daddy," she whispered.

"What don't you know?" The corner of his mouth twitched into a grin and he opened one eye, focusing on her.

"I'm the one who should be tired."

André's eyes fluttered open. "Sorry. Did you want some sleep?"

Katrina nodded. "A little would help."

André stood, stretching the sleep from his muscles before he collected his son from her, kissing her gently on the forehead in the process. He slid back in the chair, smiling down into his son's inquisitive eyes. "How long was my dad here?" he asked with a yawn.

"About an hour. The doctor came by after he left and said I'm doing well enough to go home tonight after dinner," she replied. Settling down on her side, she closed her eyes, drifting into a restless sleep within minutes.

André watched her sleep for a while, catching fragments of her dreams as he eavesdropped on her thoughts. He tore his eyes away from his wife and looked back at his son. Sam stared back at him. "Your mom has dirty dreams," he whispered, his smile morphing into a grin.

He climbed into the bed next to her with Sam on his chest and closed his eyes against the headache forming behind them. The word exhausted gained new meaning for him.

An elbow nudged his chest. "André," Katrina whispered.

"Hmm?" He opened his eyes and looked around at the change in the lighting. "How long have I been sleeping?"

"A couple hours. Take Sam for a second." She transferred Sam to André's arms and headed into the bathroom.

André sat up and swung his legs over the edge of the bed, arching his back for a moment to loosen up the stiffness. "Hey," he mumbled at his fussy son. "Momma will be right back." The door swung open and he turned his head in the direction of the intrusion.

Matthew and Linda walked in, and Linda's thoughts switched from her grandson to André. Irritation spread over Matthew's face and André steeled his expression, trying to block her evocative thoughts.

"Where's Katrina?" Matthew asked, attempting to ignore his wife's sudden change.

"She's in the bathroom."

As if on cue, the bathroom door opened. Katrina looked at the family gathering. "Hi," she said. Tension hung in the room like a patch of hot, humid air and Katrina stepped toward André.

"What happened at school today?" Matthew asked, framing the question based on some rumors that made it to his office this afternoon.

Katrina put her hands out for her son and André transferred the baby to her before burying his hands in his pockets. He wouldn't meet his father's gaze; instead, he shifted from one foot to the other, studying the tile pattern on the floor.

Katrina situated Sam with a bottle and then looked up at her in-laws. "It wasn't his fault, so back off," she snapped.

The sudden onslaught of irritation transmitting from her surprised André, and he raised his eyebrows, meeting his father's gaze. Matthew had the same look of shock that André imagined showed in his features.

She looked back at Matthew and Linda, her eyes becoming hard as steel, and her focus landed on Linda. "So help me God, I'm going to smack you if you continue looking at André like that." She sent a mental shove that actually pushed Linda back a step, gaining her full attention.

"I, uh…" Linda's gaze snapped to Katrina. "I'm sorry," she said. "I don't know what's come over me." She stumbled over the words and glanced quickly in André's direction.

"He's emitting some sort of vibe that's making us a little crazy," Katrina replied, and André caught her direct glance. "Neither of us can figure out why." She looked back at Linda. "But that still doesn't give you the right to act on it."

"I would never…" Linda began to protest but trailed off as she thought about earlier today at the house. "I wouldn't," she said, more to convince herself than anyone in the room.

Matthew sent a glare in André's direction. "You don't know how to control this thing?"

André shook his head. "I was swarmed at school, and I screwed up. Everyone in my class saw my eyes, Dad. My teacher freaked a little and I had to give him a little nudge," he drawled, the nerves getting the best of him. "They know I'm different now."

"Shit," Matthew whispered.

André shrugged. "I tried to blame it on fatherhood." His attempt at humor fell flat and he traded a glance with Katrina. "I've got another exam in an hour."

"You think it's wise to go back to school today?" Linda asked.

"He's got to finish school," Matthew replied, not giving André the option. "Just keep your...whatever...in check." He waved his hand at his son.

"Yeah, I don't want you coming back with lipstick on your face again," Katrina added.

André nodded. "I'll try."

"And no mind control shit," Matthew said.

André opened his mouth to speak but thought better of it. It was either mind control or unwanted advances. Both options sucked. He nodded, agreeing to his father's order. "I'm going to go grab something to eat," he muttered and retreated out of the room.

Relieved to be out from under the scrutiny of his parents, he wandered into the hospital cafeteria and stood looking at the menu, feeling the eyes of the female patrons heating up his backside. Ignoring the uneasiness, he walked up to the counter and ordered a cheeseburger, French fries, and two vanilla milkshakes. He paid with cash and carried the tray back to the maternity ward.

André handed the milkshake to Katrina and set the tray on the small table. He slid the chair in and didn't look at anyone as he wolfed down the meal.

"God, that smells so good," Katrina said, eyeing her husband's meal.

"Can you have normal food yet?" André said with a mouthful of French fries.

Katrina shrugged.

"Well, ask," André said after swallowing.

Katrina pressed the call button, and a nurse entered a few minutes later.

"Can I help you?" she asked Katrina, but her eyes drifted to André.

"Can I have a cheeseburger and fries too?" Katrina asked and took a sip of her milkshake.

"Hmmm?" the nurse said, pulling her attention back to Katrina.

"Can I have a cheeseburger and fries?" Katrina said in a measured tone.

"Certainly. You can call down and place your order and they'll bring it on up." She smiled, her glance again wandering back to André. She checked Katrina's pulse and measured her blood pressure, marking both on her chart before shooting a longing glance in André's direction.

"Can't you shut it off?" Katrina snapped after the nurse left the room.

"I don't even know what the fuck it is," he barked, prompting a smack on the back of his head by Matthew.

"Watch your language," Matthew scolded.

André sighed, biting down another smack-worthy response. A year ago, this kind of attention would have been a glorious ride for him, tagging each and every female who came within his radar. In that respect, Anna was right on the money, but ever since he hooked up with Katrina, she was the only one he wanted. Even so, all the silently transmitted sexual innuendo fueled a building fire within him that he knew couldn't be released for another six weeks, adding to his frustration. "I have to leave soon for class," he said. "Practice is at three. I'll be back around five."

"I thought you weren't going to practice," Katrina balked and André sent her a warning glare that shut her up.

"After everything that happened today, I need it," he said.

"Don't you think—" Matthew started.

"I need it," André interrupted, turning his fiery gaze in his father's direction. He needed some physical pounding to burn off the frustration and he knew it. If not, he might blow and that wouldn't be pretty. "Besides, they want me to keep up the strength for next season."

"Next season?" Matthew laughed. "That's going to be awfully hard to flip with a job. You've got a family to support." He crossed his arms.

"I'll figure it out," André said, standing and stalking over to Katrina. "See you later." He kissed her cheek before leaving them to talk behind his back.

A BURNING FRUSTRATION ATE at Matthew's stomach. "Sometimes..."

"He can be frustrating," Katrina finished his sentence for him. "But despite what you're thinking, André will figure it all out."

"I know he will, but what kind of damage is he going to do in the meantime?" Matthew turned and looked out the window, wondering what he should do with André and how he could teach him a little more self-control.

"You could give him a job this summer," Katrina said, addressing his thoughts as opposed to his question.

"I don't think so," Matthew replied.

"Why not? He could do office work. The hours aren't bad, and you can keep an eye on him," Katrina pushed.

"She's right, Matt," Linda said, bringing the baby back to Katrina. "Doesn't your assistant need some help?"

"Yes, but she needs real help. She doesn't need to be a babysitter."

"André doesn't need babysitting. He needs a job," Linda said. "And you're going to give him one."

"Nepotism is frowned upon in the Armed Forces," he stated.

"I don't care, Matt. You are in a position to make it happen."

"That's why I don't think it's such a good idea." Matthew turned toward Katrina.

"Dad, André still wants to go into the service. This would give him a view that most soldiers don't get to see."

Matthew laughed. "You think the administrative side is glamorous?" He read some of her train of thought.

Katrina shrugged. "My dad did pretty well and you're not doing so badly for your family either."

Matthew's eyes switched between the two women and their thoughts pressed in on him, along with the prospects of what the summer would be like if he didn't give in to their wishes. "All right. I'll see what I can do," he muttered.

Messiah Chapter 12

ANDRÉ WALKED INTO THE school and all eyes turned, watching his every move. The rumor mill must have spread through the entire student body because now everyone gave him a wide berth. He didn't know whether to be irritated or relieved and chose a seat in the very back of the class for the exam. As the students filtered in, their gazes flicked in his direction before turning toward the front of the class.

André sighed at the palpable strain in the air. The most annoying emotion hitting his filters was fear, fear of the unknown. He wanted to stand and scream at them, tell them he was the same kid who had sat next to them in class for the last six years. Instead, he clamped his jaw closed and took a deep breath.

A knot formed in the small of his back, born of the tension filling his every fiber and he shifted, stretching his muscles, trying to get the knot to loosen.

A girl who missed his brain scramble earlier in the day took a seat next to him, scanning him with the same hungry, horny expression he was getting accustomed to, and he rolled his eyes. *Unbelievable.*

He lifted his left hand and pointed to his wedding ring and she shrugged, licking her lips. *So what?*

Her glib response resounded in his head and his hands balled into fists. "No," André replied between clenched teeth, keeping the instinct to push her mind locked down. When she scooted closer, he slid his chair farther away, sending her a warning glare, one that seemed to break through the trance and she focused on the front of the class instead.

He glanced around the room, relief flooding through his flesh. He didn't want to use the influence again unless absolutely necessary.

The exam landed on his desk and he was the first to finish, dropping it on the teacher's desk before he shot out of the room, heading toward practice with an hour to spare. The empty locker room greeted him and he sat down on the bench in front of his locker, putting his tired head in his hands.

When he looked up, the cheerleading squad converged and he shot to his feet, backing into the lockers.

"You slid out on us earlier today," Anna purred.

André sidestepped several times, keeping them just out of reach until he found himself in the showers. His heart hammered in his chest as the girls peeled their tops off, tossing them toward the entrance. "Anna, come on," he said, nearly begging her to stop.

"André, I know just how good you are, remember?"

André nodded. "I remember, but you aren't Kat," he said, purposely pushing her buttons.

Anna smiled. "Normally, that would piss me off, but right now, all I can think about is screwing you again." She advanced.

"It's not going to happen," André said, but his resolve was waning. Five of the most beautiful girls in the school were stripping off their clothing in front of him.

Anna and the four other girls laughed. "I beg to differ," she said, glancing at his crotch. "You're already turned on, aren't you?" she said, taking notice of the hard shape pressing against his jeans.

André looked for an escape but they were blocking the only way out and he knew if they got their hands on him, he'd lose control. "I don't have any protection."

Anna reached in her bra and pulled out a strip of condoms. "I do." She smiled, killing his last frantic excuse.

Damn it, I should know better; she was always prepared. André scanned the shower again and his gaze landed on the showerheads and the solution to his predicament. He glanced back at Anna and willed the showers on full blast. Water cascaded out at the girls, soaking them with bone-chilling water.

In unison, they let out a collective yelp and retreated, leaving André fully clothed, dripping and shivering under the cold spray. He stayed put, letting the frigid water kill any sense of arousal before he stepped into the locker room. His sneakers squeaked water with every step and he did a quick scan of the area before he peeled off his shirt. The cold shower did nothing to wipe out the exhaustion settling in his bones and he yawned. He wrung the water out of his shirt and hung it over the side of the locker and did the same with his pants.

André breathed a sigh of relief and thanked God his football uniform was black and not white as he pulled the pants over his wet underwear. He peeled his socks off and wrung those out the best he could, slipping them back on and sliding his feet into his football cleats.

André watched the drips form on the cuffs of his pants and fall to the floor. "Dry," he whispered in the empty locker room and let out a bark of a laugh when a spot spread over the wet jeans until they were bone dry. He looked around the room to make sure he wasn't being observed and stood, reaching for his jeans. His hands confirmed what his eyes had seen. He did laugh this time, folding his jeans and opening the locker. His gaze fell on the shirt. "Dry," he whispered again and a minute later, he was folding the dry shirt, laying it on the jeans and closing the locker. He concentrated on the wet underwear and socks wrapped uncomfortably on his skin and repeated the command. He chuckled, actually feeling the fabric's heat blast.

For the first time since he landed on Earth, André wondered exactly what he was capable of. He had never exercised his powers regularly and he certainly hadn't entertained the idea of testing his limits, until now. He needed to control it without fail so it didn't exhaust him to the point of passing out.

He thought he was tired before. Now his eyelids felt like lead weights had been tied to them and he took a glance around the locker room, making sure it was empty before lying down on the bench. The minute his eyes closed; sleep pulled him into the depths of darkness.

Dreams of Katrina's hands caressing his skin and her hungry mouth toying with him took hold. He reveled in her touch until the cheering of his teammates bled through the dream. His eyes fluttered open and he gasped at Anna's predatory smile as she rode him like a professional whore.

Two other cheerleaders had his hands between their legs, his fingers working of their own accord, making them squeal with delight while his teammates cheered like they were watching a porn flick at the theaters.

Sensations flooded his mind. The pure pleasure Anna and the two girls experienced washed away his common sense and a groan escaped his mouth. Anna leaned over and kissed him hard. His mouth opened to protest but instead he hungrily accepted the kiss and his eyes clenched shut, willing this to be a dream.

Katrina's going to kill me.

The sobering thought barreled through his foggy brain and his eyes flew open, bringing him fully awake and in control of his faculties. He yanked his hands out of the cheerleaders' grip and sat up, pushing Anna off and away from him. "No," he growled in disgust. He buttoned himself up and stood, glaring at the roomful of people.

Anna reached for him again and he knocked her hand away. "This isn't a fucking game," he snapped. He felt the hands slide up his back and turned. "Get away from me!" he bellowed, breaking through their euphoria. They backed away. He shot a glare back at Anna. "You cannot have me," he said, leaning down into her face. "Understand?"

She grinned, unaffected by the rejection. "I had you a few moments ago."

"Anna, I fucked you a long time ago and that's all it was. You were just another conquest to me, just another stupid bitch willing to spread her legs wide. I never gave a shit about you; now get the hell away from me," he growled, his Southern drawl making the words much harsher.

Anna scuttled away, her eyes welling with tears as sobs tore from her chest.

André watched her run off and his gaze fell on his teammates, the anger still filling his skin, itching to be freed like a wild panther caught in a trap. He turned and walked out of the locker room onto the field, picking up a football and throwing it with all his might. An added mental shove made it sail into the top deck of the stands at the far end of the park, well over the length of the football field, bouncing between the bleachers.

"You definitely aren't one of us," Adam said from behind him.

André stiffened but didn't turn.

"We would have fucked those cheerleaders regardless of our marital status." He chuckled.

André smiled at the dig, keeping his back to Adam. "I'm sure."

"You throw like that, and we'll win every game this year." He stepped next to André.

"If I throw like that, you guys will be in the hospital." He glanced at Adam.

Adam inhaled and nodded, turning his attention to André. "What you said to Anna was pretty harsh."

André nodded. "The truth usually is." He picked up another football and twirled it in his hands. "What do you want to know?" he asked, hearing the questions rattle around Adam's mind.

"Who are you?"

"André Robbins."

"You know what I mean."

André looked behind him; the team was coming out on the field.

"I'm the quarterback and the captain of this team." He flipped the ball to Adam and walked to the sidelines.

Adam trotted up next to him. "We need to know, André," he said, looking to his teammates for confirmation. They nodded, and all eyes bore into him.

André moved his gaze over each of his teammates, seeing the questions in their eyes, too. "I've been on the team for the past year. Does it really matter?"

"Yeah, it does," Adam said, pushing.

"What are you, the new team spokesman?" André asked, trying to divert the conversation.

Adam nodded. "I've known you the longest," he said.

André could tell from their intent gazes that he wasn't going to get out of this, so he sighed. "I'm not from around here."

"Where are you from?" Adam asked.

"Ever hear of Zyclon?" André asked, knowing that none of them would have. Only people in the top echelon of the government knew about Zyclon.

"No. How far is that from Dallas?"

André laughed and considered how to answer as he took the football from Adam and twirled it in his hands. He gambled and turned toward the football field. "About a hundred million light years away." He tossed the ball in the air and caught it, turning back around to see the reactions. Eyes were bulging and jaws were slack.

"Does Katrina know?" Adam whispered.

"Yes. She was one of the first people I met here," he said, shifting under their curious gaze. He wasn't so sure sharing was a good idea anymore. The last time he felt this vulnerable and exposed, the emperor was sentencing his parents to death.

"But you look human," Adam whispered.

"Physiologically, we are almost identical to humans. There are just a couple things that are different," he explained, twirling the ball.

"The eyes," Adam said. He had seen André's eyes in the classroom earlier in the day.

André nodded. "Zyclonian eyes are red."

Collectively, all brows furrowed except Adam's.

"Are you shitting us?" Bobby asked from behind Adam.

André shook his head. He kept eye contact with Adam.

"Your eyes are blue," Adam said, stating the obvious.

André nodded again. "Yep." He tossed the ball in the air, trying to squash his nervous energy.

"Why do they change?" Adam asked, thinking he knew.

André started to laugh a little. "Up until my son was born, only Katrina could make my eyes change." He looked sheepishly at Adam, the blush heating his cheeks. He shifted and tossed the ball.

Adam caught it, laughing. "Your eyes go all laser when you're screwing around?"

"Apparently." His cheeks burned and he was sure they were as red as his eyes got when they went laser.

"How come they didn't go all red with Anna?" Kevin stepped forward from behind Adam.

André shrugged. "I was angry," he muttered. He felt the teams' curiosity. "Come on, we need to get on the field before the coach comes out."

"Does the coach know?" someone in the back asked.

André shook his head. "Seriously, guys, this is between you and me. If word ever got back to my dad..." He shook his head. "All hell would break loose."

"He's not your dad," Adam said.

"That's where you're wrong. He's the only father I've ever known," André said, sending a warning glance.

"What, are you like Superman, sent off in space when you were a baby to be saved?" Charlie Kempsey asked. He had been a comic book buff all his life.

André laughed. "No. I was exiled because I have blue eyes." He turned, leaving them with that statement, and began to warm up his arm.

"Say again?" Adam asked from behind him.

"I was six." He looked at them. "I had blue eyes and they sent me into space to die." He threw another pass into the net.

"Holy shit," Adam whispered.

"Commander Robbins found me out there," he said, picking up the next pigskin to throw. He twirled it in his hands. "This is the only home I've ever known, so, if you go blabbing this shit all over the school, I'll probably end up in a government facility where they'll study me like a fucking bug for the rest of my life."

They digested this information as they milled about on the field. Practice was uneventful and in the locker room afterwards, they collected around André again.

"What's with the girls?" Charlie asked.

André shrugged. "Kat says I'm sending off a sex vibe." He laughed at the absurdity of it all. "It started when Sam was born and I'm praying it stops soon because there's only so many advances I can ward off before I just give in and then I'm a dead man," he said as he closed his locker.

"Giving in will kill you?" Charlie gasped.

"No. Kat will kill me," he clarified, eliciting smiles from most of his teammates.

"You can die?" Charlie asked.

"I'm flesh and blood, just like you Charlie," André said, lifting his shirt and showing the scar from the stab wound. "See?" He pointed to it.

"Where'd you get that?" Adam asked. He had seen it before but never asked.

"Kat's dad," he answered. "He didn't like the fact that I got her pregnant and I ended up getting the angry edge of a knife. He was so mad he had a heart attack." André looked at his watch. "Shit. I gotta go. I was supposed to be at the hospital a half hour ago." He flew out of the school, hopping into the craft, and zoomed out of the near empty parking lot, cursing under his breath at the darkening sky.

He skidded into the room ten minutes later, gasping for air from the sprint. "Sorry I'm late," he said, leaning over to catch his breath.

"It's about time. We can go home as soon as we produce an infant seat."

"A what?" André asked.

"It's at home, André. I got one as a baby shower gift."

André dug his phone from his pocket and dialed the house. "Mom, can you bring the infant seat to the hospital? Kat's ready to go but we can't leave without it." He nodded. "Thanks." He flipped the phone closed.

"Anything else I should know about today?" Katrina asked.

André put up a barrier intended to keep her out of today's activities, but he knew he couldn't outright lie to her. "I got angry," he said. He let her see the shower scene that ended with the cheerleaders running out soaking wet.

Katrina chuckled at the image. "That was pretty quick thinking."

André shrugged. "It prompted a hell of a lot of questions from the team," he replied, leaving the real reason for the questions out of his mind.

"What'd you tell them?" Katrina asked.

"The truth."

Katrina sat down on the bed. "No, André, you didn't."

"Yes. I did," he said, wishing he had a football in his hands to twirl. Instead, he shoved his hands in his pockets.

"Your dad is going to kill you."

"He doesn't have to know."

"You're delusional," Katrina said as she pulled the portable crib closer to her, making sure Sam was still sleeping. "They are going to talk, André. It's just too juicy a story."

"You didn't."

"I know how to keep a secret," she said, glaring at him. "Those windbags don't."

"You don't know that."

"Anna." She crossed her arms.

André blocked his mind. "What about her?"

"Did you know every last one of them slept with her?"

He raised his eyebrows. "Really?"

"Anna did the whole team, André." She crossed her arms. "Including you."

"That was before I was on the team, Kat," he sidestepped.

"I'm aware of that, but she won't let up until she has you again," Kat warned.

André laughed. "She won't come near me. Not after today."

"You think a little cold water is going to deter her?"

His smile faded. "No," he said. "But the things I said will." He wouldn't let her into that recess of his mind, and he mentally threw away the key.

"What did you say?" Katrina asked.

"Let's just say I told her a different kind of truth and it was pretty harsh."

"What did you say?" she asked more forcefully.

"You don't need to know what I said. All you need to know is that I got her off my back." He walked over to his son and picked him up. "Mom just pulled in. Let's go see what we need to get out of here."

Messiah Chapter 13

ANDRÉ TENSED AS HE walked into the school the next morning. He hated it when Katrina was right, and this was no different. All eyes swiveled to him, their thoughts broadcasting a litany of questions followed by hushed whispers.

You were right. He sent the thought home and sighed.

I told you so.

Bite me, André sent back and headed in the opposite direction toward his classroom. Anna intercepted him before he could reach his destination. Her expression wavered between the wanting coursing through her veins and the anger and disgust at the rumors.

"Get out of my way, Anna," André warned.

"You're an alien?" she snapped.

André laughed but didn't confirm or deny the information. Instead, he ignored her and stepped into the classroom, thinking about how to diffuse this ticking bomb. Accusatory stares met him, and he slumped into his seat. "What is it with you people?"

"We heard you came from Mars," one of the bolder students remarked.

André snorted and shook his head. "There's no oxygen on Mars, therefore no living organisms. Didn't you learn anything in science?" He looked around the room. "No, I'm not from Mars," he clarified, seeing the questioning eyes still boring into him.

"Is that what you really look like?" the same kid who remarked about Mars asked.

André raised his eyebrows. "What the hell are y'all talking about?"

"You're an alien, right?" he asked.

"What the hell kind of question is that?" André drawled.

Professor Randolf walked in the classroom. He had heard the exchange from the hallway. "Mr. Robbins, I believe the class is curious as to the rumors flying around the school," he clarified. "Apparently, you are not from this particular planet." He mocked the class.

André leaned back in his seat, crossing his arms. "Would it really matter?" he asked, challenging the room.

"Not at this particular moment." The professor smiled. "You are all here to take an exam, not talk about what-ifs that don't exist." The professor tossed his notebook on his desk. "This year I'm doing oral exams."

The group groaned.

"Who can tell me what is required to produce life?"

"Sperm and an egg," someone called out.

The professor smiled. "More basic than that." He looked around the room and his eyes landed on André. "Well?"

"Oxygen," André answered. "Hydrogen and oxygen. You can't have life without water and air."

"Bingo." The professor pointed at André. "And are there any other planets in our solar system that have that combination?"

"No," André answered before anyone else had the chance. Astronomy was his strong suit, and he knew of two planets in space that offered the ingredients for life.

"What about beyond our solar system?" he asked the class.

A few glanced back at André, but he kept his mouth closed.

"Not to our knowledge and we have been exploring space for over two hundred and fifty years," Professor Randolf answered, and sent a stern warning glance at André. "Therefore, starting rumors about being from space is entirely without warrant."

Irritation at the indirect slam skittered across André's skin and he crossed his arms. "Just because you have been involved in space exploration for over two hundred and fifty years doesn't mean you have covered the entirety of the universe. It's huge and vast, almost endless, so how can you be so sure there isn't life out there somewhere?"

"We would have already found it," he replied.

"That's pretty damn arrogant," André snapped.

The professor glared at André.

"The human race has yet to figure out how to build a vehicle that will surpass the speed of light without falling to pieces." He leaned forward on the desk. "The sound barrier was broken over three hundred years ago, and yet, the speed of light is still a mystery. How in God's name can you believe there is nothing out there when you haven't been able to get to the other side and back in the time you've been exploring space?"

Professor Randolf pursed his lips, considering the question.

"There are millions of galaxies, Professor," André said. "Well beyond Andromeda and Triangulum." He glanced around the room. "There are 240,000 galaxy groups within one billion light years of our sun." He let that sink in. "Three million large galaxies and sixty million dwarf galaxies." He took a breath. "Mankind has only been able to get to the edge of our own solar system with manned crafts. The automated crafts lost contact about the time they reached the Andromeda galaxy." He looked around the room. "So who's to say there isn't life out there?"

"Where are you from?" a classmate asked.

"Andromeda galaxy," he answered before he could catch himself.

"So, it's true?" Samantha asked from the other side of the room.

André closed his eyes and hung his head. "Damn," he whispered, pissed that he slipped up when he was doing so well with just the scientific facts.

The questions began to fly fast and furiously at André until finally the professor yelled, "QUIET!" at the top of his lungs.

The room went silent. Professor Randolf stared at André. "Are you telling me you're that boy they found?"

"Does it really matter?" André asked.

The teacher sat down on his seat hard and just stared.

"I'm flesh and blood just like y'all," André added, looking around the room. "I laugh, I cry, I get girls pregnant."

Some of the members of his class broke out in grins.

"So does it really matter that my origin might be a billion light years away?"

"I'll be damned," Professor Randolf whispered.

"Are we done with the exam now?" André asked, looking for an escape route out of this conversation.

The professor looked at the notebook on his desk and his brow creased. "No," he said, leaning back. "No, we're going to discuss this some more instead."

Questions started to fly all at once.

"Hey!" Professor Randolf shouted, quieting the group. "I'll be asking the questions."

André picked at a hangnail without looking at the classroom. This entire situation reeked of havoc and the idea of answering more questions about his origin made him squirm in his seat.

Hands slowly lowered.

"Why are you here?" Professor Randolf asked.

André shrugged. "Dumb luck," he replied.

People shifted uncomfortably in their chairs as the blanket of silence descended.

"From what I've observed of you, there doesn't seem to be very many differences between your race and ours," the professor said. "Are there any significant differences?"

"I guess it's my eyes. That seems to be the only significant difference. Some of you have seen the primary difference, but I've been told my physical and physiological makeup is almost identical to yours."

Holly got up and crossed the distance within seconds, taking André's face in her hands and kissing him hard to the surprise of everyone in the room.

André scrambled out of his seat and away from her, looking around at the collective shock on the faces of all the males in the classroom. The females held the same hot, horny look on Holly's face. André stood with his back to the wall and glanced at Professor Randolf with a shrug.

"Holly, please take your seat," Professor Randolf ordered. Holly complied but wouldn't take her eyes off André.

"What the hell is this?" Cameron snapped, glancing between André and his girlfriend.

André let out a nervous laugh. "I don't really have an answer for you there, dude." He slid back into his seat. "Kat says I'm emitting some sort of vibe. It started after the baby was born and apparently only affects women."

Eyebrows raised across the room.

André blushed. "Man, if I wasn't married..." He grinned sheepishly, leaving the remainder of the thought to their imaginations.

Craig smiled back at André. "So, the locker room was real?"

André's smile disappeared. "We are running way off the subject here," he replied, directing the conversation away from that ordeal.

"What was your planet like?" Professor Randolf asked.

André thought before he spoke, pulling memories out of the recess of his mind where he had locked them so long ago. "Green and lush," he said, remembering some of the places his parents hid with him. "The cities were cold, though," he replied, thinking of the tall steel-like buildings. "Not temperature wise, just in lack of any sort of warmth." He didn't add that the inhabitants were just as cold as the city itself. "The cities were like steel jungles. Everything was silver, grey, and white. Severe." He homed in on the word. "It was severe." He looked around the room. "But when you got out to the countryside, it was beautiful. We had sister suns, that's what my mom used to call them." He smiled at the memory. "Two suns chasing each other from horizon to horizon." André's mind was no longer in the classroom. He was standing in a field with his mother, picking wildflowers and laughing. "Everything in the countryside was green. The grass, the trees, even the lake water had green hues, and the flowers—they were every color imaginable. And our sky was always shades of green, yellow, orange, and red. Sunsets would brighten the colors before dark took hold." His smile faded as the image dissipated. He sighed. "As beautiful as it was, that beauty was not found in the people there. Very few of them were willing to help my parents, not with a blue-eyed child in tow." He looked down at his hands. "Are we done?" He glanced at the professor unwilling to expose the reason for his exile or the torture of those years alone in the pod.

Professor Randolf studied him and then his gaze drifted across the rest of the class. "Yes."

André didn't wait for permission to leave. He got up and walked out of the room and out to the craft in the lot. He dug his cell phone out and dialed his father's office.

"Is my dad available?" he asked.

"Yes, I'll get him."

André listened to the classical hold music, rolling his eyes. He didn't think the music had ever been updated since the invention of the hold function.

"Is everything okay?" Matthew said, discarding the salutations.

André considered the question. "I'm not sure."

"André, I don't have a whole lot of time right now."

"You better make some time for damage control," André answered. "Because the secret is out and it's only a matter of time before it gets to someone who can cause problems."

"What did you do?"

André laughed. "It all started with Anna and my teacher the first day of exams." He stared at the school. "Can I come to your office?"

"I've got a meeting with the president in a half hour. I don't have much time, André."

"Maybe the timing is perfect. We can talk to the president in person," André replied. He was already in the high-speed zone, shooting toward Matthew's office.

"André, we can discuss this later this afternoon."

"Too late, Dad. I'm landing now."

Matthew met André at the entrance to the building. "I don't have the time for this."

André transmitted the entire story to his father, starting with the ambush at the school by the female population and ending with the final exam in

Professor Randolf's class during the short walk back to Matthew's office.

He stood on the opposite side of the desk with his hands behind his back and waited for his father's reaction. When Matthew turned away from the window and met his gaze, he knew there was more to the quiet response, but his father was putting up the same type of wall in his mind as André had around the locker scene.

"You didn't actually show them your powers," Matthew said.

"True, but I did acknowledge that I wasn't from here." He shifted his weight as nerves got the best of him. Not knowing what his father was thinking or feeling left him in the dark, and he hated being in the dark.

"Take a seat," Matthew said in a calm voice, and waved to the chair.

André sat down and started picking at a hangnail, unsure of how to respond. He thought his father would go on another tirade like he did when he found out Katrina was pregnant, so this calm reaction threw him.

Matthew sat at his desk and folded his arms in front of him. "We both knew this day would eventually come. I can do damage control if you want me to, but that's up to you."

André raised a questioning eyebrow.

"Either way, I think it's time I give the president a heads-up." Matthew's gaze traveled to the door.

Before André could speak, Matthew's secretary poked her head in the door. "Sir, the president is here."

"Send him in." Matthew stood.

André followed suit, turning to see the president walk into his father's office.

President Foster was a regal looking man with white hair and a rugged build hidden beneath the finely tailored suit. His dark brown intelligent eyes surveyed the room, falling on André.

"Sir." Matthew saluted.

"At ease," President Foster replied. "This is your son?"

"Yes, sir. President Foster, I'd like you to meet André," he said.

André extended his hand. "Pleased to meet you, sir."

"My pleasure." The president smiled and shook André's hand with a firm grip.

André was hit by the confident air around the president, reminding him a little of the arrogance of the emperor on Zyclon, but unlike the emperor, this man had a warmth radiating under the projected persona.

Matthew took a deep breath. "Sir, I asked André to join us today because I think it's time we discussed the matter of his origin."

The president's brow creased and he glanced at André while Matthew crossed to the safe on the wall, opened it and returned, handing the president the contents.

He waited in silence while President Foster shuffled through the papers, reading each one before trading it with a new one. Each paper brought forth a darker shade of red in his cheeks and André glanced at his father. Matthew sent an imperceptible shake of his head, telling him not to speak.

Finally, the president lowered the papers, meeting Matthew's gaze. "You have been keeping this a secret for over six years?" he hissed, tossing the papers on the desk and ignoring André for the time being.

"Yes, sir." Matthew replied.

"What the hell were you thinking?"

Matthew glanced at André. "He was just a boy, sir." He looked back at his president.

André opened his mouth to defend his father but Matthew's silent directive snapped it closed. *Keep your mouth shut.* André clammed up and sank into the chair.

"I could have you court-martialed for this."

Matthew shrugged. "I'm aware of that, sir. I ignored my orders when I boarded his ship," he said. "I kept him out of the media fiasco and hid him from the government with the help of Commander Lawrence." He nodded at the gravity of his infractions. "I raised him as my own, producing false documentation as to his identity." He looked at André. "And I'd do it again in a second, sir."

President Foster turned his attention to André, the aggravation visible in his eyes.

"He took me in and gave me something I never had before," André said.

"What was that?"

"A home."

His answer struck the president into silence, but his mind was active with aggravation and questions.

The president swung his gaze back to Matthew. "Give me one good reason why I shouldn't have you stripped of your rank and court-martialed?"

"You're a father," Matthew said. "What would you do for your child?"

"It isn't the same, Commander. You risked your career for an alien child you knew nothing about."

"André was a scared eleven-year-old boy drifting in space," Matthew responded. "I was a colonel in the Armed Forces, sworn to protect the innocent, and he certainly fell into that category. My sworn duty to protect him was in direct conflict with the orders to terminate him and I went with my gut." He paused, looking at his son. "It was a ludicrous order given the situation. Six years have passed and for all intents and purposes, that boy sitting next to you is my son." Matthew stepped behind the desk and took his seat, his jaw set in defiance. "So do what you feel is right, sir. I did, and I have no regrets."

President Foster took the seat next to André, his jaw tight and his lips pressed together in the thin line of anger. His eyes darted from Matthew to André, and he swiveled in his direction. "How old are you?"

"Seventeen."

President Foster studied André. His eyes fell on the wedding band on his left hand and his brow furrowed. "Aren't you a bit young for marriage?"

"I don't think so. But both of our parents did," André replied. He glanced at his ring and turned it slowly on his finger. He raised his eyes back to meet the president's.

President Foster let out a laugh. "I agree with them."

André stopped fidgeting. "I love Katrina and neither of us wanted to wait to be together. I did my best to respect my father's wishes up to that point, but I couldn't do it anymore. I couldn't stay away, so I married her."

"Katrina, as in Commander Lawrence's daughter?"

"Yes, sir. He wasn't happy at all with the arrangement." André looked back down at the ring on his hand and glanced over at his father. This was so much harder than he imagined.

The president blew out air and glanced between Matthew and André trying to figure out what to do with them and he focused on André. "Why did you come here?"

"I didn't have a choice as to where I went, sir. I was lucky to drift into this solar system, and that you had the technology to rescue me, otherwise I would have died in space. Which, I'm sure was the emperor's intention when he exiled me."

"Exiled? Why were you exiled?" the president asked, his eyebrows arched with curiosity and surprise.

"The emperor used an old Zyclonian myth to justify killing my parents and sending me into space to die, and because I was the first child ever to be born with blue eyes, that just gave him the fuel to manipulate the people into believing his bullshit." André ran his hand through his hair. "I don't ever remember being in one place for more than a week before someone noticed me and then we'd move on, until one day we walked right into one of the emperor's traps. Next thing I knew, my parents were charged with treason. I watched them die before they launched me into space." His voice cracked and he cleared his throat, blinking back the red tinge that blurred his vision. "There was nothing I could do to stop any of it." He met the president's gaze. "I didn't think kindness and decency existed in the universe until I arrived here."

The president swung the seat toward Matthew and took a deep breath, standing and walking to the window, digesting the points André made. "I still don't understand why you were exiled," he finally said.

"He viewed me as a threat, sir."

"How can a six-year-old be a threat?"

André sighed and closed his eyes, hanging his head for a moment. He hadn't dredged up memories of his home planet for years, but today seemed to bring on an overload of memories. "Beyond the fact he believed the prophecy was real, there was no rhyme or reason in the emperor's thinking, sir. He viewed me as a threat and went to great lengths to make sure the people shared that viewpoint."

A crease appeared between Matthew's eyes and André dropped his gaze to the floor. There was much more to the story, but even after six years on Earth, he wasn't ready to open that can of worms.

The president studied André and then turned to Matthew. "Commander, I suggest you reseal those papers."

Matthew let out his breath, unaware that he had been holding it, and traded a glance with André.

"Thank you, sir, but there's more." Matthew sighed and looked at André. "My son has certain abilities."

"What kind of abilities?" President Foster asked turning toward the two of them.

"I can read minds, sir," André answered before Matthew could. "And I can manipulate matter," he added. He was about to confess to having the ability of mind control when Matthew shook his head to keep quiet.

"Control matter?"

André looked at the chair the president had been sitting in and sent it rolling across the room in a display of what he was talking about.

President Foster watched the chair and his gaze shot back to André.

André shrugged.

"Sir, it doesn't end there. He can teach others to do the same," Matthew said.

The president glanced out the window, thinking of the ramifications and on the heels of those, the possibilities broadcasted in his thoughts to both André and Matthew.

"My dad won't let me join the military until I'm out of high school," André replied.

"He doesn't have much of a choice." President Foster turned his gaze toward Matthew.

"Sir, no disrespect, but André has to finish high school."

"He can finish at the military academy in the capital," President Foster replied.

"Denver?" André balked.

The president turned toward André. "Yes, Denver. It's the best military academy in the nation."

André looked at his father. "I don't want to be away from my son."

The president's mouth dropped. He closed it and glared in Matthew's direction before snapping back to André. "You have a child?"

"Yes. He's four days old," André said.

"This just gets better and better," the president muttered under his breath and his thoughts turned to the offspring of an alien and human with curiosity. That would be something to study, to observe, to make sure it wasn't a monster in disguise.

André shot to his feet, his eyes flashing with anger at the new direction of the president's thoughts. "No," he growled and his hands balled into fists. "You will not take him away. Not my son, you son of a bitch."

"André!" Matthew shot out of the seat. "You do not talk to the President of the United States like that!" he bellowed.

"He—"

"I know damn well what he was thinking," Matthew interrupted, glaring at André. "Now I suggest you wait outside while we finish this conversation," he commanded.

André glared at the president and then back at his father and he stalked out of the office, slamming the door behind him, his anger still simmering just below the surface.

MATTHEW SQUASHED HIS OWN anger and waited as the president played each possible scenario over in his mind. He sat back down, knowing the president did this with every major decision. He turned the chair in the direction of the president and hardened his gaze, so it was just as unreadable as his thoughts.

Finally, the president turned. "You have put me in a particularly sensitive spot Commander," he began. "There are several routes I could take to address this situation. However, most of them are as despicable as the monsters that sent that boy into space." President Foster paused and glanced at the door. "He is obviously hot-headed, but still displays a level of respect that's admirable considering he's only been in your care for six years. However, I'm troubled by the matter of teenage pregnancy." He shook his head. "I'm not so sure it is in his best interest to stay here in Dallas." He walked to the desk and leaned on it with his fists. "I want him under government control," he said to Matthew.

"André isn't something to be controlled," Matthew said, holding his ground. "He is my son and you will not exploit him. After he finishes high school here in Dallas, I will personally recruit him into the armed service, where he will report directly to me through this base," Matthew finished, pointing his finger on the desk as he stood. "Sir," he added standing tall and proud, his eyes not wavering from the president's.

Anger flared in President Foster's eyes. "I don't take kindly to my staff barking orders at me," President Foster said.

Matthew nodded. "I don't take kindly to anyone threatening my family, sir."

The president crossed his arms. "I should fire you right now."

"That's your prerogative, sir," Matthew said, his tone matching the bite of the president's.

"Goddamn it, Matt! We've known each other for years."

"Yes, we have, sir."

The president's mouth pinched with frustration. "Stop with the formalities for just a moment. Why the hell didn't you tell me when you found him?"

Matthew weighed his response. "Mitch, your first instinct was to exploit him, not protect him. It would have been the same six years ago. You would have found a way to use him as leverage in your campaign."

"Jesus Christ, you were always such a Boy Scout." The president stood, crossing his arms. "I honestly don't know whether to fire you or give you a commendation."

Matthew smiled.

"The exposure of an alien cover-up would kill my chances of a second term in office," he replied to Matthew's smile.

Matthew nodded. *Not to mention my career.* "I'll make sure this is kept under wraps for the time being," Matthew said, wondering just how he was going to pull that off with André's science teacher.

"This will have to come out at some point Matt, and I'll be the one who will deliver the message." President Foster leveled his gaze at Matthew, making his point without saying a word.

Matthew nodded, accepting the silent order. "Hopefully, at that point he will be enlisted and under my command, training an elite force of special officers."

President Foster gave a curt nod. "Commander," he said, signaling the end of the conversation. He turned and left the room.

Matthew pressed the intercom. "Please send André back in." He disconnected without waiting for a response and sent his most harrowing glare at André when he walked into the room. He waited until the door closed and then let the frustration blow to the surface. "Do you have any idea how much trouble you are in, young man?" Matthew bellowed. "You do not speak to the president that way."

André shrank into the chair, his eyes wide like he didn't expect his father's outburst.

"I want you in this office every day this summer from seven in the morning until five at night so I can keep an eye on you. Understand?"

André blinked and confusion filled his expression, creasing the space between his eyes.

"You have a summer job here," Matthew said.

"You have got to be kidding me?" André balked.

“Do you want to live in a cage? Do you want Sam to grow up the same way?” Matthew snapped.

“No.”

“Then you better damn well do as I say because if this gets out before President Foster wants it to, that is exactly where you will end up.”

“Fine,” he grumbled and left Matthew alone in the office.

Matthew closed his eyes and collapsed in the chair, relief washing the tension from his taut muscles.

Messiah Chapter 14

*J*UNE 2240

Working at the base and learning the inner workings of the military with his father proved to be more interesting than André expected. The only drawback was constantly dodging the sexual advances of the female workforce. And he truly hated getting up at six in the morning, especially after a night with a colicky baby, and tonight was no different.

"Sammy's crying again," Katrina mumbled and pushed André to the edge of the bed.

"I have to work in the morning," André grumbled.

"Can't you just go get the bottle so I can feed him?"

Her whine grated on his nerves. "Fine," André snapped and got out of the bed, crossing the room to the crib. "What's up, Sammy?" He picked up the baby and the stench drifted from the diapers, assaulting his senses. "Shit," he muttered, changing Sam's dirty diaper and sending an occasional glare at Katrina. She had fallen back to sleep, and he was now wide-awake. "I swear, she does this just to piss me off," he whispered to Sam and glanced at the clock. The display read a little after three in the morning.

Sam cooed up at his father, happy to be in a dry diaper and in his father's arms.

"You're not going back to sleep, are you?" He looked down at his son with a sigh. André took a seat in the glider and slowly rocked Sam, humming a familiar tune from the radio, the notes rumbling softly in his chest.

Katrina opened her eyes and smiled.

Her smile only served to irritate him further. He needed sleep but that didn't stop her from making him help her at night. "You can take over now," he said, getting up and bringing Sam to her. He slid under the covers and closed his eyes and within a few minutes, his breathing was even and deep, sleep taking over once again.

The shrill alarm filled the room at six and André slammed it off, turning his head away from the clock, closing his eyes.

Time to get up. His father's words echoed in his mind.

"I know. I know," he mumbled and rolled out of bed. A half hour later, he emerged from the bathroom, dressed in khakis and a dress shirt. He sat on the edge of the bed, slipping his socks and shoes on. "Love you." He kissed the back of Katrina's head, but she didn't stir.

André walked downstairs, rolling the cuffs of his sleeves up and savoring the delectable scent of bacon hanging in the air. His mouth watered in response and when he rounded the corner into the kitchen, his mother placed a full plate of bacon and eggs on the table for him. "Thanks, Mom," he said, reaching for the glass of juice next to his plate and sending her a tired smile.

"You're welcome."

Matthew folded the paper down. "I have an early meeting, so you need to get moving."

André cleaned off his plate in record time. He wiped his mouth with the napkin and dropped it on the table. After he put the dirty dishes in the sanitizer, he turned to Matthew. "I'm ready."

"Is everything all right?" Matthew asked as André climbed into the front seat of the hovercraft.

"I'm just tired," André said, rubbing his face and stifling a yawn. "Sam woke up a couple times last night."

Matthew smiled and pulled out of the driveway, heading in the direction of their office. "It isn't easy, now is it?"

Irritation prickled and André bit down on the derogatory comment that almost slipped out. Instead, he looked out the window, ignoring his father, and as they passed the lake, he sighed. *God, I'd like to just take a day and go swimming.*

"That's not an option, André," Matthew said, addressing his son's thoughts. "You need the money for daycare during the school year."

"I know," he snapped, glaring at his father. "You remind me every chance you get."

Matthew nodded. "Raising a child isn't easy."

"Please shut up. I'm already in a bad mood; I don't need you making it worse."

Matthew let out a small laugh. "I've got some paperwork that needs to be copied for a presentation that we're giving tomorrow. Think you can handle it?"

André rolled his eyes and glanced sideways at his father. "Yeah, I can handle it."

They walked into the office fifteen minutes later. As usual, the women they passed stopped whatever they were doing and stared at André. He heard every dirty thought and after the last month, he couldn't help but grin.

"Wipe that grin off your face, will ya?" Matthew said.

"You'd be smiling if their thoughts were aimed at you."

Matthew scoffed and glanced in André's direction.

"Liar," André said as they passed into his father's office.

Matthew walked to the desk and picked up a thick stack of papers. "I need a hundred copies of this put into the binders that are in the copy room." He handed the stack to André. "There should be enough paper and binders. If you run out, please see Emma; she can show you where the supplies are."

André looked at the hefty stack and back at his father. "Color copies?"

"Yes."

"No problem." André turned, the level of his irritation growing at another menial task. At least when he was working on a computer, he could stay awake, but hanging in the copy room all day wasn't a lively prospect. He yawned and slapped the pages on the copier, pressing the commands for color printing with the proper paper source.

Time dragged and every time he sat down, his head bobbed to his chest, and he popped to his feet to stave off the exhaustion. Two hours and twenty binders later, Georgia, one of the new employees in the office, came into the copy room. André looked up, surprised by the interruption.

Heat from more than the copier filled the small space and she sent a come-hither smile over her shoulder as she shut and locked the door.

"What are you doing?" he asked, but he already knew what was on her mind, and he licked his lips, stepping back into the binder-filled counter behind him.

Georgia pulled out the Oriental pins holding her hair in a tight bun, dropping them to the floor. Her thick black hair fell in curls beyond her shoulders and she smiled, her full red lips curving deliciously. "What do you think I'm doing?"

Her voice said it all. André let out a nervous laugh, his voice mysteriously absent with the stunning woman approaching him and unbuttoning her shirt. Her blue eyes rivaled his and they scanned him from head to toe and back, turning his blood into a racing river of hormones.

She stopped in front of him, standing eye to eye with him and dropping her shirt to the floor, revealing a lacy pink bra.

"I'm married." André took in her slim athletic form.

"So am I." She ran her hands up his chest, finding and unbuttoning each latch of his shirt.

André inhaled, blocking all thoughts from his mind and fighting the raging lust torching his skin. When she pressed her soft lips against his, he closed his eyes and opened his mouth, allowing her tongue access, weakening his resolve. His hands found her waist and he pushed her gently away.

"I can't do this," he whispered, opening his eyes and regretting the lapse, but the need coursing through his blood left him panting and aching to remove the rest of her clothing and do all the naughty things fluttering through her head.

Georgia smiled. "Yes you can." She reached for the front of his pants, rubbing and unbuckling and unzipping. She leaned in again, kissing him with the same fervor as before and this time he couldn't bring himself to stop her. Instead, he wrapped his arms around her, letting her silky skin ignite him. The phrase "Georgia peach" drifted through his head and he grinned under the pressure of her lips, his hands skating over her flesh, intent on exploring every crevice.

The door swung open.

André pushed Georgia away, stumbling backwards into the table and knocking over a stack of binders. The smack of the plastic on the floor knocked his senses back in place and he shot his gaze to Georgia, who remained staring at him, her skin flushed and feverish even with her boss standing behind her.

Matthew swiped her shirt off the ground and handed it to her. "My office in ten minutes." He barked the command and waited until she dressed and left the room before focusing on André.

Matthew closed the door behind him and balled his hands into fists, frustration screaming through his veins. "What the hell were you thinking?"

"Not a whole hell of a lot," André answered, glaring back at his father. He could have spouted a ream of excuses, but he knew none of them warranted his actions. "So, I kissed Georgia. What the hell are you going to do about it?"

Matthew mentally shoved André and he slammed into the back wall hard enough to see stars. He blinked to clear his vision and straightened up against the wall. "Dad, you don't want to play this game with me," André warned, his own anger rearing its ugly head.

"Why not?" Matthew growled. A box of paper went flying off the shelf in André's direction.

It stopped mid-air in the center of the room.

"Because you will lose," André hissed, and the box dropped to the floor with a thud.

The men glared from opposite sides of the room.

"What do you think this is going to do to Katrina?" Matthew asked.

The mere mention of her name slammed the fire out of André, replacing it with devastation so black it took the strength out of his legs. André slid to the floor and buried his head in his arms. He had been so frustrated with Katrina for the past few weeks that he almost tossed their marriage out the window at the first opportunity. "I can't do this, Dad."

"You can't do what?" Matthew asked.

"I can't be married and raise a family," he said, his words muffled in his arms.

"You should have thought of that last year, André," Matthew said with a voice as harsh as the truth. "I've got no sympathy for your 'oh woe is me' attitude. You're the one who created this mess and now you've got to live with it."

André raised his head, blinking away the red sheen of tears. "I can't do this."

Matthew walked over and crouched down in front of him. "No one ever said marriage is easy. If you thought it was, you are sorely mistaken. It's a lot of work, same with raising a family. I never had an infant, so I can't say I know exactly what you're going through right now, but you are not a quitter."

"How do you know?"

"Because I didn't raise you to be one," he snarled and stood up. "Button up your shirt," he added and walked out of the room.

André rethreaded the buttons and tucked his shirt back in, heading into the bathroom. He knew Georgia was only acting on the vibe he was sending out, but the thing that burned him the most as he stood looking at his reflection was this time he would have let her do everything her filthy mind insinuated if his father hadn't interrupted.

André threw some cold water on his face and wiped it with a paper towel before heading into his father's office. Matthew glanced up from the phone and pointed toward the door, his face pinched with concern.

André shut the door behind him, scanning Matthew's thoughts, looking for what he was going to do but finding something much darker: the content of his current conversation.

"Out," Matthew directed at André, covering the receiver with his hand.

André shook his head and took a seat on the couch, interested in the details he was peeling from his father's brain and that of the official on the other end of the line.

Matthew turned the chair away from André and focused his attention back to the phone call. "Where is it now?"

André stared at the back of the chair, gleaning much more of the conversation than his father wanted him to. He broke into a cold sweat.

"How long until it hits? Tell the president we will have a plan together in two hours." He swung the chair around and hung up the phone. "I really don't have time for your little lapse right now, André."

André stood on legs that felt like stilts. The latent fear hidden in his father's heart seized his muscles into a tight bundle of nerves, but he knew he could stop the ball of destruction heading toward Earth. "I can stop it from hitting, Dad."

Matthew raised his eyebrows. "Stop what?"

"The meteor," André said. "You just have to bring me somewhere so I can see it coming."

"André, there's no way you could stop a meteor of this size. I'm not sure anything we throw at it will stop it."

"I can."

"It's the size of Texas and traveling at over thirty-five miles per second."

"Yes," André said without hesitation. "Trust me, I can stop it."

Matthew laughed.

"What's so funny?" André snapped.

"I really don't have time, André," Matthew replied.

André walked over to the window. "How much does the annex to this building weigh?"

"I have no idea," Matthew said, irritation creeping into his tone. "Now if you wouldn't mind?" The sound of breaking glass and creaking metal filled the room and Matthew spun around, looking out the window, his jaw dropping at the sight before him.

The annex building, the equivalent of three city blocks, pulled out of the ground, foundation and all. The glass walkway shattered and the metal attachments twisted and broke, leaving a gaping hole between the buildings.

André glanced in his father's direction, still concentrating on making the building rise.

"Put it back, André," Matthew gasped, and the building lowered into the ground. He shot a glance at his son. "Jesus."

"So, are you going to take me up to space or what?" There would be hell to pay for what he just did, but André was ready, especially in light of the planet-killing machine vaulting toward them.

Matthew considered his alternatives and glanced at André. He turned and picked up the phone. "Emma, get me the president," he said. "I understand. Just get me the president." He hung up. "You realize this is your coming out party."

André glanced back at the building and nodded, pushing the exhaustion raking his bones away. He looked up at the sky beyond the dome and prayed he was right. "Where is it supposed to hit?"

"The Atlantic Ocean," Matthew replied.

"When?"

"Ten days."

"Where do you want the thing to go?" André said, still studying the sky.

"Pardon?"

"Where do you want it to go instead of here?" He looked at his father. "Do you want it to end up orbiting the moon or continue into the sun?"

The phone rang and Matthew picked it up. "I don't need two hours, Mitch," he said to the president. "I've got the answer in my office." He took a deep breath. "But it's going to mean that secret we discussed last month will have to be revealed." He glanced over at André. "He says he can stop it and after the little display of his, I think he may be our only shot." He smiled a little at the response. "He lifted the annex building right out of the ground, foundation and all." He listened again. "You want to fly with us?" he asked, surprise lacing his voice. "You still get airsick?" Matthew laughed at the response.

"We're going up tomorrow and will be up there for a couple days. You sure you want to float in space with us?" He nodded. "I'm scheduling take off at noon." He glanced at André. "See you then, sir." He hung up the phone. "I'll let the president answer that when we are up in space," he replied to André's last question.

André continued to look at the sky. "Don't fire Georgia," he said, without looking at his father.

"She tried to seduce a minor," Matthew replied.

André smiled and glanced sideways at his father. "Before I hooked up with Kat, I screwed anyone who'd spread their legs for me and there were a lot of willing girls at school. So, blaming Georgia doesn't fly. She's just reacting to whatever vibe I'm sending off." He paused, returning his gaze to the window. "I could have said no and that would have been the end of it." He aimlessly turned his wedding band around on his finger.

Matthew sighed and pressed the intercom. "Send her in," he told Emma.

Aggravation pulsed in his temple, and he tightened his jaw, sliding his glance toward the door as Georgia entered the office.

The door closed behind her, and she jumped, her mouth dropping with a gasp of surprise before she caught sight of André. Her demeanor changed from nervous to sensual and her stride turned sultry like a hungry panther on the prowl. She crossed to the chair and slid into it, licking her pouty lips before turning her attention back to Matthew.

"Ms. Simmons, do you know why I called you in to my office?" he asked.

Georgia's eyes wandered over to André. "No," she said as she looked back at her boss.

"You tried to seduce my son today," he said, leaning back in the seat, studying her expression.

Georgia nodded, letting her eyes wander back to André.

"He's only seventeen," Matthew replied.

Georgia's eyes widened. "Sev...Seventeen?" She looked back at Matthew.

André glared at his father. *Stop!* he silently demanded.

Matthew glanced directly at him. "You're fired."

"Dad, you can't fire her," André argued.

"I'm not. I'm firing you."

André's mouth dropped. Of all the responses he expected, this wasn't one of them. He blinked and closed his mouth. The dull throb of anger colored his vision, and he closed his eyes and clenched his fists. Before he acted on the irrational emotion overtaking him, he stormed out of the room and continued right out of the building without looking back.

Messiah Chapter 15

ANDRÉ LUMBERED DOWN THE road, his head down and his hands shoved in his pockets. *How am I going to explain this to Kat?*

Hands yanked him into a hovercraft and threw him on the floor, the door shutting behind him before he got his bearings and looked around at his abductors.

Anna laughed. "Think you can get away from me that easily?" she asked. "Go!" she yelled at Amanda.

The craft shot off like a bat out of hell.

"What are you doing?" André shifted onto the seat, looking from Anna to Liz and Amanda in the front seat.

"I've got a bone to pick with you." Anna's eyes flashed with both anger and wanting.

André glared at her. "I'm not in the mood, Anna."

"You made a fool out of me in front of everyone." Her smile faded. "I don't like to be made a fool of." She swung her fist at his face.

André grabbed her wrist before she connected with his nose. "You don't seem to get it. I'm not in the mood for your shit," he growled. The craft suddenly plummeted to the ground and stalled. The door on André's side flew open, and he stepped out, letting go of Anna's wrist and slamming the door on her shocked face. He turned and stormed off in the direction of his house.

If I can't have that son of a bitch, nobody can.

André turned and put his hand up in front of him, pushing with a small fraction of his power and the craft stopped inches from running him over. *You don't want to fuck with me, Anna.* He sent the thought at her.

Her eyes widened in recognition as his voice barreled into her mind.

That's right, you better be afraid of me right now. I could crush you like a bug if I wanted to. He smiled in satisfaction at the fear in her eyes. André stepped to the side, out of the way of the vehicle and released his hold, watching as it went careening out of control until Anna pulled it up in the travel lane, zooming away as fast as she could. He shook his head and resumed walking toward the house.

The house was empty. He didn't bother calling out, knowing already that neither his mother nor his wife and son were in the vicinity. He bounded up the stairs, stripping off his work clothes as he went and fell on the bed in exhaustion. Sleep came quick, refueling him and he woke an hour later with the sun blinding him through the window.

Rummaging through his drawers, he found his bathing suit; slipping it on along with his sneakers, he grabbed a beach towel from the hall closet. He took off for the lake, doing exactly what he had wished he could do this morning. André jogged onto the beach, slipping his shoes off and dumping the towel on top of the discarded sneakers. Ignoring all the innuendo broadcasting in his direction, he bolted into the water and dove under, coming up a few yards short of the raft. He climbed up the ladder and shot a quick look at the crowd sitting on the benches, his gaze landing on Katrina.

He wiped the water off his face and blinked, thinking he was delusional. But she was there, sending the same heat waves as the others around her, and he smiled. "Where's Sammy?" André asked as he approached his wife, ignoring everyone else in the vicinity.

"I needed a break so your mom took him for the day," Katrina answered. "What are you doing here?"

"Letting off steam," André answered and glanced around at the other girls on the raft. They were all staring at him with the same expression that Georgia had when she entered the copy room. His gaze snapped back to Katrina, and he let it drift over her. She looked particularly hot in her two-piece bathing suit. He couldn't believe she had given birth to their son only five weeks before. "Have I told you just how terrific you look?" His eyes found hers again.

Katrina blushed and stood, closing the distance between them in two strides. "No, you haven't," she answered and stopped in front of him, looking up into his blue eyes.

André leaned down and kissed her. "You look great, babe." He wrapped his arms around her waist.

"What are you really doing here?" she asked, trying to pry into his closed mind.

"I'm going on a trip with Dad tomorrow," he said, avoiding the direct question.

Katrina's brow creased. "You're hiding something."

André pulled away and stepped up onto the diving board, executing a perfect dive. He turned in the water and looked back at her before heading for shore. André walked out onto the hot sand, shaking the water from his hair, not realizing what that simple act did to the female population on the beach. He headed toward the small playground and sat on one of the swings, gently arching back and forth, digging a path in the sand with his bare feet.

Katrina approached and took the swing next to him. "What's wrong?"

"How much do you love me, Kat?" André asked, looking out at the lake.

Katrina was quiet as she studied his troubled profile. "Why?"

André looked at her. "Because I fucked up and Dad fired me today."

"But you said you were going on a trip with him?"

André nodded. "I'm going up into space with him tomorrow." He looked up at the sky and then over at her.

"I don't understand," Katrina said, her expression reflecting her utter confusion.

"Put the trip aside for the time being," André said. "It isn't related to my job." He glanced at the wedding band on his finger, still fully blocking her from getting into his head. "How much do you love me?"

"Enough," Katrina answered.

"Enough for what?" he persisted, feeling the knot in his stomach tighten.

"Enough to get through anything," she whispered.

André hung his head, letting his wet locks fall into his eyes. "I screwed up so bad, Kat," he whispered without looking at her.

"What do you mean?"

André shook his head; he didn't want to tell her. He could already feel the dread pulsating off her.

"Tell me," she insisted.

"I lost control," he said so quietly that she almost didn't hear him but he opened his mind, showing her his mistake in Technicolor.

Katrina looked back at the water, the muscles in her jaw tightening.

"She cornered me in the copy room, and I didn't stop her."

Katrina got up and walked to where she had set up her chair and towel, and quickly packed up her beach belongings. She left minutes later without another glance at André.

André stayed swinging in the playground for a few moments with his head down and eyes closed, trying to gauge Katrina's emotions. Furious didn't begin to describe it.

Another train of thought assaulted him and his eyes flew open. André bolted out of the playground, sweeping his sneakers and towel in his hands as he ran by them. He couldn't see the source of the thoughts that set him into action, but he was running at top speed, praying he would get to Katrina first.

He saw her in the distance and he shot a glance to the side in time to see the hovercraft speeding straight at his wife. "NO!" he bellowed and sent a flash of energy at the craft.

You won't make it in time to save the bitch.

Katrina spun toward the craft, her eyes going wide and she froze like a deer in headlights. André yelled behind her and the air around the craft rippled. The explosion sent Katrina backwards onto the grass, knocking the wind out of her.

André slid by her side, scraping the skin off both his knees. "Are you ok?" he asked, his breath hitching in his chest.

Katrina just stared at the wreckage. She didn't respond to André's voice or touch.

André didn't need to look. He already knew what he did, but killing Anna was the only way to save Katrina. "Kat!" he shouted and raw panic took hold.

Katrina shifted her eyes to his. "You..." She pointed at the wreckage a few feet away.

André nodded, his eyes filling with tears but he blinked them back.

Katrina's eyes followed suit, but she was unable to blink back the tears.

André nodded and took her in his arms. "I didn't mean to kill her," he said, and the shakes began. "I didn't mean to...but I had to stop her."

Katrina wrapped her arms around André, still staring at what used to be a hovercraft. Sirens wailed in the distance. "We need to get out of here."

"Why?" André asked, pulling away.

"Because you *didn't* kill Anna."

André spun toward the wreckage.

Anna sat in the driver's seat with the pieces of the hovercraft scattered around her, her eyes wide and her mouth hanging open; the only evidence of an explosion was the singed edges of her hair. She blinked, alternating between staring at the two of them and assessing the damaged pieces of her father's hovercraft lying all around her.

André slowly stood up, helping Katrina to her feet, without taking his eyes off the bizarre scene. "I told you not to fuck with me, Anna." He escorted Katrina away from the wreckage. Just before they rounded the corner, André looked back. Anna was still sitting in the driver's seat, which was the only recognizable piece of the craft. "I was so sure I killed her," he whispered.

Katrina kept her mouth shut but her thoughts reached André anyway. He would have killed Anna if she hadn't projected a protective cocoon around her the moment before the craft blew up. She had been stunned when the debris cleared, and Anna was sitting unharmed in the middle of the wreckage.

André stopped walking and looked at his wife. "You did that?" He pointed over his shoulder.

"You would have killed her." She glanced over her shoulder in his direction. "I know you were just trying to protect me." She stopped and turned toward him. "I also know you wouldn't be able to live with that, especially since she's just reacting to the vibe you're sending off."

André nodded and resumed walking.

"I'm still pissed at you," Katrina said. "You nearly frying Anna to a crisp to protect me doesn't wipe out the fact that you screwed around on me." She kept stride with him back to the house.

"I'm sorry."

"Three strikes and you're out." She glared at him. "No matter how much I love you, you do this again and I'm out of here, *and* I'm taking Sam with me. I don't give a damn that women are throwing themselves at you. If you so much as allow anyone but me to touch you..." She shook her head and sped up.

André slowed his pace, feeling both her fury and his shame course through him. He followed like a scolded puppy, carrying his sneakers in one hand and his towel in the other.

Katrina turned, swinging as her anger got the best of her. Her fist connected just above André's left cheekbone, sending him back a couple of steps. She turned and stormed back on the path to their house, shaking her head and swearing under her breath.

André watched her go, his cheek and eye burning where her fist connected. He reached up and touched the tender flesh, wincing at the flash of pain before following her into the empty house. He slowly climbed the stairs, entering their room in time to see her disappear into the bathroom.

Regret burned his stomach and he swallowed, staring at the bathroom door and debating. Impulse won out and he crossed the hall, stepping into the bathroom, peeling his bathing suit off. When he opened the shower door, Katrina glared at him over her shoulder.

"All I want is you, Kat. All I've ever wanted is you."

"Then why?"

He shrugged. "I don't know. Maybe because I can't have you right now and it's driving me crazy." He stepped closer. "I'm not getting any relief and I lie awake long after you're asleep and I'm damn frustrated." He reached out and touched her face. "So today, instead of saying no, I let it happen until Dad interrupted." He stepped closer, into the spray of the shower, pulling Katrina to him.

André leaned over and kissed her hard, burying his free hand in her hair, creating more steam than just from the shower. When he pulled away, he reached for the temperature controls, turning it into the cold territory, cooling off the heat coursing through his veins.

Katrina turned the dial back to hot and pushed him against the back wall.

"You can't," André whispered just before her lips pressed against his. *Yes, I can.* Her voice echoed in his mind. André pulled away for a moment. "The doctor gave the go-ahead?"

"It's been five weeks." Katrina looked into his eyes, her hands already stroking him.

André leaned his head back against the shower stall. "Katrina," he groaned and closed his eyes as she trailed kisses up his chest and neck. "Is it really okay?" he asked, trying to control himself.

"Yes," she said. "And your mother won't be back for another hour or so." Before she finished the sentence, André had her in his arms, carrying her dripping body into the bedroom.

Spent and nuzzling her neck, he whispered, "I love you, Katrina Robbins. You own my heart and always have." Closing his eyes, he was faintly aware that the side of his face leaning on her shoulder hurt where she had punched him earlier. Her fingers lightly traced his back, lulling him to sleep.

"André," she whispered, bringing him back to consciousness.

"Mmm?" He leaned up on his elbows.

"I think Mom's home," she said, pushing gently away from him. She rolled off the bed and headed to the bathroom to clean up.

André lay on his stomach for a few minutes, listening to the shower, content to just relax in bed until he heard his son fussing downstairs. He sighed and climbed out of bed, grabbing a pair of shorts. He caught a glance in the mirror and hand combed his hair back into place before wandering downstairs toward the sound of Sammy crying.

"Hi, Mom," he said, entering the kitchen. Sammy was in the portable crib, just starting to get that worked-up cry of discontent when André reached in and plucked him from the mattress.

"What are you doing home?" Linda asked.

"Dad fired me," André answered and turned toward her.

Concern flashed on her face, and she stepped toward him. "What happened to your eye?" she asked, touching the black-and-blue skin just below his left eye. She blinked and a crease of puzzlement appeared between her eyes. Her hand dropped to her side, and she met his gaze. "Did you say your father fired you?"

"Yes and I deserved it," he said, referring to both being fired and the black-and-blue mark on his face, but he didn't go into any more detail about either. Instead, he shrugged and glanced at his son.

"What did you do, André?" Linda asked, annoyance creeping into her voice and transitioning her features into the disappointed look she usually reserved for when he brought home a less than stellar test grade from school.

André expected the transition into the world of X-rated thoughts at any second and when it didn't come, he raised his eyebrows in surprise and stepped back. There was no hunger in her eyes or lewd thoughts in her mind and he offered a smile of gratitude, thankful for the small interlude.

"Well?" she asked as if the last five weeks never happened and she was back to herself.

"Let's just say I screwed up and leave it at that." He looked down at his son and smiled. "Hey there, Sammy," he said, tracing his son's nose with his fingertip. "Did you have a fun day with Nana?"

Sam cooed and smiled at his father, his arms and legs in perpetual motion.

"You are so good with him," Linda said.

"Thanks, Mom." It was the first real observation of his parental skills his mother had shared since Sam's birth.

Katrina came bounding down the stairs, refreshed from her shower. "Thank you so much, Mom. I desperately needed a break today." She reached for Sam.

"Not yet." André glanced at her hands. "You get him all day, every day," he added, wandering into the living room, thrilled to have some quiet time with his son. He sat in the rocking chair and began telling Sam about his day at the beach.

KATRINA LEANED AGAINST THE doorjamb, taking in André and Sam. She looked back at Linda, who was watching the same scene over her shoulder.

"Something is different," Linda said.

Katrina half turned toward her. "What do you mean?"

"André," Linda said. "Something is different with him now." She looked at Katrina. "Besides the black-and-blue eye," she added, eliminating the obvious.

Katrina turned back to André, still feeling the overwhelming need to be in his arms, but it *was* different. It wasn't that "tear off his clothes and jump him despite the crowd" urge that overtook her since Sam was born and she had almost tackled him on the raft earlier, but now it was as if the sex vibe was gone. Her eyes widened. *We slept together for the first time since Sammy was born.*

André glanced in her direction. *Don't you dare say a word.* He smiled at Katrina, making her blush, but it didn't prompt a near orgasmic reaction like it would have this morning and a new theory surfaced in her mind. One she had to test out.

Linda shrugged and wandered away.

"I need to pick up some diapers. Feel like taking a walk with me and Sammy?"

"Sure." André nodded. He stood, handing Sammy to Katrina and grabbing the stroller. He set it up outside, helping Katrina strap in their son. "You think because we had sex, I'm not sending the signal to every female in the vicinity anymore?"

"Actually, that is what I'm thinking." She glanced sideways at him with a grin.

"I don't know, I kind of like the attention. It's good for my ego."

Katrina's smile disappeared. "It's what got you in trouble, remember?"

André hooked his thumbs in his back pockets, keeping stride with Katrina as she pushed the stroller down the street. "Yeah," he said as they passed the area where Anna's craft had been destroyed. They both tried to ignore the small pieces still glimmering on the edge of the grass.

"What are you doing in space?" Katrina asked, returning to the dropped conversation from earlier.

"Stopping a meteor from hitting Earth," André replied. His cavalier attitude made Katrina stop short.

"Why?" she asked.

"Because if it hits, we're all in trouble," he said. "But I can make it miss."

"Like Anna's hovercraft?"

He shook his head. "No, it's too big to explode."

Katrina resumed walking, thinking about what André was saying. "So what are you going to do?" She looked over at him.

"If I can see it, I can push it off course."

Katrina steered the stroller across the street to the entrance of the lake, with André in tow. She could see her friends gathered on the beach and paused. "Is it dangerous?"

André shrugged. "I don't think so. I might need a week's worth of sleep afterwards, but that's it. Your friends," he said, nodding in the direction of the small clan making a beeline to the baby.

Katrina turned to the group with a smile, taking note that not one of them gave André a second glance. She smiled and picked up Sam, showing him off to the crowd of girls.

ANDRÉ STOOD TO THE side, letting Sam take center stage. He glanced around the beach. None of the women turned to look at him like they had before. There were no more lewd thoughts emanating from the strangers on the beach, nor from any of Katrina's friends. He sighed with a measure of disappointment mixed with relief.

Katrina glanced back at him and smiled.

He hated when she was right, but he returned her smile anyway. "Do you want me to run to the store while you stay here with Sammy?"

"Would you mind?"

"Not at all." He wandered away. André walked into the store and headed toward the baby supplies. He turned a corner and Anna stood next to her mother, looking at headache medicines.

She glanced in his direction and her eyes widened with shock.

André sent a nod in her direction, acknowledging her presence before disappearing around the corner.

"André?" Anna asked, stepping into the diaper aisle and approaching him.

"What?" He didn't look at her.

"I have no idea what got into me the last few times I saw you but I wanted to apologize." She studied the pattern in the floor as she spoke.

"Apology accepted," André answered. He plucked a package of diapers off the shelf and slid by her.

"Can I ask you a question?" she asked without turning.

André stopped and sighed. "No. I didn't mean what I said in the locker room," he answered without her asking the question. He glanced back. "I cared, but I wasn't in love with you, Anna." He took the diapers to the checkout, paid, and left without another word. Katrina was right; he would have never forgiven himself if he had killed her.

He arrived back at the beach a few minutes later. "Ready to go?"

Katrina nodded and put Sam back in the stroller. She smiled and waved at her friends as she headed back home with André. "It's all gone." She grinned when they were halfway down the block.

"I know," André answered. "But not with you, I hope." He glanced sideways.

Katrina smiled back at him. "I don't think it'll ever be gone with me."

"Good," André replied as they rounded onto the driveway of the house.

Linda came out on the front porch. "André, your father's been looking for you."

"Why?" André asked.

"I don't know, but he wants you at the office as soon as possible."

André nodded, assuming his father wanted to talk about the mission. He ran upstairs and changed back into more appropriate clothing and Katrina dropped him off at the base, collecting a kiss before heading back home.

He headed straight to his father's office, catching Georgia's eye as he walked by. A small, embarrassed smile appeared on her lips for a moment before André looked away. He slipped into his father's office. "You called?" he asked, startling Matthew.

"I didn't hear you coming," Matthew replied, looking up. "What the hell happened to your eye?"

"It's apparently gone," he said in reference to his father's unspoken commentary about the lack of the female office staff's lewd thoughts and completely ignored his question.

"How?"

André shrugged. "Not quite sure," he lied, but he came to the same conclusion as Katrina. Sleeping with his wife had somehow stopped the vibe from affecting the remainder of the female population. "So why did you want me back in the office?" André slid into the seat.

"The president is on his way," Matthew answered. "He wants to hold a press conference about you."

André raised his eyebrows. "Why?"

"President Foster wants America to know exactly who is saving us. He wants to give them a hero, someone to believe in."

"I'm not a hero, Dad," André answered. "I'm saving my ass, too."

Matthew chuckled. "Yes, but the president is going to make you one whether you like it or not."

"I'm not comfortable with that," André said.

"You don't have a choice, son. When we step out into the press room in a couple hours, you are going to become the most talked about person on the planet."

André leaned back in the seat and closed his eyes. "Why do I have to be there?"

"Because, I want the public to know you aren't a threat," he said. "Otherwise, our family's safety could be in jeopardy."

André sat up straight in the chair. "Why would our family be in jeopardy?"

Matthew sighed. "Sometimes you can be so naïve."

André slowly sank back into the chair. "You're talking about Zyclon all over again, aren't you?"

"No, not like what happened to you as a child. You will become more like a celebrity than an outcast, but there are still nutcases out there who will view you as a threat no matter how we spin this.

There will be fewer issues if you are seen and heard than if we keep you hidden.”

André looked out the window at the sky. “Do you really think it’s a good idea to let this out before we deal with the meteor?” He nodded toward the window.

“You told me you could move the meteor, and I believe you,” Matthew replied.

President Foster walked in the room unannounced. “Are we about ready?”

André shook his head without turning. “No, I’m not.” He stood up, turning toward the president. “I’d rather wait.”

The president studied him, and André looked down at his hands. He didn’t want to be categorized as a freak again, not here.

“Why?”

“Because I’m not comfortable with the attention.”

“Son, you’re the star quarterback on your high school football team. This will be easy in comparison. Trust me.” President Foster smiled. “Besides the press is already set up.”

President Foster led the procession to the podium. André squinted into the bright camera lights and cringed at the roar their entry spawned. The room quieted down to a low murmur, and he swallowed the bundle of nerves caught in his throat.

Relax, Matthew told his son without glancing in his direction.

This is a really bad idea, André thought and surveyed the crowd, forcing himself to stand still like his father.

“Ladies and gentlemen, thank you for coming on such short notice,” President Foster said. “In the last few hours, I’ve been briefed on a new situation that I am compelled to report to the American public.” He paused, glancing back at André and Matthew. “The astronomers at the Houston observatory advised the government that a meteor, larger than the one that caused the eastern hemisphere to flood, is on a direct collision course with Earth. By their calculation, this rock will hit somewhere in the north Atlantic in ten days." He paused and glanced across the quiet room.

Faces peered at the president, some with jaws hanging in shock, some with their hands over their mouths in an attempt to keep their horror in check and others, with wide, teary eyes.

The silence thickened before the president continued, "However, we believe we can change the course of this meteor."

It took the matter of a blink for the room to go wild. Reporters jumped to their feet and fired questions in rapid succession.

President Foster raised his palms and waited for the quiet to settle once again. "As I was saying, we believe we can prevent this disaster from occurring." He sent a glance in Matthew and André's direction.

André remembered what his father told him the first time he encountered the press. They were a bunch of filthy vultures and right at this moment, they scared the daylights out of him. He offered a halfhearted smile and shot a sideways glance at Matthew.

The president let the information he just shared with the press settle. He glanced back at Matthew and nodded, stepping to the side so they could approach the podium.

Matthew stepped forward, leaving André along the wall near the door.

The questions from the press box began to fly all at once, and Matthew held his hand up, waiting for the silence.

"What's the plan?" one of the reporters in the back called out as the room settled.

"The plan is a little unorthodox..."

A frazzled sergeant stepped onto the stage, interrupting Matthew. He hurried to the podium and slipped Matthew a piece of paper.

Gleaning the thoughts of the sergeant, André almost choked, and the slow crawl of panic started in his stomach, echoing outward like a sound wave until it penetrated every cell in his body, freezing him in place.

Matthew looked at the paper and back at the sergeant. He sent a glance in André's direction and then addressed the crowd. "You will have to excuse me for a moment."

He slipped offstage, leaving André alone with the president to fend off the press.

André stared at the chaos before him; questions shot out left and right and the president stepped to the podium. "As Commander Robbins stated, the plan is a bit unorthodox; however, if you quiet down, I will do my best to explain," he said.

The room immediately calmed. Reporters took their chairs and waited.

Of all the thoughts swirling in the president's head, André would have never guessed the one the president chose to lead with and when the words escaped the president's lips, André wanted to disappear, to sink into the backdrop and back into obscurity.

"How many of you remember the false reports of an alien in our solar system?"

Almost all hands rose in response.

The president looked in André's direction. "Those reports were not false."

Pandemonium broke out on the floor and everyone in the press box jumped to his or her feet.

André felt the heat bloom in his cheeks as a few press core gazes landed on him.

"What does that have to do with the meteor?" one reporter shouted over the rest.

"It seems that alien child has certain...gifts. Gifts such as telekinesis, and he has offered to push the meteor off course, so it doesn't collide with Earth."

Silence fell on the room and the president turned, waving toward André. "Ladies and gentlemen, André Robbins."

The room erupted. Questions flew like a hailstorm pounding the domes. André stared, unable to move or speak in the frenzy.

"Ladies and gentlemen," the president bellowed, "one question at a time." He pointed to a female reporter with the *Chicago Tribune*. "Grace."

"How old are you?" she asked André.

"Seventeen," André answered, surprised at the strength in his voice.

"Ted." The president pointed to another reporter.

"Why are you here?" Ted asked.

André didn't know how to answer that question. "Luck, I guess." He wished his father was in the room to fend off the attack.

The room exploded into questions again.

"I will end this press conference if you continue to assault this child with questions all at once!" The president stepped in again and the room quieted down. Every reporter had their hands raised, waiting for their turn like an attentive class trying to impress the teacher.

"Why did you leave your planet?" the reporter from the *Denver Post* asked.

"I, uh..." André stumbled. "I, uh, I was exiled."

Low murmurs spread through the room, but the crowd behaved by the rules the president set forth.

"Why?" another reporter called out before the president could pick the next reporter.

"Because I was different." He shifted from foot to foot, his palms clammy, and his stomach fluttering worse than Katrina with morning sickness. "That's why they hunted me down, killed my parents and sent me into space to die."

Silence slammed down on the room as loud as a judge's gavel, leaving only the buzzing of the equipment.

André looked into the camera, certain his eyes reflected the fear coursing through his entire being. Without another word, he fled the room.

Messiah Chapter 16

ANDRÉ WALKED INTO HIS father's office.

"We intercepted a transmission, André," Matthew said with an earpiece still plastered to the side of his head, listening.

"What kind of transmission?"

Matthew took a deep breath. "I'm not sure," he said. "It came from behind the meteor, and I'd like you to listen to it to confirm the origin."

André nodded; Matthew pressed a few commands on the computer screen and the voice filled the office. Four seemingly innocent words with a slight variation in inflection and pronunciation but not that far off from Earth's language: "Life in dis sector."

Four words spoken by a voice André would never forget.

A voice responsible for carrying out all manner of horrors. André's face and hands went cold with recognition. He shivered. "It's Zyclonian."

Matthew studied him and André shifted in the seat under his father's stark gaze. He shut down his mind, closing it off, keeping his thoughts under quarantine. "If they find out..." He closed his mouth and glanced at his father. *If they find out I'm alive, the meteor will be the least of our worries.*

"It's been over ten years since you were exiled," Matthew said, standing and walking around the desk to face his son. "I don't think you have anything to worry about."

"Did you see the press conference?" André pointed to the screen on the wall, still broadcasting.

Matthew shook his head. "No. Why?"

"The president announced I'm an alien."

Matthew's eyebrows rose.

"And they are out there." He pointed toward the window, the slow burn of panic lacing his skin. "Satellite feed, Dad. If they know I'm alive, they *will* come to destroy me."

Matthew's phone squawked and he pressed the intercom. "Yes?"

"Sir, we intercepted another transmission from the alien craft," the voice notified Commander Robbins.

Matthew looked at André. "What did it say?"

"André lives."

Messiah Chapter 17

"HE CAN'T GO WITH us," André said, nodding toward the president. "It's too dangerous now."

The president stared at André. "I've been in dangerous situations before."

"But not with someone who can kill you without even seeing you, sir," André said, "and I'm not so sure I can protect you from that."

"You can move a sixty-thousand-ton rock but you can't protect us from another person?" the president asked.

André shrugged. "I don't know." He ran a hand through his hair and sighed. "I don't know how strong an adult Zyclonian is. All I know is I couldn't stop them from killing my parents when I was six. I think I'm a hell of a lot stronger than I was then, but I really have no reference point, sir, and I'd prefer not to put your life in jeopardy." He looked between the president and his father. "Or yours either," he said to Matthew.

"You've got no choice, son," Matthew answered. "There's no way I'm letting you go up there alone."

President Foster nodded and turned his attention back to André. "I'm going up there with you and your father." He looked at his watch. "And we are leaving in less than an hour."

André's jaw fell. He glanced at his father and received a nod, confirming the decision. "With all due respect, sir, I do not want you up there."

"André, the president and I can take care of ourselves," Matthew said.

André clenched his fists and glared at the two of them. "Really?" He exercised a fraction of his strength, slamming them both back against the far wall and cutting off their airway with a slight tilt of his head. "For me, this is the equivalent of a five-yard toss," he said, putting a reference point on his effort. He counted to ten; just about the time their eyes started to bulge from the lack of oxygen, he released them, watching as they crumpled to the ground. "That's nothing compared to what could happen up there."

Matthew stood and stared at his son, the shock written in his expression, and he turned to the president. "Mitch, maybe you ought to stay here," he said.

The president's breath still wheezed but he stood and straightened himself out before answering Matthew. "I am going," he said, dismissing any argument and stared André down.

André broke eye contact first. "Y'all're nuts," he drawled looking back at his father and the president. He put his hands on his hips and took a deep breath, shaking his head. "You better bring Captain Grey."

"Who the hell is Captain Grey?" the president asked.

"He's a medical officer and he knows about André," Matthew answered. He walked over to the phone and picked it up, summoning Cal to his office.

"Let's go get our asses fried in space," André snapped and turned away. *Figures. I'll probably die up there. That's exactly what they wanted anyway.* He stared at the sky through the window.

"Mitch, will you excuse us for a moment?"

President Foster nodded and slipped into the outer office.

"André, you can't go up with that attitude," Matthew said.

"Now or later, what's the difference? I've basically sealed the fate of this planet." He looked back at his father.

"You don't know that." Matthew crossed the room. He put his hand on André's shoulder.

"The son of a bitch up there knows I'm here." He glanced at the sky again. "He told them I'm alive and he knows I'm coming after him," André whispered. "Please convince the president not to come with us. I can't protect both of you."

A soft knock at the door interrupted their conversation.

"Come in." Matthew barked the command.

Cal walked into Matthew's office and the president followed.

"Captain, I gather you saw the news conference," Matthew addressed him.

"Yes, sir." Cal stood at attention. He saluted both Matthew and the president.

"At ease," the President said as he crossed the room and took a seat on the leather couch under the television monitor.

André turned to Cal. "Hi."

"You can really stop the meteor?"

André nodded and looked over at his father.

"André thought it would be a good idea to have a medical officer on board with us," Matthew said.

Cal's brow furrowed. "Why?" he asked, looking back at André. "Will doing this hurt you?"

"Pushing the meteor off course won't," André answered.

"But the Zyclonian space explorer might," Matthew added.

Cal raised his eyebrows. "There's another ship out there?"

"Yes," Matthew answered. "And it's not friendly."

Cal looked around the room and nodded. "When do we leave?" he directed at Matthew.

"In less than an hour," Matthew replied.

"Okay, I'll meet you at the outer base with the medical supplies I'll need for the three of us," Cal answered.

"Four," President Foster said. "I'm going as well."

"Three," Matthew corrected and gave a dismissive nod to Cal.

Cal glanced at the three men, his gaze lingering on André before he left the room.

Matthew waited until the door closed and turned to the president. "Mr. President, you can't go with us," he stated, throwing down the gauntlet.

President Foster stared in disbelief. "Bullshit."

"Mitch, you can't," Matthew addressed him as a friend instead of as a subordinate. "You have a responsibility to steer clear of a known ambush. That is what we are doing. If we were just going up there to move a meteor, then yes, I'd welcome your company. But we know there's a hostile presence up there. One aimed at killing my son." He paused and glanced in André's direction. "If his little display earlier is a preview of what could happen, then I have to stand firm on this. I will not clear you to be on that ship."

"Then I'll fire you and get someone who will clear me."

"That is your prerogative, sir." Matthew stood up. "I'll clear my things from this office." He began to stack his personal belongings in the center of the desk.

"Goddamn it, Matthew!" President Foster snapped.

Matthew looked up at him. "Am I fired?"

President Foster glared at Matthew. "No," he spat. He looked between André and Matthew and then stormed out of the room.

"Thank you," André said.

"There are still three of us on board," Matthew said.

"I'm aware of that." He glanced at his father. "Do I need to get a change of clothes or something?"

"No, we have flight suits," Matthew replied.

"Change of underwear?" André raised an eyebrow and offered a smile.

"No," Matthew answered, his expression stern enough for André to ditch any further attempt at levity. "Let's go," he added and led André out of the office to the hovercraft in the parking lot.

Outer base was twenty minutes away on the southeasternmost point of the dome wall, and André tried to focus on the task ahead, but all he kept hearing was that voice in the speakers and he shivered.

"You don't seem concerned that Captain Grey will be with us."

"Cal will be fine," André said, studying the transitioning scenery.

Matthew glanced at his son. "You know the captain's first name?"

André nodded without looking at Matthew, keeping his mind blank. "We talked quite a bit this summer."

Matthew remained quiet, casting glances in André's direction, a crease appearing between his eyes. "You opened his barrier, didn't you?"

André pressed his lips together, irritated that his father could read him so easily.

"André, it's not safe to open barriers of just anyone."

"He's a medical officer and he's known about me since day one." André turned toward his father. "He saved my life once already, or did you forget?"

Matthew's face went red. "I didn't forget."

"I trust him," André said. "So should you. He's worked the powers in his mind to the point he is almost as strong as Katrina."

Matthew looked in his direction. "How powerful is Katrina?"

"She saved Anna's life today," André said, looking out the window again. "Anna was going to kill Katrina, so I blew up her craft." He summed up the event, glancing at his father again. "Kat put a barrier around Anna so she wouldn't get hurt in the explosion."

"You tried to kill someone?"

"I reacted. She intended on killing Kat, and I had to stop her," he answered.

"Why the hell would she want to kill Katrina?"

"Because my vibe drove her over-the-edge crazy," André said. "Can we talk about something else?" He glanced at his father. "Please?"

"You told Katrina what happened this morning?"

André sighed. "Yes."

"And that's all she did to you?" He nodded toward André's face.

"Yes," André answered, and his mind traveled to the shower. He couldn't wipe away the thoughts or the grin that formed fast enough.

Matthew swerved, glaring at André. "In my house?"

André blushed.

"I could just wring your neck."

"I'm sorry, but she's my wife. Besides, it broke whatever spell I was transmitting." André sensed the resignation in his father and met his sideways glance.

Matthew sighed. "I'm glad I won't have to be privy to *that* anymore."

André nodded. "Me too," he answered as they pulled into the outer base.

MATTHEW MARCHED DIRECTLY TO Cal as soon as they arrived at the base. "I understand you allowed my son to convert you."

Cal nodded. "Yes, sir."

Matthew scanned the captain's mind and sized him up. He found nothing that would prevent him from coming on the trip, quite the contrary. This man would die to protect André, just as Matthew would. "Fine," he replied, satisfied with what he dug out of the captain's mind.

"He's a special kid," Cal replied.

"Yes he is." Matthew followed Cal's gaze to where André stood. "It's been a tough year, though." He looked back at Cal.

Cal nodded. "I imagine so, but at least he had honorable intentions."

Matthew smiled. "Not always," he said. "Sometimes he's just a rebellious, impulsive teenager."

Cal laughed. "I can see that, too. I have no idea how I would have dealt with the collective female population throwing themselves at me."

Matthew shook his head. "I'm with you there. I probably would have tagged every single one of them," he said, voicing what he would never admit to his son.

Cal chuckled and nodded. He headed toward the situation room with Matthew.

André sat in a gray and blue nylon flight suit with a matching gray baseball cap on his head, waiting for them.

Matthew turned on the monitor and dimmed the lights. A satellite image came up on the screen, showing the path of the meteor through the galaxy. "The meteor will be passing by Saturn in a few hours. We'll be intercepting it just beyond Jupiter."

He pushed another button, showing the projected path of the meteor. "We want to push this thing a few hundred kilometers off the current course." He pushed the button and showed the new path of the meteor, missing Earth and eventually colliding with the sun. "That is our primary directive." He looked at his son. "This must happen before we intercept our visitor."

André nodded acknowledgment.

"We believe the explorer is following in the meteor's wake, hidden from our satellites," he explained. "When you shove this thing off course, he'll be exposed." Matthew looked at both men in the room. "That's when I expect all hell to break loose."

"What's the plan?" André asked, looking at the path of the meteor replaying behind his father.

"Capture and detain," Matthew said.

André laughed. "You're shitting me?"

"No," Matthew answered. "I'm not going out there with the intent to kill anyone, and neither are you."

André looked at the floor.

"Wipe those thoughts out of your mind, André. That's apt to get us killed," Cal said. "If our visitor perceives us as a danger, then we're already dead."

Matthew nodded. "We're going to act very surprised when we see the ship. Understand?"

André looked at his father. "Bluff?"

"Not exactly," Matthew said.

André looked at him, his eyes widening, and he shook his head. "You're out of your fucking mind, Dad."

"You have to wipe all traces of knowledge of him out of your mind right now." He looked at Cal. "And out of our minds." He looked back at André. "Do you understand what I'm telling you?"

"I understand, but I don't know if I can do that," André said.

"You have to wipe out everything from the point we left my office to go to the press conference and

Cal's memory from the point he entered my office this afternoon."

André stood up in protest. "It screws with your brain," he said.

"This is the only way this will work and if you need to grasp a bright side here, I won't remember you and Katrina slept together under my roof today."

André blushed and picked at another hangnail. Taking a deep breath, he gave his father a slight nod without raising his eyes.

"You can fill us in on why we are here, minus the visitor," Cal piped in.

"You're going to be disoriented," André said.

"It's all right." Matthew approached André. "I trust you, remember?"

"Yeah, I remember. Can you sit down?"

Matthew sat as André requested.

André focused on Cal first, his eyes transitioning to that neon blue Matthew had seen dozens of times, but he had never seen the full transition of power that turned André's eyes into a laser red flash. "You remember coming to my father's office and being told we're going out into space, but that's it. Next thing, you are here."

Cal winced and blinked, glancing at André and Matthew, a puzzled crease appearing between his eyes.

André smiled. "Go change into your flight suit, Cal."

Cal nodded and headed to change.

"Damn." Matthew watched Cal walk off. "It's a complete blank." He glanced back at André.

"Are you sure you want me to do this, Dad?"

"It's the only way I can keep you safe." Matthew inhaled, wondering if there were any nasty long-term side effects to the mind erase he was agreeing to.

"Besides a possible stroke?" André asked, worry painting his gaze.

"I will be fine, André. Just do what you have to do," Matthew said.

ANDRÉ INHALED AND CONCENTRATED. "You fired me, and I took off. You called me back for the press conference, the president announced what we were planning and explained who I am." He paused and raked his palm over his face. "You have no other memories since I left the office outside of the meteor." He pushed gently and his father reacted the same way as Cal. "Dad, we're getting ready to go."

Matthew looked around, blinking and confused.

"The meteor." André pointed at the repeating trajectory on the screen behind him. "You said we need to knock it off base by a couple hundred kilometers?" André asked. "Does it matter which direction?"

Matthew shot his eyes between the screen and André. "No. Either direction will take it out of Earth's path. Think you can do that?"

"Sure, Dad." André kept his mind as blank as a new sheet of paper.

Matthew looked at his son, his brow furrowing. "What the hell happened to your eye?"

André shifted. "I told Kat about this morning. She was a little angry."

Matthew barked laughter. "I'm surprised you're still breathing."

André smiled. "Yeah, well, she forgave me."

Matthew shook his head. "You are one lucky son of a bitch." He stood. "Linda would have shot me if I pulled what you have."

André glanced at his father. "I don't intend to screw up like that ever again."

"I hope not because I'll throttle you myself. She's not someone you want to lose, André." Matthew headed off to change.

André closed his eyes, collected all the memories relating to the visitor in space and jammed them in the room in the back of his mind, closed the imaginary door and locked it. He prayed that would be enough. When he opened his eyes, his gaze landed on the shuttle, studying it from a distance and remembering the last time he flew.

"This ship is a little bigger than the last one you were on," Cal said as he stepped next to André, wearing the same flight suit.

"Seems like a lifetime ago." André let the silence fill the space between them.

"How's Sam doing?" Cal asked after a few moments lost in thought.

André smiled. "He's finally sleeping through the night now." He turned toward Cal. "It's been a long ass summer."

"Just look at it this way, you'll be under forty when your boy is out of college."

Forty. André couldn't comprehend being that old and let out a laugh. "There's something to look forward to."

Cal smiled. "It's not that old."

André smirked and huffed.

"Hey, I'm not that far from forty," Cal pointed out.

"You're over thirty?" André asked.

"Yes."

"I thought you were younger," André said.

"I've got a medical degree through the service, André. That means eight years of school, followed by two years as a resident. I was in my second year as a resident when you first arrived," Cal explained. "You do the math."

"Thirty-four?" André answered.

Cal smiled. "Not bad."

"You're twice my age," he marveled.

"Okay, now you're pushing it."

"Sorry, Cal," André said. "It's just that I thought you were, like, twenty-five."

Cal laughed. "Your dad isn't even forty yet."

André turned and watched as Matthew crossed the floor. "Yeah, but he turns forty this year," he said before his father was at their side.

"Commander." Cal saluted.

"At ease, Captain."

Cal relaxed and smiled. "Your son thinks forty's old."

Matthew shrugged with a small smile on his lips. "What does he know?"

Cal laughed and followed Matthew onto the ship.

André looked around the hangar and then followed them on board, trying to lock the trepidation out of his mind.

Matthew glanced back at his son. "You all right?" he asked, sensing his son's unease.

André nodded. "I'm just a little nervous to go back up there."

Cal turned in the co-pilot's chair, his brow furrowed as he caught the lie. He glanced at Matthew, and then back at André.

"Let it go," André said to Cal.

Matthew looked between the two of them. He went to speak and closed his mouth, turning to the controls. He glanced at Cal as he turned the ignition over, rolled the ship to the exit gates, and waited for the hangar door behind them to close so the vacuum seal could take hold before he opened the outer gate.

Rolling down the runway, he revved the turbo engines and accelerated. As soon as they were airborne, he took the ship up at a seventy-degree angle through the atmospheric layers. Once in space, he set the jets to maximum speed, hitting close to ninety thousand miles per second. He programmed the course into the computer and turned to his passengers.

André watched the stars trace by in bright lines, awed by the view. He had been so sick when Matthew found him that this was lost on him the first time around. Time passed in silence as both Cal and André stared at the celestial visions filling the windshield of the spacecraft.

"You did your thing to Cal," Matthew stated, breaking the silence after they approached Mars and Jupiter loomed in the distance.

André's gaze shot to his father's. "Yes." He didn't hesitate to answer. He glanced back out the window. "How much longer?" he asked, feeling the dread wrap around his heart.

"An hour or so," he answered. "When?"

"Hmmm?" André asked, not taking his eyes from the awe-inspiring sight.

"When did you do it?"

"Early this summer," Cal answered. "I asked him to."

Matthew focused his attention on Cal. "What did you hope to gain?"

Cal smiled. "Knowledge."

Matthew leaned back. "So what can you do?"

"Cal already had a touch of ESP before I opened the gate," André said.

Matthew looked back at André. "While you are on this mission, you will refer to him as Captain Grey, understand?"

André snorted at his father. "What the hell are you babbling about?"

Matthew swung the chair full around and stared down his son. "This is not a game, son. It is a military mission and while you are under my command, you will act accordingly."

"Yes, sir," André mumbled.

Matthew turned back to the controls. "So, Captain, what can you do?"

"I can move things and read minds." Cal turned, studying André, a crease appeared between his eyes. "What's eating you?" he asked.

André shook his head. "Nothing." He looked up through the window as they passed the red blur of Mars.

Matthew and Cal exchanged a look.

"Just let it go. All right?" André said.

Matthew turned toward André. "What is wrong?"

André looked out the window. "I just had a bad day," he answered, trying to find something other than the truth to focus on. The door in the back of his mind was straining against the pressure. "The thing this morning, the fight with Katrina." He shrugged and looked at his father. "I just have a lot on my mind."

"What happened this morning?" Cal asked.

"Georgia happened this morning," André said.

After a moment, the crease between Cal's eyes faded and he said, "Damn, no wonder your wife slugged you."

André shrugged. "Yeah, I screwed things up royally." He looked down at his wedding band. "If things had gone differently today, she would have never forgiven me." He looked back out the window.

"I'm amazed she forgave you at all," Matthew remarked.

"I saved her life today," André said, gaining the attention of both men. "And inadvertently, she saved mine."

"What happened?" Matthew asked, concern replacing some of his irritation.

"Anna tried to kill her," he explained. "She tried to run Kat over with her hovercraft."

Matthew raised his eyebrows, remembering Anna as one of the many girls André had dated his sophomore year. "Why?"

André sighed. "The vibe made her a little psycho."

"What'd you do?" Matthew asked.

"I blew up the hovercraft before it got to Kat," André answered.

"You killed Anna?"

He shook his head. "No. But only because Katrina saved her ass." He took a deep breath. "I reacted." He studied the control panel, not meeting his father's eyes. "Badly," he added. "So, I've got a little bit on my mind right now."

"Jesus," Matthew said, turning back to the controls.

André felt Matthew's disappointment pressing down on his chest. He closed his eyes, succumbing to the gravity of what he did.

"You lost control?"

"No. I knew exactly what I was doing," he answered. "She was gonna kill Kat."

The silence fell over the three of them, no one knowing quite what to say.

"Let's go move a meteor," Cal said, breaking the awkward silence that settled on the cabin.

Jupiter was now within sight and Matthew eased back on the controls, changing the direction of the ship so the meteor was now in full view. "Do you need to be closer than this?" he asked, looking back at André.

"Probably," he answered, "and more to the side as opposed to head-on." André considered the situation. "Do you have the exact coordinates of where it is, so I know which way to push it, Dad?" Nerves jumbled in his stomach.

Matthew pushed a button on the control panel and a monitor slid down to the right of André. After a moment, the screen came to life with the data of the current projected path of the meteor and then the projected corrected path required to launch it into the sun's orbit. It showed the distance differentials between the original path and the changed path as well as probable margin for error.

André digested the information while his father navigated the craft where André requested. He glanced out the window, feeling the first tentacles of thought scans by the intruder. He shut down his mind, concentrating on the task at hand. "That should be good enough," he said.

Matthew slowed the craft, turning it toward the meteor. "What do you need from us?"

André bit his lower lip and looked between the window and his father. "I need the co-pilot seat," he said, glancing at Cal.

Cal stared out the window. A deep crease appeared between his eyes as he studied the meteor and André knew he felt the mind scan as well.

"Captain, do you mind?" Matthew asked.

Cal looked at Matthew. "I'm sorry, what did you say?"

"André needs your seat."

He nodded, glancing back through the window as he unbuckled and relinquished his seat.

André settled into the co-pilot's seat and took a deep breath, settling his nerves and concentrating on gathering the energy within him into a tight ball in his chest. His skin tingled with the power and his pulse pounded, tingeing everything in front of him with a pink hue. His eyes burned with the effort. He clamped his eyes closed, focusing the explosive energy.

When the tingling sensation transitioned into scorching pain, he opened his eyes, letting the power beast loose, aiming it at the meteor. Space rippled in a straight line from their shuttle, closing the distance to the meteor in a blink of an eye.

The meteor vaporized, leaving a billion dust particles floating in space and shock registered in André, dropping his jaw just before the world went black.

MATTHEW STARED AT THE dust particles in awe and turned to witness André slump in the co-pilot's seat, with only the whites of his eyes visible and his skin as pale as the day Katrina's father stabbed him.

"Jesus," Matthew shouted, ripping his seatbelt off and jumping to André's side. He lifted his son's limp head. "Oh, sweet Jesus," he whispered at the slackness in André's face.

Cal shoved Matthew aside and felt André's neck for a pulse. "He's alive," he said over his shoulder to Matthew.

He closed his eyes in a silent prayer until a heavily accented voice filled his head and both he and Cal spun to the windshield and the approaching spacecraft.

"Holy crap," Cal said, his eyes going wide. He forgot about his unconscious ward for the moment.

Matthew took a step, blocking André behind him in a protective reflex before he picked up the transmitter. Trading a glance with Cal, he pressed the button and said, "State your intentions." The only other spacecraft Matthew ever came in contact with was André's and he wondered if this ship was from the same origin.

"Peace." The voice barreled through the cabin in a low baritone that shook the interior of the spaceship.

Matthew had no tangible reason to doubt the alien's motive, but his internal alarms sounded anyway, and an unspeakable apprehension gripped him. "Permission to board?" Matthew asked, glancing at Cal and swallowing the sudden onset of nerves.

"State your intentions?" the voice boomed.

"Same as yours," Matthew replied.

"Permission granted." The craft dipped below and out of sight, followed by the familiar sound of the airlock whistle signaling a successful docking.

"Think he'll be all right?" Matthew asked, looking at André.

"His heart rate is strong, and his breathing is regular," Cal said. "I think he just expended more energy than any of us expected. I'm sure he'll come to in a few." He looked at the docking cabin. "I thought I felt something out there," he said.

Matthew studied the docking cabin as well, debating as he met the captain's gaze. "You coming?"

Cal smiled. "Hell, yeah."

After an atmospheric scan validated the alien craft would sustain them, Matthew opened the air lock and stepped into the docking station, closing the door behind him.

"Our visitor needs oxygen just like we do." The discovery did nothing to settle his internal alarms. A snarled nerve bundle settled in the pit of his stomach. He glanced back toward the cockpit and André, still reading a big blank.

Cal gnawed on his lower lip, surveying the air lock to the other ship.

"Here goes," Matthew said, and with a deep breath, he released the air lock to the visitor's craft and entered with the captain in tow.

A man towering close to seven feet stood in the front of the craft with his back to the air lock, his hands clasped loosely behind his back.

Matthew knew he was tracking them in the reflection, but he wasn't prepared for the image when the alien turned toward them. Red eyes shimmered from an otherwise human form. Matthew stopped in his tracks, his gaze landing on the scar on the alien's cheek and all the stories André told of his homeland surfaced. This was the Zyclonian commander who carried out the order. The one who sealed André in that death pod.

Anger blushed in his cheeks, and he saw the nuance of a change in the man. The calm, friendly smile changed, turning feral and dangerous.

"You have something I want."

Matthew laughed at the sheer irony. He had longed to be in the same room as this man, to kick his ass to the other side of the universe and back. But with André so close and no idea of how powerful this man was, he couldn't take the chance. "I have no clue what you are talking about."

"He vaporized the meteor," the Zyclonian replied.

"You can't have him," Matthew said, his internal alarms now sounding louder than the pounding of his heart.

The Zyclonian laughed until he lost his balance, taking a step back against an invisible shove and his gaze swung to Cal.

"You can't have him." Cal echoed Matthew's sentiments. His hands balled into fists and his head hung low. His eyes narrowed into glaring slits aimed at the alien standing at the bow of the ship. He clenched his teeth, trying to let the anger build, to fuel his power. "You can't kill him," he clarified, gleaning the stranger's deepest thoughts.

Cal slammed against the wall with enough force to daze him. He slumped to the ground, struggling to his hands and knees.

"Who are you to stop me?" he asked, glancing in Matthew's direction.

"I'm his father," Matthew growled.

The stranger laughed again. "You aren't his father."

"Bullshit," Matthew spat.

"I killed his father," the Zyclonian laughed, taking a step toward Matthew. "Just like I'm going to kill you."

Pain seared his entire body and Matthew fell to his knees, struggling to pull in a breath against the invisible hand crushing his chest.

THE COLD HAND OF fear wrapped around his heart and André sat up like a bolt of lightning, his eyes darting around the ship, disoriented.

André, wake your ass up now. Cal's thoughts invaded his mind, jolting him out of the chair. He followed the silent beacon, out through the air lock. His father's pain slammed into him like a tackle from a blind side. He stumbled, trying to catch himself. Fury enveloped him and he stormed around the corner, his gaze landing on the man causing his father's suffering. "Let him go," André growled.

The man glanced at André. "Hello André. It's been a long time." His eye twitched.

Matthew's shoulder split open, and his scream of pain echoed on the walls.

André stepped in front of his father, interrupting the power flow.

Matthew collapsed on the floor, his breath no longer gasping, but coming in harsh pulls as the air flowed in.

Cal crawled over to Matthew and began assessing the damage.

André glared at the man, recognition settling deep in his gut, bringing with it a raw blinding rage. "I know you," he hissed.

"I never imagined you would live long enough to be saved." The man laughed.

Hatred flared, along with memories of his parents' dying screams. "You're the son of a bitch who killed my parents."

"I killed them slowly, painfully, without mercy. And now I'm going to do the same to you." His eye twitched.

André's left shoulder split open and he clenched his teeth. "Is that all you got?" André asked, using the pain to fuel the building power in his soul. With a tilt of his head, he released a bullet, sending the man flying back against the glass. André took a step forward with murder in his heart.

"Don't, André," Matthew gasped.

André paused, his father's labored plea taking some of the fire from him. "He killed my parents," he said, justifying his intent.

"That doesn't mean you get to do the same," Matthew said, his voice a little more controlled.

André ground his teeth, glaring at the man, still holding him against the glass with a fraction of his power. "He was also the one who sealed me in that tin can to die." The glass behind the man began to crack under the pressure. "Get my father out of here, Cal," André ordered, glancing over his shoulder. "Now."

Cal picked Matthew up, backing out of the room and into the airlock. It closed at André's direction, sealing them out of the deadly space before he focused back on the Zyclonian. He wanted to feel this man's bones break under his fists. He released the alien from his mental grip.

The man fell to the ground but was up on his feet within a heartbeat.

"Captain Trevor, what the hell are you doing in my galaxy?"

"Looking for another world to conquer." His eye twitched again.

André put his hand up, stopping the flow of power aimed at him. The alien's eyes widened in surprise. "Have you ever used your hands to kill?" he asked. "Or are you just a fucking coward?" He pushed the power back in the direction it originated, knocking Captain Trevor back on his ass.

"I'd love to tear your head off with my bare hands and bring it back to the emperor." Captain Trevor stood, advancing at the implied invitation.

André smiled and without warning, threw the first punch. It connected with Captain Trevor's chest, sending him flying onto his back. "That felt good." He turned so he led with his right shoulder, protecting his injured shoulder, both fists positioned in front of him like a boxer. "If you knew I was coming, why didn't you just take out the ship?" he asked as the captain got to his feet.

Captain Trevor charged.

André sidestepped and threw an upper cut, connecting with the captain's rib cage, knocking him across the ship. "Is it because you aren't as strong as I am?"

"I'm going to take great pleasure in seeing you die," Captain Trevor said, standing up.

André shook his head. "Sorry to disappoint you, but I promised my girl I'd come home from this trip." He centered himself again.

"Your girl?" the captain asked.

"Yeah, I got a girl waiting for me. But you, you've got nothing waiting for you but a world of hurt."

The captain lunged, this time swinging and connecting with André's jaw.

André stumbled back, catching himself before he lost his balance completely, but it wasn't quick enough to prevent Captain Trevor from reaching him. A hand as strong as the vise in his father's garage clamped down on André's throat, lifting him off his feet and slamming him into the wall.

"Looks like your girl is going to be disappointed after all," Captain Trevor growled in André's face, and dug his thumb into the cut on André's shoulder with his free hand.

André cried out in pain. "Son of a bitch," he gasped, throwing a weak punch into Captain Trevor's side and planting a kick with everything he had, right between Captain Trevor's legs. He dropped instantly; the captain sunk to his knees, holding his balls, red tears welling in his eyes.

André didn't wait for the captain to regain his composure. He slammed his fist into the captain's upturned face, smashing his nose. He threw a second punch, connecting with the captain's eye. Crippling pain ripped through his thigh as it split to the bone and he yelped, stumbling back to the center of the room before slipping to his knee.

Anger raged, twirling and binding with the pain, and André forced himself to his feet.

Captain Trevor leaned against the wall, his nose gushing blood from between his hands. His eye twitched again, slamming André across the room into the far wall.

Fire flared in his side, and he nearly doubled over, his hand pressing against the wet fabric of his flight suit, pushing the torn skin together. Wrath boiled through every vein, pounding and pulsing until it merged in the center of his being. Like a rocket, his power fired, accompanied by a roar that echoed off every surface in the room.

Captain Trevor catapulted toward the window of the aircraft and the glass crumpled against the shove André let loose. Both Captain Trevor and all the oxygen in the alien craft were sucked into space.

The air hissed out of André's lungs, and he lunged for the air lock, mentally pressing the release valve, opening the door to the cargo bay beyond. It took all his effort to pull himself out of the space vacuum and into the cargo bay, leaving him just enough energy to slam his palm on the door controls.

His lungs stung with the lack of oxygen, and he fell on his hands and knees, crawling toward the shuttle door as white spots filled his vision. It took a moment to understand the high-pitched wheeze wasn't the replenishing of oxygen; it was coming from him. Pain and panic filtered into his consciousness, and he reached for the shuttle door. "Dad," he exhaled with the last of the oxygen.

THE DOORS SWISHED OPEN, and Matthew turned to see Cal drag André into the spacecraft. Matthew sat at the controls, his shoulder bandaged and throbbing, but not as much as the fear lacing the lining of his stomach.

"Get us out of here, Commander," Cal said.

Matthew didn't need to be told twice. He unlatched the ship from the alien craft and headed back toward Earth. He caught a fleeting view of the Zyclonian and wondered if he was dead. A closer look at the crystallized face confirmed it, and Matthew glanced over his shoulder. "How's my son?"

Cal didn't answer directly, but the barely concealed curses jolted Matthew along with the intensity of how Cal worked. Blood flowed in pulses from André's thigh, and Matthew swallowed hard. He'd seen that type of wound before. An arterial bleed, the kind that requires transfusion to keep the patient alive and his head snapped toward the body of the Zyclonian who hurt his son.

He turned the ship around.

"What the hell are you doing?"

"Getting my son blood," Matthew replied and slowed the ship as he passed the floating corpse.

Cal nodded before continuing his patch job on André's thigh, brandishing his laser like a wizard wields his magic wand. "We need to get him back home, as fast as you can, Commander. He's lost a lot of blood."

Maneuvering the ship, he trapped the dead body in the outer bay, and then he resealed the doors and pressurized the air lock.

A thud followed as the body hit the floor.

"Tell me when it's safe," Cal said, taking a sample of André's blood and cataloguing it in his handheld computer. He pulled out a syringe and a bag, setting it aside until Matthew gave the word and went back to patching André up.

"Okay," Matthew said, and opened the air lock.

Cal disappeared into the loading bay and returned a few minutes later with a collection bag holding a little under a half pint of frigid blood and gave Matthew a nod. "It's close enough to André's."

Matthew closed the air lock and depressurized the loading dock, allowing the temperature to drop and freeze dry the corpse just in case they needed more. He put the ship into overdrive and sped toward home. He spared a quick look, in time to capture Cal setting up the transfusion line.

"How much longer?" Cal asked.

"An hour. I'm pushing the limit on this thing," he said, pulling his attention away from André and concentrating on getting them home. He maneuvered the ship through space at a speed he never dared before, and it took every ounce of focus to reach their destination in one piece. Earth sped toward him and true to his word, an hour later they skidded to a stop at the outer base bay.

"Tell me my son is okay," he said as he drove the ship through the doors and into the hangar. Red strobe lights of the ambulance reflected in the otherwise dark hangar and Matthew was thankful they returned much earlier than expected and there would be no added complications of getting André the help he needed.

"I don't know if he is, sir," Cal said, looking down at the unconscious boy. "He stopped shaking about twenty minutes ago, but his pulse is still all over the place."

The doors to the ship opened and medics converged. Matthew ordered the body in the back of the ship cryogenically preserved and tagged as an organ donor for André and trusted they adhered to his directive. He didn't wait to oversee the collection; instead, he climbed into the waiting ambulance, wincing with every motion, the pain wracking every nerve now that the adrenaline had died.

"You need to be checked out when we get there," Cal said.

He nodded and dug his phone out of his pocket, calling the house. "Hi, Linda," he said, exhaustion lacing his voice and he cleared his throat. "There's been..." He traded a glance with Cal. "There's been an accident and André's hurt."

"What?" Linda's voice carried the disbelief he expected.

"André is seriously wounded." He squeezed the bridge of his nose. Voicing the words brought burning tears of fear to his eyes and he squeezed them back. "We're on our way to St. Vincent's. Bring Katrina."

He disconnected the call and took a calming breath, pushing away the fear of losing André and concentrating on his earlier feat. Meeting Cal's gaze, he finally voiced his awe. "He vaporized that meteor."

"Yeah. And he saved both our lives."

Please, God, don't let my son die. Matthew offered a silent prayer, hoping the Lord would spare him this kind of pain.

"I'll do my best to make sure that doesn't happen, Commander," Cal said.

Matthew nodded, blocking the thought from his mind.

"MATTHEW, I GOT HIM. You need an x-ray," Cal said as they climbed out of the ambulance. He gave a nod to an orderly, who escorted Matthew away.

Cal gave the rundown to the emergency room doctor as they wheeled André into a private triage room. He worked side by side with the doctor to clean and cauterize all the wounds, including inspecting the laser patch job he did in space.

"You saved this boy's life," Dr. Schwartz stated as he inspected the artery. "Nice job."

"Thanks, but he isn't out of the woods yet," Cal said, checking the readout on the machines.

The doctor glanced over his shoulder at the numbers. "Those can't be right," he said.

Cal glanced over his shoulder. "They are."

"But his heart rate…"

Cal glanced at the register, the sporadic and slow beat unlike any healthy human. It resembled the beginning of a cardiac arrest and the doctor flipped on the defibrillator.

"Dr. Schwartz, that is not necessary." Cal reached over and turned off the machine. "He isn't in cardiac arrest."

"But the readout?"

"If he was human, I would agree, but he's not and I've seen this before," Cal said, praying he was right. He didn't know what an electric shock would do to André, and the kid had slipped into what looked like a coma.

The doctor blinked and stepped back as if André were a ticking bomb and his eyes widened. "That's the alien from the president's press conference?"

"Yes."

"Did he—"

"Yes, he stopped the meteor," Cal answered before the doctor finished his question. "And now that he's stabilized, I'd like him moved to the intensive care unit and kept under observation while I talk with his family."

Dr. Schwartz nodded.

"If anything changes, please page me," Cal said, writing his pager number on the chart. "And please make sure a security detail is put in place. I don't want the press to get wind that we are here."

Dr. Schwartz deflated a bit, but he nodded and Cal gave him a quiet glare.

"Consider this part of doctor-patient confidentiality. If you leak any of this to the press, I'll make sure the only job you can get is wiping babies' butts in the local shelter medical unit."

"Yes, sir." Dr. Schwartz wheeled André toward the ICU.

Cal stripped his gloves and threw them in the trash before heading to the emergency waiting room in search of Matthew's family. He stopped at the registration counter. "Excuse me, can you tell me where Commander Robbins is?"

"He's still in the x-ray department," the nurse said.

Cal nodded and entered the waiting room, peeling off his surgical hat. "Mrs. Robbins?"

Both women looked at Cal.

THE CONCERN IN CAL'S eyes, along with his flurry of thought, sent Katrina's heart racing. Panic tried to steal her voice, but she pressed through it and asked, "Is André all right?" Despite her best efforts, tears clouded her vision.

Cal pulled up a chair. "He's in a coma," he said, keeping eye contact with Katrina. "He sustained trauma to his shoulder, leg, and abdomen. He has several bruises on his back and neck, but thankfully nothing is broken." He offered a hint of a smile. "He also went without oxygen for a few minutes and that's what we believe precipitated the coma." He glanced at the sleeping baby in the carrier in front of Katrina. "The bright spot is that he still has brain activity and is breathing on his own." He raised his gaze back to hers.

Katrina blinked and hot tears cut paths down her cheek. "Coma? André's in a coma?"

Cal nodded.

"How?" she started, and then her eyes widened. The question brought a stream of memories from Cal, walking her through the horror.

"Y'all knew there was a Zyclonian explorer behind the meteor and you still went up there?" Katrina said, her voice shaking with the anger that flared.

Cal tilted his head and his eyebrows scrunched together. "I, uh..."

Katrina's eyes narrowed. "Dad asked him to erase your memories?"

Cal shut his mouth, the crease between his eyes smoothing out and his eyes widening as well. "I guess he did."

"Then why the hell do you remember it?"

He shrugged. "I got knocked around a bit too."

Her anger diffused, replaced by panic, and she held her fiery response at bay. She couldn't lose André, not now, not when their son was so young. "When can I see him?" Her voice cracked under the stress rattling through her.

"Right now if you'd like," he replied.

Linda cleared her throat, capturing their attention; her face was pale and her eyes peered out from dark circles of worry. "Where's Matthew?"

"In the x-ray department. He was banged up a bit too," Cal said, leading them into the hallway.

Katrina stared at the matted mess at the back of Cal's head.

"Did anyone check you out?" Linda asked.

"No. Why?"

"You have blood on the back of your head," Katrina said.

Cal reached up and touched his hair. He pulled his hand away and looked at the tacky blood on his fingers. "Huh, look at that."

MATTHEW GLANCED UP FROM the x-ray table when Cal entered the room. He slipped his shirt on with a wince, pain still flaring even with the elasticized belt strapped around his midsection. "Six cracked ribs," Matthew said. "How's André?"

"Coma," Cal said.

Matthew hung his head. "I should have never taken him up there."

"Commander, he's breathing on his own and still has brain activity," Cal said. "So, stop kicking yourself. He wouldn't want that."

Matthew inhaled and held the deep breath, waiting for the sharp stab to dissipate before exhaling slowly. "Cal, I wanted to thank you."

"For what?"

"For saving my life and André's."

"It's my job, sir."

Matthew nodded. "Well, this was above and beyond, and I think that warrants a promotion." He stood. "Colonel."

"Thank you, sir," Cal replied with a humble smile. He led Matthew to André's room.

When Matthew stepped in the room, Katrina sat holding André's hand. Tears rolled down her cheeks unchecked while Linda rocked with Sam in the corner, humming in the baby's ear. Her gaze met Matthew's, conveying the level of concern in her heart. "Hi," she said, standing and crossing the room to kiss his cheek.

"Hi, hon," he replied.

"What happened?" Linda asked.

"André took care of the meteor and then we were ambushed by a Zyclonian spaceship." He glanced toward the bed. "If I had known the son of a bitch was out there, I would have never gone near the ship," he said, looking at his son.

"You knew that bastard was up there." Katrina turned on Matthew. "You knew he was behind the meteor, and you knew he wanted to hurt André."

Her words hit harder than the Zyclonian's fist, and Matthew inhaled, feeling the sting in his ribs. "There's no way—"

"Take a look at Cal's memories," she said, cutting off his rebuke and pointing toward Cal.

He swung his gaze to Cal. His mind was open, and the events of the last twelve hours transmitted in a matter of seconds, giving Matthew a full account of conversations that seemed to be non-existent in his own mind. "I ordered him to wipe out our memories?"

"Yes. You did it to protect us, sir. You believed we wouldn't get the chance to address the meteor if the alien knew we were aware of his presence. In light of what happened, I'd have to say that was a smart move."

Matthew narrowed his eyes. "Why can you remember, and I still draw a complete blank?"

Cal touched the back of his head. "I guess the bang on my head must have jarred the memories back."

"Jesus." He turned his gaze to the hospital bed.

Katrina glanced at all of them. "I'd like to be alone with my husband, if you don't mind," she said, tears shimmering on her cheeks. "Please."

They shuffled out of the room and closed the door behind them. Matthew took a seat on the bench in the hallway and put his head in his hands. "What kind of father am I?"

"You are a good father," Linda said, taking the seat next to him with Sam on her shoulder.

Yeah, right. I walked him right into the devil's lair.

KATRINA PUT HER HEAD on André's stomach and sobbed. "If you don't come back to me, I'll kick your ass worse than that alien son of a bitch did," she said, sitting up and sniffling. "You hear me?"

The edges of André's lips twitched into a smile. "You gonna spank me or what?" he croaked. His eyes fluttered open, and his vision slowly came into focus on Katrina's face. He went to lift his arm to touch her cheek and the pain in his shoulder made his vision double and his hand dropped back on the mattress. "Ouch." The blackness threatened again.

"Stay with me, André."

The panic in her voice helped him focus instead of allowing himself to drift back into the cloud of oblivion. He shifted and pain seared through his entire body. "I hurt like hell."

Katrina smiled a little and her eyes dropped to his neck. Without warning, the tears began to flow again.

"Don't." He gritted his teeth, lifting his hand to wipe the tears off her cheeks. The effort pushed him beyond his current limit, exhausting him.

"You came back to me."

He nodded, dropping his hand. "I always will." He stared at her and then turned his attention to the hospital room, scanning the machines and intravenous drip before bringing his gaze back to her. "I knew him, Kat." He closed his eyes against the red sheen now covering his vision. "It was the son of a bitch who killed my parents and sealed me in the spaceship." He paused and squeezed his eyes tighter, denying his tears a chance to escape. "I wanted to kill him with my own hands. I wanted to feel his bones break under my fist." His voice cracked under the flurry of emotions slamming into him. Fear, anger, sorrow, regret all combined and he opened his eyes, staring into her teary green gaze. "I'm sorry."

"Why are you apologizing?" Katrina asked, wiping her face.

"Because it was selfish and almost got us all killed," he said. "I should have just taken him out when I walked into his ship."

"I'm not sure you had the strength when you first walked in, André," Cal said from the doorway. "I think you needed that level of fury to do what you did." He walked into the room, followed by Matthew.

André turned toward the door, wincing at the pain the movement caused. "What I did was stupid."

"Maybe." Matthew crossed to the bed. "But not as stupid as allowing you to go up into space that far, knowing he was there. I'm sorry for putting you in that situation."

André stared at him. "I knew the risks." He scanned his father's mind. His memories still had the blank spot. "How did you find out?"

Matthew's gaze drifted to Cal and back. "It doesn't matter. All that matters is you're okay. For a little while there, we weren't sure, and that scared the daylights out of me." He messed up André's hair. A grimace of pain flashed, and he dropped his arm to his side.

"Your ribs are broken?" André asked.

Matthew nodded. "I'll live. I have to wear this thing a few hours a day." He pulled up his shirt, showing André the elastic wrap. "And my shoulder will take a while to heal, but considering the alternative..." He shrugged.

André lifted his right arm and looked at his hand, flexing it. His knuckles were bruised and swollen, but it didn't hurt the way the rest of his body did. "At least my throwing arm is okay," he said.

Matthew and Cal laughed.

"You aren't going to play football for a while," Cal said.

"You have to be kidding me! Practice starts in two weeks."

"Your thigh was sliced open to the bone," Cal replied. "That alone is going to take at least a month to heal properly."

"A month?" André balked.

"André, I almost lost you on the way back," Cal snapped. "You almost died. So, taking a month to let your body heal is not the end of the world."

"They will just have to play without you the first couple of games," Katrina added.

André didn't speak, but the disappointment was enough to force a sigh from his chest and he nodded assent. He glanced at Katrina. "Where's my son?"

"Your mom has him in the hall," Matthew answered.

"Can I see him?" he asked.

Matthew opened the door and waved Linda into the room.

"Thank God," Linda said, handing the baby to Cal and coming to the side of the bed. Her eyes immediately filled with tears. "You are not allowed to scare me like that," she scolded and gently put her hands on André's face. "Understand?"

"I'm okay, Mom." André tried on a smile but from the sadness in her eyes, he was sure it was more of a grimace than a smile and he sighed, covering her hand with his good one and giving it a little squeeze. Sometimes he didn't need words with her, and this was one of those times.

Linda patted his cheek. "I can see that." She blinked the tears back and glanced around the room.

Cal smiled down at the baby in his arms before he raised his eyes. "You have a beautiful son."

André found the controls for the bed and raised the back to a sitting position. The only visible sign of pain he allowed was the tightening of his jaw. "Bring him over here." He reached his arm out. He didn't care how much it hurt; he wanted to hold his son.

Cal brought the sleeping baby to André's side and put him on André's chest, so Sam's head was resting on André's right shoulder. He stepped away as André wrapped his arm around his son.

"Thanks, Cal," André said. He kissed Sam's cheek. The sweet clean baby smell emanating from his son brought a lump to André's throat and he closed his eyes, leaning his head back on the pillow. Tears of gratitude stung his throat; he didn't dare open his eyes because this was the type of moment that crumbled into reality and he was sure if he opened his eyes, he'd still be in that god-awful death pod.

Katrina's hand caressed his cheek, breaking the spell, and he nuzzled against her warm skin. Hot tears squeezed from the corner of his eyes, sliding a warm path down his cheeks and the soft fabric of tissue wiped the tears from his cheeks.

"Thank you," he whispered to no one in particular.

Messiah Chapter 18

ANDRÉ CAME HOME FROM the hospital three days later in a wheelchair. A sea of paparazzi greeted him with flashing cameras and microphones jammed in his face.

Matthew pushed him through the crowd to the front steps, where he stopped. "Shit," he mumbled. He hadn't thought about how he was going to get André up the stairs and onto the porch.

André looked up at him. "They know that I'm not from Earth, right?"

Matthew snorted. "Yes."

"Let's give them something to write about. Let go."

Matthew let go of the chair, smiling a little as it rose in the air and rolled onto the porch. The crowd went silent. He climbed the steps and resumed pushing the chair into the house. "You are such a troublemaker." He grinned, slamming the door behind him.

André turned the chair around. "If you had planned it right..."

Matthew chuckled. "I can roll you back out on the porch." He went to open the door.

"No, don't," André said, believing his father's bluff. "How long has it been like that?"

"Since the news got out that we were back," Matthew answered. "I chose St. Vincent's because I knew the media wouldn't get past the guards."

"How long do you think they'll camp out?"

Matthew shrugged. "I don't know. I hope once you grant an interview, they'll lose interest but I'm not even sure that will do." He moved the curtain and looked out at the group of reporters. "Think you're up to an interview?"

Katrina came out of the kitchen with Sam in her arms.

André raised a questioning eyebrow. "Should I?"

Katrina thought for a moment. "If we want any peace and quiet, I think so."

"You think I'm presentable enough?"

Katrina pressed her lips together, trying to stifle a laugh, and shook her head.

"I love you too," André said, adopting the same slight grin that now graced her face.

Katrina smiled. "The clothes aren't too bad, but the hair leaves a lot to be desired."

He rolled into the bathroom and propped himself in front of the sink, laughing at his reflection. "I look like shit." His hair had the distinct quality of a mad scientist, and his face was pale and blotchy. His eyes stared back, bluer than usual due to the contrast of the red veins slicing through the whites of his eyeballs. Turning on the water, he threw some in his face and hair, grabbing the towel before the water dripped on his blue polo shirt. He ran the comb through his hair until he was satisfied with the image. Lowering himself back in the wheelchair, he rolled back into the living room. "Better?"

"Yes," Katrina said.

André rolled to the recliner and winced as he shifted into it. "I don't want to give an interview in the wheelchair," he said, meeting his father's gaze once he settled into the comfortable seat and raised the footrest.

Matthew dialed a number on his phone and disappeared.

"Are you sure about this?" André asked, reaching for Sam.

"I think so, but I certainly don't want Sam on camera," she said.

"I'll give him back before they finish setting up, okay?"

She nodded and handed Sam to him.

"Commander, I want to thank you for this exclusive," a voice said from the hallway leading to the garage. André traded a glance with Katrina, trying to squash the nervous flutters in his stomach.

"Joanna, if you exploit my son in any way, I will make sure this is the last interview of your career," Matthew said, his eyes hard and unyielding as they stepped into the living room. "He is still only a teenager."

André took a deep breath and glanced up at Katrina. She put her hand on his shoulder and he smiled at her, silently thanking her for the support before he gazed back at the beautiful blonde reporter and the cameraman who stood stock still staring at him.

Joanna Cassidy stopped in her tracks and shot a glance at her cameraman. "Commander, I didn't know you and your wife had a child recently."

"We didn't."

Her smile never faltered, and she turned toward André and Katrina, crossing the living room and offering her hand to André. "Hello, I'm Joanna Cassidy."

"Nice to meet you, Miss Cassidy," André said, shaking her hand. "This is my wife, Katrina," he said looking up at her.

"Your wife?" Joanna asked, raising her eyebrow.

"Commander Lawrence was my father," Katrina said, shaking the reporter's hand and trying not to let her disgust show. André thought she did a pretty good job, considering how much she hated reporters.

"And this is our son Sam." André looked down at Sam, smiling.

"He is adorable," Joanna said with less than a fleeting look. "I want to thank you for letting me interview you," Joanna directed to André.

André nodded. "Thank my dad." He swiveled his gaze to the staring cameraman. "What's your name?"

"Um, Tim." He shifted his weight from one foot to the other.

"I won't bite," André said. He felt the fear radiating from Tim. "You ever cover the local football games?"

Tim nodded.

"The Sabers?"

Tim nodded again.

André smiled. "I'm the quarterback."

Tim's expression changed. The fear of the unknown transitioned to recognition and a smile formed. "You have a hell of an arm."

André felt the heat rush into his cheeks. "Thanks, man."

"Seriously, I heard your name come up more than once during the pro draft," Tim said.

André's eyebrows arched and his heart skipped. *The pro draft? Damn. I hadn't even entertained that option.* "Really?"

"Yeah, they want to see what you do this year to make sure last year wasn't just a fluke," Tim said, setting up the camera.

André's smile faded. "It'll be a while before I can play." He glanced up at Katrina. "You want to take Sam?"

"No, keep him in your arms," Joanna said.

"I don't think so." Katrina plucked Sam out of André's arms. "You are not here to exploit my son." She walked out of the room.

André watched her leave. He smiled and shrugged a little as he looked back at Joanna. "I don't want my son on camera either," he said. "This is about me, not him."

Joanna smiled. *That's what you think.*

A cold anger burrowed into his skin and André dropped the warm façade, staring her down. "Yes, that is what I think, and I'll ask you to leave if you bring it up in the interview."

Joanna's jaw hung askew.

"And I'll make whatever you have recorded disappear," he added. "Understand?"

Visibly flustered, Joanna smoothed her skirt and nodded.

"Are we ready?" André asked after a moment, adopting the friendly smile again.

Joanna looked at Tim for confirmation. He nodded and flipped on the lights.

André squinted at first as Joanna took the seat to his right. He blinked, letting his eyes get used to the bright camera light.

"André, can you tell the viewers why you are here?"

André took a deep breath. "Sure. It was dumb luck," he answered, knowing that was not what she wanted to hear.

"Can you expand on that a little?" she asked, with the same winning smile.

André almost laughed at the thought of expanding on dumb luck, but he kept his expression neutral. "I drifted into this galaxy and Commander Robbins found me. He saved my life."

"Were you alone in space?"

André nodded. "Yes."

"For how long?"

"I figure about five years," he answered.

"Why were you in space alone?"

"Because I was exiled."

Joanna gasped, but André could tell it was all for the camera. Her mind was working overtime and

André had to bite down on the growing unease filling him.

"Why?"

"Because the emperor was a supreme nutcase and I happened to be an easy scapegoat," he said, directly to the camera. He shrugged, trying to brush it off but the truth bit at him, getting under his skin. He shifted in his seat.

"Pardon?" Joanna asked.

André sighed. "It's a long, involved story, but the bottom line is the emperor considered me a threat, so he executed my parents and sealed me in a space pod and sent me into space to die."

Joanna's composure slipped for a fraction of a second and her mouth dropped open. She popped it closed and focused on the story that just got a little hotter. "Are you?"

"Am I what?"

"A threat?" Joanna answered, pleased that he had walked right into this line of questioning.

Irritation bloomed and André smiled, hiding it for the time being. He shook his head. "No. Especially not to Earth." He glanced past the camera to where Katrina stood. "This is my home." He looked back at Joanna. "The only home I've ever known."

Joanna took a deep breath, disappointed at the way André was working the interview. "Is that why you volunteered to stop the meteor?"

André nodded. "It was the right thing to do."

"Even if it meant coming out to the world?"

"Yes. I'm not that different from the next guy," André answered with a shrug. "I bruise when I get hit." He pointed to his face. "I'm not invincible," he said.

"And yet you can vaporize a meteor the size of Texas," Joanna said. She had been privy to some of the data that had been collected by NASA prior to their return. "It vanished into thin air."

André shrugged. "I've got a more developed level of extra-sensory perception than most humans."

"That sets you apart. Humans can't do that."

"That's where you are wrong. You have the capability inside; you just don't know how to break down the barriers in your mind to open the floodgates." He smiled. *Do not elaborate on that, André.* Matthew's voice boomed in his head.

"And how do you know that?" Joanna asked.

André smiled at her. "Do you follow your hunches?" he asked her, turning the tables on her.

"Yes," she answered with no hesitation.

"There you go," André said. "Hunches, instinct—whatever you want to call it—is a form of ESP."

Joanna laughed. "You are comparing a hunch to completely destroying a meteor?"

"What else do you want to ask me?"

Joanna glanced at her cameraman. "How did you get hurt?"

"What has the media been told?" André asked. He wanted to know how much he could say. *They were told that we had a run-in with an alien craft. The fact that it was Zyclonian was not disclosed,* Matthew's voice informed him.

"We were told that you ran into trouble in the form of an alien space craft." Joanna echoed what Matthew had silently told him.

André sighed. *How much can I say?* he sent to his father. The answer came a second later: *As much as you want.* "Yes," André answered. "Ironically, it was from the planet I came from."

Joanna couldn't hide the surprise fast enough. "Really?"

"Bastards are looking for more worlds to conquer," André answered. He shifted in his seat, sighing as he looked between the camera and Joanna.

"Did you know they were coming?" Joanna asked.

André shook his head. "No."

"Did they know you were here?"

"No." *But they do now.* "Not until the press conference the day we left to stop the meteor. The explorer picked up the satellite feed. He knew we were coming."

"Why did they hurt you?"

André looked squarely at her. "Because they still want me dead," he replied, trying to keep the bitterness out of his voice, but not doing a very convincing job. "They wanted to bring my head back to the emperor as a gift," he added for shock value.

Joanna recoiled in disgust. "The word on the street is that you saved your father and a medic on board."

André shrugged. "I guess," he said, shying away again.

Matthew strutted into camera range. "My son is being modest. If he hadn't stepped in, we would have died." He put his hand on André's shoulder. "In the process, he was almost killed."

André twisted his wedding band, studying the way his finger molded around the metal.

"What happened, André?" Joanna asked, feigning sorrow.

He raised his eyes to the camera. "We fought; I killed him. End of story," he concluded, closing the door on further questioning.

"The alien body was brought back. Can you tell us why?"

André raised his eyebrows and shot a glance at his father.

Matthew took a deep breath. "His blood type matched my son's."

André blinked. "Huh?"

"You needed blood." Matthew looked down at him.

"So, you..." He trailed off, getting the picture out of Matthew's mind. He sighed and closed his eyes. He hadn't realized just how close they came to really losing him. The slow rush of blood out of his face left him cold and dizzy.

"We brought the body back for organ donation if André ever found himself in a situation where he needed a heart, liver, or kidneys," Matthew explained.

Joanna glanced at André. "You didn't know how bad off you were, did you?"

André shook his head.

"I bet you were glad to see your wife and son when you woke up," she commented, taking advantage of his instability.

André's head snapped in her direction, his face transitioning from shock to anger. "I told you to keep them out of this interview," he said, wishing he could storm out of the room.

"I'm sorry," Joanna said. "But the American public has a right to know that an alien and an American have created a child."

Tim switched the camera off. "Joanna, I'm not taping this," he said, glaring at her.

She swung around, her face a mask of surprise. "It's a Pulitzer. An alien mix breed."

"Get out." André stood, pointing at the door and ignoring the sharp pain in his leg. "Now!"

Matthew grabbed her by the arm and escorted her to the front door. "If you mention my grandson, I will ruin your life," he threatened and opened the door, shoving her out onto the front step and closing the door on her. He turned to Tim.

Tim disassembled the camera, muttering under his breath about how much of a bitch Joanna was.

André lowered himself into the chair, wincing.

"Are you all right?" Tim asked, looking up from his camera case.

André returned his stare. "No. My leg is bleeding again," he said. A red spot on the leg of his sweatpants spread on his thigh.

"You really got hurt?"

André nodded. "My leg, stomach, and shoulder were split open. You heard my father. I lost a lot of blood," he said, leaning his head back against the chair, controlling the pain. The air hissed between his clenched teeth.

Tim picked up the tripod and the camera. "You are a hero," he said to André.

André laughed despite the pain. "No I'm not," he said, thinking about how he toyed with Captain Trevor.

Tim smiled. "Whether you know it or not, you are." He turned to leave and paused. He glanced back at André. "I won't let her turn you into a circus freak."

"Thanks," André said. He gripped the armrest, sweat lining his palms and tacky on the small of his back.

"Take it easy, kid." Tim left by way of the front door.

As soon as the door closed, André let out a roar of pain. "This fucking hurts!" He gripped his thigh.

Matthew glanced at him. "You shouldn't have stood on it. The doctor told you not to put any pressure on your leg for the next two weeks," he said. He ran upstairs and grabbed the bag of bandages the hospital gave them. "I don't want blood all over my chair," Matthew said as he came back down stairs, retrieving the wheelchair and lining it up so André could switch easily. He cut the sweatpants, ripping the severed pant leg off and looking at the blood soaked bandages. "Jesus," he cursed under his breath.

"I don't want to sit in a pool of blood either," André remarked.

Matthew glared up at him. "Suck it up." He removed the bandage and grabbed the bottle of iodine Cal had given them to apply with each dressing change. He poured a thin line into the stitched wound.

The iodine burned and André clamped his teeth down on a yelp, gripping the armrests so tightly the color drained from his hands.

Matthew covered the cut with the bandages and sat back on his heels.

"Why the hell didn't they seal the cut like they did with my shoulder and stomach?"

"We've been over this, André. The cut was too deep. You have to wait until it heals naturally." Matthew turned toward Katrina. "Kat, grab the pain medicine, please."

She disappeared into the kitchen and came back with the pain pills and a glass of water in her free hand, handing them to Matthew.

Matthew poured two pills into his hand and handed them to André with the glass of water.

André downed them and put his head in his hands, trying to control his breathing and the pain.

Katrina rubbed the back of his neck.

"Get away from me," André said, the tears dripping onto his lap, staining the fresh bandage and the remaining pant leg.

"I'm just—"

"Get the hell away from me!"

Katrina backed away. Sam began to cry in her arms.

Matthew gathered the soaked bandages and stood, disappearing into the kitchen.

"You shouldn't yell at Katrina like that," Matthew said when he returned with clean hands.

"You put that bastard's blood in me?"

Matthew nodded.

"You should have let me bleed out."

Matthew sighed. "André."

"You should have let me die," André screamed.

The mental slap shot out of Matthew before he could stop it.

André's head rocked to the side with the power of it. A pink handprint appeared on his cheek, and he touched the still stinging skin.

Matthew approached him. "I don't give a damn how much you hated that bastard. He was the only option I had of saving you." He towered over André. "I took it, and I will not apologize for saving you," he growled down at his son. "And if I ever hear you talk to Katrina in that tone again, I will knock you on your ass. Understand?"

André swallowed, his own anger and pain diminished by the shock of the slap.

"We set up Linda's office as a bedroom until you can climb the stairs," Matthew said. "Katrina brought down some clothes for you. Go change your pants." He pointed toward the makeshift bedroom.

André nodded, rolling the wheelchair down the small hallway. He wheeled in and stopped in the middle of the room. The shakes began and with it came the sobs, the entire ordeal finally hitting home.

André didn't react when Katrina came into the room and closed the door. The sobs kept coming, ripping through his chest with a force that clamped his lungs, leaving him gasping and shaking enough to rattle the wheelchair. When she wrapped her arms around his neck and pressed her lips to his cheek, whispering, "Shhh" he reached up, wrapping his hands around her wrists and holding her close, like a drowning man clutching his only life jacket.

Katrina kissed his temple. "I love you," she whispered into his ear.

He opened his mind to her for the first time since he got home and gave her the playback of the entire ordeal.

Katrina laid her head on his shoulder as the assault of his memories swarmed in her mind. "Oh, babe."

"They put his blood in me," he said when the sobs subsided.

"Think of how much that would have pissed him off," Katrina answered, putting a spin he hadn't thought of.

André turned toward her, wiping his face. He let out a small laugh. "It would have royally pissed him off to know he saved my life."

Katrina smiled. She disappeared into the adjoining bathroom and ran some warm water on a washcloth. She walked back to André, handing it to him.

He wiped his face and hands and handed the cloth to her. "Can you help me out of these?" he asked, waving to his stained sweatpants.

"Sure." Katrina helped him stand on his good foot.

"I'm going to need underwear and another pair of sweats," he said, standing on his good leg, looking at the seat of the wheelchair. "And something to clean that up with."

Katrina leaned over and wiped up the seat. She disappeared again. This time she came back with both the wet washcloth and a dry towel. She dried off the seat and looked at him. "Are you going to drop the pants or what?"

He smiled. "I figured you'd give me a hand with that."

She returned the smile. "I suppose you want me to clean the blood off your ass too."

André nodded, the heat crawling into his cheeks. "If you wouldn't mind."

Katrina turned the chair and locked the wheels so he could steady himself on the handles. She pulled his pants and underwear down to his ankles, taking them completely off his hurt leg and leaving them bunched around the ankle of his good leg. She ran the wet washcloth over the back of his thighs, and despite the situation, he felt the flood of heat flare, his libido taking over at the smooth strokes of the cloth.

"Next time I'm gonna rinse this with cold water," she muttered from behind him.

"Sorry." He sent an innocent grin over his shoulders.

She finished cleaning the blood off his buttocks and wiped around the front of his good thigh. "You can sit now." She pointed him to the dry towel sitting over the chair.

He slid into the seat. She pulled the dirty garments off his good foot, disappearing into the bathroom with the soiled clothing and the dirty cloth. She came back with a clean cloth and cleaned up the front of André. Her touch excited him now that the drugs silenced the pain.

"André," she said, the sharpness in her voice relaying her less than thrilled response.

"Katrina," he replied in the same tone, a smile spreading on his lips. He ran his hand into her hair. "Come on," he whispered, pulling her toward his now clean lap.

Katrina pulled her head out of his grasp and sent a glare his way, tossing him a pair of clean underwear.

"Come on, Kat," he said, smiling up at her as the full effect of the pain pills settled into his muscles, relaxing and leaving him languid in the chair with the exception of the stiff member standing at attention in his lap. "You know what I want," he slurred.

"Cut the shit, André," Katrina snapped and tossed him a clean pair of shorts.

André pouted and shimmied into his underwear, before glancing up at Katrina, trying to send her that "come-hither" look that always got her going.

She rolled her eyes and the edges of her lips stretched into a grin. "You need your rest and don't you dare give me that look."

"What look?" he said, shrugging and widening his eyes with mock innocence.

"You're high as a kite right now, aren't you?" She chuckled and pecked him on the cheek as she left the room.

André slid the shorts on and rolled himself out into the living room, his cheeks aching from the silly grin plastered on his lips. "Sorry for yellin'," he said, his words forming slowly under the influence of the medicine.

Matthew nodded. "You want to watch the ball game?" He pointed to the television.

"Nah, I'm hungry." André rolled into the kitchen. He looked at the kitchen cabinets and they all opened, making him giggle. Surveying the food, his gaze stopped on a box of chocolate chip cookies and with a tilt of his head, the box landed in his lap. He closed the cabinets and rolled out into the living room with the full box of cookies. Pulling the wheelchair next to the couch, he transferred himself to the soft cushions, lounging and facing the television. "Want some?" he asked with his mouth full of cookies, offering the box to his father.

"No thanks," Matthew said. "Don't get crumbs all over the place."

"'K," André replied. Each cookie just fueled his hunger until he reached into the bottom of the box and found nothing but crumbs. He sighed and closed his eyes.

MATTHEW GLANCED OVER AT André as a light snore interrupted his concentration. The empty box of cookies lay on André's chest, teetering each time André inhaled. Matthew got up and retrieved the empty box, tossing it onto the coffee table before sitting down again. He wondered how long the medicine would last this time. In the hospital, it only lasted a couple of hours with intravenous injections, and by the time his next dose came around, he was an irritable mess. The instructions on the bottle said one every six hours, but Matthew doubted one pill would do the trick, so he had slipped André two in the hopes it would quiet him down after the interview trauma.

Katrina came down, holding Sam. "He's asleep?"

Matthew nodded. "I gave him a double dose of the medication and it knocked him out." He smiled. "I have a feeling this is going to be a rough two weeks."

Katrina laughed. "It's going to be a rough couple of months. He's going to hate not playing football," she said, lifting Sam up in the air. "Your daddy's not going to be the star quarterback this year." She smiled at her son.

"Bullshit," André's groggy voice interrupted. He smiled a little and shifted to get more comfortable. "I'll be playing in a month." His breathing drifted back into the even rhythm of sleep.

Matthew and Katrina exchanged a skeptical look.

"How are you feeling?" Katrina asked as she plopped down on the small couch opposite André.

"I'm fine," Matthew answered. He wasn't one to complain even though his ribs still sent sharp twinges of pain any time he moved.

"Who are you kidding, Dad?" Katrina said, glancing at him. "Every time you move, you get this horrible grimace on your face."

Matthew shrugged. "Complaining isn't going to make it heal any faster."

"How long are you out of work?"

"The doctor said at least two weeks."

"Ah," Katrina said. *That ought to make for a fun house the next couple weeks.*

Matthew sent a disapproving glare in her direction.

"You and André laid up in the same house. Duh." Katrina rolled her eyes.

Matthew laughed. "We'll be fine."

"Yeah, right," she said under her breath.

"We will," Matthew said, trying to convince her.

"Whatever," Katrina said, focusing on Sam.

"Don't you have somewhere to go?" Matthew asked.

"Not with those vultures out there," Katrina answered.

A knock at the front door interrupted the conversation.

Katrina looked at Matthew expectantly as she played with Sam.

Just like a teenager. Matthew sighed and closed the recliner, getting up slowly. He opened the door and raised his eyebrows. "Mr. President." He glanced at the media frenzy on the street and stepped aside, allowing the president to enter.

"Commander." President Foster nodded as Matthew closed the door. He glanced around the living room, nodding at Katrina.

"To what do I owe this visit?" Matthew asked.

President Foster focused back on Matthew. "I came by to say thank you to your son."

Matthew nodded. "He's resting right now. He had a rough morning."

"I saw the footage," President Foster remarked.

"I know, but it took a lot out of him," Matthew said, glancing at his son.

"I also saw the footage from inside the ship," President Foster said.

"He almost died, Mitch," Matthew said, looking back at the president, showing his guilt and regret to one of his oldest friends. "My son almost died because I let him get near that alien bastard."

The president put an understanding hand on Matthew's shoulder.

ANDRÉ OPENED HIS EYES. "No, Dad. I almost died because I wanted to pummel that son of a bitch with my own hands. Stop beating yourself up for my immaturity." He slowly sat up and swung his legs over the edge of the couch, rubbing the sleep from his eyes. "Good afternoon, Mr. President," André added.

"Good afternoon, André," the president said, crossing the room and extending his hand.

"Pardon me for not standing, sir," André said as he took the president's outstretched hand. He smiled a little. The discomfort had returned, and he knew in a little while it would be back full throttle to gut-wrenching pain.

"I understand." He reached into his pocket, pulling out a velvet jewelry box. "I have the distinct honor to present you with the Congressional Medal of Honor," he said, flipping it open.

Awe filled his sleepy mind and he glanced from the ornate medal to the president and back. A Maltese cross surrounded by a laurel wreath hung below a bar reading VALOR. The medal featured the American eagle in the center, its open wings spanning the length of the cross arms. André reached out and traced the decoration with his finger. He raised his eyes, meeting his father's gaze.

"There's an inscription on the back," the president said.

André turned the medal over and inscribed in formal script were the words:

Medal of Honor Recipient: André Robbins.
July 4, 2240

André didn't quite know what to say. He knew this was an unprecedented honor. This award hadn't been given out to a citizen in over a hundred years, if he recalled his history correctly. The magnitude of the gesture rendered him speechless.

Matthew crossed the room and looked at the medal. "You earned it, son," he said, blinking back tears of pride.

"I'd like to formally present it to you in front of the press."

"You mind if I change into something else?" André asked after surveying his shorts and t-shirt.

"By all means," President Foster said.

André looked at Katrina. "Do I have anything other than sweats and shorts down here?"

Katrina shook her head. "No, but I'll go get your gray suit." She stood with Sam on her hip and looked at President Foster. "Do you mind holding Sammy for me?"

"Not at all." President Foster smiled and took the little boy in his arms while Matthew retrieved the wheelchair for André. "Your son is adorable," President Foster said.

"Thanks." André hauled himself into the wheelchair.

"Your wife and son should join us for the presentation," President Foster stated. It was not posed as a question.

"No, sir," André answered as if it was an option.

President Foster looked down at him. "That wasn't a question."

"I'm sorry, but I would rather not have Katrina and Sam subjected to the media," André answered.

"I agree with my son," Matthew said. "I don't think it is prudent to flaunt his child to the world. There are some crazy people out there, Mitch, and André is already at risk. I don't want to put his wife and son in the same situation."

"Why would Katrina and Sam be at risk?"

"André, you are not from Earth. That makes you a curiosity to most of the population and puts you into instant fame status, along with your family," Matthew explained. "That's a potent cocktail for crazy people and they're the ones I'm worried about."

"Don't I have a say in the matter?" Katrina asked. She was holding André's gray suit along with a pretty summer sundress.

"No," André answered.

"I agree that Sam should not be out there, but I'll be damned if I'm not standing by your side when the president gives you that medal." She marched into the first-floor bedroom without another word.

The three men looked in the direction that Katrina disappeared. President Foster glanced at André. "She's a pistol."

André sighed. "Yeah, tell me about it." He rolled to the bedroom, gauging Katrina's mood as he went. He pushed open the door and caught her as she slipped the dress over her head, covering her smooth bare skin. "You can't be mad at me for wanting to protect you," he said as he shut the door behind him.

"André, I can protect myself now. Remember?"

"I seem to remember you weren't the one to stop Anna's craft," André pointed out as he slipped his shorts off and reached for his suit trousers.

"I could have stopped her," Katrina said.

André let out a laugh. "Not." He shuffled the pants up and stood on his good leg to pull them the rest of the way. He stripped his shirt while still standing and put the white oxford on, buttoning the bottom and tucking it in. He sat down after he buckled himself up, exhausted from the exertion. He reached onto the bed and grabbed his jacket, slipping it on. "How do I look?"

Katrina smiled and waltzed up to him, the hem of the skirt swaying gently with her sultry hip movement. She leaned down and kissed him. "You look hot." She moved around and took the handles of the wheelchair, pushing him out into the living room.

President Foster nodded as the two entered the living room.

Katrina took Sam from his arms and set him in a portable crib in the corner of the room, popping a pacifier in his mouth. "Ready?" she asked, turning.

Everyone nodded. The president was the first to step out of the house. Matthew pushed André out, carefully maneuvering the wheelchair over the small step and moving him to the side of the door, facing the president. Katrina took her place by his side taking his hand as they looked out on the sea of reporters on the front lawn.

"Ladies and gentlemen, it is my distinct pleasure to be here today." President Foster surveyed the crowd. "As you already know, the threat of the meteor has been extinguished, thanks to the young man in the wheelchair behind me. What you may not be aware of is there was also an alien presence in space, using the meteor as a shield against us. When André destroyed the meteor, the alien attacked their ship with harmful intent." He glanced back at Matthew. "This young man defended his adopted father and an Armed Forces medic, saving their lives from the alien invader, but he was seriously wounded in the process." He turned toward André. "The United States of America owes you a debt of gratitude," he said. "On behalf of the citizens of the United States of America, I am proud to present you with the Congressional Medal of Honor." He made a great show of presenting the medal to André.

André took the medal. "Thank you," he said, maintaining eye contact with the president.

The president smiled and reached into his pocket, pulling out a legal certificate and addressing the crowd. "Before the nuclear holocaust and the meteor strike in the Arctic Circle, the United States had a tradition for welcoming those from other cultures and countries across the world into her fold. Many strived to become citizens of this great nation." He paused and glanced over at André. "In the tradition of our ancestors, I am officially granting you citizenship to our great nation." He turned and handed the paper to André. "You are now one of our own."

André looked at the certificate, more touched by this gesture than receiving the medal. The certificate said he belonged; he was a part of a society, not shunned for being different. He looked up at the president and tried to smile, blinking the tears back, but he didn't succeed at either. "Thank you," he whispered, grateful beyond words.

Katrina squatted next to him. "You okay?"

André nodded, glancing at her and then beyond at the crowd of reporters, cameramen, and photographers. He slowly stood and reached to shake the president's hand. "Thank you, sir," he said, holding both the medal case and certificate in his left hand. "It is my fortune and honor to have found such a wonderful place."

The president shook André's hand.

André lowered himself back into the wheelchair.

The press had been waiting silently until the moment André sat back in the chair. The flurry of questions engulfed the porch.

André looked up at Katrina. *Get me out of here.*

She nodded and turned the wheelchair toward the front door, rolling him into the house and away from the chaos. André put the medal down on the coffee table and stared at the piece of paper blinking back the red sheen covering his vision. He kept his back to the door when both Matthew and the president entered the house until he got a handle on his emotions and then turned, meeting the president's gaze. "Thank you," he said.

"You're welcome." President Foster turned to Matthew. "When will you be back to work?"

"Two weeks," he said.

President Foster nodded and turned back to André. "I would like you to start thinking about a military career young man."

"I need to graduate first, sir," André answered. "But after that, it is my intention to join the Armed Forces."

President Foster smiled. He turned toward Matthew. "Commander."

"Mr. President." Matthew saluted and waited until President Foster left before he turned to André. "I'm proud of you."

"Thanks, Dad," he replied and leaned back in the wheelchair, wiping his face. His thigh throbbed overtaking the moment and he closed his eyes. "My leg hurts again."

Matthew glanced at his watch. "You still have a little over three hours before you can have any more medicine."

André glared in his direction. "You're kidding."

"Afraid not," Matthew answered and picked up the medal and certificate from the coffee table, bringing them upstairs.

Messiah Chapter 19

JULY 2240

Insistent knocking woke Matthew from a sound sleep, and he blinked, trying to orient himself with his surroundings. His gaze dropped to the daily brief in his hand and then to the clock on the wall. It had been hours since Katrina and Linda left the house, and he couldn't blame them. The second he was cleared to drive, he was out of there, too.

The last two weeks consisted of sleep and battles with André over the stupidest things. Between Katrina and Linda running interference and André's whining about how much his leg hurt, he was more than ready to get back to the office.

He glanced over at André and sighed. The knocking hadn't disturbed his drug-induced sleep and a measure of irritation bloomed. Rubbing his eyes, Matthew struggled out of the chair and crossed to the door, opening it without so much as a second thought. Barrels of several guns pointed in his face; any cobwebs in Matthew's mind dissolved instantly.

André! He sent the thought to his son and backed up a few steps.

ANDRÉ SAT BOLT UPRIGHT on the couch and looked at the small band of thugs entering the house, their guns trained on his father. He glanced to his right; Sam still slept in the crib, undisturbed, and a small wave of relief washed over him.

"What do you want?" Matthew asked, but he already knew and so did André. They wanted his son.

André stood up and limped the distance to stand next to his father, despite the barrels wavering between he and Matthew. "Get out," he said.

The guns targeted him, but no one retreated.

"Get out or else!" André clarified, the anger rising like flood tides, burying the dull throb in his leg.

"Not so fast, alien," someone said from behind the line of gunmen. They parted and a man came into view, dragging a dazed Katrina with him, a knife pressed to the soft flesh of her throat.

André clenched his fists, brushing away the fleeting instance of shock that stopped his heart at the sight of Katrina's terrified gaze. Instead, he calmed the urge to annihilate, and calculated the number of weapons and the energy required to unarm these assholes.

"Where's my wife?" Matthew asked; the shake in his voice gave away his barely contained fury.

"If you don't give us the alien half-breed, we will slice their throats open."

Another man stepped into view with Linda and a knife edged against her larynx, her shirt draped in tatters, revealing bruises on her arms and ribs. Her face held the same ugly black-and-blue tones and both her knees sported trickles of blood. The brutality of her injuries set André into a whirlwind of wrath and the ball forming in his chest let loose when his gaze focused on the thin line of blood coming from the knife pressed to her neck.

His fists clenched and sent a silent command, yanking the knives away from the soft flesh of Katrina and Linda's necks. The click of triggers filled the room, but no lasers released from the barrels.

Instead, André used the heat and inertia from the multiple lasers to home in on the guns themselves, melting the metal around each gunman's hands, binding their wrists together in burning steel.

He focused on the man who dared to cut his mother and with a low growl, he shoved the power outward, catapulting the man through the living room window.

Screams replaced the shattered glass, and he focused back on the rest of the men. "If you ever come near my family again, I'll kill every last one of you. Now. Get. Out!"

The small band bolted out of the house and André slammed the door shut behind them, focusing back on the man lying on the front lawn, the leader of this band of thugs. The one who beat the daylights out of his mother. His anger swelled.

"Don't," Katrina spoke loud enough to break through the haze of fury.

André glanced back at her. "He hurt both of you."

Matthew had the phone in his hand, dialing the emergency number. "This is Commander Robbins. I need both the police and ambulance sent to my residence. We've had a break-in."

André turned toward the front of the house in time to see a large hovercraft containing the broken band of thugs speeding straight for the house. The driver flashed his teeth at André in a triumphant suicide-bomber smile that made André's skin crawl. His rage overflowed, shooting out from the center of his chest.

The craft and everyone inside blew to bits, showering bloody vapors onto the front lawn.

André stared at the particles raining down, shocked by the fine dust but not feeling a bit of remorse for those he killed. He glanced at his father. "Oops."

Matthew hung up the phone. "Oops? All you can say is oops? Are you out of your god damn mind?"

André shrugged and took a few steps back to the recliner. Slumping in the chair, the exhaustion wrung the energy from his muscles. "It got away from me."

Matthew raised his eyebrows. "Just beautiful. You killed those men and all you can say is '*It got away from me*'?"

"They were going to kill us, Matthew. All of us," Linda said, calling Matthew's attention. "They deserved what they got."

"They followed us to the store and jumped us," Katrina said. "Knocked me out cold, otherwise..." She paused and swallowed, reaching to touch the lump on her temple. "Otherwise, I would have stopped them."

"Stopped what?" Matthew asked with trepidation.

André closed his eyes; hearing the accusation was far worse than gleaning it from Katrina's mind. He glanced at his mother and gritted his teeth against the memories of their brutality. What he saw jump-started his adrenaline and he stormed out of the house, ignorant of the pain in his leg. He lifted the unconscious body and slammed his fist full in the man's face, breaking bone with the power behind his punch.

Matthew pulled André off the unconscious man before André killed him. "Enough," Matthew said, pushing him back. "He will pay, I promise, but not at our hands. I know exactly what you're feeling, André, and I would love nothing more than to kill the son of a bitch myself, but we can't. We can't."

André stared into his father's eyes and tears blurred his vision. He sat on the grass, putting his head in his hands, fighting the raging beast inside, the one that wanted to crush the life out of the unconscious bastard. His son's wail brought him out of it, and he raised his gaze to the broken bay window where Katrina stood consoling Sam.

Her gaze met his in a mixture of devastation and anger, the combination boiling inside her, swirling and leaving André helpless to stop the tears leaking down his cheeks.

The cops descended in full force. André remained sitting on the lawn with his head in his hands while Matthew ran interference. Two ambulances were dispatched, one for the madman on the lawn and the other for Linda and Katrina, along with a group of female officers and a psychologist who swarmed the house.

André blocked all thoughts, creating a silent barrier in his mind so he could grapple with the anger bruising his soul. When an officer squatted next to him, he finally turned his face out of the crook of his arm.

"You have the right to remain silent..." the officer started.

André stared at him. "You're arresting me?"

"Excuse me, Officer Sanders, but what the hell do you think you're doing?" Matthew asked as he approached.

"Your son killed those men by your own admission," Officer Sanders replied, glancing at Matthew.

"He was defending our family," Matthew interjected. *Keep your mouth shut, André.*

"That will be decided by a court of law," Officer Sanders replied, hauling André to his feet, and cuffed his wrists behind his back. "You have the right to remain silent. Anything you say can and will be used against you in a court of law. You have the right to speak to an attorney, and to have an attorney present during any questioning. If you cannot afford an attorney, one will be provided for you at government expense. Do you understand these rights as I have stated them?"

André nodded.

Before he could say a word, Katrina screamed, "Don't you take my husband!"

André turned in time to see her running down the steps and Officer Sanders, pushed by an invisible hand, landed on his ass on the lawn.

"Kat, it's okay," André said. *Don't make it worse, baby.* He leaned down and kissed her cheek.

"It's not okay." She threw her arms around his neck. "They were going to kill us, André. They were going to kill Sam." She cried against his chest.

"I know, but you've got to let them take me to the station."

Officer Sanders stood up and grabbed André's arm. "Let's go."

"I'll be back as soon as I can," André said, limping away with Officer Sanders. When the officer directed him toward the same craft that the now conscious thug sat in, André stopped. "If you put me in the same vehicle as that son of a bitch, he won't make it to the station alive."

Officer Sanders glared at André.

"He raped my mother and my wife." André clamped his mouth shut, grinding his teeth so hard his jaw ached.

Officer Sanders redirected André to the second craft. After settling André in the back seat, the officer climbed in the front and started the craft. "Did you want to tell me what happened?"

André opened his mouth and then thought better of it, his father's command to keep his mouth shut still clear in his mind. "No," André replied. "I want to talk to a lawyer." His shoulders throbbed from the angle of the handcuffs. He closed his eyes, willing the cuffs to unlatch. The sharp click was undercut by the officer's radio squawking on the dashboard.

Rubbing his wrists, André rolled his shoulders, shifting in the seat to find a comfortable position. The movement brought a wave of pain from his thigh, signaling the pain medicine was wearing thin and soon any sort of comfort would be impossible.

The craft stopped and André pried his eyes open. His headache throbbed in time with his leg.

Officer Sanders stared at him. "How did you get out of those?"

"They weren't very comfortable."

"I didn't ask whether they were comfortable—I asked how you got them off."

"If I wanted to escape, these things wouldn't be able to stop me," he said. "Besides, I've got no reason to run."

Officer Sanders's face pinched, and he turned away from André. With a curt nod he said, "Just don't try anything. Understand?"

"Yes, sir," André replied. His eyes drooped and before the officer pulled from the curb, he drifted into darkness despite the ache in his leg.

At the station, André pressed his fingers on the screen scan, his fingerprints cataloged along with his mug shot before the officer led him to a jail cell. Across the hall sat the man who attacked his family, the one who defiled his wife. The bastard had the nerve to grin at him like a sick Cheshire cat.

"Your wife was such a good fuck." He laughed at André.

André glared, afraid to speak, afraid of the rage clawing at his stomach.

"I took my time with her, too. I figured she needed a real man."

The fury broke free, and André stood, crossing to the bars and grasping them tightly, his knuckles turning white under the grip. His eyes burned with rage, and he ground his teeth together, willing the man's privates into the consistency of jelly.

A high-shrill scream filled the jail, and the man grabbed his crotch, falling to his knees.

The louder the scream, the wider André's smile of satisfaction became. He turned and walked back to the bench, taking a seat again, crossing his legs at the ankle, and folding his arms over his chest, and watched the bastard continue to scream. He took a deep breath and released his hold.

The man sobbed with his forehead on the concrete, holding his crushed privates. He vomited on the floor and fell on his side, gagging and gasping for breath.

André remained smiling. The son of a bitch would never hurt another woman again.

Officer Sanders appeared. He looked at the man on the floor and then over at André.

André kept eye contact, daring him to say something, anything that would give him cause to lash out.

The officer unlocked André's cell. "Come with me," he said, glancing back at the thug.

André limped down the hall, following the officer to an interrogation room. He took a seat, glancing at the two officers in the room. "Where's my lawyer?"

"I'm not sure an alien is entitled to the same rights as a citizen," Sergeant Bill Farrow said.

André sighed. "In case you were not aware, the president of the United States granted me citizenship. Therefore, I do have the same rights as the next person." He leaned back and crossed his arms. "So, I'd like a lawyer if you don't mind."

"What did you do to Ben?" Officer Sanders asked.

André raised his eyebrow. "Who's Ben?"

"The man in the cell across from you."

André looked between the two officers. "I'd like my lawyer now," he said. The fact that they used the man's first name said more about them and their views than even their thoughts did.

"Not so fast," Sergeant Farrow began.

André shot his gaze in the detective's direction. "I don't think you get it. I'm still a minor, and you are violating the rules by questioning me without either my parents or a lawyer present," he said.

Sergeant Farrow laughed. "I don't think you understand. You are an intruder on this planet."

André's eyes narrowed and his fists clenched again. "You condone the attack on my family?"

"No, but I share the same sentiment. You don't belong here," Sergeant Farrow said.

André realized neither one of the officers in the room accepted his existence. They both harbored the same hostility he remembered from his home planet.

Sergeant Farrow glanced at Officer Sanders and back at André. "You killed those men."

André glanced in his direction, shutting his mouth against the words that wanted to come out, the muscles in his jaw taut with aggravation. He squashed the urge to let loose on both these men. They were officers of the law and as such, required respect, no matter how much they disliked his existence. He sat back in the chair and crossed his arms in protest.

"Do you realize how much trouble you are in?" Sergeant Farrow asked.

"Do you?" André returned the question.

Sergeant Farrow raised his eyebrow. "Do I what?"

"Know how much trouble you're in."

"Why don't you tell me?"

André smiled. "You are questioning a minor without representation," he stated. "I have asked repeatedly for a lawyer, and you have refused every time, and you have basically stated you agree with the attack on my family." He leaned forward, cocking his head to the side. "I think that's grounds for a hell of a discrimination lawsuit."

This kid is shrewd, Sergeant Farrow thought. "What makes you think they will let you out of here?"

"Since when is protecting your family against armed intruders a crime?"

"It isn't, but they weren't in your house when they died, now were they?" Sergeant Farrow said.

"They were heading toward the living room in their hovercraft with the intent to kill us all," André replied. "I stopped them."

"By making the hovercraft explode?"

André glared at the sergeant. "I did what was necessary to protect my family," he said between clenched teeth.

The interrogation room door flew open, and Matthew stepped inside, wearing full military dress, followed by three others in full military garb, two of which were lawyers and the third, André immediately recognized.

"You have violated due process," Matthew snapped and glared at the sergeant. "I am taking my son home. You can discuss the situation with my lawyers."

Cal approached André. "How's the leg?"

André shrugged. "It hurts a little," he lied. It was throbbing and he was in need of another dose of pain medication.

Cal smiled. "Don't bullshit me," he said as he helped André to his feet and led him out of the room.

Matthew turned on his heels, following Cal and André out of the room, leaving Sergeant Farrow and Officer Sanders at the mercy of the two military lawyers who had been given orders to grill them for hours.

Matthew drove home in silence, with Cal riding shotgun and André in back. He glanced at André as he pulled through the newly formed sea of reporters in their driveway. "It's been a madhouse since the police left," he said.

André stepped out without a word and hobbled to the house as reporters shouted questions. He ignored them all, entering the house and slamming the door behind him. He headed for the stairs, ignoring his leg.

"André, you aren't supposed to climb the stairs yet," Cal said.

André never acknowledged the warning. He continued up the stairs, wincing with every step. He limped down the hall and opened the door to their bedroom.

Katrina lay on the bed with Sam in her arms. She looked up when he opened the door, tears tracking down her face in a steady rain.

"I'm sorry," André said, as fresh tears slipped down his cheek. None of this would have happened if they weren't associated with him. He crossed the room, sitting on the edge of the bed, wrapping his arms around both her and his son.

Katrina sobbed on his shoulder. "This isn't your fault," she sputtered, feeling his guilt.

"Yes it is," he said, taking ownership of the whole ordeal.

She pulled away from him, wiping her face and looking down at Sam. He was still sleeping. She got off the bed, laying him in his crib. "What happened today is not your fault, André." She turned as she spoke.

André stared at her, the despair scratching deep as he tried to block the visions he had seen in his mother's mind.

"I already saw what happened to me," Katrina said. "Your mom isn't that good at blocking her thoughts." Her chin began to quiver as fresh tears slipped from the corner of her eyes. "I was knocked out cold. And he still..."

André crossed the distance quickly and took her in his arms, kissing the top of her head as she sobbed into his chest.

"Did you kill the son of a bitch?" she asked.

"No," André answered. "But he's a soprano now."

Katrina looked up at him.

"He will never hurt another woman that way ever again." He met her gaze. "Actually, he'll never have any kind of sex ever again." A satisfied smile surfaced, and Katrina looked away.

"I want to move," Katrina said.

André stepped back. "What do you mean?"

"This house is too accessible," she said. "Too vulnerable to attack."

"Where do you suggest we go?"

"My parents' house," Katrina answered. "I've got enough money to support us, and the house is ours since the will settled. Besides, the security system is top rate and there's a gate around the entire border."

André considered the idea as he sat on the side of the bed. He looked around his bedroom and then back at her, torn between the need to be with his parents and the need to protect his wife and son. His eyes landed on Sam, sleeping peacefully in the crib and the decision was made. "All right," he answered, looking back at Katrina.

"Really?"

"Yeah," André answered. "Really."

"When?"

André sighed. "When do you want to go?"

"Right now," Katrina said. "We can pack up some things for tonight and come back tomorrow for the rest of our stuff."

"Kat. I can't just up and leave after what happened today. I've got to give my parents a little warning."

Katrina swallowed hard and studied her hands.

"I'm staying up here with you tonight. I want to know you and Sammy are safe." André closed his eyes, finally letting the day's events take their toll. Tremors started in his feet and hands, working their way through his entire body until every fiber shook, rattling his teeth together.

"Are you okay?" Katrina asked, suddenly so close he could smell her shampoo.

André shook his head. "I need a pain pill," he whispered with his eyes now squeezed shut against the pain lacing its way through his bones.

"Something's wrong with your leg," Katrina said.

André opened his eyes and looked at his right thigh. The fabric of his jeans darkened from the spot over the cut and spread out like a drop of water soaked into a paper towel.

"Take off your jeans," she said, unbuckling his belt.

André slid his jeans over his hips and laid back, allowing Katrina to pull them off the rest of the way. He didn't have the energy to sit back up.

"Jesus," Katrina whispered as she looked at his leg. She bolted out the door. "Cal!" she yelled down the stairs.

Cal came bounding up the stairs. "Where is he?"

Katrina pointed and followed him into the bedroom.

The bandage was soaked but not with blood; it was stained a greenish color, which wasn't the initial cause of Katrina or Cal's alarm.

"Jesus." Cal repeated Katrina's sentiment as they stared at the red veins covering the skin of his thigh, spinning out from underneath the bandage. "Go get my bag, now."

She immediately complied, disappearing out of the room.

"What the hell have you done?" Cal said, stepping closer to André.

"That bad?"

"Your leg is infected." He looked at André. "How long has it been like this?"

André propped himself up and looked at his leg. "It wasn't like that when I woke up." He lay back on the bed, dizzy and weak. "My dad changed the bandages this morning."

Katrina came in with the medical bag and put it down, scrambling for the antibiotics inside at Cal's silent instruction. She filled a syringe and handed it to Cal.

Cal didn't hesitate; he plunged the syringe into André's leg at the tip of the cut and pushed the antibiotic into André's vein, ignoring André's hiss of pain.

André stiffened, the pain raking his form, spiraling out from the wound and encompassing him to the molecular level.

"Another one," he barked and handed Katrina the empty syringe.

Immediately, the second one was placed in his hand. This time, Cal grabbed André's arm and plunged the needle into another vein, emptying the contents.

"I'm going to need an IV line." He ripped the bandage off André's leg before turning to Katrina. "Get me a couple clean towels, now."

She disappeared, reappearing moments later with two clean towels.

"Put one under his leg, please." Then Cal slipped the IV in André's hand and plunged a third syringe full of antibiotics into the line.

"Is this necessary?" André asked. The flurry of activity layered with a hazy veil and his mind wandered close to darkness.

"Yes," Cal answered and rifled through his bag, finding the iodine solution but waiting a minute for the antibiotics to run through André's system. He counted to sixty and then dumped the iodine on the puss-filled cut.

The shot had been a soft pat in comparison to the iodine saturating his wound and the haze disappeared, replaced with acute pain. André let out a yell loud enough to wake Sam. His breath hissed between his teeth and he squeezed his eyes closed, trying to shut out the discomfort as Cal cleaned out his wound, scraping the infected skin away with a scalpel.

Cal rinsed the open wound with saline solution and squeezed out a thin line of antibiotic ointment down the length of the cut before using his laser to seal it. "It's over now," he said, putting his hand on André's chest.

André panted, taking control over his body and pumping the blood through his veins and arteries as fast as he could without risking a heart attack. The medicine flowed in and he felt it attacking the infection in his leg, his body breaking out in sweat as it fought the foreign bacteria.

Within five minutes, the IV bag was empty and the red lines receded until nothing was left but inflamed skin around the cut.

André slowed his breathing to a normal pace. "Jesus." He traded a glance with Katrina.

Katrina handed Sam to her mother-in-law and stepped into the room.

"You have to stay off this, André," Cal said. "Completely, not half-assed like you've done for the past couple weeks."

"How long?" André whispered.

"A full week, no pressure on the leg at all." He looked at the group in the doorway. "Does everyone understand?"

Katrina, Matthew, and Linda nodded.

Cal looked back at André. "If you don't do as your told, I'll admit you to the hospital and have you strapped to the bed for a week." He lifted the sleeve of André's shirt. "How's the arm?" He pressed gently around the laser mark.

"It aches," André answered.

"How about your abdomen?" he asked, lifting the shirt and examining the laser mark along the length of his stomach.

"It itches. All the time."

Cal smiled. "That's good. It's healing."

"Can I have a pain pill now?" he asked, ignoring the comment.

"How many are you taking a day?"

"Six."

"You should only be taking two a day," Cal said. "One in the morning and one before you go to sleep."

"No way." André gawked at Cal. He needed that medicine. It was the only thing that got him through the day.

"It's an addictive narcotic, André; cut back now before you get into real trouble," Cal said.

"But..." André started.

"Take aspirin if you're uncomfortable." Cal stood, packing up his medical bag.

Irritation snaked over his skin. "I want a pill."

Cal turned toward André. "Not until tonight."

"Fuck you." André started to get up.

Cal exercised his power and pushed André back onto the bed. "I'll haul your ass to the hospital if you get up on that leg."

"I need medicine," he said through clenched teeth.

Katrina approached the bed. "I need to get out of here," she said. "Neither one of us are going to get what we want right now."

His hands curled into fists as frustration raked through him. He considered using the influence to get his way, but one look at Katrina stopped him. Her eyes glared a warning, like she knew what he was considering. "You don't understand," he whispered. "I need it."

"No, you don't." She sat on the side of the bed and Cal slipped out of the room, leaving the negotiations to Katrina.

His eyes welled up with tears. "I hurt."

"So do I. But you don't see me filling up on narcotics."

André blinked at her words. "You hurt?"

Katrina nodded. "I was raped today," she said. Tears slid down her cheeks. "And he wasn't gentle."

André forgot about the pain in his leg and the insane need for medication. He sat up and wrapped his arms around her. "I'm sorry," he whispered, gently rubbing her back with his fingers. He put his forehead on her shoulder. "I'm so sorry."

"I want to go home."

"When I get my walking papers, we will go. I promise."

She nodded against his shoulder.

He moved to the side of the bed and pulled her down next to him, spooning her while she cried. He ran his fingers through her hair, willing himself not to think about medication or pain, just to concentrate on the feel of her body against him and the soft strands of her hair flowing through his fingertips. She relaxed against him, and her breathing slowed as sleep took hold.

"I love you." His eyes closed, exhaustion pulling him under the blanket of sleep.

Messiah Chapter 20

ANDRÉ FOLLOWED CAL'S ORDERS, staying on the upper level and relying on the wheelchair to go between the bedroom and bathroom. André's refusal to take any medication left him virtually intolerable and Katrina began to think he'd never kick the attitude. She knew he was determined to squash the addiction before he drowned in it, but that knowledge didn't help when all he did was rant and rave about how much being in the house sucked.

Relief flooded Katrina on the fourth day when he finally stopped complaining. She had her own issues to deal with and his emotional unavailability wasn't helping. For her own sanity, Katrina began taking small excursions to their house, bringing a little at a time without notice. She hired a housecleaner to make sure the place was livable again and contacted the utility companies to set up their power, television, and communication services so they could just move in when André got word that he could walk.

"I'm sorry," André said as Katrina carried his dinner into the bedroom. He turned from the desk to look at her, his hair wet from taking the first shower since the morning of the incident.

She set the tray on the desk and glanced sideways at him. "You've been a real prick."

"I know." He put his arm around her waist. "I think I'm through the worst of it." He offered her a smile.

"You better be, because if you keep treating us like you have, we'll let you starve up here."

She stepped away and he moved the chair back, turning to face her. "I'm surprised you haven't done that already."

"Yeah, well..." She trailed off.

"My parents wouldn't let you."

She nodded. "If it had been up to me, you would have been shot."

"Ah."

He rolled toward her, and she took a step backwards, sitting on the bed as he approached. His eyes sparkled with humor and a slow smile spread on his lips. The kind of smile that used to drive her wild, but now it only irritated her. "Stop looking at me like that," she snapped and stood up. She found herself sitting back on the bed a moment later with André blocking her in.

"You wanted to shoot me?" he said, tilting his head and grinning.

"Yes." The irritation slunk back a notch and her cheeks bloomed with heat. "Either that or duct tape your mouth."

He put his hands on her knees. "Really? What about right now?" he asked, sliding his hands up her thighs.

"Stop," she snapped, brushing his hands away.

André sat back, his smile disappearing. "Are you okay?"

Katrina sighed. "No, not really."

"What's wrong?"

"I'm having a tough time dealing with what happened." Her hand fluttered to the small scab on her throat where the knife nicked her. Tough time was an understatement. She didn't want to be touched, not even by André.

He pulled her onto his lap anyway, even wincing as she shifted to avoid his bad leg. He ran the back of his knuckles over her cheek. "What can I do?"

"I honestly don't know." She leaned her head on his shoulder. His sudden focus on her produced a grapefruit-sized lump in her throat and she swallowed it, feeling the pressure all the way down to her stomach. "Just be there when I need you to be."

André nodded, holding her against him. "I still want you."

"Thanks," Katrina said, biting back the tears. He didn't know how much those four words meant to her, especially after the way he treated her the past few days.

"You thought I wouldn't want you after what happened?"

Katrina shrugged.

"Kat, I want you twenty-four-seven for the rest of my life." He pulled her away so she could see his face. "No matter how much of an asshole I am, I love you and will always want you. The idea of having you in my arms each night has gotten me through the past few days." He smiled. "You, on the other hand, may end up not wanting me when all of this is said and done."

Katrina bit her lip and blinked back tears that threatened. "I'll always love you."

"But?"

"But right now, I don't want you to touch me," she whispered. "I don't want anyone to touch me." The tears came.

"I can make it go away," André said.

"Erasing my memory won't help."

"It's just a suggestion," he offered, closing his eyes. "I wish I still had that vibe, just for you."

"I don't know if even that would help," she admitted.

André smiled and raised an eyebrow. "You sure I can't make you forget for a little while?" His hand slid down her arm to her waist, stopping at the comfortable curve of her hip. "I'm pretty good at making you forget."

Katrina closed her eyes. "You are, but right now isn't the right time."

He pressed his lips to her cheek, his breath minty, and his wet hair tickled her eyelids. His hand caressed the line of her hip and he wrapped his arms around her, just holding her even though she knew he wanted more. He wanted to prove he could still make her want him despite all that happened, but his silent acceptance of her was far more healing than a romp in bed would have been.

André kissed her shoulder and unwrapped his arms. "I love you."

"I love you too," she replied against his neck. "I need to go feed Sammy." She slid off his lap and left him sitting in the chair, staring after her.

ANDRÉ TURNED TO THE tray of food, his stomach growling for nourishment but his mind preoccupied with Katrina and her reaction to his touch. Whenever he reached for her, she flinched and her mind broadcast flashbacks: flashbacks she picked up from his mother's memories, not her own.

He sighed and dug into the meal Katrina brought, resuming his Internet surfing.

The door opened behind him, and he could see her standing in the doorway. André sent her a halfhearted smile as their eyes met in the reflection.

"I figured your son needs some daddy time now that you're more yourself," Katrina said.

André swung the wheelchair around. "I would love to have some time with Sammy."

Katrina crossed the room and handed the baby to André.

André lifted Sammy up in the air. "How's my boy?"

"You better be careful, or you'll wear his dinner," Katrina warned.

André pulled Sammy to his shoulder and looked at Katrina. "You okay?"

She smiled. "Thank you for not pushing the issue." She leaned over and kissed him.

"Anytime," he replied, rubbing Sam's back as he snuggled against his father. "How much stuff have you moved?"

Katrina's eyes went wide.

André laughed. "Come on, babe, I know what you're doing—even in my withdrawal stupor, I knew. I'm surprised my father hasn't picked up anything."

"We have less than a week's worth of clothes left," she said. "The rest has been moved."

"You've been busy."

"Yeah, well, I had to get away from you and your wild ranting."

"Ah," he replied. "So did you take any of my clothes?"

"Of course." The smile spread. "The downstairs den is completely cleaned out. That was the easiest stuff to move. You have no clue how hard it's been. Between your father and the media, it's been crazy, but the house is clean and the utilities have been switched on. We only need to pack up the rest of Sammy's stuff and the things from this room that you want to bring."

"Bring where?" Matthew interrupted from the doorway.

Katrina spun around.

"Take Sam downstairs," André said, handing the baby to her.

Katrina slipped out of the room.

"Where are you going?" Matthew asked.

"When I'm given the go-ahead to walk again, we're moving into her family's house," André said.

Matthew raised his eyebrows.

"Katrina doesn't feel safe here and they've got that fancy security system."

"I'm not sure that's such a good idea," Matthew began.

"Dad, I'm going with my wife and son."

"How are you going to afford a house like that?"

"Kat's got the money her folks left her."

"You are only seventeen," Matthew said.

"I will be just fine," André said. "Besides, you and Mom aren't that far from our house."

"You are still in high school."

"I am aware of that. So is Katrina."

Matthew sighed and looked at André. "I could just say no."

André let out a slight laugh. "You know you can't stop me."

Matthew took a seat on the edge of the bed. "I can't stop you," he agreed. "But I can try to talk the two of you out of it. We now have around-the-clock protection."

"It's not enough," André said. "Kat doesn't feel safe here. They got to us once..." He trailed off.

"And being at her house will?" Matthew asked. "You're kidding yourself there, son."

André shrugged. "Maybe, but it's what she wants."

"What about you?"

"I want to be wherever she is, and I want her to feel safe again."

Matthew nodded slowly. "But if I hear you two are skipping school..."

"I want to graduate and so does Kat."

"This is going to kill your mother."

"I know." André twisted his wedding band. "I haven't seen her much lately."

"She's been spending a lot of time with the therapist. She isn't doing so well with what happened."

"I can wipe out the memory," André offered.

Matthew shook his head and sighed. "She's the only reason you're not in jail right now, André. If you take away the memory of what happened, they will lock you up and throw away the key."

"So she suffers for me," André said.

"Yes," Matthew replied. "You would do the same for your son."

André glanced at the empty crib and nodded. He would do more than suffer; he would gladly lay down his life for Sam.

"That's how we feel about you," Matthew said.

"Why? I brought all this on you. Why would you be willing to die for me?"

Matthew thought about how to explain it to André. "Just because you don't have our DNA doesn't mean we love you any less than if we had given birth to you."

"But I've only been here for a little over six years."

"Sam's only been here for a little over two months."

"That's different."

"No, it's not." He walked over and put his hand on André's head. "You're my little boy." He smiled and messed up André's hair.

"Cut the crap," André said, knocking Matthew's hand away and laughing.

"I hope Sam grows up to be just like you," Matthew said, laying the parental curse on his son.

"That's just what I need." André grinned. "Another pig-headed, competitive son of a bitch who thinks he knows everything."

Matthew chuckled as he walked out. "You're not a son of a bitch," he said over his shoulder. "I'll talk to your mother," he added as he disappeared around the corner.

Messiah Chapter 21

MAY 2255

"Dad?"

Matthew turned to see the man André had become. Standing at a little over six-five with a hard, powerful build, he still seemed impossibly young to Matthew. He was very different from the skinny, scared boy he found twenty-two years ago. Only two things remained constant over the years: his eyes were just as blue as the first time they met and he had never looked at another girl the way he looked at Katrina in all his years on Earth.

"What's wrong?" Matthew asked.

"We're going to lose a lot of good people," André replied, his eyes distant. "You might be one of them."

"No way, kiddo." Matthew laughed. "I'm indestructible, remember?"

"Yeah," André said. A troubled smile found his lips.

"Don't worry, André; I know how to take care of myself," Matthew said as they walked out of the auditorium. He stopped and faced his son. "If anything does happen to me, you are the next in line for command."

"But—"

Matthew cut him off. "I don't want to hear it. We've discussed this plenty of times."

"But that was theoretical," André said. "This is real."

"Damn straight it's real and I expect you to live up to my expectations," Matthew snapped. He turned on his heel and continued walking.

ANDRÉ WATCHED HIS FATHER, frustrated for a moment. He wasn't ready to step in and lead this fight. He wanted his own revenge on a very personal, very private level. He sighed and caught up with Matthew again. "We can't fight them in the domes," he said, reverting back to the strategic planning. "It's too dangerous for the civilians."

"I was thinking about that," Matthew said.

"Washington DC?" André asked, reading his father's mind.

"Yes. The team is used to the training grounds we built out there and if we can get the Zyclonians on the ground outside the domes, there may be opportunity to overtake them while they acclimate to the lack of oxygen." He looked at André. "I'm betting they'll come after us first considering we're their biggest threat." He opened the door to his office.

"They'll go wherever I go," André snapped. "The emperor still wants me dead." He glanced at his father.

Matthew sighed and flipped on the monitors, watching the warriors hone their skills. Collectively, they held the power to wipe out mankind if they so desired, but their call was to protect the United States and that was what each and every one of them was thinking about as they exercised their abilities, training for imminent danger.

Life-size mannequins evaporated into dust. Water bottles boiled and exploded. Brick blocks levitated and burst into flames until they became cinder and microscopic grains. Sharp objects hurled across the room at targets with frightening accuracy. Each task executed with precision and without the touch of a human hand.

"Pack your gear and report to the transport station," Matthew said, his voice booming over the loudspeakers. The arena cleared quickly, and he turned toward André.

"There's something you're not telling me," Matthew said, staring at André and trying to read what was just behind the iron curtain in his mind.

André closed his eyes and turned his back on Matthew. His nod was almost indiscernible, but Matthew caught it along with the sigh.

"What is it?"

André looked back at his father. "The real reason I was exiled."

Matthew narrowed his eyes, digging in André's mind but he still came up empty. "You've been lying all these years?"

"No, not entirely. As far as the people on Zyclon know, I was exiled because of my blue-eyed mutation and the relation to the lore the emperor manipulated. But it was all bullshit. The emperor exiled me because I have legitimate claim to the throne."

Irritation snaked through Matthew, burning in the pit of his stomach. "Why would you keep that from me?"

André laughed. "It meant nothing here, and it would only serve to muddy the waters. And honestly, I wanted to block out the horrors we endured on the run. After the emperor branded my parents criminals, no one would help us. We were starving and desperate, but he didn't give a damn. To him, I was a threat, even at six, and he coerced the public into believing his warped version of the prophecy just to suit his greed for power. So, in essence I didn't lie; I just didn't give you all the details."

André's vibrant blue eyes shined with anger. "They exiled a six-year-old child." He took a deep breath. "They sent me into space to die because the emperor was a power-hungry nutcase." André turned and left the observation area.

Matthew caught up with André, keeping pace and letting the silence fill the space between them, turning over these new facts. It still didn't change the way he felt about his son; in fact, it only added to his fury toward the Zyclonian emperor.

"And now he's come to finish the job," André said.

"I won't let him," Matthew said.

André met his gaze. "I'm not sure you can stop him."

Matthew sent a reassuring smile in André's direction. "Maybe not alone, but with the team, we're a pretty powerful force."

André offered a nod.

"Now get going." Matthew gave André's shoulder a squeeze. "Just make sure you swing in and say goodbye to your mother before you leave."

André glanced at Matthew; something in his tone struck a chord. "Sure, I'll go over with you."

Matthew shook his head. "I've got some things to wrap up here before I head home to pack; besides, you're going out with the first wave. I'll be heading up the second group."

André stopped in his tracks. His instincts tripped on high octane, screaming that this was not right. "Dad."

Matthew glanced at his son. "You'll be fine."

"It's not me I'm worried about," André replied.

Matthew smiled. "I'll be fine. I know how to take care of myself."

André nodded, but deep down in the pit of his stomach, he knew this was the last time he would see him alive. His eyes glossed over with tears, and he blinked them back, leaving a thin red film over his eyes.

"Cut the crap, André," Matthew snapped. "I'm going to be just fine."

André nodded and impulsively hugged his father. "I love you, Dad," he said, pulling away just as quickly.

"I love you too, son. Now get moving."

André nodded and took a last look at the man who raised him with more love and honor than even his own parents had given him. "Bye, Dad."

"Don't forget to stop in and see your mother," Matthew called after him. André waved acknowledgment just before he disappeared around the corner, heading toward the parking lot.

Messiah Chapter 22

MATTHEW SAT IN HIS office, looking at the pictures on his desk. He took a deep breath, praying to God they would survive the attack.

He stared at the latest communication from the warship.

Surrender André or face destruction.

"Bullshit," he said under his breath. He knew better. The Zyclonian army was poised to attack, their intention was to wipe all traces of life from this planet, regardless of whether he handed André over or not.

Cruelty, malice, and hatred echoed in every statement received. Matthew knew there was no alternative, no peaceful solution. Closing his eyes, he ran his hands over his face before refocusing on the communication on his computer. The data being displayed worried him. They were closing in faster than he expected.

Dread wrapped cold hands around his heart. *If the Zyclonian soldiers are as strong as André is...* He shook his head, clearing the negative thoughts. If they didn't prevail, the human race would be extinguished.

He put the paperwork on his desk and walked into the outer office, where his secretary sat filing her nails.

"Emma, I'm heading out." He stopped by the side of her desk. "You've been a wonderful secretary."

Emma looked up at him. "Sir, please don't talk to me like that."

"Like what?"

"Like you're never going to see me again."

"I just..." Matthew trailed off.

"I know, Commander," Emma said. "It has been a pleasure working for you all these years." She smiled, stood and gave him a quick hug before she scuttled away.

Matthew walked out of his office with his head held high, saluting the staff members who stopped to pay their respects. He stepped outside the building and slid into his hovercraft. He took a moment to stare at the building he had worked his entire career in before shifting the craft in gear and heading home.

Parking outside his house, he inhaled and exhaled slowly, glancing around the neighborhood before he stepped onto the driveway. The door to the house opened and his grandson stepped out to greet him. Fifteen-year-old Samuel Matthew Robbins was the spitting image of his father, right down to the piercing blue eyes, with one exception: his sun-bleached blonde hair.

"Hi Papa," Sam said. "Mom's inside with Nana." He pointed his thumb over his shoulder.

"Your mother's here?" Matthew raised his eyebrows. He thought Katrina went with André and the first wave of soldiers.

Sam nodded. "Dad wanted Mom to go with you."

Matthew ruffled his grandson's hair as he walked into the house. "I'm glad you're here." His grandson always reminded him that what seemed impossible was actually achievable.

Katrina and Linda sat in the living room; they stood as Matthew entered.

"Sir." Katrina saluted.

Matthew glanced at her. "You don't have to salute me in our house, Kat."

Katrina nodded. "Sorry, Dad. Habit."

Matthew glanced at Sam.

"Dad told me what's going on," Sam said.

Matthew nodded. "You need to stay with your grandmother."

"But—"

"Your father doesn't want you to get hurt, Sam," Katrina answered.

"I am not bringing you with us," Matthew said.

"But—" Sam began.

"No buts." Matthew put his hand up in the air. "I'm in command and you are too young."

Sam tilted his head in disgust. "Too young?" He sighed and looked between his grandfather and his mother. "You know I'm stronger than all of you combined, right?"

Matthew bit the inside of his lower lip and sent a glare at his grandson. "I don't care. I'm not walking you into battle at your age, Sam."

Sam's lips pressed together, frustration outlining his eyes to the point a single laser red line encircled his iris, but he nodded in obedience and flopped down on the couch.

"How long do you have before you have to leave?" Linda asked Matthew.

Matthew looked at his watch. "Not very long." Their eyes met. Matthew would have liked nothing better than to sweep her off her feet and take her to their bedroom, but he didn't have time for that right now.

"Come on, Sam, let's give your grandparent's a minute." Katrina led her son out of the room, leaving Matthew and Linda alone.

Matthew put out his hand and Linda came to him without hesitation. He held her, afraid to let go. "Linda, you have no idea how much I love you." He kissed her forehead.

Linda lifted her gaze to his. "I do, Matt, and I don't have to be psychic to know how you feel. I see it in your eyes every time you look at me."

He kissed her gently. "I have to go," he said, taking her face in with his eyes, before unwrapping his arms from around her and heading upstairs to change into his battle uniform.

She followed and sat on the edge of the bed, tears shining and leaking from the corners of her eyes, streaking her make-up. "I love you, Matthew," she whispered.

Matthew nodded and looked back at her from the bedroom door. "I'll see you later, honey." He smiled and closed the door behind him. Slowly, he descended the stairs. As much as he wanted to stay with his wife, he couldn't. He was the Commander of the United States Armed Forces and didn't have the luxury of holding onto those he loved while doomsday descended.

Messiah Chapter 23

"KAT, YOU COMING?" MATTHEW called.

"Yep," she answered, trotting out onto the steps.

Sam followed. "Be careful, Mom." He gave her a hug, something not normal for the fifteen-year-old; usually he treated her like a leper. "I love you," he said, and then pulled away.

Katrina smiled and ruffled his hair. "I love you, too."

Matthew drove the craft away, his glance drifting to the house. Katrina could feel his heavy heart.

"It's going to be all right, Dad," Katrina said, putting her hand on his.

"I hope you're right, Kat," he said, glancing in her direction.

"We're a pretty sharp unit, thanks to André," she said.

He stared out the window, doubts lacing his thoughts; even as he tried to justify their strength, he knew. He knew they didn't have a prayer against an army of Andrés.

Katrina swallowed and stared out the window, his thoughts a constant assault on her conscious, chipping away at hope like a pickax breaking through a glacier wall. "They sent another message?"

Matthew nodded. "Surrender André or die."

"Was it from the son of a bitch who exiled him?"

"I don't know," Matthew admitted. "I haven't told André about the last message."

"Why?"

"They want us to hand him over and I can't do that." He shook his head. "If he knew…"

"He would give himself up for the rest of us," Katrina finished the sentence.

Matthew nodded. "And they would kill us all anyway."

"And then there's Sam," Katrina said, looking out the window, sighing. "He would never stand by and watch his father be taken away."

Matthew glanced at Katrina. "Precisely. Sam's powers leave all of ours in the dust, including André's, and I'd hate to see what hell that would unleash."

"Do you think he could stop this?" Katrina glanced back at Matthew.

"I'm not bringing Sam into this. He's too young."

"He's almost the age that André and I were when we got married."

Matthew laughed. "You know that doesn't mean much, Kat. You two were way too young to be married. I'm amazed you made it through the growing pains those first couple of years."

Katrina joined him, laughing. Their senior year in high school was the hardest time of their marriage, living on their own with Sam and fighting constantly about money, about their future, about football and jobs and whose turn it was to watch the baby. It still amazed her that they got through it without killing each other. "If you had told me then we would still be happily married fifteen years later, I would have laughed at you."

Matthew smiled and focused back in front of him, his smile fading at the sight of the outer base and what lay ahead. "André warned us; I just didn't believe it would ever happen." He gripped the wheel.

"Fifteen years." He shook his head. "It took them fifteen years to get here."

"You didn't know," Katrina said.

"But he did," Matthew answered, closing his eyes. "André knew." He rubbed his face and doubt rattled in his thoughts.

"Dad, you can't do this now," Katrina said, capturing his attention. "They need their commander, not André's father." She pointed toward the building, referring to the team waiting for them.

Matthew nodded. "Let's go."

They walked into the launch bay and their conversation died. Zyclonian warriors surrounded them, blocking their exit. The remaining Armed Forces personnel knelt in the center with their arms pinned behind their backs by invisible restraints.

"Commander Robbins, I presume?" A voice broke the silence.

MATTHEW TURNED TOWARD THE voice. He thought André was tall at six-five, but this man had him beat. He had to be over seven feet tall and was built like a bulldozer. He wore a uniform decorated with similar medals and sashes as his own. He looked into the red eyes of the Zyclonian intruder. "Who the hell are you?"

"I am the emperor of Zyclon," he answered. "And I believe you have something I want."

"What would that be?" Matthew asked, his heart pounding in his chest, the adrenaline drying the saliva from his mouth. He hadn't even felt their presence when they approached the building. God help them, these bastards had the ability to cloak themselves, to appear as vapor to the senses.

"The lost Zyclonian."

"I have no idea what you are talking about," Matthew said.

The emperor looked over at the line of soldiers.

The closest officer screamed, his hands flying to his temples; seconds later, the scream cut off as the soldier's head exploded. The body flopped on the floor, headless.

Matthew's eyes widened, registering a fraction of the shock gripping his muscles.

"He's not here," one of the men shouted from the back of the group.

Matthew's jaw tightened. *Shut up.* He sent the thought to all the men kneeling and felt his knees buckling beneath him. A powerful force lowered both he and Katrina to their knees, and he turned toward the source.

The emperor tilted his head and smiled before turning toward the man who spoke. "Tell me."

"Sergeant Murphy, keep your mouth shut," Matthew ordered.

"I can inflict the most interesting types of pain without even touching you," the emperor said to Sergeant Murphy.

Sergeant Murphy's hand flew toward his face, but it didn't make it in time. A scream peeled from the sergeant's throat and his eye burst into a bloody mess, leaving a vacant hole in his face. His good eye stared at the emperor, wide with the pain and horror of what just happened.

"Tell me," the emperor said again.

Sergeant Murphy's good eye shot to Matthew and back to the psychotic intruder in front of him. "He, uh, he led the advance team. They left about a half hour before you arrived." His whole body shook. Sergeant Murphy never felt the invisible knife that ended his life. His head rolled on the concrete tarp as his body fell backwards.

The emperor switched on the screen. "We tracked and intercepted them." He headed in Matthew and Katrina's direction.

Matthew watched the massacre of the advance team, his heart breaking when André's craft turned into a ball of fire, plunging into the Caribbean Sea just east of Houston. Hope evaporated, replaced by a fury so engrossing that he roared and struggled to his feet, rebelling against the invisible hand pushing against him. He let the anger grow, his teeth gnashing together in concentration as he stared at the emperor, wishing him dead.

The emperor's laugh echoed against the hangar walls.

Matthew ignored Katrina's whimpering sobs and growled, "That was my son." Power escaped, aimed at the emperor.

Knocked back a couple steps from the invisible shove, the emperor's laughter stopped, and his eyebrow rose in Matthew's direction.

The blow hit Matthew in the center of his chest, knocking the wind out of him and sending him flying into the wall at the far side of the hangar. Pain flared in his head, and then the blackness sucked him under.

KATRINA SOBBED, HER DEVASTATION paralyzing her in place. *André! Dear God, please not my André.* Her mind repeated the thought like a broken computer loop.

The emperor walked over and crouched in front of her. "You said his name," he said, tilting her chin up.

"Fuck you!" She managed to spurt between sobs, jerking her chin from his grip.

"Perhaps." He smiled, letting his gaze flow over the front of her uniform.

She shuddered. "Never," she growled, letting anger replace the emptiness at the center of her soul.

The emperor ran his finger down the front of her uniform and the buttons unclasped in the advance wake of his approaching fingertips.

"Don't touch her!" one of the officers yelled, gaining the attention of the emperor.

"Why not?"

"She's André's wife," Officer Jones said between clenched teeth. Seconds later, he fell to the floor, his body convulsing on the concrete and blood spurting from his eyes, ears, nose and mouth. At last, he laid still, no breath, no sound—just silent trails of blood flowing from his dead form.

The emperor turned his attention back to Katrina. "André's wife." He smiled and grabbed her by the hair.

The pain in her scalp overrode her anger for a moment and she scrambled to her feet even as he pulled her up, her hands locking around his wrist, willing the pain to dull and it did. But with the dulled sensation, the bitter anger returned, scraping her tongue with the sour taste. She swallowed and glared at the emperor.

His grip on her hair loosened and he studied the consistency of her blonde locks before returning his red-eyed gaze back to hers. He swept her shirt open, staring at the black lace bra with interest.

"Don't touch her!"

The emperor turned his head toward the soldiers and waved his hand in a dismissive gesture.

Katrina felt the death of each soldier as they fell to the ground and with each one, a little piece of her sanity shattered. They were doomed and she shut her mind off, not allowing her thoughts to drift to Sam. Maybe he could survive, if she didn't slip up and let this bastard know he existed.

Maybe.

His gaze landed back on her, driving all thoughts into a black hole of despair.

A sadistic smile graced his lips. "André's *wife.*" His eyes narrowed and he again swept her shirt aside, running his fingertips from her lips down her neck, approaching the crest of her cleavage.

"Get away from me." His touch was like a hundred spiders slithering over her skin and she shuddered, revolted, but she couldn't break the invisible grip.

The sound of ripping fabric filled the hangar and Katrina gasped as her camouflage drifted in shredded tatters to the floor, leaving her standing in black lace panties and matching bra with her army boots. The hunger etched in the emperor's face struck terror in her, heightening her powers and she broke the spell holding her in place and took a step back.

The emperor licked his lips and said the words again, but this time, they were laced with disgust and hatred. "André's wife."

She tried to take another step away, but the grip tightened, pulling her forward instead. His hand shot out, the back of his knuckles connecting with her cheek and dropping her to the ground at his feet. Pain bloomed like a hot iron branding her skin and she blinked back the blinding flickering haze in front of her eyes, refocusing on the bastard before her.

Acute agony assaulted her head, his mind scan prodding but she held the wall to her memories intact. She cried out, the paralyzing sting reminding her of when André broke her psychic barrier.

The emperor smiled. "You *will* give me what I want."

"No," she said between clenched teeth, keeping him from controlling her mind. The sudden exit of his influence left her muscles rubbery and weak, and she collapsed onto her side, the cool floor welcoming in comparison to the hostile enemy standing over her.

The emperor crossed his arms, gnawing on his bottom lip in a familiar habit she had seen André do a thousand times when he contemplated what to do next. For the first time since they walked through the door, she really looked at the emperor, blinking back tears of shock at the similarities between this psycho and her husband. She glanced at the other Zyclonians guarding the entrance, waiting for their next command. None of them had the same features. Different shapes and sizes, just like humans. But this man, this monarch, he could have been André's father.

The emperor's eyes narrowed. "*I* didn't sire that abomination."

Katrina clamped down on her mind again, shaken that the emperor had read her train of thought. "André's going to kill you."

"If he survived, all the better. I'll finally have his head mounted on a trophy plaque over my mantel. But before I kill him, I want him to watch you and his '*father*' die." He made quotation marks with his fingers as he said the word father along with a distasteful smirk. He turned and nodded at his men. They converged on Katrina and Matthew pulling them to their feet and escorting them into one of the Zyclonian fighters. The emperor took a seat facing the two of them. "The world is going to watch you die on live television."

Messiah Chapter 24

ANDRÉ PULLED CAL ONTO the shore. "You okay?"

Cal nodded. "Just having a bitch of a time breathing," he said.

"Slow your metabolism down," André said as he looked around for anything that had survived the Zyclonian attack and his counterattack. "We have to get back to the base before it's too late." He put his hand out to help Cal up.

Cal accepted his hand and stood beside him. "How?"

André sighed. "I don't know." He looked back at the ocean. "I don't think there's anything left." He looked inland. "There are a few trails that way." He pointed to a couple distant plumes of black smoke. "Think you can make it?" he asked.

Cal nodded and they began walking.

"Thanks," Cal said after a couple of miles.

"For what?" André asked, keeping his eye on the target ahead.

"For saving my ass."

André shrugged. "You were lucky enough to be in the jet with me." He glanced over at his friend. "I wasn't able to save anyone else." He blinked back the red film covering his eyes, the weight of the words slamming into his chest hard enough to stop the breath in his throat. He stopped, closing his eyes, forcing himself to relax. He'd be no good to Katrina and his father if he died out here in the desert. When he opened his eyes, he scanned the horizon, his eyes homing in on a hunk of metal. "What the hell is that?"

Cal cocked his head. "Well, I'll be damned."

"What is it?"

"It looks like one of those antique solar trucks."

André didn't understand. He looked between the vehicle and Cal. "What does it do?"

Cal ignored André and jogged over to the vehicle, opening the door.

André followed, skirting around to the other side of the cab and opening the passenger door. The smell that wafted out of the cab made him gag. In the back seat lay an old human skeleton lying on some blankets that had been infested and long deserted by all manners of creatures.

"This is an antique." Cal ran his hands over the big round wheel in front of him and dropped his gaze to the push pad on the dash. "We're in luck. Hop in." His breath wheezed and he smiled.

André saw the light of possibilities in his friend's eyes and the excitement rattling his heart. "Easy, Cal, you have to conserve oxygen."

Cal nodded and closed his eyes, gathering his wits and doing as André said. When he opened his eyes, they focused on the gearshift. "This could get us there if it still works." He reached for the pad and pushed. The truck lurched forward. "No way," he said, looking at André.

"Do you know how to work this thing?"

Cal studied the gears and the pedals. "I drove one once when I was in high school. They had it at a fair in Kansas." He pushed the clutch in with his left foot and turned the ignition. The truck made a screaming noise as the gears that hadn't moved in two hundred years were asked to move. "Shit."

André opened the glove compartment and pulled out the manual. He flipped through it quickly and then put his hands on the dash. "Try again." He closed his eyes, concentrating on what he read, breathing his power into this behemoth of a vehicle.

The engine turned over and Cal let out a whoop.

"Hang on," André said, jumping out of the cab. He looked at the pin holding the cab to the rusted-out trailer and pulled, releasing the cab and making it lighter for travel. He jumped back in the passenger seat, smiling. "Do whatever you do to make this thing move."

Cal shifted into first gear, released the clutch and pushed the gas pedal. The cab rumbled forward. "I don't know how far we'll get," he said, as he shifted the gears. The engine screamed again but kept going. Cal looked at the instruments. "At least there seems to be a charge." He tapped the solar charge indicator to make sure. The needle stayed put, showing the vehicle had half of its battery life. Cal got through the ten gears and had the vehicle flying down the road at a lumbering hundred miles an hour.

"Can't this thing go any faster?" André asked.

"To be honest, I didn't think it would go faster than fifty. It had to have been sitting there for a couple centuries." He glanced at André. "It's a miracle it's moving, never mind going close to a hundred miles an hour."

"Just drive," André said, closing his eyes and concentrating as he gripped the door handle. His breath came in the same shallow rasps as Cal's, his lungs burning from exertion and lack of oxygen. He lowered his head and the engine revved, pushing the truck faster. He opened his eyes, watching as the needle on the speedometer buried itself beyond the one hundred and sixty mark.

"Don't use all your strength, André," Cal said, taking a quick glance in his direction. "You'll need some juice when we get there."

André nodded, dialing back a little. The wheels spun on the empty highway, going over a hundred and fifty miles an hour between the actual mechanics of the truck and André's silent mental strength.

"How much longer?" André asked, his energy level tipping toward the empty mark like the energy needle on the dashboard. He knew he should conserve, but he needed to get home to make sure Katrina and Sam were safe.

Cal's hands were on the wheel so tightly his knuckles turned white. They could see the dome in the distance now. "Less than a half an hour." He glanced at André. "Don't exhaust yourself to the point that you can't recover. We're gonna need you as strong as possible."

"I need *you* alive in case I get into trouble." André glanced at Cal. "And we're pushing the limit on that."

Cal took a shallow breath. "I'll be fine," he said more to convince himself than André.

André closed his eyes again and pushed. The truck lurched faster, now making noises in protest of the speed André was making it go.

The next fifteen minutes seemed to take forever.

"Ease up, André," Cal said as they approached the outside of the outer base.

André pulled the power back inside and the truck sputtered, stalling a few hundred yards from the door.

Cal sat back in the seat, wheezing and staring at the hangar. "I think someone's inside."

André closed his eyes, concentrating, putting feelers out there and coming up empty. He glanced at the crease between Cal's eyes and the worry lines etched in his face. "If they are here, I can handle them." He took a small breath. "Can you make it to the door?"

Cal nodded. "I think so," he said as he looked at the cameras.

"They aren't working at the moment. Haven't been since we hit the horizon," André said with a smile. "Come on." He tumbled out of the cab. They met in front of the truck and started walking toward the door.

"You look like shit, André."

André chuckled. "You don't look much better, buddy."

"I'm serious. You look like the walking dead, like you haven't slept in months."

André shrugged. "I'm a little tired, but I'll manage."

Cal stumbled.

André caught and steadied him. He kept his arm around Cal's waist for the remainder of the trek.

"Thanks," Cal hissed as André leaned him against the wall by the door.

André put his hand on the doorknob and hesitated, trading a glance with Cal and steeling himself for a battle. "If they are in there, they'll know we're here the minute this door opens. Get in and get behind me, understand?"

Cal nodded.

André mentally unlocked the door and turned the doorknob, swinging it open. The rush of air pushed him back a step as he entered with Cal in his wake. The door shut behind them.

It took a second for André's eyes to adjust and comprehend the two sets of red eyes running in their direction. His heart tripped into overtime, running adrenaline through his tired body, fueling the sudden fury etching his skin. André lashed out, the power exploding from him and eviscerating the intruders like he did to the meteor so many years ago. He sucked in a huge breath of oxygen, shaking from both the rush of relief from his lungs and the power expenditure.

Stepping farther into the hangar, his gaze rose to the screen and his heart dropped. "Oh God." He broke into a run.

Messiah Chapter 25

THE ZYCLONIAN FIGHTER JET blasted through the hangar walls and into the dome, traveling faster than any earthbound vehicle, arriving at the Dallas football arena within a matter of minutes, crushing the crafts it settled over. Inside the stadium, the clueless fans cheered as the Dallas Cowboys advanced on the Denver Broncos.

Katrina traded a glance with Matthew. The chains binding her wrists dug into her flesh with every yank from her captors. The emperor led the procession, killing anyone who dared intercept his march. Katrina had time to study the machines they rolled in with them and it took a few minutes, but then she understood their use and a cold fear plunged into her stomach, turning her bowels into watery fire.

They were death machines, instruments of torture meant for her and Matthew.

The band of Zyclonians converged into the stadium, unchallenged, even with their torture chairs within clear eyeshot. They stopped at the entrance to the field and the emperor turned to one of his subordinates. "Keep us on the air," he commanded.

Katrina clenched her teeth, knowing Sam was home watching the game. She prayed for André, for him to be alive, to find a way back, to get to Sam before this madman did.

The emperor turned and stared at her, and a crease appeared between his eyes.

Katrina shut down her thoughts, closing his small window of opportunity.

He swung his gaze back to the spectacle before him and marched their band onto the turf, disrupting the final minutes of the first half.

Katrina had a moment to smile, this arrogant bastard's entrance diluted by the crowd's screams as Dallas's quarterback launched a Hail Mary toward the end zone. Her smile vanished when the ball burst into flames in mid-air, stunning the crowd into silence.

"What the hell?" the announcer's voice filled the stadium.

Messiah Chapter 26

SAM STARED AT THE television, his mouth open in shock at the sight of his grandfather and mother dragged onto the football field in chains. Panic throbbed through his bones, and he scanned the room, his gaze landing on the key rack, stopping on the single set for the craft parked in the driveway.

After a moment of hesitation, he glanced toward the kitchen and his grandmother lost in the process of preparing dinner, trying to forget what lay ahead for her family. It didn't take a genius to understand why she was so engrossed, and he took advantage of the situation.

Sam flipped the television off, peeled the keys from the peg and headed out of the house.

Guilt made him pause at the door. "Grandma, I'm going out for a little while," he yelled. "The game's a blowout. I'll be back before dinner." He closed the front door and bolted across the lawn, jumping into the hovercraft before she could intercede.

Without another glance, he sped away, praying the cops wouldn't pull him over and the usual Sunday drivers would stay the hell out of his way.

"Come on, you piece of shit," he muttered, pushing the craft to its limit, driving much more aggressively than he ever would with his parents in the craft. But the thing was not fast enough and he gave it an added mental push, catapulting into

hyper-drive, the sonic boom shaking the craft and
everything in its wake.

Messiah Chapter 27

KATRINA STRUGGLED AGAINST THE soldiers holding her in place, but she was no match for four men, each with strength equal to André's. One grabbed a handful of her hair and yanked her head back.

"I will enjoy seeing you torn apart," he whispered in her ear.

"Fuck you!" she growled.

The emperor sent a glare over his shoulder. With it came an invisible gag, silencing her.

The emperor took the microphone from the official. "Ladies and gentlemen. I am Viktor, the Emperor of Zyclon, ruler of the known universe, including this secluded galaxy." He gave a nod to the soldiers with the chairs, and they dragged the machines to the fifty-yard line and parked them side by side.

With another nod, the soldiers surrounding Katrina each grabbed a limb, carrying her to the first of the two machines. She twisted in their grasp but couldn't break free. As the gag was lifted, her screams and curses echoed in the stadium. She freed one of her hands and scratched a soldier's cheek, drawing blood. Her moment of satisfaction ended with a hard smack that left her dazed enough for the men to strap her to the table. She glanced at Matthew and his cool demeanor as his wrists and ankles were bound, wondering how in God's name he could remain so calm. He met her gaze and the muscles in his jaw jumped, giving away his fury.

"I am looking for a traitor from my planet," the emperor said, looking into the cameras, touching the scar on his face. "His name is André, and I will kill anyone who gives him safe harbor." He turned toward Matthew and Katrina.

Katrina let out a wordless roar, pulling against her bindings, her anger too much for her to contain. "You exiled a six-year-old, you bastard! He wasn't a traitor. He was a child!"

Matthew didn't fight; instead, he glared at the emperor. "My son is not a traitor." He projected his voice above Katrina's wild shrieks, loud enough for the microphone to pick up his words, and the emperor spun on his heels, matching Matthew's glare.

The wound in Matthew's shoulder split open and he gritted his teeth but did not cry out. "You can go to hell."

"You both granted him safe harbor and this world will see what happens to those who open their doors to this traitor," the emperor said, crossing toward Katrina. "This whore not only opened her door, but she also opened her legs, so I'm offering a treat to anyone who wants a piece of this filthy bitch." With a nod, the table split, stretching her legs wide and she cried out in pain. He smiled, waving toward her, opening the invitation to the entire coliseum.

"You bastard," Katrina screamed, and her gaze darted to the crowd. At first no one moved, but then she saw a group of Hells Angels glance at one another. The feral smiles that surfaced slammed the fight right out of her, replacing it with the memories of the brutality visited on her years ago, and with it came the debilitating fear.

Matthew cursed under his breath and returned his gaze to the emperor. "You are a sick bastard."

The emperor turned back to Matthew with a smile and a shrug.

The first man to approach Katrina staggered and fell on his ass. "Stay away from my daughter," Matthew growled at the man without moving his eyes from the emperor.

Katrina's gaze jumped from the man to Matthew in time to see his cheek split. He winced but that was the extent of the visible emotion, but she knew. She felt his fury growing steadily inside him and the memories of the attack on Linda fueled it.

The perverted fantasies of the approaching men overrode everything else, and Katrina snapped her gaze toward the group of men. Her skin crawled at their thoughts, and she fought against the bonds, frustrated at her inability to break both the physical restraints as well as the mental commands holding her in place. A sob escaped and she hated herself for sounding so pathetic.

"André is going to tear you apart, and I hope he does it slowly," Matthew said.

Matthew's anger-fueled power sweep past Katrina, tingling her nerves.

The man's scrotum exploded, and he screamed, grabbing his crotch and backing away from Katrina, a red stain spreading over the lap of his pants at an alarming rate. One look at the results, and the rest of the men backed away.

The emperor's face split open in the same spot André tore so many years ago and Katrina turned toward Matthew and his smile of satisfaction at the emperor's gasp of pain.

The emperor's hand shot to his face. When he pulled his bloody palm away from his cheek, Katrina's soul filled with terror.

SEARING PAIN SPLIT HIS abdomen and Matthew screamed. It felt like a wild cougar raked his claws through his torso and blood spurted out of the gash. Matthew closed his eyes for a moment, slowing down his heart rate like André taught him. The pain was unbearable, but he had to keep himself alive and conscious.

As long as he was alive, the emperor wouldn't hurt Katrina.

The emperor laughed and Matthew opened his eyes.

"You really think that as long as you're alive, I won't hurt her?" He approached Katrina and ran his finger down the length of her arm, slicing the skin like a scalpel.

Katrina whimpered, but did not cry out; instead, she kept eye contact with him, and the hopelessness reflected in her irises seared his soul.

I'm sorry. I failed you, he thought.

Katrina shook her head, and her voice filled his mind. *No, you didn't, Dad.*

Matthew glanced back at the emperor. "I wonder. What will André tear off first?" He sent a mental punch to the most tender of manly regions.

The emperor doubled over.

Matthew's legs split open, tearing both femoral arteries. Dizziness overtook him and the pain receded with each ounce of blood pouring onto the field. *André, if you can hear me, hurry.*

I'm going as fast as I can. Just hang on.

André's response made Matthew smile and the knowledge that he lived allowed Matthew to harness what was left of his strength. *Love you, kiddo.* He pushed the thought to André and with the last vestige of his strength, he focused on the emperor, willing whatever damage he was capable of inflicting.

The emperor's forearm split to the bone, bringing forth a roar of pain and frustration.

Matthew's throat burst open, but he was beyond pain. He forced a smile of satisfaction before the darkness dragged him away.

Messiah Chapter 28

"**NO!**" SAM'S VOICE ECHOED with heart pounding panic. The sight of the arterial spray arcing from his grandfather's throat unlocked his paralysis and he stepped into the shadows as the emperor's gaze passed over where he stood.

Hide, baby, please hide. His mother's voice assaulted his mind.

He swallowed the lump of fear in his throat, blinking back the sudden burn of tears. His grandfather's passing hit him harder than a sucker punch, leaving a hollowness in his stomach. The injustice and brutality of his murder bloomed, bringing with it an anger that straightened his back and set his jaw tight.

If he had been a few seconds faster, his grandfather wouldn't have died, and he was damned if he was going to let this monster kill his mother, too.

"No, Mom, I won't hide." He stepped into view.

The emperor's reaction brought a smile to Sam's face.

Fear.

He saw fear in the bastard's eyes. His smile faltered when the emperor stepped behind his mother, using her as a shield.

You coward.

His anger morphed into hatred. Hatred so strong that it sprung a life of its own, traveling through his bloodstream like a ravaged monster, and he took a step in the direction of the field, reveling in the power flashing in his veins.

"Well, well, well," the emperor said, staring at Sam. "You were hiding something after all."

"Don't hurt my baby," she whispered, the microphone picking up the plea and broadcasting it through the stadium.

"I'm going to take great pleasure pulling him apart, piece by piece." He stood, his words producing a fear in his mother's face, one Sam couldn't abide seeing.

With each step, he felt the power coiling into a tight ball, like a cobra ready to strike. He didn't need to scan the crowd to pinpoint where the rest of the Zyclonian army stood; he felt them, sensed their stalking, murdering eyes watching him descend the stairs in the silent arena.

Protect yourself, the panicked voice of his mother whispered in his mind. Their eyes met and hers went wide. Pain filled his mind as her scream carried through the stadium.

ANDRÉ RAN THROUGH THE entrance, his heart throbbing in his chest and his lungs screaming from exertion. Katrina's scream filled his head and echoed throughout the stadium, cutting off abruptly.

"NO!" Sam's scream overrode Katrina's, and André emerged onto the field in time to see Sam crossing at full tilt, an angry mask of murder transforming his young face. Instead of attacking the emperor, André ran straight at his son, tackling him before the emperor could gather another targeted strike.

Sam's fury radiated off him as much as his building power and André shuddered at the consequences if Sam let that ball loose. He held his flailing son tightly to his chest as they rolled and whispered in his ear, "I need you to control your power, Sam."

"They killed Mom," Sam said when they stopped rolling.

"I know," André said. He stood, facing the emperor with his arms still wrapped around Sam. He pushed Sam behind him and out of the emperor's strike line. Fury, raw and wild, snaked through him, almost getting away from him as his peripheral vision picked up the remains of his wife and father.

A Zyclonian soldier stepped forward.

"Watch out," Sam whispered.

André felt a stinger of power escape from his son.

The soldier screamed.

"Don't torture him, Sam," André said, his eyes never leaving the emperor's. "Just kill him."

Sam obeyed his father and the soldier's chest exploded.

"You killed my wife," André said, not allowing the lion's share of emotions tied to that statement to surface. Fury was the only allowance.

Another Zyclonian soldier stepped onto the field.

André raised his hand and the soldier evaporated to dust, the level of controlled power erupting a gasp from Sam.

"How very humane of you," the emperor said stepping into the open space between the two halves of Katrina, forcing André to see how his wife died.

André looked at the halved remains of his wife and shock racked his brain. The bastard had split her right down the middle from head to crotch. A clean slice like he had run her through a particularly sharp industrial table saw. On the heels of shock came the full force of loss, punching him in the gut.

He shoved aside the urge to crumple to the ground and let the emperor kill him.

The only reason he remained standing was the boy behind him. "You bastard," he whispered, blinking back the tears. His shoulder split open.

The emperor smiled. "Emotion still rules you, just like your parents."

"Perhaps, but this time, you are on my turf. This is my country, my planet," he growled taking another step forward. "This is the United States of America, and it is *not* for the taking." He stood a fraction taller, the words like his own personal talisman projecting his powerful voice through the silent stadium.

Cheers erupted.

"Take the soldiers out, Sam," André said over his shoulder. "Just like I did."

Sam wasn't as humane or as clean as André and the soldiers exploded.

André tilted his head and glared at the emperor. "It's just you and me now."

"And your son," the emperor said.

Sam cried out and André twirled catching him before he hit the ground. Sam whimpered, grasping his leg, holding the wound the emperor created. He set Sam on the ground meeting his gaze.

André stood, turning back toward the emperor with his thoughts on lockdown. He needed to put distance between the emperor and his son and the only way to do that was offering himself as bait.

"I bet you wouldn't be able to take me with just your bare hands," he growled, playing on the emperor's vanity and giving Sam time to glean the plan from his mind. He had a way of stopping the emperor, but he needed his son's superior control because his was just about tapped.

"The thought of squeezing that scrawny throat of yours until you die is tempting."

"You don't have the guts," André spat, positioning himself so he was blocking the emperor's direct line of sight to Sam. He caught a glimpse of himself in the side projection, his bright blue irises outlined with laser red, reminding everyone in the viewing audience that he wasn't human.

The emperor laughed and took a step toward André.

André circled as the emperor approached, putting his wounded shoulder behind the line of his body, trying to protect Sam as long as he could. He left his hands loose, and elbows slightly bent so he could strike out with his fists if the emperor took the bait. In his mind, he replayed the scene fifteen years before, the way his fists felt punching Captain Trevor and feeling his nose break, broadcasting the little show so the emperor picked it up instead of the underlying current between André and Sam.

When he stepped to the side, leaving Sam unprotected, his heart leapt into his throat, and he taunted the emperor. "Come on; let's see what you've got." The words rumbled from his chest.

The punch came from nowhere and tossed André onto his ass. He scrambled to his feet. "I figured you wouldn't play fair." André smiled; his eyes moved past the emperor and met his son's. "Now, Sam."

The emperor fell to his knees under the power Sam unleashed and André felt it sizzling in the air, begging to do more than just hold the emperor in place, containing the emperor's power to a six-inch radius around him.

"Sam, just hold him there," André said, still meeting his son's gaze. *I promise the bastard will pay, but not at our hands.* A part of André smiled at the same words his father said to him years ago, and then he focused back on the emperor.

He rubbed his chin. "Now, what was the reason you exiled me at six?" he inquired, tapping his finger on his lips. "Oh, now I remember." He looked at his son. "It was the prophecy. Supposedly a boy with blue eyes would either rule or destroy Zyclon." He glanced back at the emperor.

Sam pleaded with his gaze and André shook his head. He wanted everyone on the battleship to hear this. He wanted his home planet to know what their emperor was made of. "The prophecy was bullshit, wasn't it?"

The emperor glared at André and sent the silent command to the warship to send the fighter fleet.

"You shouldn't have done that." André looked up at the sky, unleashing the power and fury inside him before the battleship could fire on the domes. The air in the stadium changed, rippling around André as a powerful blast shot out through the opening in the stadium ceiling, passing through the solid sphere of the dome and annihilating the fighter planes. He took it a step further and destroyed the flight deck on the warship, disabling their ability to fire on Earth.

The stadium roared as the television screens switched to show the disintegration of the fighter jets in space.

André staggered a step and shook the cobwebs of exhaustion from his head. He glanced back at the emperor. "Tell them the real reason you killed my parents and sent me packing," he demanded, circling again. "Tell us all." He looked around the stadium, his eyes falling on the remains of Katrina and Matthew. His face contorted with rage, pushing the tiredness from his bones. He stepped closer to the emperor, slamming his fist into the man's face. "Tell them!"

The emperor glared at André, blood gushing from his broken nose.

"Since you seem to be without words, I think I'll clue everyone in on just how much of a bastard you really are." André stepped away. "You manipulated Zyclonian prophecy to suit your own needs. The prophecy that I read stated a mad tyrant would destroy Zyclon, not a blue-eyed boy. Not the heir to the throne."

The emperor struggled to break free of the invisible bonds that held him in place.

"You conveniently targeted my blue eyes, because I was different," André growled. "It didn't matter that I was your nephew. It didn't matter that I had legitimate claim to the throne. All that mattered to you was power and control, and with me and my parents alive, that threatened all you built. All you stole." André looked around the stadium and up at the displays. "So, tell me, Emperor," he said, his voice filled with bitter sarcasm, "did you fulfill the prophecy? Did you destroy Zyclon?"

Silence fell over the crowd, and he looked up at the screens, feeling the pause of the warship crew.

"You are an abomination," the emperor hissed.

André laughed. "You killed your own sister and sent your nephew into space to die. I think you've got the corner on that market." He looked in the direction of his dead wife. "I've waited over twenty-five years for payback," he said, glancing over at Sam, "and you've destroyed almost everything I cared about." His vision clouded with red tears. "And as much as I want to see you die for what you have done..." He trailed off as the tears spilled. "I can't kill you in cold blood. That would make me no better than you." He walked toward Sam. "And my father taught me better than that." He stopped behind the emperor. He put his hand on the back of his head and with a vicious mental yank, he slammed the barrier in the emperor's mind closed, shutting all traces of his inhuman power.

The emperor cried out in pain.

"But I can take away your power." André dropped his hand and turned toward his son.

"He killed Papa and Mom," Sam said as André approached.

André nodded. "But that doesn't make it right for me to kill him. Too many have already died."

"He declared war," Sam whispered.

"He did more than that, Sam. He destroyed Zyclon," André said, looking at the display now broadcasting the interior of the warship control room, and received a nod from the acting commander of the Zyclonian fleet. "It's over now and he'll stand trial for his crimes." He put his arm around Sam, turning him away from the carnage. "Let him go."

SAM RELEASED THE EMPEROR, squashing the urge to shatter the bastard's bones to a pulp where he stood. His gaze fell on his mother and tremors started in his stomach, spiraling outward while sobs ripped from his chest.

Cal's wide eyes caught his attention and then his father lurched forward onto his knees, his breath a wincing wheeze of an exhale. No inhale followed and his father fell forward with a dagger sticking out of his back.

Sam spun around, fury lining the power, transforming it into a wild beast, and he let loose.

The skin peeled from the emperor, his scream a fraction of a second too late, but when it came, it echoed like a frightened little girl.

Sam crossed the distance and plunged his hand inside the man's chest. "You won't be needing this, but my father will." He ripped out the emperor's heart. He stood in the center of the football stadium, holding the muscle in his hand, reeling in his power and focusing it on keeping the heart beating and strong.

The emperor keeled backwards, dying like he lived—heartless.

Messiah Epilogue

THE SOUNDS OF THE heart monitor and the swish of the ventilator registered in his fog-ridden brain. André's eyes fluttered open. The bright lights of the operating room made him squeeze his eyes shut again. He welcomed the darkness.

You can't stay, her voice whispered in his ear.

But I want to be with you, he said, straining to see her in the mist.

Katrina stepped into view. *We will be together again someday. But right now, Sam needs you.* She leaned forward and kissed his cheek. *I love you.* Katrina faded, mixing in with the smoky mist.

"Don't go!" André yelled and sat up in the recovery room.

Cal looked up from the chart. "It's about time you came back to us."

"Kat," André whispered, looking around the room. He glanced back at Cal. Slowly, the events of the past couple of days filtered back into his consciousness. André lay back on the pillow and covered his face with his hands. "She's dead," he said, finally allowing the despair to take hold.

Cal put the chart down. "We thought we lost you, too."

"My father's gone."

"Yes."

"Please tell me Sam's okay." He looked beyond his fingers.

"Sam's just fine." Cal smiled. "He's with your mother. They're waiting to see you." He handed André a wet washcloth and let out a small chuckle. "I'm not sure what to call you. Is it Commander or Your Highness?"

André glared at him. "Don't go there, Cal," he said, wiping the bloody tears from his cheeks. "Did anyone else from the team make it?" he asked, diverting the conversation of his true lineage to another time.

"No, you and I are the only ones who are still alive."

André wiped his face and took a deep breath, stepping into the role of commander as easily as his father had. "We need to arrange a national memorial service to recognize the sacrifices our team made, as well as my father's leadership in protecting the country."

"I already made that suggestion to the president and he is waiting for word on your condition before he finalizes the plans," Cal said.

"What about the remaining Zyclonians on the spaceship?"

"Peaceful negotiations are underway and they haven't shown any signs of hostility since your showdown. The president has included Sam in the negotiations and Sam confirmed their peaceful intent. He says they just want a place where they are welcome."

André nodded and closed his eyes, letting the emotions back in. "Can I see Sam now?"

"In a second," Cal said. "I need to tell you the extent of the damage and what we had to do." He sat on the edge of the bed, taking a deep breath. "Do you know what happened?"

André shook his head. "The last thing I remember was leading Sam away."

"Your uncle threw a dagger and it went through your heart," Cal said. "I tried to push it away, but I was a little late on the draw. I was only able to move the trajectory a little, enough to save your life, but not enough to save your heart."

André looked down at the bandages on his chest and back at Cal. "Okay, so whose heart do I have?"

"Your uncle's," Cal replied.

Surprise sputtered a shiver up his spine and André's eyebrows creased. He had left the emperor alive on the football field.

"Sam killed him," he replied to the unspoken question in André's eyes. "He ended up being a perfect match to your blood and tissue type. Better than the one we had on ice."

André closed his eyes and nodded. "Where's my heart?"

"Probably still in the operating room. Why?"

"I want it buried with Katrina," he said. "She's the one who owns it." The tears fell again. "It belongs with her."

Cal nodded. "I'll make sure that happens." He stood up. "There haven't been any complications at this point and no sign of your body rejecting the organ."

André opened his eyes, meeting Cal's. "I don't know how I feel about this," he said. "I hated my uncle; he was a cold-blooded killer."

"André, it's just a muscle that pumps blood. You are still André Robbins, no matter whose heart is in your body." Cal tapped his temple. "It's what's up here that counts." He headed for the door. "Besides, it's an ironic twist of justice," he said over his shoulder. "He wanted you dead; instead, he ended up saving your life."

André swallowed the lump in his throat and sent a sad, lonely smile in Cal's direction. "That's something Kat would have said."

The End

529

Armageddon

I SAT ON THE cold sand, staring at the reflection of the strange sky. It looked like a rainbow erupted, leaving a trail of blood across the spectrum. The mighty Pacific, reduced to a still and death filled lake—no surf, no quiet lapping of the sand—just choked silence. The rotting stench of death tinged by the salty sea filled the air.

I turned, wincing at the pain in my strained lower back, and scanned the beach and the burning building in the center of the concrete parking lot. I blew a stream of air from my mouth and the fabric of the handkerchief fluttered from the disturbance.

I still don't understand why I'm alive. Nine lives used up, so to speak, spared from the disease and subsequent acts of sheer stupidity. By all accounts, I should have died a thousand times over by now.

The disease.

Like a spear piercing my liver, I folded over from the memory. Burning tears mixed with smoke from the funeral pyre scathed my eyes. I closed them against the soot, against the memories, against the pain. But they came anyway, taking me hostage.

The last television program I saw was months ago. A dying scientist examined the biological weapon, explaining the hybrid concoction to the masses. Anthrax, Ebola, cancer, meningitis, and a particularly virulent strain of swine flu had been successfully combined into an airborne disease that spread like wildfire.

And a fanatical faction in the Middle East released it in a coordinated attack on both Europe and the United States.

Crazy fucks thought it would stay localized.

Crazy fucks never grasped the full scope of what they created.

Crazy fucks didn't know when they released the virus they sentenced the Earth to die.

Had they known, would they still have released it?

Obsessed by the question, I let it dominate my mind, leaving no room for the more crippling thoughts. But it wasn't the television program that brought the pressure down on my chest like a two-ton boulder, restricting my lungs and folding me in half whenever something barreled through the brick wall surrounding those taboo memories.

No, it wasn't the television show at all.

That dying doctor droning on about the virus was secondary to the boy in my arms.

My Daniel, my six-year-old angel, lying in my lap, suffering, sobbing through the bloody coughs, his skin as hot as the pavement in Phoenix at noon, his torso covered in bruises from internal bleeding, his organs turning to liquid as the disease ate through his body.

And there wasn't a damn thing I could do.

I knew what was happening, I had watched the virus take my husband earlier that day and I knew Danny didn't have much longer. He was suffering and God help me, I couldn't end it for him.

That iota of hope still clung to me: if I could kick it, certainly my child could.

But that's not what happened.

He died in my arms just as surely as my husband did hours before.

And this disease, this hell unleashed on Earth, didn't stop destroying when the host died. Not right away. No it kept eating until all that remained was a gelatinous skeleton, covered in a bruised layer of skin or fur or scales or feathers and a slow escape of fermented liquid, blood, and pus ripe with disease, drained from every pore.

The smell of rotting corpses descended over the town like a shroud and in those early days, I found myself vomiting more often than not at even a hint of the vile scent.

Frantic, I went house to house, searching for survivors, but there was no one but the ghosts of the dead. I found myself on the town green, exhausted, drained, and numb, and I sank to the steps. I couldn't wrap my head around the devastation.

Just when I thought it couldn't get any worse, I scanned what used to be a scene right out of a Norman Rockwell painting and blinked. If it weren't for the colorful homes lining the once vivid town green, I'd have thought I just stepped into a black-and-white movie.

The trees dripped with large black drops of decay, some already cast to the ground, unable to support their own weight. The mighty oak in the center of the town green was nothing but petrified wood, surrounded by shriveled dry grass now completely devoid of color, a pale gray fur on the deep brown soil. I rubbed my eyes, trying to wipe away the horrific illusion and glanced to my right. The potted plant next to me, once a colorful bloom of petunias, was now a sludge pile.

That was the first time I realized the true horror of the airborne virus. It killed more than just humans and dogs and cats and deer and birds. Anything it came in contact with it attacked, morphing into the perfect blend of viral bacteria aimed at destroying whatever it clung to before moving on to the next victim. It didn't discriminate; it didn't care whether the host was a member of the plant or animal kingdom: this nightmare strain devoured everything it touched.

The world was dying, and I was the only witness.

There had to be someone out there whose fever broke before the worst of the symptoms hit, whose bruises faded away like shadows formed by clouds passing on a sunny day.

Someone who had no understanding why they were spared.

Someone like me.

Surely, I couldn't be the only human left on the Earth, could I?

That thought got me moving. Well, that and the rumble in my stomach.

I had left my home on the Connecticut shore on a warm spring day, the car packed to the hilt with water, canned goods, pasta and anything that wouldn't spoil. I had a suitcase of my most comfortable clothes and my purse. The only snag in my oh-so-perfect plan was the gas gauge. The needle hovered just above the *E*, which meant I had just enough to get me to the nearest gas station.

I pulled out of my driveway, weaving between the fallen trees and strewn cars. A little shortsighted considering, but I was naïve, not realizing that when I ran out of gas, that was it.

I don't know how many times I scanned my credit card. It must have been at least a half-dozen scans: stare, sigh, and scan again. I varied the ritual, sprinkling streams of swears between each step, staring at the dead pump, fully expecting it to roar to life just for me.

I guess you could say I was in a state of shock and when the reality came, the card tumbled through my fingers falling to the ground. I almost followed it, too. My legs turned to jelly, and I grabbed for the side of the car to steady myself.

No electricity, no gas.

Such a simple concept and yet the most complicated one in my world at the time. I had no clue how to get the pumps working and had less of a clue how to siphon gas from the cars around me.

How was I supposed to get the hell out of dodge without my car?

I thought my capacity for panic had dulled, but this flipped the switch, and I had a full-out attack, sinking to the ground against the side of my tire, hopelessness stretched endlessly before me. My chest fought for each fragment of air, the ragged wheezing grating on my nerves enough to snap me out of it.

"Get moving, girl." My shaky voice broke the silence and the sound on the flat air startled me, loosening my lungs.

I climbed to my feet and slid back into the car, pulling out of the parking lot.

I slammed the brakes, my eyes locking on the sporting goods store at the far corner of the plaza. I had an *aha* moment, an epiphany.

"A bike." *Yeah, that's what I need—a bike.*

I threw my car in reverse and pulled forward into the street-side mall. Of course, the store was locked, but that didn't deter me. Nope, so intent in my mission, I didn't even blink when I tossed the small shopping cart through the display window.

Daintily, I stepped inside, righting the shopping cart and scanning the dark store. The bikes were in the back, lining the wall and floor, but I diverted to the camping supply section.

I grabbed anything I thought I would need and hesitated in front of the gun counter. A small voice in the back of my head urged me to grab one of the guns; however, I wasn't versed in firearms, so I stood surveying and debating. When my gaze locked with my reflection, another realization hit.

"I'll probably end up shooting my foot off or something." A nervous, almost crazed cackle came from the wells of my chest and I quickly turned away from the reflection.

Instead, I opted for a heavy aluminum bat and a small hatchet that fit in one of the compartments of my handlebar bag for protection. Not that I was expecting to encounter much, but I figured those two things would be more useful than a gun.

The last thing I grabbed was a fleece throw with my favorite football team emblazoned in the soft fabric. A relic, I realized, but one that brought me comfort.

Outside the store, I packed up the storage bags and fit them on the bike along with a large lockable trailer that carried the camping supplies I grabbed. I did an inventory: tent, sleeping bag, Coleman stove, propane tanks, flashlights, batteries, canned goods, cooking utensils, matches, water, vitamins, food, and snacks. It had been years since I went camping and I wondered if I had enough to sustain a long ride.

I crossed into the grocery store and pilfered the energy bars, bringing as much as I could carry out and dumping them in the trailer. *There, I think that should do the trick.* And with that, I started on my great adventure, my quest to find others like me.

For each town I passed through, a notch of enthusiasm died and more sores marred my ass. Exhaustion took hold but I pushed on, day after day, despite the almost constant nausea accompanied by crippling despair.

No survivors.

Anywhere.

No animals, no birds, no vegetation: just a dusty gray landscape everywhere I traveled, marred only by man-made structures. I tried to keep to the more populated routes, the ones with the Wal-Mart's and the large grocery chains, replenishing my supplies as I went. But there are large gaps in the Southwest. Larger than I anticipated and the heat, even in late fall, was oppressive. Dry heat, my ass; it was life sapping and sweat rendering and it nearly did me in. It took weeks to cross the Mohave Desert and even though I stocked up in Phoenix and then again in Blythe following Route 10 all the way west, my meager supplies ran out long before I hit Indio.

Hallucinations gripped me through that horrific leg, and those few random gas stations became my utopia, my saviors with mold-encrusted refrigerators housing the few bottles of water and soda and the paltry pickings of snack food that they had left on the shelves that kept me alive. But most of the time, they were just a nasty mirage that propelled me forward.

I thought Indio was a mirage, too, but when I rolled off the highway into the town, I started sobbing at the sight of the local mega-grocery store. I sat in the dark, drinking bottle after bottle of water until I was satiated.

And then I stood in the center of the aisle, scrubbing every inch of my skin with antibacterial soap, alternating between lathering and rinsing with the gallon jugs, sloughing off the layer of dust that had built on my skin.

When I emerged, draped in clean clothing, I felt new hope. I took my time on the ride to Santa Monica, searching for any sign of survivors.

And again, I found none.

But I did find a house on the shoreline that utilized solar power. Leave it to the environmentalists to build a self-sufficient house. I had electricity and running water and propane stove. And the best thing about the house? No dead bodies. The place was empty, clean and by some miracle, it was unlocked when I found it.

A mall and several shopping centers were within walking distance, and I had enough supplies at my disposal to last a couple of years without going farther than Santa Monica.

It took me a while to clean up the neighborhood and I glanced back at the funeral pyre. The work I did to finally settle in here: cleaning up decayed corpses—the meager remains of the dead—and bringing them to that small building, and then the lighter fluid and the sudden whoosh when the match hit the pile.

It's been burning all day, fire licking the sky, sending thick black plumes of smoke into the atmosphere and layering a stench of cooking flesh over the landscape.

I turned back toward the ocean, the memories receding again, lifting the weight off my chest, but not quite all the way. I still have one more adventure.

One that strikes terror in my heart.

Seven months of traveling, of scrapes, of bruises, of sores and bone-weary exhaustion, only helped to increase that fear.

Movement under my hand pulls my attention from the flat sea.

"I know, I know. I'll head back in a bit."

I run my fingers over my stretched, swollen belly, trying to soothe the baby kicking at my ribcage and I can't help but wonder, will the air kill her too?

The End

Abyss

"I HEARD THE GULF stream are full of striper," Rob said as we got off the bus.

I peeled my sweaty shirt from my back, the mid-October Indian summer bringing the last onset of sweltering heat with it before the winter closed in. "My dad already pulled his boat in for the season."

"Yeah, but yours is still on the river, right?"

My eyebrow rose. "You want to take that piece of shit out on the open ocean?"

Rob grinned and nodded, his eyes dancing with the devil within. "I snagged a case of beer and have it hidden in the shed. I say we go."

I bit my lip and glanced at our house and Rob's next door. The shed in question bordered our property and we passed by it on the trail to our dock.

"Come on, Matt. This is probably the last nice day till spring. You want to wait that long to go fishing again?"

No, I didn't. I wanted to be buzzing around on the water, whooping it up one last time before the winter set in. "Okay, fine, but I have to grab a couple things."

"A plastic bag for your cell?" he asked, rolling his eyes at me before he took off to change.

No matter how many times Rob razzed me about it, my dad drilled it into me ten times over and as I slipped on a pair of cut-offs and a t-shirt, his voice invaded my mind. *When you're out on the water, a dry phone and a book of dry matches could save your life.* With a sigh, I grabbed a Ziploc bag, slipping my phone inside along with my Swiss army knife and a book of matches from the kitchen cabinet before burying it in my pocket. I also grabbed a bagful of snacks for the afternoon to munch on between casts; otherwise, I might get too drunk to drive the boat home and that would not be a good thing. I'd be grounded until my seventeenth birthday, and I could forget about Friday's fall ball with Melissa.

I figured we had a good four hours before we'd have to head home and I scribbled a note saying I went fishing on the river and would be back for dinner.

I half-filled the fish cooler with ice and met Rob in my backyard. We stopped at the shed and dropped the beer cans into the ice.

"Grab your cooler in case we get lucky."

Rob grabbed the smaller cooler and smiled. "Good idea. We're gonna need this."

The kid was forever optimistic and this time the sparkle in his eye gave me a chuckle until we settled in the boat, and he pulled out the chart, pointing to the spot he wanted to go.

"You're kidding, right?" I said, pulling the boat away from the dock and heading toward the mouth of the river. The Gulf stream line he pointed to was well beyond Boone Island and a far cry from the mouth of the York River.

"It's supposed to be the best fishing spot around. My Uncle Charlie swears by it."

I took a good look at the map and brought my hesitant gaze to his. He raised his eyebrow and cocked his head in his familiar silent dare, waiting for me to agree. Rob had a way of getting what he wanted, when he wanted, wherever he wanted and sometimes it irritated me, especially when he was shoveling a load of shit, but the fact he invoked Uncle Charlie's name told me he spoke the God's honest truth and like always, I agreed to the crazy adventure.

My boat lurched on the choppy seas, but we made it to the mark on the chart and dropped anchor in the path of the Gulf stream leading out into the heart of the vast Atlantic.

"Here's to crazy fishing!" Rob opened his first beer and tapped it against mine.

From the first cast, the fish were biting. Crazy fishing was dead-on and by late afternoon, we had a cooler full to prove it. Between the beer, shooting the shit, and the heat of the afternoon sun, we lost track of time. It wasn't until the first crack of thunder reached my ears that I turned toward the open sea.

The magnificent sunset painted the clouds with broad brushstrokes of yellow, orange, magenta, and purple, bouncing colorful reflections that mixed with the whitecaps. In the distance, dark clouds lined the cold front overtaking the sky, rolling across the waves at a pace I knew I couldn't outrun. Lightning crashed to the ocean like a stealth strobe crawling closer and closer with every breath and I swallowed hard, the bitter taste of beer lining my throat.

I glanced at my best friend and then back at the closing storm, regretting the decision to take my used fifteen-foot speed boat out on the open ocean. It was made for river and lake cruising, not for outrunning a violent thunderstorm churning the seas. The crappy engine topped out at twenty-five miles an hour on a good day on the sedate York River, but I'd be lucky if I hit fifteen miles an hour on a rolling ocean.

"Shit." Surveying the seascape, I realized just how far we drifted. The rope to the anchor wasn't very long. Certainly not long enough to drag on the bottom and stop us from drifting. When I dropped anchor, Boon Island had been within a mile of where we sat and now I estimated the distance closer to three miles.

Maybe we'd be safe if I could reach the pile of rocks housing the lone lighthouse.

Maybe.

"I don't know, Rob."

"No way to ride it out?"

I laughed. "Not in this piece of shit. We'd be instantly fried." Looking toward land, I could barely make out the Maine shoreline through the thin layer of fog that cropped up. "We might be able to make Boon Island."

"That's nothing but a bloody rock."

"I know, but it's either that or the storm." I turned, pointing at the fast-approaching lightning. A bright bolt with spindly arms reached from the cloud to the surface of the water. The crack of thunder reached us and we exchanged a glance.

"Those options suck," Rob muttered and dropped his empty in the beer cooler, rooting around for another one.

"No shit." I grabbed the rope and started coiling it on the bottom of the boat, hauling up the useless anchor.

"Lot of good that thing did." Rob pointed and tipped the newly opened beer to his lips.

Shrugging, I dropped the anchor in the middle of the coil. "Yeah, well, at least we got a good run of fish." I leaned one knee on the driver's seat, flipped the ignition key and blew out a stream of air at the rough putter of the motor. I turned the bow toward Boon Island.

I glanced back at the storm and my mouth went dry. Fierce gusts of wind blew my hair into a frenzy, the edges whipping at the corner of my eyes, and I wished I had listened to my dad and gotten a damn haircut. Thunder boomed with a baritone quality that resonated through the frame of my boat and the electrical current in the air left a bitter metallic tang in my mouth, making me crave another beer.

I had just a little under a mile to go and I pushed the small engine, revving it to the point it screamed over the now constant rumble. Another quick glance over my shoulder told me what I already knew. The storm was faster than my boat, but I was determined to get us to the rocky island before we were fried by a bolt of lightning.

"You might want to put on that life vest." I pointed my chin toward the neatly stowed vest, sounding much calmer than I felt. My heart raced in my chest, pounding against the security of the life vest encasing my torso. My palms slid on the steering wheel despite the death grip I had on it, and I met Rob's questioning stare. I never went out on a boat unprepared, and Rob never ceased to rag me about any of it either, but now I saw a fragment of regret in his eyes just before he turned aft.

"Holy shit!" Rob's reaching hand shot faster toward the life vest, his exclamation driving my gaze to the back of the boat.

A wall of water headed toward us and my eyes nearly shot out of my head. "Oh fuck!" I yelled, feeling the stern dip a few feet into the curve of the wave.

Time halted, transitioning into the sluggish slow motion of a nightmare.

The back of the boat lifted into the body of the wave and both coolers tumbled over our heads. Empty cans of Budweiser scattered on the water in front of us before being sucked into the crest. The fish cooler dropped like a hundred-pound weight, barely missing Rob as he frantically tried to get the life vest unzipped and over his head.

He held onto his seat with one hand, screaming like a girl as the boat rose toward the crest. It struck me funny until the anchor whipped into the air and hit him in the forehead, leaving a bloody welt and knocking him out. He slumped and his body tumbled from the seat, suspended in the air for a brief instant.

My laugh turned into the same high-pitched shriek, and I let go of the seat reaching for him, the fabric of his t-shirt grazing my fingertips before gravity yanked him away. He fell over the bow into the water and my head snapped around, focusing on the rogue wave, my scream dulled by the roar of the thunder.

Gravity won the fight with my boat and it plummeted bow first before capsizing at the base of the wave, plunging me headfirst into the icy ocean. I had the presence of mind to close my mouth shut before it filled with cold sea water.

The pull of the wave tugged at me as it sailed over the capsized boat. The motor sputtered and died from the rush of saltwater entering the engine, yet I still had the steering column in my grasp. The white rope attached to the anchor dangled into the blackness below. Drifting down beside the rope was Rob's body; his eyes were closed and his lips slightly parted, leaving a thin trail of bubbles as seawater replaced the air in his lungs.

Fear and the buoyancy of the life vest kept me pinned to the seat. I let go of the steering wheel and terror swept through me. I tried twice to reach Rob, but my life vest stunted my progress and taking it off in the rolling waters wasn't an option my panicked brain would entertain. My lungs burned, and if I didn't get to the surface soon; I would give in to the need to take a breath.

I kicked hard, feeling a twinge in my calf as I pushed to get clear from the tumbling boat. I headed for the last slivers of light reflecting off the surface before the storm stole them from me.

Surfacing, I gasped, drawing a deep breath of air along with a stream of salt water. I sputtered, coughing, spraying water from my mouth and drew wheezing air into my lungs. I bobbed in the rough waves, trying to get my bearings. Thunder pressed against my eardrums, even though the heart of the storm was still close to a mile away.

The shakes gripped me, and a sob escaped. Frantic, I dove in the water, trying to kick my way down again, trying to reach Rob, to save him but I didn't have the strength and the life vest pulled me back above the surface.

Rob's death crashed into me harder than the wave that capsized my boat. Yeah, Rob could be a pain in the ass, but he and I had been best friends since the second grade. "Sorry, Rob," I sobbed, and the survival instinct took over, shaking the grief out of my head before it yanked me under and left me for dead.

I turned in a slow circle and spotted Boon Island a few hundred yards to my right and started a slow crawl stroke, trying to get to the rocks I could see jutting out of the ocean. Harsh sobs hitched in my chest, drowned out by the thunder overhead.

The cold water bit my skin, draining me of heat, draining me of energy, and I cursed, pushing myself forward against the battering of waves and the urge to give up. By the time I edged onto the rock, my fingers were frozen in stiff claws, too cold to bend or straighten without shooting pains and my toes were as good as gone. The stiffness crept along my limbs, throbbing all the way to the bone and I figured it would take years to feel warm again.

I crawled toward the safety of the granite lighthouse; the driving rain pelted my back as I made my way forward, stinging my semi-numb skin. The bitter wind raked over my body, making me colder than I thought possible. Being struck by lightning was a distant thought surrounded by the very real possibility I might freeze to death instead.

A small patch of soft sand sat next to the base of the lighthouse, and I inched onto it. A sliver of radiant warmth still locked in the grains caressed my cheek and I closed my eyes. I don't know how long I lay like that; I think I passed out because when I opened my eyes again, all was quiet except for my chattering teeth.

The storm had passed and the deep clear night sky filled my vision. I could see the Nubble Lighthouse and all the tiny lights along the southern coast of Maine.

My breath came in plumes of white fog on the cold air, I tried to push myself to my knees, but my muscles seized and I groaned, falling back onto the sand. I rolled onto my back, digging my hand into the damp pocket of my jeans.

"P-p-please God, p-p-please don't let the battery be dead."

I shimmied the bag out and my hands shook so bad it took me three tries to open the zipped bag. Finally, my numb fingers wrapped around the phone, and I pulled it out, flipping it open.

My chin trembled and my eyes blurred with tears. The display showed bright in the darkness and I had never been so thankful to see the two slim bars showing I had service. I dialed home, sobbing as my mother picked up the phone.

"JESUS, MATT, WHAT THE hell were you thinking?" my father ranted in the hospital room even before they took the warming blankets off. My teeth still chattered, and my burning eyes swung from my angry father to my crying mother.

"Stop it John. He's lucky to be alive." My mother sniffled in his direction.

The nurse said it was a miracle I survived, that I hadn't bled to death or died from hypothermia.

Under the blanket, my leg throbbed to life, the stitches coming alive, morphing to a burning pain lining my calf from ankle to knee where the engine blade sliced to the bone. The cold water stunted my circulation enough to slow the bleeding and kept me alive long enough to be rescued.

"I know he's lucky to be alive, but it was still irresponsible to take that boat out as far as he did alone."

"I wasn't alone." My voice rose above the pending argument and both their heads swiveled in my direction. Tears brimmed before I could find the rest of the words.

"Ah, Matty, what have you done?" my mother asked.

EVERY DAY, THE SOFT whisper of the water lapping the rocky shore reminds me that I killed my best friend. Whenever I close my eyes, I still see him falling into the abyss with bubbles drifting from his mouth.

In my nightmares, he's pulling me down with him.

I haven't been in the ocean since.

The End

Grayson House

SILENCE ENCOMPASSED THE CUL-DE-SAC where the Grayson house sat. No one in the yard moved, and the surrounding twenty acres of dense forest felt unusually still. Nothing we would have expected for our annual neighborhood Halloween bash, even for the pre-party setup, which in the past, rivaled the noise of the actual party.

We were late. The rest of the neighborhood committee had gathered a couple of hours ago to begin setting up, but I got held up at the station. Linda, my wife, wouldn't go down to the Graysons' without me, not since the episode with the Graysons' son last year. He freaked her out, decorating the lawn with wax creatures that scared the crap out of all our children. I almost arrested him for the temper tantrum he threw when we made him put the figures away. To this day, Linda swears one of the statues was our neighbor's dog that went missing a few weeks before Halloween, but I never found proof to support her theory.

Linda and I exchanged a glance as I stopped half a block away. The clumps of unmoving bodies coupled by a distinct odor hanging in the air sparked my intuition. The scent was familiar, and it took a moment to pinpoint what it was. Instinctively, I reached for my Glock, but instead of the reassuring metal, my fingertips grazed my shirt.

Shit.

My gun was at home in the safe.

Maybe it was just a dead animal. Either way, I didn't want my children to see the source of the odor. "Take the kids back home," I said.

Linda grabbed Alex and Alyssa's hands, turning them away.

Alex yanked his arm, trying to break Linda's grip. "But I want to go to the party!"

I forced a smile and crouched down to his level. "We're a little early. I'll come get you when everything's ready."

The crease between Linda's brows deepened as I stood back up. Her eyes pleaded with me to accompany them back home. I held her steady gaze, and after a moment, she gave me a slight nod.

"But Dad?" Alex and Alyssa both began.

"Go," I said, pointing back toward our house. "Or no trick or treating tonight!" They stopped struggling and I watched them trudge back the way we came. Before disappearing around the corner, Linda shot me a worried glance over her shoulder.

I turned my attention back to the Graysons' yard. Still, no one moved from their places on the front lawn. As I moved closer, the breeze shifted and the scent of spoiled meat became thicker.

I halted in the middle of the street, my mouth suddenly so dry my tongue stuck to the roof. It was definitely more than just a dead animal but the ancient oak tree at the end of the driveway blocked most of my view. I inched forward, pulling the phone out and dialing 911.

"This is Trooper Josh Reynolds with the state police...I, uh...," I trailed off as I approached the yard, my brain unable to wrap around what I was seeing. This year, it wasn't wax figures propped in front of the house. I took shallow breaths but the stink still permeated into my mouth, leaving a vile taste at the back of my throat.

"What is the nature of the emergency?" the operator asked reminding me that I had placed the call.

"Drop the phone." Paul Grayson, a six-foot-three, two-hundred-pound teenager stepped into view with a rifle pointing at my chest.

I moved the phone away from my ear, holding both arms away from my body. "Easy," I said, but I didn't close the cell phone.

The rifle report broke the silence. My phone flung away in pieces, the bullet tearing it out of my hand, leaving a bloody trail across my palm.

"Shit!" I yanked my hand to my chest. "What the hell are you doing?"

A small chuckle erupted from Paul as he centered the gun on my chest. He gave a nod toward the front yard. "Like the art *this* year?"

I turned toward the carefully propped bodies. The putrid stench radiated from his dead parents. They were positioned at a small card table with empty plates sitting in front of them. Each body held a fork in one bloated hand and a knife in the other. The serving plate caught my attention. Bile rose in my throat and I swallowed hard, forcing it back. The head of Paul's younger sister, Mabel, sat in the center of the serving plate with a dead black bird stuffed into her gaping mouth.

Beyond the Graysons were the members of the setup committee and this time I wasn't able to stop the vomit from escaping. I turned and spewed on the road. Paul skewered four entire families into the ground, posing them into warped adaptations of Hansel and Gretel, Billy Goats Gruff, Rumpelstiltskin, and Little Red Riding Hood and my family would have been added to the grand spectacle had I not been running late.

When I finished emptying the contents of my stomach onto the asphalt, I spit and wiped my mouth on my sleeve, straightening up. "You've been busy." My voice shook, despite my attempt to control it.

"And you ruined my fun." Paul stepped further into the open, the rifle still trained on the center of my chest. "You were supposed to bring your family with you." He moved the rifle slightly to his right and pulled the trigger.

The bullet tore through my left shoulder, knocking me to the ground.

Harsh sounds came from my chest as I caught my breath and scrambled to my feet, holding my ruined shoulder. I attempted a round house kick as he crossed the distance, but he sidestepped and jammed the rifle barrel into my thigh, pulling the trigger again. The round was muffled, but my scream wasn't. I collapsed on the ground.

Paul grabbed the back of my shirt, dragging me down his driveway toward the garage as he whistled a tune from *Snow White*.

Slaughterhouse was the first thing that popped to mind as he dragged me inside. Blood dripped from the ceiling, streaking the walls. The floor was covered in a slick layer that he navigated easily in his work boots. Multiple chairs were arranged around the biggest pool of blood and he yanked me through it, hauling me into the farthest one.

"You made me take down the fairy tales last year," he muttered, binding my arms behind my back and ignoring my shriek of protest.

When he moved in front of me, I kicked him in the shin. Paul rammed his fist into my bloody thigh and I howled in pain and frustration. He shoved a bloody rag between my lips, muffling my angry outburst. I gagged as the coppery taste filled my mouth.

"No one's telling me to take them down this year." He tied my good leg to the chair and stepped away, lifting his phone to his ear. "Mrs. Reynolds, hey, it's Paul Grayson. Your husband asked me to give you a yell to ask if you wouldn't mind bringing a salad bowl down." Paul cupped his hand over the phone's microphone, cutting off the muffled noises I was making behind the rag. "He's outside helping my parents tap the keg. Okay. I'll tell him. See you in a few." He folded the phone, smiling at me.

I wanted to smash his face in as I thrashed in the chair.

His smile faded and he regarded me with a quizzical expression, tapping his lips. "I may have to rethink your family's fairy tale." He plucked the rag from my mouth.

A stream of steady swears spilled from my mouth between the dry heaves. I was able to spit most of the blood from my mouth as he reloaded his rifle.

"Time to get your family." Paul picked up the rifle and trotted out of the garage. He pushed a button on the remote and the garage door slid down behind him, drowning out the last of my warning cry.

The blood-ridden soundproofed walls absorbed my roar. I struggled, gritting my teeth against the pain in my shoulder and rolling my wrists in a circle, testing the binds. They were plastic and my hope of escape vanished. Sweat slid into my eye, making it clamp shut against the sting.

Gasoline fumes and coagulating blood filled the garage. I glanced around until my eyes landed on the chainsaw. Bits of flesh, bone, and hair clung to the blood-soaked blade. My stomach rolled and I quickly looked away.

Taking a deep breath, I assessed my condition, shifting my weight as the shattered bones of my left thigh ground together. My stomach lurched and I had to take a deep pull of foul air to keep it in check.

I studied the spackled egg crate pattern in the ceiling before looking back at my leg.

At least blood wasn't gushing from the wound.

Yet.

The sharp laugh from my chest caught me by surprise, further degrading my already shot nerves.

I jumped at the first muffled gunshot; three more rang successively. Then silence filled the garage and I stared at the door. Tears burned my eyes, blurring my vision before rolling down my cheeks and sliding into the corners of my tightly clamped lips. I hung my head and prayed for a miracle. I prayed my family wouldn't suffer. I negotiated with God until the garage door rattled on the frame.

My eyes shot open, and I waited. Minutes passed before the garage door opener whirled into action. Inch by inch it raised, revealing the blood-soaked driveway, but Paul was nowhere in sight.

My muscles trembled and I kept my eyes on the gaping opening, waiting for Paul to drag my family down the same path he dragged me. A figure swung into view, aiming a gun between my eyes. It took my embattled brain a second to comprehend who was in the opening.

"Josh!" Her shaky breath reached my ears as she lowered my gun.

A slight sound escaped from my throat. I couldn't form words as renewed tears blurred my vision.

Linda ran to me, sliding through the muck on the floor. She threw her arms around my neck as sobs ripped from her chest. "You're alive!"

I nodded, still staring at the door. "Is he?" The words came out in a raspy whisper.

"No," she said in my ear. "I killed him."

Sirens howled in the distance.

"How?" I asked as she pulled away.

Placing my gun in my lap, she knelt to untie my leg. Her voice trembled when she spoke. "All I could think about were Paul's threats last year. I asked

Jenny to watch the kids until the party started." She covered her mouth with the back of her hand as her eyes surveyed the garage before falling back on me. "I grabbed your gun and headed back this way. I figured if I was wrong, we would have a good laugh." She offered me a slight smile before her eyes welled up again. "I saw him shoot you and I hid in the woods." A sob interrupted her, and she couldn't continue.

"Shhhh," I said, thankful she had the combination to the safe and knew how to handle a gun.

Linda shook her head, her jaw clenching and forcing the sobs to stop. "I shot him when he walked past the oak tree. I thought you were dead, Josh. I thought he killed you, and I just kept shooting." Another sob escaped her lips as they pressed against mine.

I silently thanked God for the miracle.

The sirens came to rest outside the Grayson homestead. Red and blue lights filled the twilight creating shadows on the garage walls as officers and emergency technicians converged on us.

The End

Iron Rain

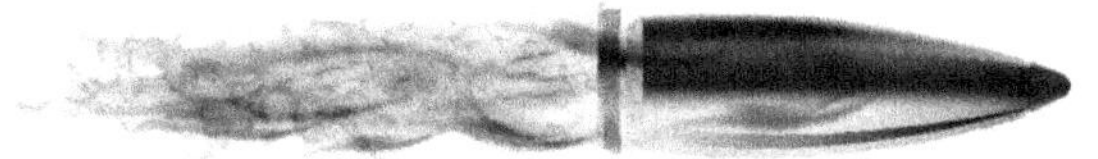

MY STOMACH RUMBLED AS I turned the page. A half hour left before lunch. I almost groaned out loud when the hand clicked backwards on the library clock before settling in place just before the 11:17 spot. Do all the clocks at school do that?

The grass outside the cafeteria was calling, a much more suitable reading environment, vaguely like the scenery in *Wuthering Heights*. Okay, the Rockies are a tad more jagged than the rolling moors of Scotland, but hey, a girl can dream. Besides, Johnny would be out there, and I loved it when he read to me. His smooth deep voice was hypnotizing under the late April thaw, especially when he pulled off a plausible Scottish brogue imitation. I mean, seriously, how sweet can it get?

My friends were studying at the table next to me; every now and then a whisper interrupted the silence of the library, pulling me out of the story. I gave them a crooked smile and got a shrugging nod in return. If I hadn't detoured to the bathroom, I'd be sitting with them. Oh well—you snooze, you lose.

A rumble like thunder echoed through the hallway outside of the library, sending vibrations through the floor and up my flip-flop clad feet.

Out of place for a high school, but it was getting close to graduation. Probably just a firecracker in some poor freshman's locker, like last year. God, what a mess. It blew the locker open, spewing flaming notes across the hallway. Who knew a pencil could become a flying projectile, piercing that poor unsuspecting sophomore's ass? Both Principal Ramsey and the fire chief blew a gasket, hauling us all into the auditorium and ranting about the dangers of M80s, especially in an enclosed space like a locker.

The second report was closer, reminding me of my father's hunting rifle. A metallic tinge tainted my saliva like I'd taken a giant bite of tinfoil and I shivered.

Ms. Nielson pushed through the doors, her face flushed and her eyes like those of someone caught in the crosshairs of a grizzly with nowhere to go. Her chest wheezed as the air barreled in and out of her lungs. "Get down!"

We all blinked, exchanging a quick glance.

"Everyone get down now!"

The panic in Ms. Nielson's voice was enough to jumpstart my frozen muscles. I slid under the table with my friends. The five of us—Lisa, Lauren, Jeanna, and a younger girl named Kelly— were huddled together, none of us understanding what the hell was going on.

"I bet some idiot put M80s in the lockers again," Lauren whispered. "Everything's going to be just fine." She waved her hand like swatting a fly, but her blasé attitude quickly changed.

They stepped into the library, two pair of denim cargo pants alongside shiny rifle shafts. The rake of a zipper and shuffling nylon followed by plink. *What the hell were they doing?* My question was answered moments later when a small explosion rocked the library, sending broken books in different directions.

"Get up!" Their voices blended into one boom, the order filling the air as thick as the smoke from the burning books.

My muscles seized in place, planting me to the spot under the table. Lauren's arm slung over my shoulder, tightly pulling me next to her. Her other arm pulled Lisa close, Jeanna and Kelly across from us. Our bodies shuddered uncontrollably. Our eyes darted from one to the next, none of us daring to speak, daring to move, daring to breath.

"Get out from under the tables, now!" The report of the rifle broke the strained silence and I saw the first student fall. I think his name was Kyle, his Walkman headphones askew on his head with music blaring from the speakers as he hit the floor. Blood pooled, seeping into the carpet, maroon spreading inch by inch over the beige fibers.

I don't want to die! The thought continuously looped through my mind, competing with my prayers for God to make us disappear, become one with the floor or a solid piece of impenetrable furniture. Anything to go unnoticed, to have them pass us by.

They opened fire as they walked from table to table, getting closer. A bullet whizzed by my face, close enough that I could smell the gunpowder still clinging to the metal cylinder. Lauren gasped, tightening her grip on me for a moment before she slumped in my grasp. Kelly backed away, sliding out from under the table and making a run for it.

Two steps. That's all she got before they gunned her down.

This wasn't happening. I wasn't holding my best friend's dead body and staring at Kelly's lifeless form on crimson carpet. I wasn't surrounded by the stench of burning books, gun smoke, urine, and blood. It must be a nightmare. It had to be.

"Enough!" My voice boomed over the wails of the injured and before I knew it, I had stood, turning in the direction of the spray of bullets. One grazed my temple and hot liquid slid down the side of my face, stinging my eye and shrouding half my vision red. A second pierced my abdomen, searing my insides, doubling me over. My hand grasped the corner of the table, the fine grain wood smooth and reassuring under my fingertips, giving me the strength to remain standing. "Enough!" Hissing, I took a shaky step to intercept them.

The bullets stopped, leaving a ringing silence above the moans.

Instant recognition. I had seen him skulking around often enough, but I never bothered to find out his name. His cold gray eyes regarded me, and he raised the rifle a fraction, swinging the barrel in my direction.

"Stop." I barely managed a whisper, but it was enough for the skulker to pause and study me.

"Do you believe in God?" He cocked his head, waiting for my answer.

Again, I faltered, scanning the carnage. When my eyes returned to him, I had no answer. I thought I believed in God, but this, this defied my faith. "Why?" I beckoned with my hand, indicating their destruction.

"Because it's fun."

He leveled the gun at me and smiled the kind of smile I envisioned on the walking dead. The kind of smile Lucifer embraced, and I shivered.

"Do you believe in God?"

I was still breathing, still standing. Still alive. The grace of God touched me, creating a steady thumping beat in my throat, blocking my voice. I tilted my head in a slow nod. Maybe I could buy the rest of the kids some time, enough to save their lives. I straightened, studying him as blatantly as he was studying me. "Do you?"

He hesitated, the barrel dropping slightly away, our eyes locked.

"Shut up." Another boy stepped from behind one of the book aisles to my right, casting a dark shadow over me.

I didn't turn toward the voice; I needed to maintain eye contact with the skulker. My life depended on it. When the rifle cocked, a sensation of blood rushing toward my center, retreating away from my extremities, left my hands and feet cold even as my heart thudded against the walls of my chest, struggling to push warmth from where it had just fled. I flinched when the shot echoed through the room.

Miraculously, the bullet missed.

The shadow didn't take another shot.

Skulker's eyes widened. The barrel of the rifle lowered another fraction as his gaze darted from me to the right where the rifle shot had come from.

Something clattered to the ground, triggering another round; this time, I felt the burn in my calf, but it was distant, and my bones stood fast, holding me in place.

A thud shook the floor, and I followed his gaze. The other boy lay face down in a pool of his own blood next to the discarded rifle. My ears still rang with a high-pitched whistle, leaving my thoughts in a jumbled mess but I knew I was lucky. Whether the shot ricocheted or skulker killed him, the shadow gunman was dead, and I was still standing.

I glanced back at the skulker in front of me. Saucer eyes with a matching mouth returned my stare. "Do you?" I asked again, my voice shaking as shock threatened. White noise filled my ears, drowning out the cries of the living. My skin tingled where the slow trickle of blood and piss slid, creating a puddle on the floor around my feet, bright red diluted in the clear watery liquid.

"Do I what?" He regained his composure, raising the rifle again.

A whisper, like a breath of wind, brought my answer to him. "Believe." The room spun and my knees buckled. As I sank to the ground, a black veil slipped over my eyes, the harsh rasp of my breath following me down into the abyss.

I WOKE TO WHITE light, blinking under the brightness. The haze cleared and I scanned my surroundings. An IV bag hung above my head, gaining my full attention. The scraping of a chair tore my gaze away from the hypnotizing drip. My mother slid into view, her thin hand wavering like a butterfly as it rose to her lips, tears slipping over the graceful curve of her fingers.

The End

Nightmares

SWEAT SEEPS DOWN THE small of my back as I strain to see through the mist. My eyes dart back and forth but I can't locate the source of the terrible sound echoing against the brick walls of the alley, reminding me of claws dragging against metal. Gritting my teeth, I shiver uncontrollably. My clothes are soaked, slick against my clammy skin.

Terror washes over me as his hot breath touches me from behind.

I scream...

...and am in the lobby of an old theater.

There's a coffin in the middle of the room, and I drift to the other side to see what's inside. The remains of my husband's face floats in a bath of blood. My hand flies to cover the cry of horror that is escaping my mouth. I back away from the sickening smell of death. Terror, grief, and a sense of justice fight for domination over my emotions as I stare at the gruesome sight. A scraping noise startles me out of my trance. Alarmed, I flee through the doors and into the theater.

The foul aroma of a thousand spilt sodas assaults my nostrils, the rancid decaying carpet causing me to crinkle my nose. Each step I take toward the stage makes me quiver, but I must reach the exit. A rusty creak shatters the silence of the darkened theater as a sliver of light passes by me. I spin around.

A dark form lurks in the doorway, backlit by the brightness of the lobby. He utters my name, sending his hideous breath in my direction, a reminder of rotting eggs.

My lungs constrict. *Oh God, he found me.*

My heart pounds wildly and I reach a door that leads beneath the stage. I slam it and flip the lock. The bellow of rage fills the room as he repeatedly strikes the door. I am entombed in darkness, and each strike sends me further into the blackness.

Then silence. I hold my breath—waiting, listening. The only sound I hear is the frantic beat of my heart.

A crack of light invades the darkness. Another door. I bolt, throwing my weight against it, but I'm not strong enough. The door swings open.

I stagger into the far corner, my breath coming in ragged rasps.

A low chuckle emanates from him as he prowls closer. I can see the twisted metal form that he carries and I gasp. He reaches for me, and I let out a shrill cry...

...I sit upright in bed, my hand covering the scream. It's too late; the light flips on in the hallway.

"Are you alright?" My husband steps into the room.

I nod, swallowing and offering a pitiful smile. "Nightmare."

He smiles. "You've been reading too many horror stories."

"It was a bad one."

"I could tell. The neighbors must think I'm killing you." He grins. "Either that or you're having one hell of an orgasm."

I blush as the dream dissipates.

He slowly approaches the bed, un-tucking his shirt.

I giggle like a school girl, anticipating his touch.

His hands drift over my feet and clamp down on my ankles, violently yanking me to the foot of the bed. "You didn't tell me you were pregnant."

My smile freezes as I look in his eyes. Rage gazes back at me.

"The doctor called. He asked what pharmacy he should have your prescription sent to. I got a hell of a surprise when I picked it up for you. Prenatal vitamins?" He grabs the front of my shirt, yanking me to his face. "Who have you been sleeping with?"

"Nobody!" I scream, momentarily infuriated by his accusation.

"It isn't mine." His voice is barely a whisper.

The calmness of his voice brings the terror back. "Of course, it is."

"You've been a bad girl." He punches me in the stomach, knocking me to the floor. "You need to be taught a lesson." He unbuckles his belt.

I have never seen him like this; he means to kill me. *I'm pregnant!* The scream is only in my head. I watch, horrified, as he yanks the belt out of the loops and swings it at me. The sting that flares in my cheek catches me off guard. My hand flutters to the side of my face.

"Please don't." I try to scramble backwards. The belt hits my arm this time, causing me to yelp in pain. I finally find my feet as he cocks his arm back for a third whipping.

"No one makes a fool out of me! No one!" He advances, swinging the belt as hard as he can.

It connects with my stomach, doubling me over. I drop to the floor. Before I can catch my breath, he kicks me. The moan that escapes my lips fills the room.

"I'm sterile, you bitch!" He reaches down grabbing a handful of my hair, yanking me to my feet.

Blood flows from my mouth. "I didn't sleep with anyone else." The tears fill my eyes, blinding me before they spill over.

He drops the belt and jerks my head back. "Don't lie to me." He growls in my face.

"I haven't been screwing around!" I shake in his grasp.

"Liar." He smacks me across my face and drags me to the bed, ripping at my clothes.

I almost get away, but he slams his fist into the bridge of my nose. Stars fill my eyes, and the soft fabric of the bed engulfs me as I fall, dazed. My underwear is torn from my body and then the bed springs creak. My husband mutters under his breath as he crosses to the closet.

I blink, desperately trying to get my vision to clear. Wincing, I touch my face and when I pull my hand back, there is blood on my fingertips. *He broke my nose.*

My husband rips the paper framing the hanger, tossing it to the ground and gaining my attention. He rapidly untwists the twine of the hanger, creating a crude instrument meant for destruction.

In my dazed state, understanding of his intention eludes me until he turns and smiles in my direction.

"You're not gonna have another man's child." He is on me before I can react.

I scream as he pries my legs apart, kneeling on my thighs and pinning me to the bed.

I swing to hit him, but he is faster, catching my wrist and sharply twisting it. The pain comes with the sick snap of the bone.

He drops the hanger and slaps me twice, letting go of my broken limb.

I yank my arm back to my chest, cradling it as the tears streak my face. I lunge for the discarded hanger, feeling the metal in my grip as I whip it across his face. He falls back, freeing my legs, and I kick, connecting with his stomach and knocking him off the bed.

I flee but everything is sluggish again. I reach the top of the stairs, losing my balance and pin wheeling, landing...

... in an alley. I shake my head to clear it. My arm is in a cast, and fog engulfs me.

A dead end. Nowhere to go. I back against the brick wall, feeling the rough surface with my good hand, and watch the thick fog swirl in front of me.

Footsteps approach. Its foul, rotting breath is accompanied by a low visceral growl that shatters through the mist.

I am frantic.

The beast has come for me, and I realize with horror that it is carrying a twisted coat hanger.

I scream...

...and sit up in bed.

My husband flips on the light on the nightstand, looking at me with sleepy surprise. "You okay?" He rubs my back with eyes full of concern.

I look at the familiar surroundings and burst into tears.

He sits up and pulls me into his arms.

I flinch, glancing at the cast on my arm. The understanding that I am no longer pregnant slams into my consciousness and the sobs begin to rip from my chest.

"It wasn't your fault," he reminds me. "You fell down the stairs."

He kisses my temple, holding me until I stop crying.

"Did I kick you again?"

He laughs a little as darkness flares in his eyes. "I don't know. I didn't wake up until you screamed. Try to get some sleep." He flips the light off.

I stare in the dark, listening to his breathing slow to even rhythms as sleep finds him.

I don't remember what happened.

Was it the fall?

Was it?

Eventually, I drift into a restless sleep.

The End

Pollywogs and Water Moccasins

MY FIRST GLIMPSE OF our new house was a field of grass as tall as the Kansas wheat fields we passed a few days ago on our cross-country journey. I ran into the thick of the long, silky stalks and sat down, swallowed completely from view by the green reeds.

"Jamie," Mom called.

I stood up, barely visible in the field. "Yeah?"

"You and your brother should go see the stream in back," she called, carrying Jackie, my little sister, toward the new house.

A stream? The thought excited me, and I turned in Mark's direction. His eyes caught mine and then he was off like a shot through the tall weeds. I bolted after him, my heart pumping with the thrill of a new landscape. I skidded to a halt as I rounded the side of the two-story colonial and beheld our mammoth backyard. It was almost as big as the field across from the postage stamp of a yard we had out West. Tall reeds of grass stretched to the wood line, waving a welcome. The trickling of the brook reached my ears and I followed the sound, finding my brother kneeling at the side of a small pond just inside the canopy of the woods.

Pollywogs played in the stagnant water—big ones, little ones, fat ones, and skinny ones in all stages of metamorphosis.

I dropped to my knees next to Mark and reached in, carefully palming one of the larger blobs and balancing the slick carcass as I pulled it from the water, inspecting all sides of the odd, squirming amphibian before trading it a moment later with a larger, squishy one that had both a tail and the beginnings of little frog legs. Awe encompassed me, and I glanced at my brother, who wore the same expression of intrigue thrumming through my bones. The dry hills of northern California didn't harbor anything like these creatures.

A rustle in the grass caught our attention and I scooted a fraction closer to Mark. The tall reeds parted, and Jackie toddled through the grass, executing a fast getaway from the preoccupied eye of our parents. Mark and I exchanged another glance.

He rolled his eyes, which made me laugh.

Jackie crawled to the edge of the pond next to us. Reaching in, she grabbed a handful of the mini-pollywogs, squeezing her hand into a tight little fist. The runny remains dripped from both sides of her hand, black and slimy.

My stomach did a slow roll and I recoiled away in revulsion.

"Uh-o." She opened her hand. She reached in the water for more.

It was as if we were timed jack-in-the-boxes; both my brother and I popped to our feet and yelled, "MOM!" in unison.

My mother made her way through the long grass. Her face scrunched in disgust as Jackie turned, proudly displaying the contents of her hands. Mom squatted and took Jackie's wrists, dunking her hands into the water to wash them off.

Jackie clearly thought it was a game and squealed with delight, catching more doomed pollywogs in her chubby hands.

"For crying out loud," my mother muttered under her breath, reaching her arm around Jackie's waist. Hoisting her onto her hip, she headed toward the house with Jackie's piercing scream shattering the happy sounds of the new neighborhood.

"Want to go across the street and see if we can play?" Mark pointed to the neighbor's house and the heated game of whiffle ball already underway.

I shook my head, still staring at the pollywogs. Baseball wasn't my thing.

"Mind if I go?"

"No." I watched him trot away.

The lawn mower droned in the front yard as my father began the difficult task of chopping down the field of grass surrounding our new house. I could still hear Jackie crying inside the house, where I'm sure my mother sequestered her into the playpen before continuing to unpack.

Which left me alone by the pond, and the distant call of the stream pulled me in that direction. I set out on an adventure, first slipping my shoes off, placing them on a dry rock, away from the destructive jaws of the lawn mower, and sloshed through the marsh.

The stale pond smell drifted around me as I navigated the woods toward the sound of running water. I broke through the underbrush, finding the bank of a small stream I crossed in two leaping steps. On the opposite bank, I scanned both twisting sides of the meandering stream before stepping in the middle of the brook. My toes tingled from the cold water; I carefully avoided the slippery algae covered rocks, sticking to the sandy bottom center. The current caressed my ankles, barely deep enough to reach my calves, and I headed upstream until I found a low bank clear of underbrush and stepped out of the cool water.

I meandered upstream for a couple hundred yards, stopping every so often to squat down and inspect a minnow or pick up a loose rock to see if there was anything underneath. Each hidden creature, from crawfish to minnows, was carefully examined and replaced where I found them before I continued the journey.

Around a bend, I spied the stream flowing through a drain pipe, large enough for me to walk through if I leaned over. A pungent algae and decay smell drifted from the pipe and I crinkled my nose. Ducking to peer through the murky darkness inside, I saw light bleeding from the opposite end, but even though there was an obvious end to the pipe, I didn't want to see the source of that awful smell. Instead, I climbed the embankment and crossed the dirt road bordering our property. I glanced at my dad's mower chopping a sea of grass near the road before I climbed down the opposite bank. It was steeper than I thought and I skidded down into the muck.

My feet sank into the cool mud, squishing between my toes. A sucking noise filled the air as I pulled my foot from the sludge. Giggling, I stepped into the cool stream, but after a few paces, I decided I liked the feel of the mud squishing through my toes better so I trudged through the muddy muck bordering the water.

The waterway widened as I made my way upstream.

A rock plinked off the rocks at the far edge of the stream and I jumped, my heart lurching in my chest and my eyes widening at the sudden interruption to my quiet journey. Inching farther upstream, I peered around the bend. A group of five boys around my age were pelting rocks into the stream.

"Did you get it?" one yelled.

"No, there it goes!" A boy pointed and another round of rocks hurled into the water.

I approached unnoticed and glanced in the direction of the rock assault. A thick black snake dodged the projectiles. With a quick inspection and an internal snake catalog flipping through my thoughts, I concluded that this particular snake wasn't poisonous.

The injustice of their actions set me into motion and I leapt into the middle of the water, blocking the path of their pitches. "What are you doing?" I snapped.

"There's a snake in the water," the skinniest boy yelled, pointing frantically behind me.

"Get out of the way!" another one yelled.

"You're killing it!" I hollered at them.

"Get out of the way or we'll throw these at you." The biggest boy in the group picked up a rock but the rest of the boys hesitated, giving the large kid a glance like he was shy some cards.

"No." I shook my head, staring him down even though he was easily twice my size.

He pitched his rock in my direction and it nicked my shin, splashing in the water next to me but I refused to move.

Ignoring the rock assault as if it never happened, Skinny pointed again. "Are you stupid? There is a snake behind you!"

"I know." I turned, plucking the thing from the water before another rock could be pelted in its direction. The snake wrapped its tail around my forearm and I nestled it to my chest, stroking its head with my index finger. I turned back to the group of boys.

Collectively, they stepped back with their jaws slack. Every set of eyes bulged, staring at the snake on my arm and then at my defiant face. Even the boy who threw the rock was dumbfounded. The tension in his arms disappeared and they dropped to his side. The rock he picked up fell harmless out of his grasp.

"It won't bite." I put my hand in front of the snake's face and the small tongue shot out, feeling the texture of my palm, tickling me. "See?"

"That's a w-w-water m-m-moccasin," Skinny stuttered and stepped farther away.

"They're poisonous," the rock thrower whispered. His eyes looked like they were about to shoot out of their sockets at any moment.

"This isn't poisonous," I informed the group and stepped closer. "This here's a garter snake. When we were in California, my brother used to bring home snakes this big." I spread my arms as wide as they could go. In truth, some of the snakes he brought home were twice the size of my little arm span. I pulled the snake back to my chest and gently rubbed the top of its head.

For each step I took toward the group of boys, they stepped away. "What? Yer afraid of a little snake?" I asked.

Each and every one of them nodded and I laughed.

"Aren't you?"

I cocked my head and raised my eyebrows, glancing from the snake snug around my arm to the boy who had asked the question. *Maybe the kid was daft; you never know these days.* Still, I couldn't stop the sarcastic "Ya think?" that slipped from my lips. I held my arm up a little and gave them a fake shiver followed by a chuckle and then resumed petting the snake.

"But you're a girl," Daft boy pointed out. He sneezed and wiped the snot that shot from his nose on his sleeve.

"No duh." I rolled my eyes and smiled. After a few moments of dull stares, I shrugged and glanced at the snake. "So what if I'm a girl."

"I don't know any girls around here who *aren't* afraid of snakes," Rock-chucker ventured.

I smiled. "Well, ya do now."

I turned and climbed up the opposite bank of the stream and could hear the hushed whispers as the boys grouped together, discussing the new girl in the neighborhood. The reverent tones touched my ears and I smiled, hiking the short walk home with the snake nestled against my chest.

"Stupid boys," I said, setting the snake down at the edge of the woods near the pond in our backyard, watching as it slid into the marsh, blending with the black roots.

After it disappeared from sight, I strolled into our new home, wondering where my next adventure would take me.

The End

Flight Plan

I APPROACHED THE IDLING helicopter, escorted through the safe zone by the pilot like I had been all the other times I've used the corporate ride. The wind whipped across the East River, blowing my hair, strands slapping at the corners of my eyes from the upstream created by the rotors.

The pilot opened the door for me and both of us stopped, jaws askew, staring at the scene inside the cabin.

"Harry!" The woman gasped, pushing the shoulders of the man buried under her silky skirt.

Harry pulled away from between her legs, wiping his mouth on his sleeve as he looked between the pilot and me. A small smirk appeared on his lips as he shuffled into the seat opposite the woman. She, on the other hand, was glowing like a stoplight and frantically trying to right her rumpled clothing.

I froze on the tarmac. There were no more flights home this evening, but the prospect of stepping into the cabin now was even less desirable than being stuck in New York.

The pilot cleared his throat and glanced in my direction. "Ma'am?" He offered his hand to help me into the craft.

Unfortunately, I had to get home to pick up my kids, so I took the pilot's hand and slid into the window seat on the same side of the helicopter as the woman but as far away from the two of them that I could possibly muster in the small space. The pilot gave me a quick nod and closed the door, leaving the three of us in the silent cabin.

The woman wouldn't meet my gaze. She was still crimson and flustered, but Harry—he was altogether another story. His head tilted as he studied me.

"Harry Stone," he said, extending his hand in my direction as the helicopter ascended, heading north. The corners of his mouth twitched into a hint of a smile.

I raised my eyebrows, meeting his direct blue eyes with a bark of a laugh. I wasn't playing this game. I didn't care if he was the flipping CEO; there was no way I was going to shake his hand, not when I knew where it had just been.

Harry slowly withdrew his hand, glancing at the woman across from him for a second before swiveling his gaze back in my direction. "What brings you to New York?"

"Business," I replied. "You?" I did my damnedest to keep the smirk from my lips as I posed the question to him.

The smug smile returned, along with a quick glance at the woman. He waived in her direction. "My associate and I were here on business as well."

"Ah," I offered, locking gazes with him before focusing on the passing skyscrapers.

He leaned farther back in the seat, shifting uncomfortably and capturing my attention by clearing his throat. Less cocky and self-righteous now, he met my blatant stare. The wheels turned behind his intelligent eyes and he pursed his lips, scanning me again, sizing me up. Harry crossed his arms and tilted his head, letting the silence settle in the cabin.

I wasn't going to break his stare. Uh-uh, no way, but when the pilot announced landing instructions, I broke his gaze, staring out the window as we touched down at the airport.

The woman gathered her things, uttering a muttered apology as she stepped off the helicopter.

The door closed behind her, leaving me alone with Harry Stone for the remainder of the flight. I was unprepared and the prospect of forty-five minutes alone with the man left my mouth dry. I reached for a Lifesaver stored in the door, popping one in my mouth as the rotor whine turned into the thunderous roar of take-off.

I uttered a small laugh, shaking my head as the airport shrunk in the window and we headed north once again. "You really are a piece of work."

Harry was silent and I glanced in his direction. He was still studying me, and I shifted under the blatant stare.

"That poor girl didn't even know who I was," I shot at him.

This time his smile was genuine, forming dimples in his cheeks, and he shook his head. "No, I don't believe she did."

I knew why all the women in the office had the hots for the man, and I felt the same rush of heat encompass me, but I ignored it, glaring at him. "You son of a bitch, you planned this!"

He shrugged and stretched his legs out onto the seat across from him, raising a single eyebrow, slightly tilting his head. It was an unspoken invitation, one I had seen umpteen times before.

I laughed. "You've got to be kidding me?" I returned my attention to the sunset on the horizon, shifting my gaze between the window and my watch before turning back to him.

Harry leaned forward, clasping his hands in front of him and resting his elbows on his knees. His eyes twinkled as they scanned me. "Come on," he prodded, and ran his fingers up my bare leg.

I slapped his hand away. The flash of anger in his eyes matched mine.

"I swear..." He pressed his lips together and glanced at my hands. The muscles in his jaw tightened.

I followed his gaze to my bare fingers; the white strip where my wedding rings once sat a blatant reminder of my newly single status. My eyes dropped to his hand and the gold band still gracing his ring finger. I slowly sat back in the seat and crossed my legs.

Harry inhaled, leaning back in his seat as well, and turned his attention out the window at the green hills peppered with houses. He licked his lips, glancing back in my direction.

"You thought *this* would change my mind?" I waved at the empty seat next to me.

"I wanted you to know what it felt like," he snapped.

"Harry, you've been screwing around on me since the day we met."

Harry opened his mouth to speak and clamped it shut. He studied his hands, twirling his wedding band. He inhaled and slowly nodded, owning up to what we both knew before raising his eyes to mine. "What do you want?"

"I want you to stop fucking around and give me a divorce."

The End

Savior

SAM SAT IN THE interrogation room, handcuffed to the desk with his head bowed. He caught his reflection in the two-way mirror, staring at the familiar blue-green irises surrounded by aging crow's feet and his once dark hair now peppered with streaks of white. His shoulders slumped and he dropped his warbled gaze. Tears dripped off his eyelashes onto the fabric of his jeans.

The mangled remains of his wife and children played across his field of vision every time he closed his eyes. A hollow pain in the center of his chest grew with every tear, along with the paralyzing grief keeping him immobile and silent.

The door swung open, and he stiffened, blinking the remaining tears from his eyes and regaining composure. He raised his gaze to the woman, the officer, sitting across from him.

"Tell me what happened, from the top," Detective Howard requested.

He took a deep breath, shaking his head slowly. "I didn't kill my family." His vision misted with tears, and he blinked them back, pushing the emotions down into the well of his soul.

She leaned forward on the table. "Then who the hell did?"

He ground his teeth together before he spoke. "I don't know."

She took a deep breath and the tense muscles in her jaw line relaxed. "Tell me what you do for a living."

He knew the drill and recognized her change of tactics, but her frustration still reflected in her eyes. "I'm a hunter."

"What exactly do you hunt?" she asked. The tape recorder spun, picking up every word of the interrogation.

"You wouldn't believe me if I told you." Bitterness crept into his skin and he offered a smile relaying the sentiment. The flash of aggravation in her eyes manifested and his smile disappeared. He narrowed his eyes, scanning her, looking for a sign, anything, but she was just a hick town cop. He exhaled the air locked in his chest, his muscles relaxing a fraction, even though his intuition prickled with danger.

SHE STARED AT HIM, scanning his sculpted frame and his handsome face. This man had aged well, and he stirred something deep inside her—a completely inappropriate protective instinct considering the circumstances. She had caught him with his family's blood on his hands and his prints on the knife used to carve them up. Yet she still had her doubts. "Try me." She leaned forward on the interrogation desk.

Sam glanced at the mirrored wall. "He knows." He nodded toward the glass. "Why don't you ask him?" He returned his gaze to her.

Detective Howard turned toward the mirror. "No one's in there," she said. At least there hadn't been anyone there when she entered the room.

The laugh that escaped from Sam's chest was low and menacing, producing goose bumps on her thin, graceful arms. He tilted his head to the side, moving his gaze from her to the glass and a crevice of concentration appeared between his eyes.

The sharp echo of cracking glass filled the room and Detective Howard pushed her chair back. Shock raked over her skin like a mini electric shock, raising the hair on her arms and neck and perpetuating the shiver that his laugh had started. A crack spindled out from the center of the mirror like a spider web and she was sure this man was causing the glass to crumble. Her gaze shot to Sam.

With the handcuffs no longer clasped on his right wrist, he extended his arm, his hand reaching toward the glass. Sam dipped his head further, glaring out from behind his bangs, focused.

The glass imploded, turning to dust, and she gasped at both the display of mental power and the vision of an officer standing rigid in the space behind the defunct mirror. The officer's head tilted back, his eyes rolled, showing only whites, and his mouth open in a silent scream choked off by a stream of black smoke.

Sam mumbled incoherent commands, each verse causing more black smoke to release from the officer. Sweat broke out on Sam's forehead, and dark circles surfaced under his eyes, yet he continued reciting the familiar chant.

A stream of smoke exploded from the mouth of the officer, billowing up into the ceiling, leaving a large black spot like someone took a blowtorch and scorched the material in a perfect sphere.

The officer fell to the floor, unconscious.

Sam lowered his arm, leaning back as the shackle holding his bound hand released. He mopped his face with his sleeve before returning his focus to the detective. "I didn't kill my family." He resumed the conversation as if nothing had happened.

Detective Howard's eyes darted between Sam and the observation room, where the officer was coming to. "Wha—" She couldn't form words and reached for the glass next to the recorder. Droplets of water jumped from the glass as her shaking hand brought it to her lips and she forced the cool liquid down her dry throat. A tingle in her shoulder morphed into a wild itch and she ignored it, setting the cup on the table with a steadier hand. "What exactly do you hunt?"

"Evil things."

"Was your family evil? Is that why you killed them?" she asked, scratching her shoulder.

Sam shook his head. "I didn't kill my family. I think my brother did."

"Your brother died twenty years ago. How is that possible?" Her eyes darted to the confused officer now sitting up and glancing around the observation room.

Sam offered a shrug. "Sometimes they come back." He rubbed his face. "And what returns isn't the same." His eyelids drooped as he met her gaze, deflating before her eyes as the exhaustion took hold. "It's my job to hunt them down."

Detective Howard's eyebrows raised high. "Hunt *what* down?"

He pointed toward the observation room. "Demons. Like the one that possessed him. It's my job to send them back."

"Are you saying a demon killed your family?"

Sam nodded, wiping tears from his haunted eyes. "So, unless you want to see what Armageddon looks like, you better let me do my job." He stood and walked out of the interrogation room.

She made no attempt to stop him. "He's not our guy," she said to the questioning stare of the officer. The itch in her shoulder morphed into a burning sensation and she rubbed it to quell the irritation.

Picking up the tape recorder, she returned to her office and closed the door.

Heat from her skin radiated through her shirt and she pulled up her sleeve, revealing the glowing insignia embedded in her flesh.

"That's impossible." Only one person on Earth could activate the emblem and save her soul.

He would save all their souls.

Detective Howard looked at her wide-eyed reflection and down at the cassette in her hand. Slowly, she began to pull the tape out.

The End

The Understudy

THERE'S A DIRTY WORD for you.

That's what it says next to my name on the casting sheet. No mistake. I've blinked my eyes a dozen times waiting for the text to correct itself, but no such luck. Understudy for the lead, which kindly put, means I'm not quite good enough.

Damn it.

I wonder if she's sleeping with the director.

She's standing over there, her hands fluttering at her lips, her eyes all shiny with tears, chattering away with the other leads. Her black hair cascaded down her back like a waterfall, beautiful and silky, and I hated it.

Bitch.

I'm so much better than she could ever be.

Understudy. What a slap in the face.

I turned away from the board, frustration raking over me like a deluge hitting the shore during a hurricane. Facing the rest of the cast right now would not be prudent, not with the building storm in my blood, so I headed toward the stairway, climbing into the rafters and taking a seat on the cold metal walkway above the stage.

Being in the dark, silent theater didn't alleviate the burning in my soul, so when the walkway creaked behind me, I stiffened, but didn't turn.

"You deserved that part." His voice settled over me like a warm blanket, quelling some of the fury. I glanced over my shoulder at his barely visible form just hanging in the dark like a macabre marionette.

He stepped closer, his shape more solid than shadow now, and I found myself standing, drawn to him. His dark eyes held promise, so when he reached for me, I didn't back away like I had a million times before.

The moment his hand connected with my skin, a rush of heat enveloped me, bringing to the surface the rumbling anger that had been stuck in the pit of my stomach.

"How could you," I whispered, just before his lips silenced me. His kiss was sinuous and sly, burning and ice cold, a litany of contradictions and it blackened my soul, leaving me breathless and desolate.

When the kiss broke, I glimpsed the brimstone in his eyes and within a blink they were shrouded in gray again. He had promised I would get the lead, had made an arrangement with the director, or so he told me one night over some tequila shots.

"You tricked me," I said, but the tremor in my voice made me sound like a petulant child and I clamped my teeth together against the rest of my scathing thoughts.

He patted my cheek with a gentleness meant to disarm and said, "You asked to be famous and I assure you, you will be." His smooth voice lulled me, making me grasp onto the belief that he would make it happen somehow, even though the cast list said otherwise.

"How?" I started, but he maneuvered me farther down the scaffolding until my back hit the solid wall.

When he smiled, his teeth gleamed in the darkness, and I shivered. I knew he wanted me, but now that I had been delegated to understudy, the idea of a tawdry screw in the rafters left me dizzy with wrath and I struggled under his grip.

He pressed his weight into me, pinning me against the wall.

"This was part of the deal," he hissed in my ear. "Save that fury for later, for those celebrating your downfall."

Something in his chiding tone set me on fire and I stopped struggling, meeting his hungry gaze. "What do you want?" I asked in a hushed whisper, giving in.

"I want you to worship me," he said, purring the words before his lips caught the underside of my chin, sliding over my skin like satin knives. His body pressed into me, promising the release I needed. Release from fury, from passion, from the dead-end life I led and into the world of fame.

All I had to do was honor my end of the bargain when he decided to cash in. And from the feel of him, he was calling in his chips right now.

My soul cried for me to run, to shun him, but the lower his lips went, the foggier that warning cry became. I was lost in his seductive touch, even though it burned with the hot flame of lust; he engulfed me, reveling in my muffled moans.

"Kneel."

I obeyed. The cold metal bit into my knees as the sound of his zipper filled my world. He was hard, all right, and he took a handful of my coarse hair and plunged through my open lips. His rhythm was that of desperation, like he had fantasized about this for months and couldn't quite get enough.

He took me every way possible until my knees were scraped bloody on the metal and my muscles clenched with soreness from his relentless pounding. He used his magnificent body in ways I never imagined, bringing me to heights I never dreamed I could reach, draining what little energy I had and leaving me spent on the hard metal of the catwalk.

His breath tickled my ear and he shifted. "Now, as far as fame is concerned..." he whispered, and then a small prick pinched my neck.

My gaze snapped to his before falling to the empty needle in his hand. His smile turned feral before the curtain closed and I tumbled into a black well of nothingness.

MY EYES FLUTTERED OPEN to shadows dancing on the ceiling, and I tilted my head toward the belly of the theater. Every seat was occupied, and my brain stalled, trying to find the missing hours between our torrid affair and the current moment.

Music filtered from the orchestra pit, and I dropped my gaze to the stage, recognizing they were near the end of the play. My vision blurred and then cleared, focusing on the fluid movement of the cast until it homed in on one person.

There he was.

The devil incarnate, capturing the attention of the entire theater. His empty promises of fame reverberating across the air like his charmed voice. I should be next to him on the stage; instead, I was...

I was...

Where the hell was I?

I blinked and tried to move, but restraints held me in place. A dull pain pounded between my shoulder blades and the stench of kerosene filtered into my nostrils. My gaze snapped to my right, where the prop for the finale leaned on the catwalk, discarded, delegated to witness the pending horror.

My heart flooded with shock, filtering through the rest of my being, creating a flush that crushed the breath in my chest.

I tried to move, but only my head seemed to be responding to the commands sent by my brain. The rest of my body hung on the metal chains, numb from whatever he stuck me with. I stared at the chains and craned my head back to see the tops of the giant wings attached to my back. The wires holding me in place were driven by a control box backstage and would lower the flaming angel into view at the right moment.

The truth of his promise struck fear in every cell. The prop was fireproof, but I certainly wasn't. The giant angel was made to withstand fire; flames only flickered until the accelerant burned away and it was an awe-inspiring sight. But I now hung in place of that prop, doused in kerosene.

Fumes gagged me each time I drew a raspy breath, and I calculated I had less than five minutes before I became a funeral pyre. Five minutes to review my life, to scan over the mistakes that led me to this situation. Five minutes to wonder how I could have been so blinded by the thought of fame to not recognize a psychopath.

The music rose to a crescendo, signaling the climax of the play. With a jerk, the chains started lowering me. My heart thundered and my gaze dropped, meeting his for a brief moment.

Malice lived there, along with the underlying wonder of a pyromaniac.

I tried to scream, to give an indication that the prop was alive, but my voice was nothing but a hoarse breath.

The lighter sparked on cue and hungry flames licked the air under me, igniting and crawling up my body. The chains lowered the flaming angel into view and all the actors on stage took a knee, averting their gaze as the play instructed. The audience gasped and I had a brief moment of ecstasy when all eyes were locked on my magnificent glowing form. For a brief moment, I experienced fame.

Then the flames ate through the layer of kerosene, devouring my skin, and I finally found my voice. My scream echoed and the cast snapped their gazes to me, their faces filled with the same horror reflected on each member of the audience.

Only his face held something other than horror or a hand covering his mouth in shock. His held a slight smile, one born of fascination and satisfaction.

Anger spread as fast as the flames and I threw my head back, bellowing my pain and frustration into the rafters, letting the heat devour my soul.

But I wouldn't be alone in my journey to hell.

The bucket of kerosene tipped, spilling directly over him, dousing him in a flaming shower. My last coherent thought as his burning form pin-wheeled on stage catching the curtains and wood flooring on fire was...karma is a bitch.

The End

Thank you for reading GLIMPSES.
If you enjoyed this book, please consider leaving a review!

About J.E. Taylor

J.E. Taylor is a USA Today bestselling author, a publisher, an editor, a manuscript formatter, a mother, a wife, a business analyst, and a Supernatural fangirl, not necessarily in that order. She first sat down to seriously write in February of 2007 after her daughter asked:

"Mom, if you could do anything, what would you do?"

From that moment on, she hasn't looked back.

In addition to being co-owner of Novel Concept Publishing, Ms. Taylor also moonlights as a Senior Editor of Allegory E-zine, an online venue for Science Fiction, Fantasy and Horror, and co-hosts the popular YouTube talk show Spilling Ink.

She lives in New Hampshire with her husband and during the summer months enjoys her weekends on the shore in southern Maine.

Visit her at www.jetaylor75.com to check out more of her books.

Other titles by J.E. Taylor

SHADES OF NIGHT

The Monster Defense Agency demands loyalty, and once you become an agent, the only way out is in a body bag.

When Sarah Stone and Robby Young train together at the agency's academy, sparks fly. And when they are paired as partners, they must muzzle their attraction, or they will face a firing squad.

All their pent-up frustration sharpens them into finely tuned monster hunters. Their ability to neutralize entire nests of vampires becomes the stuff of legends.

But hunting vampires has its own risks. Especially when Sarah and Robby uncover duplicity and corruption at the highest echelon within the Monster Defense Agency.

With a bull's-eye on their backs from both the agency and the vampires they hunt, Sarah and Robby's only hope is to take down the Monster Defense Agency.

But two against an ancient organization that trains monster-killers and knows all their tricks is even harder than it sounds. It's going to take all their skill and intelligence to kill this beast.

And being caught is not an option.

Shades of Night delivers forbidden mates, cool magic, and a kick-ass heroine in this fast-paced urban fantasy series.

SEASON OF THE DRAGON

**Monsters, trust issues, and a near death experience.
What else could go wrong?**

The end of life as we knew it didn't come with a nuclear blast. It didn't come with the deadly impact of a hurdling asteroid. No. It came in a wave of illness that swept the world with fear, and in our quarantined silence, the monsters awoke.

Leviathans, serpent kings, and dragons came forth from the bowels of the Earth. The season of the dragon began with fire and fury and ended with a new world order. One in which these giant terrorists held all the power.

When Mikhail St. Clare betrays the monsters by saving me from death at their claws, I cannot trust the last remaining dragon shifter. Not when humankinds' survival is at stake, and he had a hand in our near extinction.

The only thing we seem to agree on is our desire to annihilate the leviathans and unseat the Serpent

King. Our personal futures depend on ridding the earth of these murderous overlords.

We thought crossing the leviathan-patrolled city where every corner hides a hideous death was our most lethal hurdle. But building a bomb large enough to wipe out an entire species carries its own insane levels of danger.

One wrong move and we could destroy everyone living in New York instead.

A FRACTURED FAIRY TALE

Little Red Riding Hood, Cinderella, Brave, Rapunzel, Frozen, Snow White, Sleeping Beauty, Aladdin, Beauty and the Beast and Peter Pan – all fairy tales you know and love, but twisted, fractured into something new.

Shifters and magic claw through the pages of these fractured fairy tales, giving you a thrilling take on an old tale.

Will the heroine survive whatever the evil villain has in store?

Will love conquer all?

Grab your copy of A Fractured Fairy Tale – books 1-10 and find out!

A Fractured Fairy Tale books 1-10 includes:
Red, Cinder, Brave, Tanged, Frozen, Snow,
Spindle, Jasmine, Belle, and Hook

FIRE CURSED TRILOGY

Lucifer's daughter rises.

Faith Kennedy's mother hid the awful truth from her daughter for sixteen years. Until she lay on her deathbed. Only then did she reveal who sired her daughter, and the revelation terrifies Faith.

The devil may have sired her, but he only wants her beating heart ripped out of her chest. After all, that's where her angel grace fueling her fire power is stored, and that will give him what he needs to bring about humanity's fall.

And Lucifer will take down anyone who gets in his way.

When Faith is given an ancient knife that can kill the devil, she faces the toughest challenge of her young life. She must hunt Lucifer and put him down. Otherwise, the world will burn.

But if she succeeds, she may wipe herself, and everyone she loves, out of existence.

Fire Cursed Trilogy includes these individual titles:

Fire Cursed

Homecoming

Judgement Day

THE RYAN CHRONICLES

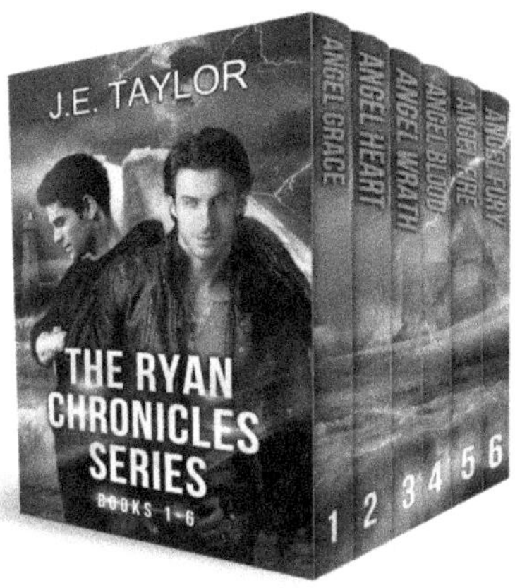

**Demons, vampires, angels, and the devil.
What the hell kind of nightmare do I live in?**

CJ Ryan was born with enough psychic power to destroy the earth. And Lucifer wants him to do just that.

Raised with a strong moral compass, CJ won't sacrifice innocent lives to protect his own, and that puts him at odds with the devil.

But if he doesn't give in, he and all he loves will become the target of Lucifer's rage.

When CJ gives his twin brother, Tom, a dose of his powers to keep him safe, it puts Tom directly in Lucifer's crosshairs.

As the final battle draws near, what will they have to sacrifice to keep their loved ones safe?

Can they survive the devil's wrath?

THE RYAN CHRONICLES includes these titles:

CJ's Story:

ANGEL GRACE - Book 1

ANGEL HEART - Book 2

ANGEL WRATH – Book 3

Tom's Story:

ANGEL BLOOD - Book 4

ANGEL FIRE - Book 5

ANGEL FURY – Book 6

Fans of Supernatural and Shadowhunters will enjoy this series.

RUNNING FROM THE DEVIL

An escaped demon and a snarky cat face off against the seven deadly sins.

Escaping from Hell was just the beginning of Phoebe's problems. In Hell, she had a position of legend. A marquis of torture. But on the human plane, she is just another New York City destitute.

Before she has a chance to get her bearings on the unforgiving streets, Fate steps in and offers her a chance at redemption, but it doesn't come cheap.

She must bring in the demons that escaped alongside her while making sure no humans are harmed in the process. In order to do that, she needs to learn to live in the human world with the help of another one of Fate's parolees, a snarky cat named Smoke.

If it means never seeing the halls of Hell again,
Phoebe will do anything, even battle the seven deadly
sins single-handed.

THE DEATH CHRONICLES II

Death is the family business, but not one I want to pursue. Thankfully, it's been passed down from father to son for generations, so it should skip over me as Death's daughter. Then I won't have to stop being alive and can actually live my life. Right?

Well, the reapers don't agree. And neither do the angels.

One thinks I'm destined to take over, the other believes I will destroy existence. Both want me dead to match their own agendas.

I have an agenda of my own, and Leviathan who has sworn to protect me. But once my family and friends start being targeted, the family business, while grim, might be the only choice I have to save those I love.

The Death Chronicles *II* includes the following
titles:
Grim's Daughter
Finding Death
Reap the Dead
Kissing Fate

THE STEVE WILLIAMS SERIES

Special Agent Steve Williams excels at his job catching the most heinous of monsters walking the earth.

Serial killers.

When his job brings him face to face with a psychic, he struggles to accept her gifts in his neat little black and white world. Armed with her visions, along with his skills as an FBI agent, he hunts the worst of the worst, but will he catch the killer before they set their sights on him?

Unstoppable, breath stealing, and terrifying all at once.

Gripping, rich and magnificent!

The Steve Williams Series mixes compelling crime thrillers with supernatural forces that will grip the reader from page one. This six-book series takes you

through some of Steve Williams darkest cases in his
FBI career.

This book includes the following titles:
DARK RECKONING
VENGEANCE
HUNTING SEASON
GEORGIA REIGN
CRYSTAL ILLUSIONS
SAVING FACE

PACK MAGIC

She's a hybrid alpha scorned by her pack, until he arrives.

Daughter of a tribrid and a flame-touched alpha werewolf, Erica Young's course in life should be set. Except no one wants a phoenix-werewolf with a taste for blood to be their alpha.

When the head of the werewolf council shows up with a possible candidate to take her place in the pack, sparks fly.

Logan Blaez, the prodigal son of the council head, is willing to challenge Erica for the role of alpha, even if that means a fight to the death. Until he lays eyes on her.

Now he wants to claim Erica as his mate and rule as her alpha.

Too bad Erica isn't willing to submit, or give up
her birthright.

THE WITCH ASSASIN

An Assassin is tasked with taking out a mythical fae king …

… In a realm that doesn't exist.

Mya's mission is to get in, obtain the fae king's DNA, and get out.

It should be easy with her gifts, except, when does anything ever go as planned?

But failing in her line of work is a death sentence, and nothing in her training prepared her for Tavin Zorander—the most powerful Elvren to ever exist. After all, it's his family's magic that's kept Eleka cloaked from the prying eyes of the universe for centuries.

When she finds herself at the mercy of the fae king, Mya has a choice to make.

Does she use her darkest power, thus compromising her mission, or should she surrender to Tavin?

Part of her wants to surrender, while the other part is terrified. For if she does, the league will only send more assassins. Then all of Eleka will suffer.

Faced with an impossible decision, what will she do?

Find these and other titles at
https://books.jetaylor75.com/